GW00399891

THE DEVIL LOOKS AFTER HIS OWN

*for Deirdre
and in memory of Joe*

Niamh McBrannan

THE DEVIL
LOOKS AFTER
HIS OWN

ARLEN
HOUSE

The Devil Looks After His Own

is published in 2018 by
ARLEN HOUSE
42 Grange Abbey Road
Baldoyle
Dublin 13
Ireland
Email: arlenhouse@gmail.com

978–1–85132–180–3, paperback
978–1–85132–181–0, Mobi
ISBN 978–1–85132–182–7, ePub

International distribution by
SYRACUSE UNIVERSITY PRESS
621 Skytop Road, Suite 110
Syracuse, New York
USA 13244–5290
Phone: 315–443–5534/Fax: 315–443–5545
Email: supress@syr.edu
www.syracuseuniversitypress.syr.edu

© Niamh McBrannan, 2018

The moral rights of the author have been asserted.

This is a work of fiction. Names, characters, businesses, places, events and incidents are either the product of the author's imagination or used in a fictitious manner. Any resemblance to actual persons, living or dead, or actual events is purely coincidental.

typesetting by Arlen House
map and illustration by Alice Bentley
cover artwork by Daryl Slein

CONTENTS

THE DEVIL LOOKS AFTER HIS OWN

Four Days Earlier

'Fifteen minutes to landing,' announced the captain of Aer Lingus Flight EI605. *'Weather in Dublin is hot and sunny, the current freak heatwave is forecast for another week, temperature twenty-eight degrees and humid.'*

Humid! They had no idea, the passenger in Seat 18C snorted. He saw the woman in the seat beside him turn her head to dart a concerned look in his direction. It was a look that asked if he was another crazy, like the old guy in the aisle seat on her right, a dumbass from Drumlish, or wherever the hell he said he was from. That old bastard had finally shut up about the goddamn teeth he got fixed in Budapest and had gone to the bathroom.

'Sorry,' the passenger in Seat 18C said to the woman. But he wasn't sorry, he was tired and it was starting to show.

'Ladies and Gentlemen, as we're experiencing some turbulence, the captain has switched back on the seat belt sign. If I could please

ask you to return to your seats ... ensure your seat belts are securely fastened ...'

The old guy was still pulling up his fly as he rushed down the aisle towards his seat.

'God Almighty, I only just made it back in time! I was telling the air hostess back there about the porcelain veneer and the implants. Bloody expensive! Had to sell off one of the apartments in the end and sure you get nothing for them these days.'

He sat down, fastened his seat belt and poked the woman passenger's arm insistently.

'But it was entirely worth it, am I right?'

The woman examined his face, a leathery mess of deep-etched lines, living proof that there was no Factor 30 in Longford when it was needed. His smile was astonishingly bright, like a UV drug light in a public toilet and just as classy.

Earlier, he'd announced to the unwilling audience of passengers and crew that his new bride had made him get some work done, starting with the teeth. Apparently poor old Maura had never complained in fifty years of marriage, but Katya had other ideas and you had to move with the times.

'I'm sure Katya will be overjoyed,' the woman passenger muttered.

'Oh, she'll be well satisfied,' he said with a dirty laugh. 'Like the girls I left back there in Amsterdam ... Whoa, what's happening?'

The plane gave a sudden lurch and began to pitch and roll violently. The three babies in various locations on board began to wail in unison.

'Hold my hand,' the old man pleaded as he grabbed the woman's nearest hand and clasped his arthritic fingers around it.

'No! Get off – let go of me!' She picked up the inflight magazine to beat him off.

'Please, I'm terrified. I can't die like this ... I'm the chairman of the County Board.'

A seat belt clicked open and the passenger in Seat 18C stood up, leaned across the woman and gripped the old man's shoulder close to his neck. He spoke quietly, in a slow drawl.

'Get your hands off the lady. And shut the *fuck* up.'

The old man's face contorted with pain and he instantly released the woman's hand. He rubbed his neck, looking fearfully at his assailant, but said nothing.

'Thank you,' the woman said, believing her rescuer had acted out of chivalry. But her words scarcely registered with him as he sat down again, having first paused to scan the rows of the passengers in front. Three men glanced back at him from separate seats. He gave the woman a laconic salute and murmured 'Ma'am' before turning to the window and allowing his head to loll against it.

As Aer Lingus Flight EI605 landed with a bump at Dublin Airport and taxied down the hot concrete runway, the woman examined the reproductions of baroque paintings in her inflight magazine. Her dental tourist neighbour glared ahead with his arms folded in resentment, ill-advisedly grinding his new implants. And the passenger in Seat 18C dozed against the window. The images flickering before his closed eyes finally slowed and settled on two places – a doomed village amongst sweltering salt-marshes, thousands of miles from a cool, dark hole in a deep green wood. And reaching into the jacket pocket closest to his heart, he thought of the small, calcified structures that linked those places, that linked all of his special places.

Day 1

Sunday

1

VULTURES

Feeding vultures is not recommended for the vulnerable. Nothing personal, but given the opportunity the average vulture will devour the hand that nurtured it. It's just their nature. Too bad some of us have to find out that kind of thing the hard way.

Seagulls wheeled and screamed as they fought over the crumbs of yesterday's bread rolls. I dodged the wings that swept too close, brushing my cheek like the casual aggressive touch of a bar-room letch. One bird crashed hard into the quayside rail and dropped to the ground, stunned. The rest descended in a squawking frenzy, pecking, tearing, clawing as the bloodied feathers flew.

I tried to remember if we'd had the same cannibalistic flying vermin back in Amsterdam, but I had almost no memories left from there. Everything had been edited out, everything from before last week. A line from an old song came to me, something about the things you can't remember and the things you can't forget. But I couldn't recall any damned songs either.

'Hey, Missus!'

A white van idled in the middle of the road, its engine wheezing like a bronchial camel, its driver leaning out the open window, his sunburnt face pink and raw, an uncooked steak topped with mirrored shades.

'For Jaysus' sake, love,' he said, his head wagging with pseudo-concern. 'D'you not listen to the news? Don't feed them bastarding birds. They'll take the eyes out of your head – and then they'll come back for your kids. Or in your case, maybe your grandkids.'

'Oh, thanks,' I said, advancing on him, rage rising in me like lava through a fully-dilated volcano. A stale rock bun hit the side of his van with a thunk.

'That's for the unsolicited *poxy* advice. And,' as another one flew just wide of the windscreen followed by the flock of screaming gulls, 'that's for the ageist gender stereotyping.'

I turned to the nearby bin overflowing with stinking food containers and dog-shit bags and armed myself. The van window rolled up rapidly, cutting off his 'it's your fucking dumb-bitch funeral ...' come-back, and the vehicle zoomed off pursued by clamouring seabirds.

I took a deep breath and slowly exhaled. Wiping my hands on my jeans I checked round quickly for any witnesses to my outburst. Not a sinner. The only evidence was the debris I'd slung about like a maniac, now scattered accusingly on the road. Slowly, I collected what I could and replaced it in the bin, muttering stern self-admonishments. As I did so, I became aware of a muffled sound of men's voices coming from somewhere close by. I leaned over the railings lining the quayside to get a better view of the swollen Liffey. Last night's deluge had come after ten days of record high temperatures. No one knew how long the freak heatwave would continue. The only seasonal certainties were increased incidents of road rage, flying ants and peculiar skin eruptions arising from carcinogenic skin conditions and STDs.

A short distance upriver, a small boat bobbed close to the quay's green walls. The man sitting at the back shouted into his phone while battling to hold the boat's position against the river's flow. A second man knelt with most of his upper body bent over the side, his arms stretched down into the water, straining to keep his grasp on something beneath the surface. The boat tipped over so far it looked like it would capsize at any minute.

I squinted to see what was in the water, but could only make out a long, dark blur. A foul smell came from upriver and I shivered despite the early morning sunshine already warming the city.

'That's your lot,' I told the two remaining gulls, crumpling my empty brown paper bag as I moved away. They ignored me, more interested in ingesting the entrails of their fallen comrade. 'Time to open up shop. And roast some Java.'

That was pure bravado. I knew nothing about coffee beans – or about running an inner city café whose only notable feature was the miracle of how it managed to elude the health inspectors. The café was opposite me at the end of a short terrace of dilapidated nineteenth-century buildings that had somehow escaped the surrounding redevelopment. The terrace stood facing the river, awkward and embarrassed by itself, like an unwanted memory. A faded plastic sign on the shabby shop-front announced, 'The Silver Bullet Café'. It could have added 'Hardening Workers' Arteries since 1951' but there was no need. The aura of stale grease that shrouded the building like a toxic cloud said everything you needed to know about the menu. The small home espresso-maker I'd installed when I arrived was as unexpected there as a Michelin star. The café belonged to my Aunt Aggie, who had opted for early retirement at eighty-one in order to focus full-time on Texas Hold 'Em. Just last week, she'd called me at my apartment in Amsterdam with her offer.

'You can have the business, Connie, if you're stupid enough to take it on.'

Contemplating the wreckage of my life, I decided that I was. I arrived two days later – a burnt-out professional the wrong side of forty-five, average in every way except, perhaps, for the asymmetrically-hacked chestnut hair. That was the result of panic and poor eyesight, my simultaneous short- and long-sightedness inadequately corrected by out-of-date contact lenses. Washed-up, broke and alone, the only thing I had to look forward to now was the menopause.

'For the love of God. What do you have to do to get a cup of coffee round here?'

It was the proprietor of the nearby Sunrise Hotel, who stood observing me as I wrestled with the café window's security shutter and whose face displayed a day's growth along with an unwelcome grin. My daily battle with the shutter required the kind of dexterity rarely seen outside the sex shows of my old neighbourhood and the last thing my contortions needed was an audience.

'You could at least give me a hand – what's your name again?'

'Pius Fogarty.'

'Yeah, your manners are as backward as your name. I suppose your poor mother called you after a pope or a priest or something.'

'That's uncalled for,' he said, looking wounded. 'She was suffering from post-natal depression. And anyway, it's a family tradition. I was called after my Uncle Pius, who was no priest.'

Fogarty didn't look much like a priest either as he watched my fumblings with the espresso-maker. One of Aggie's regulars, he was in his mid-to-late-forties, of average height, broad-shouldered with unkempt black hair streaked with grey. He wore blue jeans, a black t-shirt and the air of a man who's seen it all and didn't like it. A typical cocky local I'd decided the minute we were introduced – the type whose hard man pose concealed a mountain of insecurities and a mammy in the background saying novenas for him. By the looks of him she was wasting her time.

I spilled half of the fresh brew down my jeans as I handed him the cup.

'What's wrong with the coffee in that so-called hotel of yours?' I asked, ignoring the mess.

'The coffee machine's knackered and the kettle's gone walkabout. Thought I had it pretty much nailed down, but ... my guests are professionals, after all.'

'Ever considered rethinking your customer base?'

Pius Fogarty laughed. The way Aggie'd described it, the Sunrise Hotel sounded like a depression-era flophouse on Skid Row. Most of the guests were semi-permanent and permanently out of it, due to drink, drugs, dementia or plain old disappointment. It was like the French Foreign Legion, Hotel California and Roach Motel all rolled into one. What Fogarty got out of it was anyone's guess. It wasn't the money, that's for sure. The Sunrise was the cheapest hotel in Dublin, bar none, and seemed to be only tolerated by the authorities due to its function as a kind of human flypaper. And Fogarty's involvement didn't arise from an excess of human kindness. He had no time for people he called do-gooders and bleeding hearts. Aggie said most people reckoned he was running the hotel as a front for something dodgy, but no one had ever been brave enough to ask.

Fogarty's phone rang as he took the coffee. He listened briefly, then told the caller he was on his way. He downed the coffee on the spot, threw some change on the counter and headed for the door, turning his head as he opened it.

'Some boatmen found a body in the river somewhere around here. They're in danger of losing it to the tide and they need help. The cops are on the way.'

'So that's what they were doing,' I said. I pushed out past him and pointed. 'They're down there. I saw them a few minutes ago.'

Fogarty frowned. 'You didn't go for help?'

'How was I supposed to know that it was a *body* they were trying to hold on to? I can't see very far.'

'You could have checked.'

'Why would I check? Look, you may not realise this, but in my experience it's not usual to have to check for dead bodies in your neighbourhood on a Sunday morning. It wouldn't be considered normal.'

Fogarty stared at me for a second and, shaking his head, walked across the road. I hate it when guys do that silent head-shaking thing.

'Where's your faggot neighbour?' Fogarty called back. 'Will you get him? At least he might help ...'

But Ozzie Wolf had already appeared, his long, leather-clad form practically gliding up the basement steps of the nightclub next door. With his spiked black hair, chalk white skin, strategic piercings and fashionable Russian prison-style tattoos covering one side of his neck, Ozzie had all the signs of a nocturnal creature of the slightly upmarket variety, completed by his studied air of sexual ambiguity.

'Good morning, Ms Ortelius,' he said, nodding at the empty café. 'All go round here as usual, I see.'

I pointed across the road.

'You're needed over there. Direct order from our self-appointed leader.'

I followed Ozzie, my sudden anger with Fogarty changing, as I drew closer, to a crawling dread. My mouth was dry with apprehension, a pulse pounded in my temple. What was the matter with me? If there was a body in the river, it was sad, but it was not my problem.

'Snap out of it,' I told myself, 'remember the last time you let things get to you.'

Fogarty called to the boatmen from the quayside wall, then quickly ducked under the railings and disappeared down the steps to the river.

Ozzie and I looked down as soon as we reached the barrier. The boat butted right up against the quay wall. That long dark shape was alongside it, wrapped in a tarpaulin and secured to the boat with ropes. They must have used the tarpaulin like a net, throwing it over the body and reeling in their terrible catch with ropes. Not an easy thing to do in a tidal river. I reluctantly admitted that Fogarty had a point. Why *hadn't* I done something when I'd seen them earlier?

Fogarty stood on the lowest step above river level, the dark water sloshing over his feet. He bent down to hold the side of the boat, to pull it close. One of the boatmen rose and shouted to us.

'Hey you! Grab a hold of this.'

A heavy wet rope flew upwards, missing my face by inches. I ducked. Wrong response again. Luckily, Ozzie caught it with a deftness that was surprising for one so languid. He looped it round a pole and smiled at me almost kindly.

'Bit on the jumpy side this morning, are we?'

Fogarty shouted up at him. 'Stay there, Ozzie. I'm bringing it up. I'll need you at the top.'

They secured another rope to a metal ring embedded in the quay wall, then swung the boat around to bring the body alongside the steps. The boatman who had thrown us the rope was now on the steps with Fogarty. The man in the boat clung to the body while the current tried to pull it away. Fogarty descended the steps below the water level to get his arms underneath the body. With the water swirling around his chest, he was having trouble keeping his footing.

'I've got it,' he called after a few minutes, his arms grasping the body. 'Untie the ropes.'

Fogarty climbed the steps slowly, painfully, grappling with the sodden weight that didn't seem to want to leave the water. But the boatmen provided support from below him until he was halfway up the steps and they could reach up no further. Fogarty staggered and almost fell. He stopped and leaned into the wall for support, then clasped his burden closer and with a superhuman effort made it to the top of the steps. Ozzie was there to help him and moved to take one end of the body.

As they stepped forward carrying the body between them, a man in a high-viz vest quickly opened the gate in the railings.

'Thanks, Shay,' Fogarty muttered.

A small crowd had gathered now and the faces of the onlookers showed curiosity, concern, sadness. Not what I felt, not the cold fear that made me want to run as far away from there as I possibly could. Just then, part of the tarpaulin around the body came undone, exposing a thin, white arm. It had a frayed purple and green friendship bracelet on its wrist.

A murmur went through the group of onlookers and one or two people cried out. The men carrying the body stopped. They'd instantly realised who it was.

They gently laid the body on the ground and Fogarty sank to his knees beside it. He looked pale and sick as he placed his hands lightly on the body and bowed his head.

'Ah God, no,' he said.

2

Tragedy Central

I saw it in their faces, the same fear that I felt. Most of us had stopped breathing for an instant. I might have been the only one there who didn't know who the victim was, but even so I felt that the ground had dissolved beneath me and I was in free fall.

Ten or twelve of us stood in a broken circle around the body, with newcomers joining every few minutes. I recognised a couple of customers from the café and I saw Josie Corcoran and Viv Foley, two of Aggie's friends, as ancient as herself. They were on their way back from early morning mass in Immaculate Heart of Mary across the river. They wore their good hats and coats and their handbags rattled with holy relics and medals. Aggie told me that Viv did the flowers in Our Lady of Lourdes on Sean McDermott Street. I guessed she'd been over in Immaculate Heart of Mary checking out the competition.

A couple of joggers had stopped and an old man waited with his Jack Russell beside him on a lead. A band of stick-thin women and men in hoodies and tracksuit bottoms stood a small distance behind the main circle of onlookers.

'They're from Fogarty's place,' Ozzie whispered. 'The Sunrise Hotel.'

Fogarty rose slowly and stood, scrutinising the faces around him. His hoarse voice broke the silence.

'Where's Shane?' he asked Ozzie, who shook his head. 'Try to find him. And call Kitty. You'd better tell her before somebody else does.'

He was too late. A teenage Asian girl burst through the circle of onlookers and stood in front of Fogarty.

'Tell me what? Oh God ...'

Before anyone could stop her, she tore away the covering from the body and stood back quickly, her hands at her face.

'No!' she cried. 'Oh no.'

She threw herself on the ground beside the dead body of a boy who was as young as herself.

I stepped back almost on top of Ozzie.

'It's ... Stevie,' I said with my hand clamped to my mouth.

Stevie Hennessy practically lived in the café and Aggie, who was not the warmest of people, loved him like a son. Aggie had introduced me to a lot of people when I arrived, but Stevie stood out. The first time I saw him was when I arrived, four days ago. He was talking intently to Kitty at a table in a corner of the café. His quick smile and shining eyes were almost dazzling, bewildering to my numbed soul.

He couldn't have been in the water for very long. His body wasn't waterlogged and there were no signs of any major bruising or damage. His golden curls were dark from the river, but they framed a face that still looked like it was carved by a Renaissance sculptor. His lower lip was pierced with a gold ring, giving him a slight pout, which made him seem even younger than his seventeen years. A gold crucifix hung around his neck on a thin chain. A frayed purple and green friendship bracelet clung to his left wrist. He wore only a pair of ripped jeans and his slight, white body hadn't a mark on it. Except, that is, for one of his hands. Stevie's right hand and wrist were black and swollen and horribly disfigured.

'Holy Mother of God,' said Josie Corcoran, blessing herself. 'He's like a poor, drownded angel.'

'A martyr,' her friend Viv said. 'He was always a saint and now he's a martyr.' Her rosary beads clicked through her fingers as her whiskery lips moved in silent prayer.

Kitty threw herself across the boy's body and cried piteously. I tried to concentrate on breathing and wondered how I was going to tell Aggie. It was her own fault, she shouldn't have gone off and left me like that. I came back here for rest and recuperation, not to find myself in the middle of Tragedy Central. I had emotions of my own to nurse and I didn't need the new one I'd just acquired – guilt. The last thing Aggie'd said to me at the airport, just after she told me not to burn down the café, was, 'Keep an eye out for that lad, Stevie. I'm very fond of him.'

I'd forgotten that too until just now.

'Hey, you – get away from that body!' shouted the plainclothes police officer who'd just pulled up in an unmarked car and had pushed his way through the knot of onlookers.

Ozzie groaned, 'Brady. Detective Inspector.'

Kitty didn't move.

'Jesus Christ! Who's responsible for this? Fogarty, I might have known you'd be involved.'

Fogarty took his time responding, first shaking the dust of the ground from his knees, then slowly wiping his hands together. With eyes narrowed under his dark brows, he contemplated the police officer. When he spoke, his tone was low and even.

'Take it easy, Anto, will you? Can't you see everyone's in a state of shock?'

'Doesn't matter what state they're in – you can't be manhandling dead bodies you've decided to pull out of the river. That's way out of order, Fogarty, and you bloody-well know it.'

'The tide was turned, we'd have lost him.'

Fogarty nodded towards the boatmen. 'Those guys deserve a medal for holding on to him and bringing him to shore like they did.'

'They deserve a summons, and so do you,' Brady said. 'You've probably destroyed important evidence.'

Fogarty looked at him derisively. 'Important evidence of what?'

'Cause of death.'

'Ah. Well, if you cops get stumped, I'm sure any eejit will help you out on that one.'

Brady stepped towards Fogarty with clenched fists, a blue vein protruding in his forehead. He was well over six feet tall with short blond hair and wore light brown chinos with a long-sleeved, pink-striped Ted Baker shirt, expensive-looking shoes and a gold watch.

'I'm watching you, Fogarty. You know that, don't you? If you don't cooperate, I'm taking you in – along with all your neighbours.'

Fogarty gazed out over the glittering river and said nothing.

Brady turned to the crowd.

'I'm Detective Inspector Anthony Brady from Store Street Garda Station,' he announced unnecessarily since most of the people there knew exactly who he was. 'Move away from the body, all of you, and give me some room to see what's going on here. Fogarty, you know the deceased?'

Fogarty's eyes were on Kitty, who hadn't moved from Stevie's body. He sighed and said, 'It's Stevie Hennessy, from the Sunrise Hotel.'

The detective glanced at what he could see of Stevie's body. His eyes fixed on Stevie's blackened hand.

'Jesus Christ,' he said.

His phone went off and he answered it with a muttered curse, walking a little way up the quayside to put some distance between himself and the gathered crowd. We could still hear every word.

'No, I told you already, I don't like it at all ... Look, I can't talk now, we'll have to meet. Some members of the public have just pulled a body from the river. Yes, dead. No signs of violence, as far we can tell at this point. Blackened hand. Skin-popping, maybe snow blow or bath salts.'

I frowned at Ozzie. He whispered back, 'MDMA. Mephedrone. Legal high, illegal. Injected under the skin.'

He stopped to look around and then whispered again. 'Stevie wouldn't have. Brady's got it wrong.'

I had no idea what 'legal high, illegal' meant. I'd have to ask him later.

Brady was still on the phone.

'... positively I.D.'d as Steven Hennessy, no fixed abode. My take is accident or suicide, the post mortem will confirm. Hey!'

Something hurled itself at Detective Inspector Brady with a violent force that knocked him backwards and sent his phone spinning across the flagstones.

'Stevie would never kill himself,' Kitty screamed, her violet-streaked hair flying wildly around her face, her black eyes full of fury.

'He was clean. He was going to art college next month.'

She ran back and flung herself down again beside the boy's body and, lifting his head with her two hands, she stared into his lifeless eyes.

'He wanted to live,' she said.

She looked around desperately at her friends and neighbours. Fogarty moved closer and stood behind her protectively. Brady and Fogarty glared at one another with a deep-rooted loathing, the type that develops over a lifetime of enmity. I looked at Ozzie for some clue as to what was going on, but he was occupied with watching the smoke curl from his roll-up.

Kitty's voice was quiet when she spoke again.

'This was no accident. Somebody did this to Stevie.'

The arrival of an ambulance and two police cars distracted Brady. He dismissed the Garda Water Unit van and barked orders at the other officers. The medics got busy. Statements were taken, cameras flashed and eventually Stevie's body was bundled up, hoisted on a gurney and loaded into the ambulance. A blonde-haired girl held Kitty in her arms, both of them sobbing. I clutched the railing to steady myself as the wailing ambulance pulled off and sped away down the quays.

The sun beat down from directly overhead and the stench of the river intensified. My stomach heaved and I leaned over the railings, as if the flowing water beneath me could wash away all the bad things I felt. Although the overnight deluge had stopped many hours ago, from several openings in the green, slime-covered walls, brown fluid gushed out of ancient pipes. Not quite the healing waters I'd hoped for. I felt that if someone punctured my chest right there and then the same dark liquid would pour straight out of me.

The crowd began to disperse, but the furious voice of Detective Inspector Anthony Brady held some people, promising more drama. He'd gone back to collect the broken pieces of his phone case and now strode towards Kitty to continue where he'd left off. Not the forgive and forget type, I guessed.

'You broke my fucking iPhone,' he yelled, fumbling with the pieces as he tried to put the smashed case back together. Deep cracks radiated across the screen.

'I want your name and address. Now!'

Kitty folded her arms defiantly and drew her head back, as if she was going to spit in his face.

'Tell him, Kitty.' It was Fogarty. 'Tell him or he'll arrest you.'

Kitty swallowed and then relented.

'Kitty Lee.'

'Spell the surname.'

'L-E-E.'

'Address?'

Kitty hesitated. Like Stevie, Kitty was basically homeless, so Aggie had told me. She moved around, couch-surfing with friends, occasionally sleeping at the Sunrise Hotel.

Before she could answer, somebody said, 'She lives in the Silver Bullet Café.'

Turned out it was me.

Fogarty shot me a look of surprise. Ozzie raised an amused eyebrow. Kitty moved closer to take my hand and stood beside me, staring at the ground.

'First floor, the Silver Bullet Café, North Wall Quay, Dublin 1,' I said more confidently.

The detective was sceptical. 'Sure about that?'

Everyone nodded.

'Kitty Lee, I am arresting you under a Section 3 Assault. I'm taking you down to Store Street Garda Station for questioning.'

'For fuck's sake, Anto,' Fogarty snapped. 'She's upset – she's only sixteen. Let it go, would you.'

Brady ignored him and spoke to Kitty.

'As a minor, you are entitled to have a parent or guardian present during questioning. You may contact that person now.'

Kitty said nothing.

'If you do not have a parent or guardian, you may have another relative or responsible adult present at the interview.'

'I'll go, Kitty,' Fogarty said.

'Thanks, Fogarty. But I want Connie to come with me. Is that ok, Connie?'

'Yeah, sure,' I said with a confidence I didn't feel. Responsible adult? They had no idea. I was hardly capable of looking after myself let alone rescuing a distraught teenager with anger management issues almost on a level with my own. I'd been detached from reality lately – you could call it shock. But something had just shifted inside me. Now I warned myself, recognising a familiar needling prickle as my long-lost survival instinct came creeping back, 'Don't get involved in *anything else* until you can trust your judgment.'

And it whispered back to me that it was too late, that I was already involved – and that I had no idea what I was getting myself into.

3

A GREAT START

From the outside, Store Street Garda Station could be mistaken for a tastefully-designed gallery of contemporary art. Walls of glass brick flank the entrance and above it, the glazed upper stories curve in a graceful bow front. A double row of perfectly-carved granite spheres lines the exterior plaza, bathed by night in ultramarine light. It's the world's most beautiful barricade, a hymn to functional aestheticism. Or aesthetic functionalism. Rather than ramming it, the joy-riders probably get out and take photos.

Backing on to the poverty-stricken, drug-ravaged, crime-ridden north inner city, the police station's appearance sends a reassuring message to the International Financial Services Centre across the road and the partially redeveloped docklands further on down the tramline. The management of crime as an art form, something you could invest in. It was the perfect location for our designer detective, Anthony Brady.

'Look Kitty, can you try not to antagonise him? And stay calm. Just go along with the questions and apologise if you have to. The sooner we get out of here, the sooner we can go home and put all this behind us.'

'I'm not bleedin' apologising to that fucker.'

Kitty had finally stopped weeping and was quietly picking the remaining black polish off her fingernails.

'He said Stevie was a junkie and that he topped himself. That's a fucking lie. And,' she added, 'Brady's a fucking wanker.'

'Jesus, Kitty. Keep your voice down.'

I looked at the open door of the interrogation room where we sat waiting. Brady'd be back any minute. I had to think fast. Aggie would kill me if I messed this up. That's when I forgot my decision not to get any more involved. That's when I made my promise.

'As soon as we get out of here, we can find out what happened to Stevie.'

'What do you mean?'

'I mean we can ask questions, find out who he was with, you know ...'

'You mean, investigate?' She stared at me for a second and then grinned unexpectedly.

'Yeah, go on. Let's do it. It's not like the guards are going to do anything.'

Great, I thought. I'd got through to her. Maybe I wasn't so bad at this teen relationship thing after all. And how hard could it be to ask a few people about Stevie?

'Promise you're not just saying you'll do it, promise you'll do it for real?'

'I promise, Kitty. But you'll have to help out in the café if you want me to go out and talk to people. And you have to be polite to the nice guards.'

She nodded. She looked a lot brighter.

'It'd be as well for someone to find out what's going on,' she said thoughtfully. 'Before something else happens.'

'What do you mean?'

'Well,' she said, 'it's just the last time I saw Stevie, he said we're all in danger and we need to protect ourselves.'

'He said ... who's in danger?'

Just then, Brady appeared, accompanied by a woman officer he introduced as Detective Nuala Rossiter. She was dark and petite and doe-eyed and she smiled at us sweetly.

Brady started the recording and stated the date and time along with our names and address and the charge against Kitty. It was eleven thirty am. Detective Rossiter began writing on the yellow pad in front of her.

Brady smiled as he handed me a plastic cup of water.

'Thank you for coming.'

Minus the fury he seemed quite civilised, just a regular alpha male on his home turf. And not bad-looking either, when he wasn't behaving like a lunatic.

'Kitty, can you tell me what you were doing on the North Wall Quay at nine thirty this morning?'

'I was going to work.'

'You have a job?'

'I have two jobs. I'm a nightclub rep. And I have a part-time day job in the Silver Bullet Café, making tea and stuff, you know? Today's my first day.'

I tried to hide my astonishment. Just a minute ago I'd suggested she could help out in the café, now she was presenting herself as my star employee. A pulse pounded behind my eyes. I gulped down my water and looked round for more, but there was no jug or water cooler in the room.

'Indeed. Well, you're off to a great start there, aren't you? You and your boss in the Garda Station and you on a charge of assaulting a police officer.'

'I didn't mean it, Guard, honest I didn't. I was upset about Stevie ...' Her eyes filled with tears. '... when I heard you say that about him, you know, about the drugs and the ... Well, I just saw red and I pushed you. I didn't know you were a guard.' Kitty gave me a sidelong glance as she wiped her tears and became the picture of sincerity as she continued. 'I'm very sorry. I've never been in trouble before.'

'That's correct,' Rossiter confirmed. 'We have no file on Kitty Lee. No record of any previous arrests or misdemeanours.'

'But you hang around with criminals, don't you Kitty? Why don't you tell me what's going on out there? There's something up, isn't there?'

'How do you mean?' Kitty asked. 'Going on where?'

Brady observed her for a moment.

'Kitty Lee, were you under the influence of drugs this morning?'

'Sorry?'

'You heard me.'

'You don't have to answer that, Kitty,' I said.

Brady was trying to provoke her and I couldn't figure out why. Surely he must have something better to do with his Sunday mornings than harass teenage girls.

'I don't do drugs,' Kitty said quietly.

'Would you be prepared to take a test to confirm that statement?'

'Say no, Kitty. You don't have to take a test,' I said through gritted teeth.

'I'll take any test you like.'

'Detective Rossiter, please ensure that the agreement of Ms Kitty Lee to a drug screening is recorded in writing.'

Rossiter nodded and scribbled on the pad.

With his hands pressed on the table, Brady leaned forward and stared intently at Kitty.

'What about alcohol? Were you up all night drinking at some party? Maybe in Fogarty's place, the Sunrise Hotel? We know what goes on there. Don't we, Detective Rossiter?'

Rossiter shifted uncomfortably in her chair. Brady had hit a sore point with her. I couldn't figure out what was going on with this interview and it was really starting to bother me.

Kitty gazed at him calmly. 'I wasn't drinking last night.'

'What about that night job of yours? Is it possible one of your "clients" slipped you something?'

'That's it!' I was on my feet. 'Come on Kitty, let's get out of here. I don't know what you're hoping to achieve, Detective Inspector Brady, but I'm responsible for Kitty and your questions are completely inappropriate.'

'Hey, Connie, it's ok, chillax,' Kitty said.

Detective Rossiter gave me an encouraging smile. Brady silently examined his left hand, rotating his wedding ring. I sat down again and wondered how to chillax.

'Look, I work for one hour a night, two or three nights a week, as a rep for Ozzie Wolf's night club. Stevie did it too.'

Kitty swallowed and continued, 'We're out on the street offering people concessions to get into the club. We stamp the back of their hands or their wrists with the club stamp. By about half twelve the clubs are as full as they're going to get and we can go home. Some nights I go into the club but not last night 'cause I knew I was working early this morning.'

There it was again, the lie about working in the café. I didn't know which was worrying me more, her casual dishonesty or her relaxed demeanour. If the latter was the result of self-medication, I wanted whatever she was on. I was reminded that I knew nothing about the girl. What if she was a criminal or a cult member or a crack whore ...

'And I don't have any "clients", whatever that means,' she continued.

Brady leaned back in his chair and gazed at Kitty through half-closed eyes. I wondered if he was showing off to impress Rossiter. It was hardly for my benefit. I guessed he wanted Kitty to crack so that he could milk her for information. So far, she'd done well in the face of his provocation, but I couldn't imagine her equanimity would last. I'd lost mine quite some time ago.

'Ms Lee, I think it's time you started telling the truth about your relationship with drugs and Steven Hennessy.'

'Ok,' I interrupted. 'Why don't we just do that drug test now and put an end to this pantomime?'

'We could do that,' Rossiter said. 'All right, Detective Inspector?'

'Just a moment.' Brady hadn't taken his eyes off Kitty.

'I believe you're hiding something. There are plenty of witnesses down there on the quays who saw you attack me. That is not in question. Now,' he said, leaning forward again. 'Maybe you'd like to start again and tell me what you know. And, *don't*,' he was halfway across the table, his face right in front of Kitty's, 'waste my time with lies. Because I know where you and your mates hang out and I'll be checking up on you.'

'Whoa! That's *totally* out of order!' I was on my feet again, shaking with anger. 'Detective Rossiter?'

Rossiter put down her pen. She met Brady's eye and he nodded.

'Sit down please, Connie,' she said. 'I'd like to ask Kitty a couple of questions.'

She smiled. 'Where are you from, Kitty?'

'The Silver Bullet Café on the quays. But you know that.'

'Before the café, Kitty. Where did you come from, originally? Were you born in Ireland?'

'Oh right. Well, I'm not an illegal migrant, if that's what you mean. I was born here. My parents died when I was a baby and I was brought up by relatives. Until they went away and I was left homeless.'

A pack of lies, and not even good ones. The cops weren't going to swallow any of this. I looked over at Brady, expecting another tirade, but he was doodling on the pad in front of him, drawing boxes inside boxes. Rossiter smiled at Kitty again.

'Any idea where the relatives are now?'

'Oh, they're all back in China. Somewhere in ... you know ... China. We've kind of lost contact.'

'Ok. And Stevie. How long did you know him?'

'Nearly three years. We met when we were both sleeping rough. I was thirteen, Stevie was fourteen.'

'Can you give us a bit of background on Stevie? Where he came from, anything about his family?'

'He said he came from the West, somewhere small, way out the country. That's all I know.'

'Did he not talk about his past at all then?'

'No,' she said brightly. 'Not really, no.'

For a couple of seconds, the wall clock's tick sounded loud in the silent room.

'Thanks Kitty,' Rossiter said gently. 'That's very helpful. Stevie and you must have been very close.'

'He wasn't my boyfriend, if that's what you mean. He was totally gay. No, it was like he was my brother. He looked after me, you know? He made sure I was safe, that I had food.'

It was easy to tell when Kitty was telling the truth. It was when the tears came.

'Was Stevie in some kind of trouble, Kitty?'

'Nope. Not that I know about anyway.'

Not half, I thought, remembering what she told me before the interview.

'Like I said,' Kitty continued, 'he was gay, so there was always a danger, you know? He had some weird friends ...'

Brady looked up.

'Weird like Ozzie Wolf?'

'No!' Kitty laughed. 'Ozzie's harmless. Weird like other people I don't know but I've heard about.'

'Names?' Brady demanded.

She shook her head.

'I don't have any names. I used to be worried sick about Stevie sometimes. But he went off the drugs before Christmas and he stayed off them. That's what I mean, about the injecting or skin-popping or whatever. He wouldn't have done it.'

She was shaking her head at Brady.

'And he was looking forward to art college. His painting was going really well.'

Kitty stared at us in desperation, the tears streaming down her face again.

'What am I going to do without him?'

I squeezed her hand, fighting back the tears myself. So much love, so many lies.

Rossiter bent her head as she continued to write, one hand supporting her forehead.

'I believe we're done,' Brady said. He stood up and spoke directly to the mic, 'Interview concluded, twelve twenty-two pm.'

He gazed at me for a moment and then at Kitty.

'Thank you, Ms Ortelius,' he murmured and he left the room without looking back.

Rossiter also rose, and, picking up her pad, moved towards the door.

'Give me a minute with Detective Inspector Brady,' she said. 'I'll be right back.'

Kitty leaned over the table and buried her head in her arms. I put my arm around her shoulders and listened to the ticking of the clock on the wall.

Well, at least that's over, I thought, much relieved. It could have been a whole lot worse. Even the traffic outside seemed to have gone quiet now. So much so, that when the noise of the gunshots rang out, it sounded like an explosion in the room.

4

THE SHARK

The door to the interrogation room flew open, hit the wall with a bang and swung back again. Detective Rossiter pushed past it and entered the room, pale-faced and shaking.

'There's been a shooting outside, a hit. The victim managed to get away. He's here. He's hurt ...' She had difficulty speaking '... and you know him. It's Pius Fogarty.'

Kitty wailed and raced out the door past Rossiter.

We took off after her, Rossiter calling, 'Come back here, Kitty. You're *not* to go out there.'

We caught her in the hall. I grabbed one of her arms, Rossiter caught the other and together we restrained the struggling girl from breaking through the crowd gathered in the reception area. Worried faces turned towards us. I looked past them to the figure lying motionless on the floor. It was Fogarty. Brady bent over him, trying to talk to him while a kneeling officer applied first aid. He was still alive, for now at least.

The officer at the reception desk was on the phone to the emergency services, his voice urgent. 'Yes. The victim's conscious. He's lost some blood. Gunshot, shoulder injury, possibly more wounds elsewhere. Not sure how many times he's been hit. Sounded like there were multiple shots. Ok, he's on the floor just inside the entrance.'

He called to Brady, 'They're on their way. They'll take him to the Mater.'

Brady stood up and glowered around the room.

'Jesus, can we have a bit of room here? Today seems to be my day for moving on gawkers. Come on, some of you must have work to do. Go back to your desks, for God's sake.'

The crowd of officers and administrators moved away slowly, leaving a clear view of the trail of bright red spots splattered on the floor. It led from the glazed double doors at the entrance to the place where Fogarty had fallen.

Kitty stood quietly now, no longer struggling. I released her arm and moved closer to get a better look, ignoring Brady's command to stay clear. Fogarty lay flat on his back, his eyes closed, blood pooled around the back of his neck and shoulders.

'I don't believe it,' I said aloud.

If I hadn't got involved, if he'd been the one to accompany Kitty to the Garda Station instead of me, this wouldn't have happened. Now I had something else to feel guilty about. The victim stirred and raised his head, groaning with pain. He wanted to say something. I moved to his side and stooped down to hear him rasp, 'I didn't know you cared.'

As his head sank back again, I swear the bastard was laughing at me. I resisted the urge to give him a good kick.

Kitty clutched my arm. 'Is this what Stevie meant, Connie? About the danger?'

'God, no. This must be an accident ... a mistaken identity thing.'

My words fooled neither of us.

The ambulance crew burst through the doors and within minutes Fogarty was stretchered out and driven off at high speed, the blue light flashing, siren screaming.

The double doors slammed closed in their wake. The trail of blood on the floor was blurred now and patterned with multiple footprints. I took Kitty by the elbow and steered her around the sticky mess, heading for the exit. I pretended not to feel the suck of the bloodied lino on the soles of my shoes or the ice-cold of Kitty's flesh or the pounding of my heart. As we reached the doors, I glanced back. Detective Inspector Brady remained standing at the reception desk, watching us silently. He looked as if he might say something, but changed his mind. Instead he turned and walked quickly down the hall.

'Connie, Kitty – hold on there a minute!' Rossiter was back in official mode as she emerged from a doorway, almost colliding with Brady in her haste to catch us.

'Look,' she said, 'don't worry about Fogarty, we've just received word that his injuries aren't life-threatening. But we need to finish up with you, Kitty. Detective Inspector Brady has agreed to drop the charges against you on a couple of conditions. We have your apology to him on record. And I want you to promise me that you'll stay out of trouble. Ok?'

Kitty nodded.

'You'll allow us to take the drug and alcohol tests you promised. Right?'

'Right,' Kitty said and, following a nudge from me, 'Thanks.'

Rossiter let us leave immediately after the blood tests. She didn't say anything about results and we didn't ask. She walked us out and shook my hand on the station steps.

'Thanks for your help, Connie. It's never easy for us to deal with troubled juveniles. Detective Inspector Brady's a talented and effective officer, but his approach may not always be the most sensitive –'

'Nothing a truckload of lithium wouldn't cure.'

Rossiter smiled. 'He's been under a lot of pressure lately. This shooting won't help. Right on our doorstep too.'

I wanted to ask her about Fogarty, about who could have shot him and why. But before going there, I needed to know more about her connection with him. I opened my mouth but then stopped. She didn't look in the mood for an exchange of confidences.

'I'll be in touch,' Rossiter said, handing me a card. 'Here's my number in case you need me ...'

Her voice trailed off, drowned out by the prolonged honking of a car horn right in front of us.

A horrendously ugly vehicle waited there, obstructing the path of the trams and buses around the city's main bus station nearby. It looked like it belonged in some grainy Kruschev-era news footage showing the arrival of moustachioed politicians at a convention for war criminals. Its black bodywork gleamed in the midday sunshine and large, staring headlamps bristled in front. Its monstrous chrome grille looked like the grinning teeth of a carnivore who has just spotted dinner. The bonnet carried a huge silver emblem of a deer. Flags fluttered on either side, one with a psychedelic Mexican day-of-the-dead skull with flowers in its eye sockets, the other had a black background with yellow block letters spelling STALAG 17.

'Hop in, sweeties,' said Ozzie Wolf, unperturbed by the curses of the bus drivers and the ineffective clanging of several tram bells. He was parked right across the tracks, holding up two trams full of passengers.

I made to move but Kitty wouldn't budge.

'I'm not getting in to that,' she said. 'What if someone I know sees me? State of it.'

'Get that thing out of here right now before I have to arrest you all,' Rossiter said. She looked like she'd had enough of us for one day.

I dragged Kitty down the steps and shoved her into the back passenger seat, slamming the door after her. I got in the front, beside Ozzie.

'Thought Kitty'd need a lift to pick up some of her stuff,' Ozzie said as he started the engine. 'So why not take The Shark out for a little spin?'

Kitty rolled her eyes. 'It's an embarrassment, is what it is. I thought your other one was bad, that disgusting jeep thing, but this is the pits.'

'I phoned the station to see if you were nearly done.' Ozzie pulled out slowly, waving to the large, red-faced truck-driver who was rapidly approaching and who looked like he was planning to dismember us with his bare hands. 'So, I hear the Fogarty fella's been shot?'

'You don't seem surprised,' I said. 'Or even the slightest bit concerned for his welfare.'

'Bound to happen eventually,' Ozzie laughed. 'I'm sure he'll be grand. Can't kill a bad thing, eh, Kitty?'

She groaned. 'God, will you just get us out of here.'

The Shark continued along the tram tracks at a stately pace and, to the relief of hundreds of delayed public transport passengers, finally turned right on to Amiens Street. I looked through the rear window as we passed the corner, as if I'd see some answers to the many nagging questions about Fogarty's shooting. I opened my mouth to say something, but Ozzie smiled at me swiftly, pressed a button on the sound system and the car filled with the clamour of Russian girl punk-rockers.

On a cordoned-off area of the street, a Garda investigative unit carefully bagged evidence while the city traffic around them slowly returned to its normal level of chaos.

5

NOBODY HERE IS INNOCENT

I stood outside the café watching Ozzie's outlandish car pull away, noting the sticker beside a rear fin that said '*Mein anderes Auto ist Deutsch.*' I hoped his other car was also more low-key, but I doubted it. He and his ungrateful teenage passenger drove off to collect her belongings from multiple locations. And I had to return to my role as incompetent barista in the café that time forgot.

The minute I peered through the steamed-up window I saw that something was different. Customers. The place was full of them, occupying every one of the formica-topped tables, some actually sitting on the tables.

I'd asked Josie Corcoran, Aggie's elderly pal, to hold the fort, expecting she'd use the time to catch up on her knitting or a little light character assassination. But by the looks of it, she wouldn't have had a chance for any of that. The plates on the counter stand now held nothing but a scattering of crumbs. A solitary misshapen currant bun remained, looking lonely and rejected. Empty egg cartons and sliced bread wrappers piled up beside the sink alongside an industrial-sized baked beans tin. Nearby, the frying pan cooled, a crinkle of coagulating skin forming on its two inches of hot grease. The kitchen wouldn't have been this busy in decades. There's nothing like a tragedy to stimulate the appetite.

Josie emerged from a cloud of steam around the stove. She wore a nasty brown and yellow housecoat and a disapproving look to match.

'Aggie wouldn't like it,' she said. 'All these strangers. And the things they're asking for, I never heard of half of them. Bagels? I gave them black pudding and told them to take it or leave it. Those young ones are all right though, Stevie's friends – God love them.'

She indicated, with an incline of her head, the group sitting around two adjacent tables. I'd seen some of them with Stevie the day I'd arrived, a few of his gay friends from the nightclub and some girls from the College of Art. They were pierced, tattooed and tear-stained. Some wept, others guffawed at shared memories as the stories flowed.

I recognised a few faces at the other tables, a couple of retired dock workers and a woman with a perm and a headscarf straight from the nineteen fifties. Josie's friend, Viv Foley sat in the corner close to a man who looked both foreign and oddly familiar to me. It was those new faces that bothered Josie. I guessed she thought Aggie would hold her personally responsible if any yuppies slipped in. Like the Eye of Sauron, her reproachful glare swivelled away from the suspected undesirables and settled on me.

'The guards let you go, then,' she said.

'They did, for now, Josie. But they're on to me – they'll get me yet.'

She was not amused. 'Where's that young one you went with?'

'Kitty? She's gone to get her things. She's moving in here, temporarily. She'll help out here in the café. Maybe you can show her what to do when she comes in. Give her a few jobs. It'll be great ...'

The expression on Josie's face told me just how great she thought it would be. She pushed a full milk carton across the counter to someone who asked for a jug and muttered 'Jesus, Mary and Joseph. A tramp and a hussy. We'll be robbed blind.'

'Did you hear about Fogarty?' I ventured, hoping to change the subject.

Her eyes told me to say no more as she squeezed my arm. 'I forgot to tell you. There's someone over there waiting for you.'

She flicked her head in the direction of a slight, bespectacled, ginger-haired man who sat alone at a table by the window.

'One of them bleedin' journalists,' she hissed. 'Tell them nothing.'

He rose as I approached and put out a hand to shake mine while reaching into an inside jacket pocket for a card.

'Jimmy Mooney. Crime Correspondent with *The City Times*. You're Constance Ortelius, proprietor of the Silver Bullet Café?

'Acting proprietor.'

'Do you mind if I ask you a few questions?'

I must have looked less than enthusiastic.

'It won't take long.'

'Well, ok,' I said, sitting down, suddenly exhausted. 'I could do with a break.'

One of the students put a dented stainless steel pot of tea and a chipped white pyrex cup and saucer in front of me. Josie must have taken pity on me and sent it down. Maybe she wasn't as hard-hearted as she looked.

Mooney began to fire out questions like tennis balls from a ball launcher.

'Ms Ortelius, as a representative of small business in this area, do you have an opinion on the drug-fuelled crime explosion in this part of town and its impact on trade and tourism? Would you agree with the statement made by a city councillor that we need to get the junkies and beggars out of the city centre – relocate the drug clinics and homeless shelters?'

'Sorry?'

'Do you support the Cleaner Liffeyside Initiative?'

I wondered if Mooney was a bit on the drug-fuelled side himself. The man was wired.

'Ok, I'll come back to that. Specifically about today's events, then ... There are suggestions that the death of Steven Hennessy might not be the accident it appears. It's my job to get to the bottom of these rumours. I believe that you and young Kitty Lee were taken in for questioning by the guards this morning. Do you mind me asking you what that was about?'

'Kitty was charged with assaulting a police officer. She pushed Detective Inspector Brady ... by mistake. I accompanied her to the Garda Station at her request, as she's a juvenile. The charges have since been dropped.'

Mooney spoke into his recording device. 'Kitty Lee, homeless, Asian/Irish female – about fifteen years old?'

'Sixteen.'

'Sixteen years old. Works the streets at night around city centre night clubs ...'

'Hang on a minute –'

He continued talking, '... ostensibly as a club rep.'

'Look, Mr Mooney –'

'Jimmy.'

'I've stuff to do. I don't have time to sit here and listen to you making things up.'

Mooney looked contrite. 'I'm sorry if I've offended you.'

He switched off his machine.

'Let's start again,' he said. 'Off the record. I know you haven't been back in this country very long – just a few days, isn't it?'

I nodded.

'So here's my first question. In the name of all that's holy, what possessed you to come back here? Especially from a civilised country like Holland. Are you out of your mind?'

I moved to get up.

No, don't go – please! Here, let me do you a favour. Some information. Ok?'

'What kind of information?'

He leaned forward and spoke in a low, urgent voice.

'You'll be aware from the media that the city centre is a hotbed of drug-dealing, vice, racketeering and violent gangland activities. And that paramilitary republican groups have turned their focus to the opportunities ...'

He stopped to draw a breath. I tried to suppress a yawn.

'With respect, Jimmy, that's all very interesting. But it's not exactly news. And I don't see what it's got to do with me.'

'Here's some news for you then,' Mooney said. 'You need to be very careful. Everyone you've been consorting with in this quaint little neighbourhood is known to the guards.'

'Everyone?' I looked over at Josie, cackling with laughter at some joke with Viv Foley.

'Nobody here is innocent. Many of your neighbours and customers come from long lines of criminal families. This port, like all ports, has always been a centre for racketeering. Most of the families who live around here have been implicated for generations.'

Mooney's gaze on me was intense.

'Now it's all ramped up. There are new players – Nigerians, Chinese, Eastern Europeans. Our post-boom bust/hit-and-miss recovery has thrown everything wide open. Government agencies have been decimated by cutbacks and the guards can't cope. You know what it all adds up to?'

I shook my head, too tired to argue.

'It adds up to a land of golden opportunity for any evil bastard with a suitably sociopathic frame of mind.'

Mooney's eyes were burning. He was clearly a madman.

'Look, Jimmy,' I said, hoping to get rid of him, 'Tell you what. I'll tip you off the minute an evil sociopath comes in here for a cup of tea and a currant bun.'

'You may sneer,' Mooney said, rising to go. 'But don't say you weren't warned.'

He pushed his card towards me. 'Here. You know where to find me.'

His slam of the door was like a slap on the face. I shivered as a cold draught sliced through the muggy warmth of the afternoon.

6

HUMAN RESOURCES

The last customer departed just before six leaving me in the middle of an intergenerational war. Kitty had marched in and dumped a small mountain of bags on the floor while Josie watched her with her arms folded and a look on her that would turn a normal person to stone.

'Get that pile of rubbish out of my way this minute or I'll throw it straight in the river.'

'Then I'll have to throw you in as well, won't I, you vicious old bag,' Kitty retorted, stepping closer like she was more than ready to do it.

'Connie, you keep that little minx well away from me,' Josie snarled. 'Or I will not be responsible for my actions, so help me God.'

'Look, you two,' I said through clenched teeth. 'I'm doing my absolute best to keep it together here, but you're really not helping. I'm in a *very* delicate state emotionally and I've had *more* than enough hassle for one day. So I'm only going to say this once. The pair of you'd better try your damnedest to get on. Josie, you promised Aggie you'd help out here. Kitty, you promised me the exact same thing. So just fucking do it – all right?'

Two resentful faces looked back at me but clearly knew better than to argue with someone so obviously on the edge. For the next few minutes, Kitty ran up and down the stairs to her room while maintaining a safe distance from the Ancient One. Josie departed a little later to visit the most recent addition to her clutch of great-grandchildren and Kitty returned to the Sunrise Hotel to fetch more of her stuff.

Finally, I sat at a table by the window, alone, breathing deeply while holding my aching head. It wasn't so bad, I told myself. I'd just checked the till, expecting to see it empty. Instead, piles of notes and coins looked back at me. Even the tip jar on the counter was full. The locals must be more honest than Mooney claimed, at least when it came to paying for their tea and coffee. Maybe now I could hire someone to fix Aggie's monstrous forty-year-old coffee machine which hadn't shown a spark of life since I got here.

Feeling better, I got up and began checking the supplies like a real café manager. After all the noise of the afternoon, the place was unnaturally quiet. I had just climbed on a chair to switch on the portable TV on the corner shelf above the fridge when my phone rang. I answered it while examining the broken remote control I'd found. It was held together with sellotape. The on/off button was missing and the uncovered battery was stuck in with a lump of blue tack. Or maybe it was chewing gum.

An efficient female voice said, 'Constance Ortelius? Can you take a call from Aleka Marr, Heartbeat Services? I'll put her through.'

I'd never heard of her but she seemed to know me.

'Hi, Connie? This is Aleka, Aleka Marr.' Her voice sounded friendly, her accent American.

'I've been meaning to give you a call. Apologies for the late hour – and on a Sunday too. Heartbeat has a major event coming up on Friday so we're working twenty four-seven. I just realised that I'll be in your neighbourhood tomorrow morning and I was wondering if we could meet? In addition to housing services, I'm involved in a group that supports SMEs in the area ...'

'You support what?'

'Oops – sorry about the jargon! Small to Medium-sized Enterprises. Businesses like the Silver Bullet Café. There are a range of free supports available and I'd like to outline them to you tomorrow, if that's ok.'

She didn't sound like a woman who'd accept the usual polite rebuffs.

'Great,' I said, planning to dump her on Josie. 'Drop in whenever you're around.'

'Looking forward to it!' she said and rang off just as the TV came on unexpectedly and at full volume. Gregorian chant resounded thunderously in the room, echoing like a football stadium full of hooligan monks. Images of ancient stained-glass windows and shots of St Patrick's Cathedral illustrated a documentary about the discovery of some long-lost medieval artefact. The racket was so loud and remote control so ineffective, I had to stand on the chair again and yank out the plug to prevent myself from being deafened. It was only then that I heard the tapping at the door. I thought it was Kitty arriving back with more of her endless belongings. But a further, more insistent, tap on the window came from a bearded man in his fifties, wearing a tweed jacket and well-cut jeans. He stepped back to wait with both hands in his jeans pockets. An unusually handsome, blond young man in a dark suit stood close behind him, mirroring his stance like a more attractive shadow.

'Sorry, we're closed,' I said as I opened the door a little. Wrong move.

'We're not customers,' the older man laughed. 'We just thought it'd be nice to call by and welcome you to the area. I'm Brian Costigan and this is my associate, Dean Clarke. We're with Steyne River Securities, South Docklands – across the river. You may have heard of our director, Dessie Donlon?'

I shook my head. 'I'm new here.'

'Of course you are,' the older man continued. 'May we come in for a moment?'

His foot was over the threshold and before I could do anything, they were inside. I stood there not knowing what to do, watching as they walked around checking the menu, examining the remaining currant bun.

'You're a brave woman, running a business in this area – and all alone too.' Costigan said cheerfully.

He stood looking out the café window at the river, his hands in his pockets again. His young friend leaned backwards in a chair and began to run a pair of spoons across his outstretched fingers, back and forth. My ears felt like they were bleeding. I resisted the urge to grab the spoons and hammer them all over his handsome, rubbery, hard-boiled mug.

'Just trying to make a go of it,' I said.

'There's a lot of people out there trying to make a go of things,' Costigan said, making an expansive gesture across the cityscape, the panorama of old and new buildings crowding down to the river. He stood with his back to me for a moment, gazing out the window thoughtfully.

Then he turned and, taking a chair, indicated I should sit down too.

'These are difficult times, Constance, and people in my line of work have many unpleasant decisions to make. But I want you to know, that, in so far as possible, we'll try to ensure that the process of change doesn't impact on you unduly.'

'What is this?' I asked. His language reminded me of my last employer, a Dutch corporate so subtly manipulative that I actually felt sorry for *them* and the pain they expressed when they sacked me. 'Are you from Human Resources?'

'Human Resources?' Costigan smiled at his companion, who smiled right back at him. 'Yeah, I like that.'

He continued, 'You know, Constance, challenging times like these demand a flexible approach. At Steyne River Securities we like to think of ourselves as an agile organisation, able to respond swiftly to new situations. Do you have a flexible business approach, Constance?'

'Maybe.' I had no idea where he was going with this but it didn't feel good.

'That's great, Constance. Because we'd like to make you a proposal which will work well for us *and* for the entire community. The community is our greatest asset. Wouldn't you agree, Constance?'

'Totally.'

'Good, good,' he smiled approvingly. 'You see, up until recently things were very straightforward. Our organisation supplied traditional security-type services to businesses in the area. Our focus was entirely local and personal and our clients valued the service.' He sighed. 'You know, for years you wouldn't see a broken shop window on this row. And there were practically no fires or attacks on shopkeepers as they were locking up. I like to think we played a role in that. You know what I mean?'

I nodded. I knew exactly what he meant.

'Now things have changed, Constance. Globalisation, economic turbulence, shortage of credit to small companies ... At Steyne River Securities we want our clients to have full confidence in our services. To do that, we need to keep abreast of developments as they occur. Which brings me to our proposal.'

Oh here we go, I thought. Why doesn't he just take the money from the till and have done with it.

Costigan signalled his associate. The younger man rose and moved to the door. Instinctively, I stood up too and backed away from the table towards the kitchen, keeping my chair in front of me for protection.

Costigan stayed seated and raised both hands, palms towards me, in a gesture of peace.

'Whoa, whoa, Constance! There's no need for you to be alarmed. We're not going to hurt you. We just want to talk to you.'

He looked towards the door.

'I want Dean to keep an eye out. You see, there's a level of confidentiality involved and we don't want any unexpected interruptions. Isn't that right, Deano?'

Dean was leaning against the café door with his arms folded and a smile on his face that was less than reassuring.

'Yeah. That's right, Brian.'

I stood my ground with my back to the counter. Out of the corner of my eye I spotted a cake slice lying close-by. Not exactly your defence weapon of choice, but if I could reach it fast enough it might be better than nothing. I decided to go on the offensive.

'Look, Brian. Aggie told me that she'd refused all offers of protection and there's no way she's ever going to pay them. If that's what your proposal is about, you're talking to the wrong person. Aggie still owns this place and you'll have to take it up with her. She's in Vegas at the moment,' I added, helpfully.

'Now, Constance,' Costigan said. 'You shouldn't leap to conclusions. I'm familiar with the negotiations with your aunt. She's a fine woman and I'm sure we'll reach a satisfactory conclusion eventually. No, this is something else we'd like to arrange with you. Something that will allow you to retain your profits without us having to top-slice. And it will help keep your aunt safe.'

Oh Jesus, I thought. 'Is Aggie in some kind of danger?'

'She's fine, to the best of my knowledge,' Costigan said. 'Although, if you're talking to her, perhaps you could advise her to be careful about the company she keeps. Now, what I'd like to suggest to you, Constance, is that you simply provide us with information at the point of need.'

'You want me to spy for you?'

Brian looked pained. 'I wouldn't call it spying. But yes, we do require information. You are ideally placed to overhear conversations, pick up on gossip, observe meetings, notice who's talking to who, who's dealing to who ...'

'Who's screwing who ...' Deano grinned from the door.

'Knowledge is power,' Costigan said. 'And we need to know what's going on.' He raised his hand as I opened my mouth to respond.

'You don't need to decide now. We'll leave you to think about it for ... say, twenty-four hours? Meanwhile you might like to call your auntie. Every year people go missing from those poker classics and are never found, or so our friends out there tell us. The Nevada Desert is a big place ...'

'Someone's coming,' Dean said. 'That Chinese bird.'

'Ok, we're done here anyway.'

Kitty appeared at the door, laden with bags.

'You'd better let young China Rose in there, Deano.'

Dean opened the door just wide enough to let Kitty squeeze through, forcing her to push against him on her way in.

'Hey, Gorgeous,' he leered down at her.

'Fuck off, you disgusting letch. I've heard about you, Dean Clarke.'

Costigan moved. 'Come on, Dean.'

'Think about my proposal, Constance, ok? It's a good solution. What would you call it? Win-win?'

Win, win, for Steyne River Securities, I thought despairingly as I watched them go. Shit, shit for me.

Kitty put down her bags and turned to me.

'Lovely company you're keeping there, Connie,' she said. 'By the way, I have some news. Hey, what's up – why are you looking all weird?'

'Because *everything's* all weird,' I groaned, my face squeezed in my hands. I clutched my hair by the roots and forced my eyes open, willing the sense of darkness spiralling around me to stop.

'Kitty, your news will have to wait. I'm phoning Las Vegas.'

7

Aggie

'SORRY I MISSED YOUR CALL. COFFEE BREAK IN 2 MINS – CALL BACK.'

The smiley face at the end of Aggie's text message winked and stuck out its tongue at me. Cute. She'd really taken to her new phone. If only it wasn't permanently locked on All Caps, her messages might be less alarming.

I looked at the crappy screen on my own sad, wannabe iPhone, an emergency purchase and the only thing I could afford. I wondered how I was going to tell Aggie about Stevie. I decided to first check on her own safety – and mine – and rang her the instant my phone pinged with her 'Call me'.

'Well howdy, Connie!'

My heart sank as any hope of a sensible conversation instantly receded. She'd gone native after being in the US for less than forty eight hours.

I cut her short before she could launch into an endless account of the poker competition, how many tables were left, who was out already, who was still in and what her chances were.

'Aggie, I had a visit just now from Steyne River Securities. Two guys. Brian Costigan and Dean Clarke. Do you know them? They were trying to get me to spy for them. They said it would help to keep you safe. They said that the desert is a big place ...'

'Ah now, Connie. Don't mind that pair. Sure I knew them when they were in short trousers. That lot've been trying to snare me for years. Threatened me with all kinds of things, but I won't play ball. They know that I know their Ma's and they'd never live it down if anything happened to me.'

'Are you having me on? Jesus, Aggie, we're a far cry from the days of the short trousers and the Ma's ...'

I was about to tell her about Stevie's death and Fogarty getting shot and Mooney's warnings.

'I have to go, Connie. They're calling us back to the tables. Don't worry about me. I've made lovely new friends. I'll tell you all about it when we get a chance for another chat. Don't forget, there's people around who can help you if you need a hand ...'

'Like Aleka Marr?' I said. 'She's coming to visit tomorrow.'

'That one? She's way too interfering, with all her talk about support schemes and the like.'

'Ok,' I was a bit taken aback. 'What about the guards, then. Anthony Brady?'

'Brady's no fool, but he's very full of himself. And too pally with those yuppie types.'

'Ok. Who can help me then?'

There was silence for a few seconds. Why was it so hard for her to think of someone?

Finally she ventured, 'Fogarty's all right – up to a point. He's been good to me in the past. Just don't tell him too much. And for God's sake don't start putting the glad eye on him. It won't get you anywhere.'

'I have no idea what you're on about.'

'Yes, you do. And you'd be a sitting duck when it comes to fellas like that. You're fairly presentable when you make the effort, although I won't mention the current state of your hair. What were you thinking? And you go around all naïve and starry-eyed. Honey, they'll see you coming.'

Ouch! A stab in the front. The *modus operandi* of elderly relatives with advanced skills in undermining and disparagement. Pressing a palm over my wounded heart, I took a deep breath. 'Ok, so I *might* be able to trust Fogarty. I just shouldn't be in a room alone with him. Is that what you're saying?'

'Exactly,' Aggie said. 'And there's Ozzie Wolf. He's a decent enough young lad for a German – in spite of all they say about the drugs and the kinky sex. Just watch out for that thing he has.'

'What thing?'

'The older woman thing. It's unusual but I don't think there's a law against it. In fairness now, he's never tried anything with me. But sure Connie, you should be well able for the lot of them, with your Amsterdam experience and all.'

That reminded me.

'Aggie, did you tell people round here that I lived in the red-light district in Amsterdam?'

'Well you did, didn't you? Where's the harm in it?'

'It's just that some people seem to have got the wrong impression.'

My work in Amsterdam had been based in the anonymous high-rise offices of a multinational academic publishing company. My Dublin neighbours had latched on to an altogether different story and, from the hints I was getting, they believed I'd been offering my professional services out of a window on a street off the Zeedijk.

But Aggie wasn't interested in my reputation and, almost as depressingly, her wild west accent was getting stronger by the minute.

'Well Jeez, Connie, all publicity's good publicity, ain't that the truth? Josie – now there's a gal you can rely on. And Viv too. She's just hunky dory *and* she has connections in the Church.'

'No offence, Aggie, but between them, Josie and Viv are nearly two hundred years old. You're telling me that the only people I can trust around here are an ancient pair of daily communicants with a fondness for gin?'

I didn't mention that I was terrified of Josie or my suspicion that she and Viv viewed me as a dangerous half-wit.

'Sorry Connie, gotta go. It's the last call. Catch ya later – and quit yer frettin'!'

I stared at the silent phone in disbelief. Then I remembered what my new protectors from Dessie Donlon's gang had said, something about the company Aggie's keeping out there. Well, it would have to keep until next time.

I turned to talk to Kitty, but there was no sign of her.

'Kitty!' I called out.

No response. The café was in darkness and I was completely alone.

8

THE EIGHT BELLS

It was almost dark outside and the streetlights had come on. Torrential rain hammered down on the hot summer streets for the second night in a row. Water cascaded from the broken overhead gutter and splashed noisily on the pavement in front of the window. I shivered. It was time to lock up.

I pulled on a jacket to go out and tackle the window shutter, first calling Kitty's name again, thinking she might be upstairs. The shutter was misbehaving as usual and by the time I had it secured and locked, I was drenched. It was only when I got back into the kitchen that I spotted the chalked scrawl on the blackboard.

'Gone to pub – 8 Bells. Meet me there. *PLEEEEESE!*'

Ah, no. I'd already had enough for one day. The last thing I needed now was an unfamiliar pub filled with more of the local criminals Mooney warned me about. I poured what I hoped was soup into a mug, grabbed a hunk of bread and sat down to consider the options.

I could pretend I never saw the message, go to bed and try to forget the whole, horrible day. But I'd promised to look after Kitty. What if something happened to her? Sure, she was streetwise and knew the neighbourhood better than I did. But a sixteen-year-old girl in a city centre pub full of cutthroats and robbers? I remembered Fogarty's look of disbelief earlier on when I'd failed to act fast and get help for the boatmen. Ok, I decided. I'd go over there quickly, find Kitty and bring her home. Shouldn't take any more than a few minutes.

I slammed the door behind me and stood for an instant, considering the sheets of rain, before running across the road and over the Samuel Beckett Bridge.

In the ten minutes it took to reach the door of the Eight Bells, I got soaked to the skin, my face awash, hair dripping. I smoothed back the strands that were stuck to my forehead and felt a cold stream trickling down my back. As I squelched my way up to the bar, I left a trail of wet footprints on the bare floorboards.

'Ah, Jaysus,' the barman said when he saw me. 'Here.'

He handed me a soggy tea towel.

'There's a dryer in the ladies.'

I wiped my damp forehead to stop the water running into my eyes. Now at least I could see where I was. It was the kind of place that was meant to be seen by gaslight, that way you'd miss the damp patches on the walls and the nicotine-coloured ceiling. The sparse clientele was almost entirely what you'd expect – male, working class, middle-aged or older. They sat on the high stools at the bar, hunched over their pints with their backs to the door. A couple of what Aggie would call 'yuppie types' sat together in a corner. I guessed they were from the new apartment buildings up the road.

Two young women, with tanned legs, shorts and plastic rain-jackets, bent over the guidebooks and maps spread out on their table. Not really a place for tourists, I thought, but then I remembered that Windmill Lane Studios, where U2 first recorded, used to be nearby. Music fans from all over the world made pilgrimages there, leaving messages on a wall that became a tourist attraction in itself until it was demolished. Maybe someone should tell the girls. Or maybe they were just lost.

I spotted Kitty at the far end of the bar, talking to a man whose back was turned to me. I pointed towards the toilets and she waved back, then returned to her conversation.

The women's toilets were cold and smelled strongly of damp and the swampiness of the river. There were signs of water damage on the ceiling around the fitting for the naked light bulb. Someone had half-repaired the hole and left a folded stepladder propped against a wall and some pieces of timber and plasterboard beneath it. The two cubicles were occupied. I tried to turn off a cold tap that gushed and spluttered into a hand basin, but it wouldn't budge. The hand dryer was dead. Pushing the button had no effect and banging on it several times didn't work either. I was about to squelch back to the bar when the woman in the right hand cubicle began to talk to her friend next door, unaware that anyone else was around.

'Desperate about that young fella they pulled out of the river this morning, wasn't it?'

'Ah God, not another one,' said the left cubicle. 'How many's that over the last few months? Who was it, do you know? One of them junkie skangers or an oul' drunk from Fogarty's place?'

'Don't know. I heard Fogarty was there when they pulled him out. And that fella from the nightclub, you know, Stalag 17?'

'Him? He's some fucking weirdo! Course he's a German, isn't he?'

'A half a German or something. He has that massive tattoo going down his neck.'

'That's not the only place he has a tattoo,' said the right cubicle, authoritatively. 'I heard he has a swastika on one of his arse cheeks.'

Screeches of laughter shook the cubicles.

'Where did you hear that?'

'From the nurse down in D-Doc. I suppose she was injecting him or something. He travels a lot. Probably needs shots.'

'I heard that he runs black masses in the basement of that nightclub.'

'No way!'

'It's true! They're very popular. People come all the way across town for them. We should go sometime!'

'Handy for him that the Sunrise Hotel is only a few doors up, isn't it? Plentiful supply of fresh meat!'

'Oh, that's a terrible thing to say!' said her friend and they laughed uproariously. There was a moment's pause.

'I wonder,' said the right cubicle, 'If Pius Fogarty has tattoos in any interesting places?'

'Well you'd have to ask herself – what's her name? You know, the guard, the little, dark one. Didn't they have something going on?'

'You're right! And you could ask that one who's minding the café for Aggie Moran while she's away – her niece, isn't it?'

I went cold and it wasn't because of the damp. They were talking about me.

'Yeah, Fogarty's in there all the time now, like a fly around shite.'

Charming, I thought.

'I heard she's one of them high class hoors, or she was until recently. Back from Amsterdam, you know.'

'With all the tricks of the trade! And knowing Fogarty, he wouldn't be backward in coming forward in that department, if you know what I mean. You should ask *her* where he has his tattoos!'

Their laughter turned to outraged shrieks as they were plunged into darkness. I pocketed the hot light bulb, now wrapped in layers of tissue, and smiled grimly as I went back to the bar. The piece of timber I'd wedged under the door should keep them there for a bit. We'll see how funny they found being stuck in the cold and the damp. When I got back, the barman was pondering two large, untouched Bacardi and Cokes on an unoccupied table.

'Are they gone? ' he asked me.

I shrugged. 'Must be,' I said and watched him clear the table.

I ordered a drink with a sense of some satisfaction, a feeling that faded the minute I saw who Kitty was talking to.

9

The Blackening

The lunatic reporter, Jimmy Mooney, rose to go to the bar as I approached.

'What're you having?' he asked.

'Nothing from you, thanks,' I said. 'I just ordered. And Kitty's fine too, she's underage.'

'That'll be a strawberry mojito for me, Jimmy,' Kitty told him. 'And a packet of peanuts.'

She turned to me. 'The barman's doing a course in mixology – he's not bad. You should try one.'

'Just get her the nuts,' I snapped at Mooney. 'Then please go away.'

Mooney took my order surprisingly well and moved to the bar, staggering a little.

'What are you doing, Kitty, talking to a journalist? Are you crazy? I hope you didn't give him any information. He'll twist everything you say.'

She hissed back at me. 'You're just as bad as that Josie one. The pair of you are so negative, it's doing my head in. I mean, one of us had to do something, right? Mooney might be able to help me find out what happened to Stevie. So, he's creepy and kind of loopy but at least he's interested. The cops don't give a shit.'

Mooney's only interested in getting a big, juicy story for himself, I thought, regardless of the consequences. God knows what she'd told him.

My hot whiskey arrived. Unseasonal, but necessary to ward off my impending pneumonia. I cupped my hands around the glass, inhaled the spiced fumes and took a careful sip. Finally, I stopped shivering and examined Kitty's face.

Her eyes were full of tears again. Beneath them, the purple rings were black against the paleness of her skin.

'You need to get some sleep, Kitty. You're wrecked.'

'I'll go home as soon as I talk to Fogarty. I want him to tell me where Stevie's stuff is.'

'Fogarty? Even if he's not at death's door, he won't be released from hospital yet,' I said, thinking back to when we skirted the pool of his blood on the Garda Station floor earlier on.

'Nah, he's grand. Discharged himself.' Kitty looked around. 'I actually thought he'd be here by now. He texted me earlier.'

'You don't think that several gunshot wounds would delay him just a bit? Is he indestructible like the Terminator?'

'No!' Kitty laughed as if I was being deliberately ridiculous. 'He wasn't hurt bad. He was wearing a vest, wasn't he? One of those Kevlon things.'

'Kev*lar*,' I said, deeply shocked. 'Why was he wearing a protective vest? Where would you even get one of those?'

'Down in the market. Fella sells them out of a black plastic sack. Loads of people have them.'

You'd think we were discussing the availability of umbrellas. I hoped she hadn't told any of this to Mooney. I glanced towards the bar to check his whereabouts.

'Looks like your journo pal has taken the hint and he's staying up there to talk to someone,' I said.

Kitty squinted over my shoulder at the men at the bar and caught Mooney's eye.

'Hey thanks, Jimmy,' she called and deftly caught the packet he threw her.

'That's Brady he's with. You know, Mr Shit-Hot Detective Inspector. Did you not recognise him?'

She watched Brady carefully for a moment. 'He's had more than a few pints. Must be off-duty. I didn't think you'd forget him in a hurry – I bet he hasn't forgotten you!'

'I've a minor problem making out faces in the distance. Need to get the eyes checked. Anyway,' I said, 'finish what you were saying about Fogarty.'

'Why?' she asked, with a sly smile. 'Are you worried about him?'

'Not particularly,' I said, wishing she wasn't such a little brat. 'Am I the only one who finds it strange that a neighbour – who just happens to be wearing a Kevlar vest – gets gunned down on the street, practically on the guards' doorstep, is rushed to hospital, and is then expected to stroll into the pub a few hours later as if nothing happened.'

'Ok,' Kitty said. 'Here's all I know about Fogarty. He was wounded in his arm or shoulder, nothing serious, just lost some blood. The other shots missed him. He left the hospital after a couple of hours and went back down to Store Street for questioning.'

'Do they know who shot him?'

'Nah. Could have been anyone, really,' she said as she shook the small bag at me. 'Nuts?'

'No, thanks. It could have been anyone? But it was broad daylight on a busy street, who's going to do that? There must be witnesses.'

'Loads of them. But no one could give a decent description. Maybe the CCTV will show something. The guards are looking for the car. I heard it was a jeep but I bet it was stolen as usual. They'll never trace it.'

'You seem very sure.'

'It's just the way things are. Fogarty will know who's behind it, or he'll be able to narrow it down.'

'He's got that many enemies?'

'Everybody's got enemies. I bet even you have one or two.'

If she'd asked me that question twenty-four hours ago, I'd have told her she was crazy. I hadn't an enemy in the world, or, I corrected myself, at least not in this part of the world. But today's events had changed that and I seemed to have clocked up a respectable number of foes, even for this neighbourhood.

'But Fogarty will never tell,' Kitty said. 'He's a dark horse.'

'Unless he can explain himself, that dark horse can trot off to another café for his morning coffee,' I said. 'I'm not having the place turned into a gangsters' den. Pius Fogarty can get himself gunned down someplace else.'

'Jesus, Connie, it's hardly his fault that he got shot. And you talk about journalists twisting things. I've a good mind not to tell you what I found out now. God knows what you'll say.'

'Here's what I'll say, Kitty: full disclosure or look for somewhere else to sleep tonight.'

'I don't think I like you anymore,' she said sulkily but changed her tack when she saw me yawn loudly and get ready to leave.

'Ok,' she said quickly, 'so when Ozzie dropped me off at the Sunrise Hotel I went to get some things I'd left in one of the lockers. I only sleep there on and off, but I use the lockers for storage. Last week I stayed with my friend Ruth on the North Strand. Her flat's tiny but she gets lonely when her boyfriend's away.'

'He's back now?'

'Finished his sentence. He'll be back inside before long though. Always is.'

She took a drink from the clear liquid in her glass. At least it wasn't a strawberry mojito. I hoped it was water and not some noxious alcopop.

'The thing is, I thought I had something in the locker, a small backpack Stevie gave me and asked me to keep safe for him. But it wasn't there today. Then I thought I'd left it in Ruth's. But it's not there either. I had a quick look in Stevie's room in the Sunrise, but it was cleaned out – nothing left.'

'Fogarty might have done that. Or maybe the guards.'

'Not the guards. They're not interested. That's why I need to see Fogarty. He can tell me what happened to the things in the locker – and where Stevie's other stuff is.'

'Any idea what was in the backpack?'

'I took a quick look when Stevie gave it to me. All I saw was a couple of sketchbooks and a pencil case.'

'So why do you think he gave it to you?'

'I don't know. He just told me to keep it safe. I did a crap job on that one, didn't I?'

She'd been unconsciously banging a beer mat against the corner of the table as she spoke. Now she brushed away another tear and started shredding the cardboard into confetti.

'Could it have been an accident, Kitty? Maybe Stevie just fell into the river ...'

'... when he was out of it on drugs? I already told you, he was off everything for months, from way back before Christmas. Except for maybe the odd bit of weed. Art college was a really big deal for him. He wouldn't have topped himself on purpose, Connie. And he wouldn't suddenly lose it and start injecting bleedin' bath salts.' She shook her head violently. 'No way would he do that.'

'But as soon as people saw Stevie's body this morning, they decided it was drugs.'

'Because of his hand. Remember what his hand was like when they pulled him out of the river, remember it was all black?'

I nodded. I'd never forget it.

'Girl I know, her feet went black from skin-popping snow blow, you know, injecting it under her skin. Same thing happens with injecting bath salts, coke, all that. Disgusting,' she shuddered. 'So when they saw Stevie's hand, they just made up their minds. Like Brady did – you heard him.'

I'd read about bath salts – the drug, not the unimaginative Mother's Day gift – in lurid media stories about legal highs and the head shops that sold them.

'So they're saying Stevie's hand was black because he injected drugs. And then what ... they think he fell into the river when he was high and drowned?'

I didn't want to say it, but that version of events did make sense.

'Yeah, but he was *off* drugs. And anyway, there's something else. That's what I wanted to tell you. I talked to some of the people in the Sunrise. They're really scared.'

'What do you mean?'

'They said there's a disease going round. They say it's really contagious. Once you get it, you're finished, there's nothing any doctor can do for you.' She paused. 'They call it the blackening. They're saying that Stevie had it.'

'They're saying Stevie died of a *disease*? Besides drugs and drowning there's *another* thing that could have killed him?'

'I don't know, Connie. I'm trying to make sense of it. I saw Stevie's hand up close. There was something wrong about it, different to what you see from skin popping. His hand and wrist were all black, and ... rotten, like ... like a piece of old fruit under a market stall.'

She wasn't making it up, she was way too scared. But that disease theory of hers didn't explain how Stevie ended up in the river.

'You're saying his hand was black because of this disease, not because of drugs?'

'Not drugs.' Kitty's eyes gleamed with absolute conviction. 'If they find drugs in his body, we'll know that someone killed Stevie.'

'Oh God, Kitty. Promise me you didn't tell any of this to Mooney.'

Kitty's eyes focused on the desiccated beer mat on the table as she mumbled. 'Just the last bit. But I think he knew most of it already.'

10

FITTING IN NICELY

'I need another drink,' I said. I looked over at the barman. He and I seemed to have an understanding. He gave me a wink and started to warm a glass.

'You stay,' Kitty said, as she moved towards the bar. 'I'll get it.'

I gave her some money and told her to get herself something. I wanted to think. About the fear on the streets, the bad drugs and that disease, the one she called the blackening. I thought about Stevie's hopes for the future and how he was clean. About his missing backpack and why, if Kitty was right, anyone would have harmed him. Maybe there didn't have to be a reason. Or maybe Kitty didn't know Stevie as well as she thought.

Angry, raised voices at the bar distracted me. The journalist and the detective were having a serious disagreement. They'd been sitting quietly conversing until a moment ago but now a heated argument was in full force.

Both men were on their feet, faces inches from each other, fists clenched and fingers pointing.

'You fucking bollocks, Brady. We had a deal.'

'We had no such thing. You're on your own, Toe-Rag. See how far that gets you,' Brady said, practically spitting into Mooney's face. The reporter stepped backwards and almost stood on Kitty.

'Get off me, you drunk fool,' Kitty shrieked, pushing him away.

Mooney turned and grabbed Kitty round the waist.

'Can't keep your hands off me, can you, darlin'?' he slurred. 'Here, give us a kiss.'

His mouth opened as his face came down on hers.

The barman acted instantly and was around the front of the bar just as Brady reached to seize Mooney by the collar and yank him backwards. But I got there first. I twisted the journalist's closest arm, stamped sharply on his instep and pulled Kitty out of his grip as he roared in pain. Kitty ran off in the direction of the toilets as Mooney's arms flailed about dangerously. He managed to free himself from Brady's grip and glared around to see who had attacked him, his face purple with rage.

'You bitch!' he roared, reaching for me. 'I'll fucking kill you!'

'Come on now, ladies and gentlemen,' the barman intervened, trying to create some space between us. 'Get back to your seats and settle down or I'll bar the lot of you.'

I felt an arm going around me as I was pulled close to a solid male body and held there firmly. Brady kept me secured with one arm while using his other outstretched arm to keep Mooney at bay. Mooney was still roaring, his fists up, ready to strike.

'I can't breathe!' I gasped. He was holding me unnecessarily tightly.

Brady grinned down at me, while keeping one eye on Mooney.

'You're all right,' he said. 'I'll look after you.'

At that moment, the door opened and a blast of sea air filled the room. Fogarty walked in, his left arm in a sling. He stopped at the entrance, taking in the scene in front of him. The look on his face was impossible to read as he addressed me.

'Well, I can see that you're fitting in nicely.'

The interruption was enough to diffuse the situation. The barman managed to get Mooney to sit down, although he was still muttering angrily.

'You can let me go now,' I said to Brady.

'Pity,' he said, as he released me. 'I was enjoying that.'

'Oh, please.' I was aware that Fogarty's eyes were still on me.

Brady kept a hand on my shoulder as he bent down to whisper. 'Seriously, I need to have a talk with you. Off duty and off the record.'

'Are you asking me out?'

'Would you like that? You know I'm married, but I don't mind if you don't. I'll give you a call. I have your number.'

Of course you do, I thought. You've got any amount of information on me. Before I could answer him, I heard more loud, furious voices. This time they were female. I'd forgotten all about the women in the toilets. Kitty must have let them out. They'd been trapped there all this time and they didn't sound happy about it.

Their voices got even louder as they clumped up to the bar. The smell of damp followed them like a stalker. Black cobwebs streaked their faces and laced through their hair. White skinny jeans were patterned with dirt. A dress was torn and filthy. Clearly they'd been trying to escape.

The barman caught my eye as he addressed them, 'Ladies?'

He knew what I had done, I just hoped he'd say nothing. I moved away from Brady and positioned myself better to see the women. Both were blonde and thirtyish. One was short and busty, the other tall and looked older than her friend. They'd been all dolled up for their girls' night out, looking forward to a bit of a laugh. But they weren't laughing now.

'Someone locked us into the fucking jacks,' the tall one shouted at the barman. 'Did you not hear us calling? We were in there for fucking hours.'

'In the fucking dark!' the short one shrieked.

They'd actually been there for less than an hour. But in fairness, I thought, it had probably seemed like hours.

The barman spoke to them gently.

'Well, that's terrible. We had a bit of bother here in the bar and I'm sure that's why nobody heard you. Could you not have used your phones and called for help?'

'I lost my mobile – it fell down the fucking toilet. And Tanya's wasn't charged. You never bloody charge it, do you Tanya?' The tall one gave her friend a filthy look.

'Ok, Karen, I get the message, you've told me a million times,' the short one said. 'But who locked us in there and knocked off the light? And where's our fucking drinks?'

The barman put two sad-looking Bacardi and Cokes on the counter, their ice cubes long melted. They'd be sure to be completely flat and watery by now.

'I held on to these in case you came back. Would you like some more ice?'

Karen growled something incomprehensible as she downed the drink practically in one gulp.

'Disgusting,' she said, wiping her mouth. She looked around at the few of us remaining in the bar. 'When I find out who locked us in there, I'll fucking kill them.'

'Ah, I'm sure it was just one of those things,' the barman said. 'It happens sometimes, you know? The light goes, the door gets stuck.'

'A light bulb doesn't just disappear into thin air, John,' Karen said. 'And the door wasn't just stuck. Something was jammed underneath it. I know 'cause that Chinese young one over there had to pull it out. Hey you,' she shouted over at Kitty who was sitting down quietly at the end of the bar, 'isn't that right?'

Kitty nodded reluctantly.

'The door didn't jam something under itself, John, now did it? I'm not fucking stupid.'

The barman gave me a quick look and I thought I saw the flicker of a smile.

Fogarty's voice was in my ear. He was right behind me.

'Did you have something to do with this?'

I ignored him and kept my hand in my pocket, holding on to the light bulb.

The barman should have been working for the UN.

'Well, I'm not saying you're wrong, Karen. But I guess we'll never know.'

Karen swivelled round and surveyed the bar again, her lips pursed. Her gaze was slow. It moved across the empty tables where the yuppies and the Americans had been. It passed over Kitty on the bench seat at the end of the bar and over the two old men on their bar stools who were quietly enjoying the entertainment. She glanced at Mooney, sitting on his stool, holding his jacket and more than ready to leave. Her scan flickered over Detective Inspector Brady, who was leaning against the bar counter with a little smile on his face, and the word 'bastard' automatically formed on her lips. It lingered for a second on Fogarty, before passing onwards, and then back to where I stood. The attention of the group focused on me like a searchlight.

'Who is that one?' she said.

I opened my mouth and a little cough came out.

'Connie Ortelius. From across the river. I'm just back from Amsterdam ... nice to meet you.'

Her eyes were small and blue, heavily outlined with black eyeliner and weighted down with extra long false eyelashes. They drooped downwards as if her rage had diverted the energy required to lift them.

'Right. I know who you are now.' She came up close to me and stabbed a sharp, French-polished talon in my face.

'I'm Karen Donlon. And if I find out that you tried to make an eejit out of me ...' her face was right next to mine, eyeball to eyeball. I caught the sweet sour smell of Bacardi and stale foundation, 'you're fucking dead.'

She picked up her handbag, took out a packet of cigarettes and snapped it shut.

'Come on, Tanya.'

They swept out into the night, swiftly followed by Mooney who'd been waiting for the opportunity to go.

'Well, you know how to make friends in all the right places.'

For the second time today, Pius Fogarty shook his head slowly as he looked at me. 'That was Karen Donlon. Dessie Donlon's wife. *"Gangland leader, Dessie Donlon"* as our friend Mooney would put it. You'd better watch yourself, Constance Ortelius – or I won't be the only one around here with the bullet holes.'

Using the fingers of his one free hand, Fogarty picked up a couple of almost empty pint glasses off a table and went to put them on the counter.

'There you are, John. Oops, sorry, Anto!' he said as the dregs from one of them sloshed out and landed on the front of Brady's white shirt, just beside the little polo-player logo.

'You think that's funny, Fogarty, do you?' Brady seethed. 'Well, I don't have time for your little games. You know that I'm on to you, don't you? You'll be hearing from me very soon ...'

He shook on his jacket and stopped at the door.

'Call you tomorrow, Connie. Ok? Looking forward to it.'

The door slammed behind him.

'Why?' I accosted Fogarty. I'd had enough of their stupid antics. 'Why would you go and deliberately antagonise a bloody guard? As if there wasn't enough trouble round here already.'

Fogarty bent down to my ear and spoke quietly.

'Because I can, Connie.' Then he grinned broadly. 'Would you like to see what else I can do?'

'No. Jesus! What's wrong with you? I thought you were supposed to be hurt. Could they not have done the community a favour and sedated you for a few days at least?'

I called out to Kitty. 'I need to go now, are you ready?'

'Hold on. Any sign of Stevie's stuff?' she asked him as I waited by the door.

'I found a few of his things and put them back in his room. Someone had gathered them up thinking they were being helpful. There's no backpack like the one you described, though. You can have a look tomorrow.'

'Thanks,' Kitty said, perplexed. 'Night.'

Fogarty stood at the open door, watching us run across the bridge. The rain had almost stopped now, just a few isolated heavy drops plopped into the black, tumescent river.

'Night,' he replied, eventually.

11

GREEN SPOT

'You know what would be good with that coffee cake? The truth, Kitty. Just for once I'd love to hear something from you that I can actually believe.'

'How do you mean?' Kitty mumbled through a mouthful of crumbs.

'Oh, come on. I didn't want to bring it up earlier, but now that it's just the two of us – you really don't expect me to believe that fairytale you cooked up for the cops, do you? All those missing relatives "somewhere in China"? And you not knowing anything about Stevie's past?'

'That's nobody's business but mine and Stevie's. Not Brady's. And not yours, Connie. So just leave it, will you?'

The girl sat back in her chair, her tired face suddenly belligerent. This was not a good time to push her, but I needed to know more about who I was living with.

'And anyway,' she continued. 'I know fuck all about you too. You could be a big bleedin' lezzer for all I know. So we're even, right?'

'That's extremely rude both to me and to lezzers. And I am *not* a lezzer'.

But she had a point. I sighed and looked round the empty café. The cracked lino gleamed in places, hopefully less from decades of grease and more from the cleaning fluid I'd doused about liberally. The chairs were upturned on all of the tables but ours, a clearing in a forest of wooden legs. The window blind drawn down unevenly against the darkness was randomly patterned by street light shining through holes in the shutter outside. Stalag 17 remained open but only occasional revellers came and went at this hour.

Inside the café was quiet except for the ticking of the wall clock, the constant shifting sounds of the old building and the whispering of its ancient pipes. I couldn't see the clock but I guessed it was around one a.m. The only internal light came from the kitchen. It cast a dim semicircle over the corner where we sat, throwing deep shadows across the face of the girl. She looked like a little hunted creature, bristling with defensiveness. I guessed I looked like the Hag of the West and about five hundred years old.

We should have gone to our beds a long time ago but something kept us up, something like tea and coffee cake and not wanting to be alone.

'Ok,' I said. 'So you know nothing about me. What do you want to know, Detective Inspector?'

Kitty giggled. 'Why do I have to be the dickhead? Why can't I be Nuala Rossiter?' Then she pushed her hair behind her ears and tried to look fierce while rotating her silver thumb ring. 'Ms Ortelius ... is that how you say your name? So what kind of a weird name is that?'

'It's the name of a street in Amsterdam. A street where we lived, once upon a time.'

'And who is "we"?' Kitty demanded, warming to her task.

'Me and my husband. Ex-husband.'

I really wasn't ready to talk about this.

'Names?' Kitty barked. Now this was getting scary.

'Me: Constance Moran. Him: Henk Van Gorp. When we married we both changed our names. We did it for fun, but I suppose it was silly ...'

Kitty was giggling. 'Not silly at all. Connie Van Gorp!' She tried to copy my attempt at the guttural Dutch 'G' and triggered a fit of coughing.

'Yeah, yeah. Now it's my turn.'

'That's not fair – I'm not done.'

'The Detective Inspector can continue in a minute.' I smiled Nuala Rossiter's sweet smile. 'Now I'd like to ask Kitty a question.'

She looked peevish and folded her arms.

'So, Kitty, would you like to tell me about your family and where you come from? And it'd be lovely if you could try something a bit believable this time.'

'That's cheating,' Kitty muttered. 'You're acting more like Brady than like Rossiter. Next thing you'll start roaring "Answer the question!" at me.'

'No, next thing I'm going to see if I can find a drink anywhere in that kitchen. You can be thinking about your answer while I'm doing it.'

I'd opened most of the cupboards and rummaged at the back of the shelves before Kitty spoke.

'The shelf beside the cooker. Behind those notebooks.'

Bright girl. She must have checked the place out pretty thoroughly when she was here earlier on. I reached behind some tattered old jotters and felt a bottle. When I held it up to the light, I almost fell to my knees in thanks.

'Well, hallelujah!'

I'd no idea what Aggie was doing with a half-full bottle of Green Spot, but I knew what I was going to do with it. I got a glass and poured.

'How about me?'

'Forget it. This'd be wasted on you. Have more tea.'

'You're so mean.'

Kitty sipped her tea without enthusiasm while I sat down triumphantly with my glass, keeping the bottle within easy reach.

'Things are looking up,' I said, raising my glass to her. 'This, my dear, is one of the world's finest whiskeys. Produced in limited quantities by Midleton distillery for Mitchell's, the famous Dublin wine merchants. It is nectar, pure and simple.'

'Whatever,' Kitty said with an eye-roll.

'So, where were we? Ah yes, you were going to tell me your life story.'

'Ok, if that's what you want. My parents were smuggled here from Germany in a container. I don't know anything about them, they died soon after they arrived. I was a baby and I was put into care. It was terrible. I ran away when I was thirteen and that's it. Happy now?'

I cogitated for a moment.

'Not really, Kitty, I'm not happy. Because you're still not telling the truth.'

Thousands of asylum-seekers had came into Ireland from the late nineties onwards by various means, including by ship, hidden in containers. Her story was possible, but there was something in the way that Kitty said it, it just didn't ring true.

'Too bad,' Kitty said. 'My turn again. Constance Ortelius, where do you come from and where's your family?'

'Fair enough.' I took another sip and savoured the whiskey's golden smoothness.

'I'm from a village in south County Carlow, you wouldn't know it.'

'Never heard of Carlow, know nothing about it.'

'Nobody does. It's not famous for anything ...'

For the first time in many years, I pictured rich fields, tall trees, billowing grasses, deep dark rivers, a little white church nestled with its churchyard into a mountainside ...

'... Nope, there's nothing much there at all.'

'Go on,' she said.

'My father died over ten years ago, my mother followed him two years later. Sister's in Canada, married with kids. Haven't seen her for years. We live in different worlds. Aggie's the only one I have here now.'

'No kids?'

'I haven't a maternal bone in my body. And between me and Henk ... our combined genes would've made a lethal genetic cocktail. They should give us the Nobel Peace Prize for not reproducing.'

I paused and Kitty waited expectantly.

'And Amsterdam?' she prompted.

'I went there after college and got sucked into the whole corporate thing – you know?'

She looked at me blankly.

'I mean working all hours, rarely taking holidays ... I lost touch with my friends, didn't notice things ... things about Henk. When I finally copped on, it was too late. I cracked up pretty spectacularly. Lost my job – everything.'

'No way! What didn't you notice about Henk? How did you crack up?'

'I'm not prepared to go into that at the moment,' I said, reaching for the bottle. I hadn't intended to say so much. I hadn't even told Aggie the few details I'd just related, but I felt a little better now. Or maybe it was just the whiskey.

'Over to you. Tell me about Stevie.'

I expected more resistance from Kitty, so it was a surprise when she quietly began to talk.

'We met when I was thirteen and he was fourteen. He came from County Roscommon. Single, teenage mum – she gave him up when he was born. He never knew his dad. He was put in the orphanage in Galway city. Later on, they fostered him out loads of times, but it never worked out. He said he was too gay, even when he was a little kid, that he didn't fit in. He said he always felt like an alien waiting for the mother ship to come and beam him up.' She smiled.

'He was a magnet for the pervs – being so alone in himself and looking like a little angel. The abuse started with the Christian Brothers and then with the bigger boys and in some of the foster homes.'

'How did he end up in Dublin?'

'That was later. When he was around ten or so he was fostered out to an old couple who had no kids of their own. They lived way out the country, right beside a turlough. Do you know what that is?'

I half-knew about turloughs but shook my head. 'Tell me.'

'It's a disappearing lake, that's what Stevie called it. One day the lake is there, with frogs and ducks and things in the water. The next day, the lake's gone. The water disappears down a kind of a plug hole – Stevie called it a swally hole. Swally hole sounds funny, doesn't it?' she laughed. 'Like it'd swally you up!'

'So for weeks or months, it's dry and you think it's a meadow with grass and flowers and stuff, and then the lake fills up again all of a sudden through the swally hole and all the frogs and things come back. I'd love to see all that. Stevie said he'd take me sometime.' A sigh rattled through her thin chest.

'He loved it there and he loved the old couple. The man put the thatch on the old houses that people bought for holiday homes. The woman made baskets out of ... reeds? Would that be right?'

I nodded. 'That'd be right. Go on.'

'Stevie started drawing and the old man bought him paints. He used to stay in after school some days for an art class. One day when he was walking home from school, he saw that the lake was up. I mean, it was full of water. The quickest way home was to row across in the little wooden boat they had. But the boat was all broken up. Stevie had to walk around the long way and when he went into the house, he found the old couple were dead. They'd been beaten to death and the house was all wrecked. There was no phone and Stevie had to run a couple of miles to the nearest neighbour. They called the guards and told Stevie to stay there because the guards would want to ask him questions. Stevie panicked, and as soon as he got the chance, he ran away. When he got to the main road, he hitched a lift. He ended up in Dublin, all alone. Years later, he heard that they'd got someone for the murders, it was robbers who were roaming the countryside attacking old people. But by that time it was too late for Stevie to go back. There was nothing there for him anymore.'

We sat in silence for a couple of seconds. I could see why she hadn't related this to Rossiter and Brady. Running away from a crime scene would not endear poor Stevie to the guards.

'So Stevie used to talk to you about his past?'

Kitty nodded.

'I'd get him to tell me about the turlough anytime I was scared and trying to go to sleep.'

She paused and fixed her eyes on me while I watched a large coffee-coloured moth batter itself repeatedly against the kitchen lightbulb. It was too high up and too far gone for me to save it from itself.

'Connie, you *are* going to help me find out what happened to him, aren't you? You're going to keep your promise, the one you made earlier?'

'Sorry?' I said vaguely.

She stood up, marched over to the sink and slammed her crockery into it with a crash, before turning back to me.

'Unless you were just lying to me to get me to go along with the cops? Was that it? You were just pretending, weren't you? You're not going to do anything to find out about Stevie. You're going to shaft me, just like everyone else.'

God, she was volatile. I wondered if all teenage girls are like this or if it's a new thing. I couldn't remember what I was like when I was sixteen, but then my memory was faulty, along with so much else. I stood up and approached her with my arms outstretched.

'I won't let you down, Kitty. Come on, give me a hug.'

She relented stiffly but pulled away almost instantly.

'We'll work out a plan tomorrow,' I said. 'But first we both need some sleep, ok? Come on.'

I led her upstairs to the first landing and left her there as I continued to the next floor. My hand was on my bedroom doorknob when I realised she was still standing below.

Her thin, strained voice came to me out of the darkness.

'There was no container and no aslyum-seekers. I was adopted when I was a baby, adopted from China by my Irish parents. I was loved. And then I wasn't. I'm not saying any more.'

The door clicked as she went inside and closed it softly behind her.

12

GOODNIGHT, CARLOW

It came from outside my bedroom window, a sharp and irregular tapping. And there was something else, a deeper, more prolonged sound from further away. I was way too scared to go over there and look.

I lay awake, unable to sleep. I'd been like that for some time, watching the shadow of ripples on the ceiling projected from the river across the road. I hadn't slept properly for years but tonight my insomnia hit a new low. It wasn't helped by the relentless beat from Stalag 17 next door and the occasional shouting in the vicinity of the Sunrise Hotel from what sounded like a series of vocal domestics.

After the day I'd had, I should have collapsed into a coma, but instead, the fear I'd felt at the quayside that morning returned, gnawing at my insides like a hungry rat. I lay there, trying to get things straight in my head, trying to categorise the multitude of dangers, threats and warnings I'd encountered since the morning.

There was Stevie dead and everyone in danger and Mooney's dire warnings. The threats from Steyne River Securities and the insinuation that they'd got Aggie and they meant to do her harm. Karen Donlon's death threat, Fogarty getting shot and all those undercurrents between Brady and Mooney ... and Brady and Fogarty ... and Fogarty and Rossiter ... I couldn't keep up. That was before contemplating the teenager downstairs, a possible runaway with ill-advised expectations of me. I couldn't even think about the perverted satanist next door and what he might be getting up to. My brain started spinning again. I briefly considered getting out my laptop and putting it all on a spreadsheet before deciding that would be weird, even by my standards. I'd do it in the morning.

My throat was so dry my tonsils felt like mothballs. I got up for water and, as I returned from the bathroom, I heard the tapping again, more insistent this time. I crept towards the window. The lace curtains moved slightly in the breeze and I remembered that I hadn't been able to fully close the bottom part of the sash window. No wonder it was so noisy.

Lights shone through the yellowed lace: the streetlight and the moving headlights of taxis coming and going from the night club. A shape moved on the windowsill outside. It tapped on the glass. With shaking hands, I lifted a lace corner and peered out. An over-sized seabird as big as a goose was out there on the windowsill. It examined me balefully with its yellow eyes before stabbing at the glass again with its enormous beak. Maybe it was a gannet. I remembered hearing somewhere that gannets have larger beaks than the average seagull. This one looked like it had been specially contracted to knock a hole through the window.

I banged on the glass, hissing 'Shoo, gannet! Stupid bird – piss off!'

The bird marched to the other end of the window and started tapping again.

I put both my hands under the window's centre bar and heaved upwards with all my strength. The sash shot up with a juddering protest and the bird reluctantly swooped over to the nearest lamppost, where it positioned itself to watch me with a familiar reproachful look, the one common to most of the males in my life.

'Have we met before?' I asked him.

With the window open to the night, the smell of the river and the tide filled the room. Looking down, I saw the light of the night club entrance next door. A burly bouncer leaned against the wall, talking in a low voice to someone, probably the other bouncer, inside the entrance.

The burning end of a lit cigarette glowed from the edge of the quay across the road. A tall, dark figure stood alone, smoking and facing up-river. He turned and glanced up as if he knew I was there all along. It was Ozzie Wolf, his face pale and serious, his black hair swept back from his forehead, dark eyes glittering. He raised a finger to his lips and slowly moved the hand with the cigarette in the direction of something up the road.

I leaned further out the window to see what he was pointing at. Now I saw the source of the strange noise. It came from close to where Stevie's body had been raised from the water. Figures were moving there. In the dark it was hard to see how many, maybe seven or eight. Most of them were standing, some swaying gently. One or two knelt on the ground and rocked backwards and forwards or were bent over with their foreheads pressed to the pavement, arms wrapped around their heads. The ragged shapes of their silhouettes reminded me of the group from the Sunrise Hotel who had quietly witnessed the recovery of Stevie's body. I was sure it was them out there now or others like them. The sound they made was a painful, gut-wrenching lamentation. It was amplified by the water and I imagined it carried all the way down the river and out to the wide sea beyond. In all my life, I'd never heard a sound like it. Even so, I didn't need to be told what it was. Keening, the keening of those who are left behind to carry on, bereft. It was the primitive, feral expression of loss and anguish and it made the hair stand up on the back of my neck.

The silhouette of a man stood apart from the others, also observing them. He seemed familiar, but I couldn't see his features. As I watched, he walked slowly and deliberately towards the river, paused for a moment, then climbed through the railings and stood there swaying perilously close to the edge. My heart pounded and the sound of the lamentation faded into the background. Surely he wouldn't jump? I couldn't bear to take my eyes off him but I wrenched them away to look back to Ozzie, to see if he'd do something to help. But Ozzie was gone, and there was no sign of the bouncers either. Most of the mourners had departed or were drifting away swiftly and quietly, in ones and twos, like dry leaves scattered by the wind.

Only the man remained, standing there at the river's edge. He took another small step forward and I thought he was gone.

'No!' My cry was involuntary. It was loud enough for him to hear and turn his head in my direction. The streetlight reflected on his glasses. It was Jimmy Mooney, the journalist.

'Stop,' I shouted. 'Get back from there.'

He muttered something I couldn't make out and reached for the railing as his legs seemed to buckle beneath him.

'Hold on!' I shouted. 'I'm on my way!'

I threw on a hoody over my pyjamas and ran down the stairs and out the door. I stopped to look across to the quayside. He was still there, just about. If he lost his grip on the railing, he'd fall right down into the river. And if he was as drunk as I thought he was, when that happened he wouldn't have a chance.

'Hold on, Jimmy,' I called again as I ran over, slowing down as I got closer.

Mooney's glasses were crooked and half-falling off his face. His hair was stuck to his forehead. His face gleamed with sweat.

'Jesus, not you,' he said. 'That's all I need. Queen of the fucking cupcakes. Piss off, will you.'

He tried to straighten himself but his legs crumpled and he dropped heavily to his knees, losing his grip on the railing. He began to fall backwards and would have gone over the side but at the last minute he managed to grab the railing with one hand and save himself.

'Jimmy!' I shouted. 'Help! Somebody help!'

But the quayside was deserted, there wasn't a car or a person in sight. I was terrified to take my eyes off him even to phone for help. If I had a phone. It was on my bedside table.

'Come on, Jimmy,' I tried. 'Come in from there. Please. You don't want to do anything stupid.'

'Stupid! I've already done something stupid. Stupid, stupid, stupid ...'

He whacked his forehead repeatedly with his free hand, before turning his crazed eyes on me.

'Will you just leave me alone?'

'I can't do that, Jimmy. I can't leave you like this. Will you come back here and talk to me?'

He wasn't listening, he was staring down into the dark water below, mesmerised. I needed to get his attention fast.

'Jimmy, I have some information for you. It's important. It's about Stevie Hennessy. No one else knows it.'

His eyes were still on the water but I knew he'd heard me.

'You're the best crime reporter in town, Jimmy. Remember you offered me information? Well, I have some for you now. Come and sit down over here and I'll tell you.'

Mooney turned his head and studied me. He spoke slowly, slurring.

'Information about Stevie Hennessy?'

'Yeah. I have to give you that information, Jimmy. You're the only one who'll understand it. I need your help.'

He maintained his stare for several minutes. Then he sighed, fixed his glasses on his face and started to pull himself up. I went over to help him clamber through the railings but he brushed me away.

'Get your hands off me. Fucks sake, I'm all right.'

Somehow he managed to climb between the metal bars. I retreated to a steel street bench a little way back and sat down. It was cold and wet and damned uncomfortable. Contemporary street furniture, designed to give you a cold in your kidneys.

A wave of weariness and misery washed over me. I wanted to be back in my warm bed, not out on the side of the quays with a suicidal journalist on my hands. I wondered what information I'd give him when he finally got round to asking for it. Which would be any minute. He was starting to look almost sober now. Boy, was he going to be pissed off if I didn't give him something worthwhile. You can't save someone from suicide just for nothing. I started to think fast.

He staggered a little as he moved towards me and I noticed for the first time how very thin he was, gaunt even. No wonder I'd hurt him when I kicked him in the pub earlier on. Maybe I should've been feeling guilty about that now, but I really didn't, you kind of had to be there.

He collapsed on the bench beside me and buried his head in his hands.

'Oh God,' he moaned.

It was quiet, or at least as quiet as it got around here at night. The music from the club was fainter now, but you could still feel the constant bass, pulsing slow and steady. A car with a flat tyre flapped its way up the road on the far side of the river. Sirens wailed distantly from all across the city. The river water slapped against the quay walls, washing up and down the steps beside us, the steps Stevie's body had been carried up. Tide must be coming in, I thought.

'Right. What have you got for me?'

All of a sudden the campaigning journalist was back in action as if nothing had happened. His fierce attention focused one hundred percent, his burning eyes trained on me like lasers.

'Come on,' he said. 'I haven't got all day.'

'Night,' I corrected him. 'Well, you've bounced back, haven't you? Ok, let's see ... People are saying Stevie had that disease, you know, the blackening. Others say he was skin-popping drugs ...'

'Tell me something I don't know.'

'... but he was off drugs, so that can't be true.'

'Says who?'

'Well, his friends ...'

He was not impressed.

'I've been trying to piece it together. Something happened on Thursday night. Stevie wasn't himself on Friday, he was scared. He said everyone's in danger ...'

So much for saying nothing to journalists. But now I had his attention.

'Everyone's in danger? Are you sure that's what he said?'

'Yeah, why – do you know what he meant?'

Mooney ignored me. He stood up and walked away a few paces, then turned back.

'What else did he say?'

'Nothing, I don't know. He moved out of the Sunrise Hotel, packed his stuff up and left. But he gave a bag to someone to mind and it's gone missing.'

'What's gone missing?'

'Sketchbooks. I don't know what was in them, but they've disappeared.'

'I have to go,' Mooney said. He fumbled in his jacket pocket and brought out his mobile. 'Need to call a cab ...'

His hands were shaking so badly I thought he'd drop it.

'Let me,' I said, reaching for the phone and was surprised when he allowed me take it. I scrolled through his long list of contacts and found a number. It answered immediately and I gave the address: North Wall Quay, a street bench. Classy.

'He'll be here in five minutes,' I said, handing back the phone. 'Before you go, are you ok? I mean, that looked pretty serious a little while ago. You could have ended up in the river yourself.'

He looked back towards the edge of the quay and his face twisted as if he was in pain.

'It would have been better if I had,' he said. 'But I'm a bloody coward, too chicken for that. I made a mistake, you see. I was taken for a fucking ride. Never happened before, in all my years as a journalist. But don't you worry ...'

His finger stabbed the air like a gannet's beak.

'... I know what I have to do.'

'Taxi?'

I whirled around in surprise.

The car had pulled up behind us quietly while I was focused on Mooney.

'Phibsboro,' Mooney said to the driver. He got in and closed the door. As the car pulled off, he rolled down the window. 'Hang on,' he told the driver.

'Look,' he said to me out the window. 'Will you tell the young one I'm sorry, you know, for earlier on. It was the drink ... and other stuff. I'm not myself sometimes. You were right to give me a kick. Should have gone for the balls.' He laughed mirthlessly.

'I'll bear that in mind for the future, Jimmy.'

He gazed at me for a minute.

'You do that,' he said with what was almost a smile. 'You're not really from Amsterdam, are you? Where are you from?'

'Carlow,' I said.

'Good night, Carlow.'

I watched the taxi's red tail lights recede into the darkness and felt any energy I had left drain away with it.

Day 2

MONDAY

13

THE CITY TIMES

My nemesis was waiting for me when I came downstairs in the morning. Aggie's monstrous coffee machine sat on the counter sulking malevolently and daring me to try to start it again. After the night I'd had, I was in no mood to take any nonsense from a machine. I'd need a steady supply of high quality caffeine to have any chance of surviving in this place and that stainless steel scourge would have to shape up or ship out.

I knew how to fix it now, or I thought I did. I'd woken up after only two or three hours of sleep, brushed the moths off my face, checked the windowsill for giant birds and then went online. Within a few minutes I'd downloaded *Coffee Machines for Cretins* and started perusing diagrams of the innards of various devices, not one of which resembled the ancient object in the kitchen, but at least I got the theory.

Shouting, 'Morning Kitty!' back up the stairs, I checked my notes, then poured water into the machine's reservoir-thing and confidently flicked the large red switch. I retired to a nearby vantage point to observe the results.

'I've fixed the coffee machine,' I informed Kitty when she appeared in the doorway, pale and bleary-eyed. 'We'll use mine until this one warms up or whatever it's supposed to do.'

A constructive start to the day, I thought as I went out to raise the shutter. I planned to fulfil my promise to Kitty and ask a few of the neighbours about Stevie. I had no doubt I'd hear that Stevie had fallen back into his drug habit and if that was the case, Kitty would just have to accept it. Sad, but in this part of the world I imagined accidental death while under the influence was a pretty commonplace tragedy. And then, as soon as I could, I'd get back to my own agenda, whatever that was.

Miraculously, the shutter rolled up smoothly and I was back in the shop, drinking tea with Kitty, and leafing through Aggie's order book when Pius Fogarty strode in with a dark frown and a grim set to his face. My automatic response to moody males kicked in, which is to completely disregard them and focus upon my own needs.

'*Gur* cake?' I asked loudly with my finger on the page. 'What in God's name is gur? Anyone know or do I have to go online again?'

I looked up when the silence became impossible to ignore. Fogarty stood, holding up the full front page of *The City Times*. With her hands clasped over her mouth, Kitty's eyes darted across the text. I leaned closer to see the headline.

Flesh-Eating Infection Ate Teen Junkie's Hand!

Fogarty slammed the paper down on the table in front of me.

'That bastard, Mooney. What the hell did you say to him, Kitty? I heard you were talking to him last night. And you, Connie – he interviewed you, right?'

'Now you hold on just a minute, Pius Fogarty,' I shot back at him. I was about to continue but bit my tongue when I saw the look in his eyes. Clearly now was not a good time to confront him about his propensity for getting shot, nor would it be wise to divulge anything about my nocturnal adventures with Jimmy Mooney.

'Before you start with the allegations,' I went on, picking up the paper, 'let me read this properly. If you want coffee, go ahead and make it yourself.'

I held the paper close to my nose and scanned the front page. Kitty pointed Fogarty towards the espresso-maker.

'**Property Prices Rise as Recovery Continues**' trumpeted the lead article, juxtaposed with another one headed '**Caution Urged on Welfare Increases**.' A colour photograph close by showed our nation's leader shaking hands with a US country music singer.

The bottom half of the page was dominated by that screaming headline about Stevie Hennessy's death. Slowly, I read the article aloud, with an growing sense of unreality.

Flesh-Eating Infection Ate Teen Addict's Hand
The body of Steven 'Stevie' Hennessy (17) of no fixed abode, Dublin, was recovered from the river Liffey early yesterday morning. The post mortem is expected to confirm that Hennessy drowned on Saturday night, possibly while under the influence of drugs. Our exclusive source has revealed that the youth was infected with deadly *necrotising fasciitis*, a bacterial infection which spreads rapidly and can destroy the body's soft tissue within hours. A reported discolouration of the victim's hand is consistent with injection of drugs, compounded, in this case, by the spread of infection.

'Lies!' Kitty exploded. 'All that crap about drugs, calling Stevie an addict ... How could Mooney write that? And that disease – it's true then, what people are saying about it.'

'Read the rest,' Fogarty said. 'Jesus, wait till I see that irresponsible, lying gobshite. This is all we bloody need. The clean-up-the-streets crusaders will have a field day.'

He dumped the ground Arabica into the filter basket without bothering to measure it. I read on.

> The youth may have caught the flesh-eating infection after injecting 'bath salts', a widely available synthetic drug. Aleka Marr, CEO of Heartbeat, the inner-city housing agency, warned that as injecting 'bath salts' gains popularity amongst the homeless population, the city's medical personnel will need to be alert to what might be a new and possibly extra-virulent strain of deadly *necrotising fasciitis*.

Flanking the main story was a shorter piece. It stated that the post-mortem report would not be released for at least another week but that the immediate evidence pointed to death by misadventure. There were no outward signs of violence and the quantity of water in the lungs was consistent with drowning. It was expected that drugs would be found in the victim's system but this had yet to be confirmed.

'Where did Mooney get all this medical information?' I murmured to myself.

'It had to be someone in the Coroners' Office,' Fogarty said. 'Sounds like the results of a preliminary analysis.'

'Detective Inspector Anthony Brady is quoted here saying that the post mortem results will determine whether a police investigation is necessary.' I looked up as Fogarty snorted. 'There's no love lost between you and Brady is there?'

'Anto?' Fogarty gave a short, harsh laugh. 'He's a well-known bollix – from a long line of bollixes. But hey, you seem to be on pretty close terms with him yourself, judging by last night. From where I stood, it looked like the pair of you were getting on like a house on fire.'

'It's none of your bloody business what I was doing or who I was with. And getting back to the point,' I fixed Fogarty with my most glacial look, 'haven't you noticed that this article is all about drugs? As in, completely contrary to what Kitty's been saying about Stevie? So don't bother trying to blame her for this. Look, last night in the Eight Bells, Mooney and Brady were having a big heart-to-heart just before Mooney went ballistic. Maybe Brady was Mooney's exclusive source.'

'If that's true, Brady won't be pleased being named in the paper like that. Not that he's averse to the limelight, but he likes to control his public image. So, when did Mooney file that story – before or after the pub?'

Fogarty, his eyes thoughtful, rubbed a hand across his cheek with a sound that rasped like sandpaper. I met his gaze with studied vagueness. Based on events in the dead of the night, I was sure Mooney had filed the story before he went to the pub and I was equally sure that he had subsequently regretted it.

Kitty shook her head, peering at the paper. 'Brady's not his source for this – he's not interested in Stevie. Remember when he was questioning me yesterday? He wanted other information from me. Same as Mooney did.'

Fogarty turned his attention to Kitty. 'What kind of information?' His voice was quiet but serious.

'Oh you know, all that word on the street, what's goin' down' kind of crap. I told him ...'

I cut in before she repeated Stevie's warning that everyone was in danger or said anything about Stevie's sketchbooks. I wasn't at all sure we could trust Fogarty.

'You told him you knew nothing, isn't that right, Kitty?'

'That's what you told me to say,' she said, nodding at me carefully.

Fogarty folded his arms and regarded us with a sigh.

'So, Kitty,' he said, 'did you tell Mooney or Brady what condition Stevie was in the last time you saw him? Because when I talked to him, on Saturday morning, he really wasn't himself.'

Kitty eyes filled with tears as she shook her head violently.

'He was sick. And he was upset. It was on Friday, the night before he disappeared. He was coming down with something, like a fever. And he kept rubbing his hand, said it was really sore. But there wasn't a mark on it that I could see, nothing like those massive bruises he sometimes had. He said he'd been at a party ...'

'Thursday night?' Fogarty kept pushing her.

She nodded. 'But he wouldn't tell me where it was or who he was with. I just thought he'd had a bad night.'

'Did you tell any of this to Mooney?' I asked.

'No. And the guards didn't ask.'

'So, contrary to the intemperate allegations that were being bandied about earlier,' I gave Fogarty another filthy look, 'all Kitty did was repeat to Mooney that Stevie was clean. The precise opposite to what's suggested in this article.'

'Ok, you've made your point,' Fogarty said. 'Apologies for the intemperate allegations.'

'Accepted. But if there's really evidence of drugs and "death by misadventure", as the article says, there'll be no further investigation into Stevie's death, right?'

'Yup,' Fogarty said. 'If there's any political mileage in this, it'll be exploited. But after that Stevie will be old news.'

'Speaking of news, I would have thought you'd feature somewhere in the paper yourself, "Dramatic Shooting Outside Garda Station" or something. But maybe you're not important enough.'

'I'm on page two,' Fogarty said, taking up the paper and folding it under his arm. 'The crime section. And if you get round to reading that article, *don't* go and swallow it whole and jump to all kinds of conclusions. It's a load of shite.'

He took a sip of the coffee he'd just poured into a takeaway cup. 'This is not too bad, if I say so myself. Definitely an improvement on the usual.'

Arrogant git, I thought. He's a fine one to talk about jumping to conclusions. And then he goes and insults my coffee.

'I'm sure we'll be far too busy today to waste our time reading about you,' I said. 'And you can pay for your coffee on your way out.'

He dropped a few coins on the counter, slapped a lid on his cup and headed for the door. As he opened it, he turned.

'In case you're interested, I'm going to find Mooney.'

'And do what?' I asked, alarmed.

'Force him to write another article. Try to fix some of the damage he's done. And after that, Connie, since you're so curious about gur cake, maybe I can introduce you to some of the local cuisine.'

The door closed behind him. Before I had time to figure out what that last cryptic comment meant, I saw that Kitty's face was buried in her hands and she was crying again.

'Oh don't mind him,' I said. 'Or that stupid article ...'

'That's not it,' she said, wiping her eyes and sobbing at the same time. 'I feel so bad. I didn't tell you or Fogarty or anyone – that night, the last night I saw Stevie – we had a fight. When he said everyone's in danger, I told him to stop going to those parties and mixing with those people. But he said I wouldn't understand and he walked away. And that was the last time I saw him. I feel terrible. I just wish I could talk to him again.'

'I know, Kitty, that's completely natural,' I murmured, patting her shoulder and wondering what else my little lodger had forgotten to tell me.

A thin, slightly-hunched shadow appeared at the opaque glass of the door.

'Oh Lord, here's Josie,' I said. 'Why don't you go upstairs, Kitty? Come down again when you feel better.'

She quickly dried her eyes on a tea towel and darted up the stairs just as Josie bustled in the door to take command of the kitchen.

'Just give me a minute, Josie,' I said picking up the iPad I'd liberated from my previous place of employment. I googled the *City Times* and scanned the front page again, looking for a link to the article on page two that I was far too busy to read.

14

DUBLIN'S DARKEST DAYS

Unsurprisingly, the flesh-eating disease was top of the 'Most Read' links on the *City Times* website. Viewed online, it looked even more like a horror movie tagline. Two photos accompanied the article, one of our handsome and resolute poster boy for law-and-order, Detective Inspector Anthony Brady, the other a photograph of a concerned-looking Aleka Marr, which I examined with interest. There was no picture of Stevie.

I scanned down through the 'Most Read' list:

'Flesh-Eating Virus Ate Teen Addict's Hand'
'Tortured Body Found of Suspected Crime Lynchpin'
'Garda Raid Yields Multimillion Contraband Haul'
'Shot Man Staggers into City Centre Garda Station'
'Missing Medieval Memorial Found'

'Shot Man Staggers into City Centre Garda Station' – it could only be Fogarty. I tapped the link and saw a photograph of Store Street Garda Station beside a short article suggesting that the shooting was widely regarded as gangland-related and that the victim, Pius Fogarty, had a criminal record from some years back.

'Not good, Fogarty,' I said, my suspicions confirmed. 'This does not look good.'

Almost automatically, I clicked on the editorial entitled 'Dublin's Darkest Days.' Referencing the flesh-eating disease story, it spouted the usual law-and-order homily with the predictable exhortation to say 'no to drugs'. Somewhat wasted on the paper's middle-aged, middle class readership, I thought. But what did I know? Maybe the whole country was shovelling chemicals into its collective veins, regardless of age or class.

The editorial reminded its readership that 'bath salts' were involved in the notorious Florida case where, under the drug's influence, a man had eaten part of the face of another living man. It ended with the question, 'In Dublin's darkest days, is the next stop cannibalism?'

I shuddered and looked up, suddenly aware that someone was standing directly in front of me. As she removed her large sunglasses and pale peach trilby and shook out her hair, I recognised her from the newspaper. It was a concerned-looking Aleka Marr.

'Constance Ortelius? I'm Aleka Marr. Heartbeat Housing Services. This is such an amazing place! It's so authentic! Sorry – I know that sounds ridiculously corny. But *look* at it!'

I followed her gaze, taking in the yellowing wallpaper printed with copper kettles and baskets of fruit, the black peg board menu with so many missing letters you'd have to be a cryptographer to read it, the profusion of formica on most of the surfaces, the greasy, peeling contact paper on the remainder. I sighed and looked at her instead.

She was tall and slim with shoulder-length honey-blonde hair. She wore a well-cut, pale blue pants suit with a pretty lilac blouse. She placed the oversized shades and hat on my table as she pulled up a chair. Generic executive type meets rock chick. Mid-thirties, I guessed, with the confidence and perfect dental work that comes with long-standing affluence. She radiated energy and well-being, while I seeped bitterness and fatigue.

'Thanks ... Aleka.' I reached out a clammy hand to shake the one she offered. Hers was warm and smooth and purposeful, just like the rest of her.

'Nice to meet you,' I said. 'Sorry, I'm a bit stunned – this editorial ...' I tilted the tablet to show her the screen.

'Shocking.' She didn't look shocked. 'So sad for the community,' she continued. 'We're doing what we can to help, but ...' She shook her head, resignedly, then perked up. 'Look, at least maybe I can help you, link you in with those business supports I mentioned on the phone?'

'I need all the help I can get! Have a seat. Tea or coffee?'

She gave the plastic bottle in her hand a little waggle as she pulled up a chair. 'Water's fine for me, thanks.'

She sat back, still taking in the surroundings.

'This is *so* much the new Dublin, isn't it?' she said. 'Multicultural, mixed generations and classes. I love that *diversity*. Brings its challenges, of course, but it's all good. You know we work to help the community too?'

'I'm looking forward to hearing all about it,' I told her insincerely. I had a sudden flashback to my old corporate team and the mountain of proposals and reports we churned out. I shuddered again.

'Great,' Aleka said, pushing a glossy folder across the table. 'Here's an information pack detailing the available schemes and incentives. All the contact details are there, including my personal mobile number. I've a special interest in supporting women in business. So call me, won't you? Even if it's just for a chat.'

'That's very kind of you.'

I made a polite show of flicking through the folder. A flyer fell out, a promotion for something called the Bicknor Programme. I picked it up.

'Oh, I love that one. It's called after Alexander de Bicknor,' Aleka said. 'Archbishop of Dublin back in medieval times. Maybe you've seen the news? His brass memorial has just been discovered in Temple Bar after being missing from St Patrick's Cathedral for *centuries*. He was such an innovative guy for his time. We named our programme after him. It's a set of really exciting projects.'

'Is this one of them?' I asked, holding up a printed card for the Cleaner Liffeyside Enterprise Initiative. 'What's that about – dredging?'

'No,' Aleka laughed. 'That's a group of business people who want to present a better image of the area. You know, less begging and crime, more ... um ...' she grinned mischievously, '... hanging baskets. We partner with them sometimes. But between ourselves, they go in for a lot of whining and hand-wringing – and *interminable* meetings.'

'I don't do meetings,' I said firmly, replacing the card and flyer in the folder and closing it. To be read later, possibly. Or more probably, never.

'I totally agree – life's way too short. Look ... do you mind if I ask you something?' Aleka said, lowering her voice and pulling her chair a little closer. 'I'm not going to beat about the bush and you don't have to say anything, obviously. But are you being pressurised to pay for so-called security services?'

'Nope,' I said, neglecting to mention my recent visit from the same so-called security services. 'Aggie has a long-standing objection to that. She sends them packing whenever they try it on.'

'Really?' Aleka seemed surprised. 'Steyne River Securities, I suppose. And your aunt has resisted them? That's so great.'

'Aggie's been here a long time,' I said. 'She has her own way of doing things.'

'Good for her,' Aleka said. 'That's exactly the kind of independent business spirit we want to support. And what about her niece?' She touched my arm lightly. 'There's a lot of colourful characters around here. Any problems with the neighbours? Or concerns about crime?'

'Should I be worried about crime?'

'We get complaints about the number of addicts and vagrants and the associated robberies and assaults. It's a problem everywhere in the city but a bit more so in this area.'

'Doesn't seem much different from anywhere else I've been.'

'You've just arrived back from ... Holland, is it?

So Aleka had made enquiries about me. Well, you'd expect that from someone in her position. But she couldn't have done anything in-depth. If she had, she wouldn't be sitting there smiling at me.

I nodded and smiled back. Tell them nothing, as Josie would say.

'Dublin's become a lot more complicated than it was,' she said. 'It's no longer a case of a handful of hobos wandering about or a few of the town drunks kicking up a racket.'

Another lecture on the crime wave, I groaned inwardly. But Aleka apparently included mind-reading amongst her talents.

'Look, I'm not part of the law-and-order brigade, if that's what you think.' Her eyes sparkled. 'Despite my legal background, not at all. Let me explain.'

'It's fine. I believe you,' I said. She could have been the Chief Justice of Ireland for all I cared, but she was determined to win me over.

'The thing is, I achieved my professional goals and made my money years ago, back in Chicago before I was thirty. My investments look after themselves now, leaving me free to pursue my other interests. You know what I'm interested in, Connie?'

'Counting your cash?' I ventured. I have a deep aversion to success stories.

'Doing cool stuff, Connie. Having fun and maybe making the world a better place while I'm at it. You can't spend your life behind a desk, can you?'

Not if you're me and you get handed your marching papers, I thought.

'That's why I'm here. Back in the States, I used political contacts and celebrity friends to organise fund-raisers – benefit concerts, all that stuff. It was very satisfying and a hell of a lot of fun,' she laughed. 'But the sorry tale of the old country kept appearing in the news. The dismal national saga of rags to riches to rags to shaky recovery – and the same mistakes being made over and over. Remember those boom and bust Celtic Tiger stories in *Time* magazine, *The Economist*, *Newsweek*, each one more depressing than the last?'

I nodded, pretending it hadn't all passed me by.

'It was impossible to ignore, right? So I decided to do something – my people came from here originally, you know? I knew I could put my experience to work and, well, try to give something back.'

'You mean your experience in law?' I was half-listening and completely lost.

'And expertise in networking, raising capital, property management – the world I'm familiar with. A lot of people over here have lost faith in the system, obviously with good reason. But that's like losing faith in gravity or the solar system, in the way the world works. You just need to understand it, right?'

I could see how Aleka Marr had become so influential. She exuded confidence and know-how and *passion* and was so admirable and lovely that, if I couldn't be supportive, at the very least I should have been envious. But I just felt tired. Slightly ashamed, I tried to make an effort and feign some interest.

'So, your company – Heartbeat? What does it do?'

'It's a public-private partnership with the city council and other state-run agencies. We operate in the context of the remaining encumbered city properties tied up in debt and lawsuits, some of it taken over by the State – alongside the need for accommodation for those who can't afford a home and those not sober enough to know what they need.'

'Ah,' I said, blinking, still in the dark. 'And your approach is different ...?'

'We're not the only agency working in this space. What makes us unique is our joined-up thinking across the public and private sectors. We rely on personal contacts and a lot of goodwill.'

She took a sip from her water bottle while gazing at me earnestly.

'Like I said, I'm not in this for the money or to push some kind of agenda,' she smiled. 'If I wanted a career in politics, it wouldn't be in this country.'

'Too small for you?'

'I'm just used to operating on a different scale. Having said that, in this country you can work at a much finer level of granularity.' She saw my look of incomprehension.

'What I mean is, here everything is personal. And the devil, as they say, is in the detail.'

'So that's the reason that someone in your lofty position can take an interest in the death of a homeless teenager?'

If Aleka noticed my sarcasm, she ignored it. She was probably used to begrudgery.

'Something like that,' she said. 'I'm afraid that your dead boy is just one of many. More than thirty homeless people die every year in Dublin and more than half of them die on the streets. Those are the ones we know about. Many of them simply disappear; they're presumed dead and it never gets reported. So when Jimmy Mooney pushed me for a comment, I decided to highlight the danger of drug-related infections – in the hope of preventing similar tragedies.'

Finally, something I was interested in. 'You really think that Stevie had that ... disease?'

Aleka Marr was no longer smiling. 'Make no mistake about it, Connie. That disease is very real.'

But before I could ask her any more, we were loudly interrupted by a furious voice coming from the counter area.

15

LOCAL CUISINE

'Piss *off* Ozzie,' Kitty yelled. 'I told you – I'm *not* coming back to work until you pay me. If you don't watch out, I'll go and rep for the competition. You know how many nights you owe me for now? It's nineteen, Ozzie, I've kept a record. Stevie told me you owed him too. Last time I saw him he said that he'd marked your cards and he'd rat on you if you didn't pay him.'

'Cash flow issues, darling,' purred Ozzie. 'Haven't you heard we're still emerging from a global recession? Connie, if you get a chance at all, do you think you could have a little chat with Kitty about the national economy?'

He was unperturbed by her outburst. While he was as deathly pale as always, he still didn't look as if he'd been awake all night. Maybe the rumours were true and Ozzie Wolf belonged to the legions of the undead. I pictured him dozing in a coffin next door surrounded by black candles and a couple of goats. The image of a tattooed buttock floated into my head and had to be banished instantly. I really wished I hadn't heard so many strange things about Ozzie. It made it very difficult to concentrate.

'The club went through a temporary difficulty,' he continued. 'But we're back on track now.'

He produced a thick roll of notes from his pocket.

'Here's what I owe you, Kitty. And I've thrown in a little extra for goodwill. I appreciate your patience and understanding.'

Kitty snorted. She took the wad of notes and counted them carefully. It didn't look like all that much to me but she seemed satisfied.

'About bleedin' time too,' she said.

'Why don't you take Stevie's pay too?' Ozzie said. 'Oh go on! It's no good to the poor little bugger now, wherever he is. And you seem to be the closest he has to next of kin. Now, come on, Kitty. Give us a hug!'

'Get away from me, sleazeball.'

But she took the money. 'I'll do something for Stevie with it.'

'You're more than welcome. And speaking of sleazeballs. You do know that I wasn't the only one round here to get a piece of Stevie's mind on Friday? Our loveable rogue from the Sunrise Hotel got the sharp end of his tongue too – so much so that Stevie got thrown out of his ratty little room there and was told not to come back.'

'No way – Stevie would have told me.'

'Actually, I can confirm what Ozzie said is true.'

Kitty and Ozzie looked over to see who had spoken. It was Aleka Marr, still sitting at the table opposite me.

'My staff informed me, as soon as they heard the reports of his death, that the young man had booked into one of our hostels for Saturday night. Promising artist, I believe. Too bad these kids seem to slide back so easily ...'

It was clear that Ozzie knew Aleka but hadn't seen her sitting there. Now he greeted her rather too effusively.

'Well! Fancy seeing you here! Really, Aleka, it's been far too long! What an honour for us to have you back in this neck of the woods. And how's the world domination going?'

'It's coming along nicely, Ozzie, thanks for asking. How's the club? No more injunctions about the noise, I hope. You're on your final warning, right?'

Obviously there was history between the two of them. I wondered about that 'thing' Aggie said he had, the thing about older women. Aleka and Ozzie? Surely not. Aleka seemed so cool, so *together*, it was hard to imagine her throwing caution to the wind. But then again ...

She and Ozzie were smiling dangerously, each watching the other closely like a couple of alley cats who could decide to spring at any moment and tear each other apart.

I felt the pulse in my temple starting to throb and wondered if I should be worried about having a stroke.

'No bloodshed in the café,' I was about to tell them. The insurance probably wouldn't cover it. And I didn't need any more stress.

The door opened and a small freckled boy with a ginger buzz cut walked in and came straight over to me. He held out a white ceramic pudding bowl covered in a blue checked tea-towel.

'Hey, missus. Are you called Connie, missus? I've a delivery for you from Mr Fogarty.'

I took the pudding bowl from him and lifted the tea towel. The rising steam blinded me for a moment. I waved it away to view the contents. Four pink and glistening pigs' feet nestled in a pool of jelly, their dainty little hooves looking prepped for a pedicure.

I slowly replaced the tea towel and looked at the curious faces around me.

'Fogarty said he'd introduce me to the local cuisine.'

'Well darling,' said Ozzie as he started to leave. 'What do you expect from an unreconstructed male like himself? No fucking finesse.'

At the door, he stopped and directed a carefully fabricated look of sincerity and a tentative thumbs-up to Kitty, 'Back tonight, please? The usual place.'

She laughed and returned his thumbs-up.

Aleka waited until Ozzie was gone and then rose also.

'It's been great meeting you, Connie. But I can see you're busy. You've got my card with my number. Promise you'll call me – I'm sure I can help. And I really hope we can be friends. We blow-ins have to stick together!'

She gave me a smile and a conspiratorial little wink, then rose and shook my hand. She stopped by Kitty on her way out to say a quick word of commiseration, then gave me a wave from the door. She really was very attractive. And you have to like someone who gives you conspiratorial little winks.

Josie had already taken command of the pudding bowl.

'I'll have the pigs' feet. They're lovely in the coddle.'

The old coffee machine gave a series of alarming clanks and a loud hiss. A spurt of steam blew off a small metal part that flew across the room and lodged in the ceiling light shade.

'I think the coffee machine needs a bit more work there, Connie,' Kitty said, grinning.

'Well, it'll have to wait. Can you and Josie manage without me for a while longer? It's time to visit the Sunrise Hotel. I need to have a word with Fogarty. And this place is bloody dangerous.'

16

THE SUNRISE HOTEL

A rush of torrid air greeted me the minute I opened the café door. It felt hot and tasted of diesel and rotting seaweed. The sky hung low and heavy, threatening more rain. Beneath it, the river gleamed like mercury.

I ran past the silent Stalag 17 and a series of boarded-up doorways to the crumbling brick portico of the Sunrise Hotel. A couple of unsteady, purple-faced men raised themselves off the entrance steps as I passed them.

'Morning,' I said. 'Know where Fogarty is?'

One of them blurted something incoherent and gesticulated in the direction of the bridge.

Must be out, I thought. Good, I can take a look at Stevie's room without his interference. It would save me a lot of trouble with Kitty if I could find those missing sketchbooks. Better still, if I could find something to confirm that Stevie had gone back on the drugs, that would put an end to her wild accusations. With any luck, I'd be in and out of there in a matter of minutes.

I walked through the open double doors of the Sunrise Hotel into a dim hallway. Battered cornices edged the ceiling and dark green paint peeled off the walls. Light filtered through the cloudy fanlight and illuminated the bank of chipped lockers along one wall and the motes of dust slanting upwards from the cracked black-and-white tiled floor. A once-grand staircase curved upwards, uncarpeted and missing half of its banister rods. To my right, a door opened on to a reception room full of mismatched furniture around an ancient fireplace, rusted curtains hanging in ribbons from the shuttered double windows. To my left was a closed door marked Private. Further back the hall, to either side of the stairs, a corridor ran in both directions.

The building smelled of socks and stale cigarettes, of dampness and despair. The only sign of life was the distant clatter of plates from somewhere to the rear of the hallway. There was no one about.

I'm not sure what I'd expected. Only someone who has never been in one could call this place a hotel; only someone who could afford nothing better would choose to stay here. Light years away from free wifi or complementary bathrobes, this was a dosshouse, pure and simple. I looked around for something that might resemble a reception desk.

I spotted it close to the stairwell, a small wooden table and a chair inside a roofed cubicle made from thick steel bars. The table held a desk lamp and an old push button telephone. A ledger lay open, probably the hotel's register of names and dates.

A voice from the gloom under the stairs made me start.

'They put in the cage when the last fella got battered. Ended up paralysed and on life support. Poor fucker.'

The voice was cracked and thick with alcohol. It belonged to a dead-eyed man wearing a crumpled hat who sat in semi-darkness beside the reception cage. He cradled a guitar, fingering its loose strings noiselessly and mechanically.

I examined the metal bars encasing the reception desk. A cage? I couldn't think of a better place for Pius Fogarty.

'Come here to me,' the seated man said, reaching out with a gnarled hand, 'come here till I tell you something.'

I moved closer to the desk so that I could get a better view of him while carefully keeping out of arm's reach.

'What is it?'

'Where's the bar in this hotel?' he demanded. 'Do you know where it is?'

'I don't,' I said, surprised. 'Is there a bar here?'

'There bloody well isn't!' he roared, then looked around furtively. 'But,' he whispered, 'I know where we can get ourselves a drink.'

'Thanks, but maybe later,' I said. 'I'm actually looking for someone's room. Maybe you can help me? Do you know which room Stevie Hennessy stayed in?'

'You're wasting your time,' he said. 'He's brown bread.'

With an open palm, he slowly banged on the side of his head, as if he was trying to clear it. 'Elvis has left the building.'

'I know Stevie's dead,' I said. 'I'm sorry if he was a friend of yours. I just want to see his room. I'd ask Fogarty but he doesn't seem to be here ...'

'Fuck Fogarty!' the man shouted, making me jump. 'Are you one of his fancy women?' He glared at me. 'Never you mind about him. The room's down there.' He waved his hand towards the passageway on the right. 'Down at the end.'

'There's nothing there,' he added.

I skirted round him, murmured thanks and darted down the dingy corridor, hoping he wouldn't follow.

The mutterings continued from his outpost in the hall, 'Fuck Fogarty' and again, more loudly, 'Where's the bar in this hotel?'

The doors lining the corridor were painted in cream gloss, with room numbers stuck on in adhesive black vinyl letters. Despite the layers of repaint jobs, carved initials of former residents still scored each door like ancient scars. Amongst the sounds of snoring and muffled voices, radio music and the chatter from a small party came from one room. Passing another, I heard someone quietly sobbing.

At the end of the corridor, a toilet door was labelled 'Gents' with more adhesive letters, this time in gold, the function of its interior further advertised by a combined stench of bleach and urine. The door next to the toilet was ajar. Guessing it was Stevie's room, I entered it quietly.

It wasn't much bigger than a prison cell, maybe eight feet by ten, windowless. The low ceiling had stipple-effect tiles. I tapped the light partition walls. No insulation. I could imagine the racket at night. There was just about enough space for a bed and a tiny bedside table. I remembered the bank of lockers in the hall. That must be where the hotel residents kept their belongings. Kitty said she'd checked the lockers for the missing backpack and it wasn't there. Stevie could have taken it back to his room. Fogarty hadn't found it but maybe he didn't look hard enough.

The back of the bedroom door had a simple slide bolt on the inside but no other security. Pretty lax for a place with above-average levels of substance abuse and financial desperation.

It didn't take long for me to check out the room. The only personal belongings lay on the stripped bed: a couple of books and a small, light blue holdall. No backpack, no sketchbooks. I examined the books, both of them old, thick and dog-eared. *The Dictionary of Subjects and Symbols in Art* had a writhing mass of Renaissance nudes on its cover. The other book was Vasari's *Lives of the Most Eminent Painters, Sculptors and Architects*. Standard textbooks for any art student, they were incongruous in these surroundings.

I unzipped the holdall and lifted out a white t-shirt and a pair of worn jeans. A toilet bag contained soap, a razor, a toothbrush. I replaced the contents and closed the holdall, then stopped and sniffed the air. I'd smelled something when I entered the room, something familiar but unidentifiable, something chemical. Now I got it again. I went to the door and closed it, shutting out the noxious fumes wafting in from the Gents. The smell was definitely there, weaker at the door, stronger around the bed. I raised the mattress, then replaced it and felt it all over; I turned it and did the same on the other side. I pulled out the bed, examined the bedside table and checked the floorboards. I pressed my hands against the walls and tugged at the skirting boards. But I found nothing. And then I looked up. Directly over the bed, the edge of one of the ceiling tiles beside the central light fitting looked a little loose. I stood on the bed and reached up with both hands. I could just about touch the tile with my fingertips. It was definitely coming away from the ceiling. The smell was stronger up there too. If only I was taller. I got down, stacked the art books on the bed and placed the up-ended bedside table on top of them so that I could use its upturned legs to steady myself when I stepped up on it. Teetering on top of the pile, I forced myself to overcome my vertigo and open my eyes. I reached up again and pushed my fingers under the tile. It came away easily and dropped down on the bed. I stretched up further and fumbled around blindly inside the cavity until my fingertips encountered something. I edged the object towards me and, keeping my eyes downwards to avoid getting dust and dead flies in my contacts, lifted it out. A wooden paintbox.

The box had a lid that swivelled upwards to act as a small easel. Inside were a few used tubes of oil paint, an unlabelled bottle containing a clear fluid, a stained rag, a palette knife and some brushes, including the kind of six-inch paintbrush you'd use for home decorating. I opened the bottle and sniffed. White spirits, that's what I'd smelled, that and oil paint. Not drugs.

Disappointed, I dropped the box on the bed and looked up again. I saw the corner of something else in the darkness inside the hole. Stretching up again, I pulled at the object and two more ceiling tiles detached and fell, covering my hair and face with black soot-like dirt. I spluttered while easing from the hole a flat piece of hardboard, maybe just over two foot square. Paint had been applied on its rough side. An art catalogue might have described it as 'Oil on board, unframed'. I lowered it with one hand to get a better look, steadying myself with my other hand pressed to the ceiling.

It was a portrait of a sensuous young man with an expression of pain on his face. The name, 'Stevie H.' was neatly inscribed in a bottom corner. The picture's subject and treatment looked familiar. It reminded me of a portrait by Caravaggio, one of his series of works with titles like *Boy with Fruit* or *Boy with Basket*. Or the one where the boy's been bitten by something, a snake or a lizard.

This boy was golden-haired, pale and gentle looking, with a small, pink rose in his hair, tucked behind his ear. It was Stevie himself. His round red lips were parted in pain, the white tips of a bottom row of even little teeth just visible in the blackness of his open mouth. His eyebrows twisted in outrage and surprise. I couldn't see the cause of his pain. I needed more light.

'Well, make yourself at home, why don't you?' said Pius Fogarty as the door swung open.

Just then, the structure beneath me collapsed and, as I fell, the electric light fitting and a good section of the ceiling came down with me, followed by a small nest of spiders.

17

SPIDERS

'Don't come near me,' I said from the broken bed, feeling myself for injuries while brushing off the debris. 'Just go away and leave me alone.'

'I've no intention of going near you,' Fogarty said. 'You're guilty of breaking and entering private property, committing an act of vandalism and possible larceny. God knows what else you're capable of. Plus there are things crawling in your hair.'

'*You're* accusing *me* of criminal activity?'

'No, I'm calculating the money you owe me in damages. I reckon about five hundred should cover it.'

'The only thing that would improve this dump is a demolition squad. I'm sure we can organise a neighbourhood whip-around to pay for it.'

Ignoring me, Fogarty bent down and picked up the painting.

'You found this here?'

I nodded. 'Hidden in the ceiling with a box of paints. I was looking for Stevie's sketchbooks. *Don't* start shaking your head at me now. Have you seen that painting before?'

Fogarty examined it carefully.

'A self portrait.' He shook his head. 'No, I've never seen this one, but it's definitely Stevie's. It's different from his other stuff though. There's a couple of his works hanging in the dining area. Would you like a look at them?' He handed me the painting as I studied him suspiciously.

'And I'll give you a personal tour of this fine establishment while you're here. To make up for my past transgressions. Did you get your delivery this morning, by the way?'

'Yeah, yeah. Introduction to the local cuisine. Very funny.'

'I hope you weren't expecting dinner for two in some bijou restaurant offering locally-sourced specialities,' he said with fake concern. 'I'd hate to disappoint you.'

'All I expect from you, Pius Fogarty, is juvenile behaviour and general stupidity,' I said with dignity. 'You did not disappoint.'

'Well, I hope the poor little piggies didn't go to waste. Did you put them on the menu?'

'You'll be glad to know that they're already in Josie's coddle. You'll have some tomorrow morning instead of your coffee. No, no, I insist. I won't take no for an answer.'

'If that's a threat,' he said, 'I'm quaking with fear. Look, I'm sorry about making fun of you like that. I won't do it again. Truce?'

His repentant look was not convincing.

'Fine,' I said, moving towards the door with the painting under my arm. 'Show me Stevie's other paintings, but it'll have to be quick. I don't have much time.'

The man with the guitar was still in the hall, half asleep, when we passed. He stirred and sat forward when he saw us, pushing his hat back on his head with one hand.

'Ha!' he said. 'Would you look at the pair of them.'

'Be nice, Marty,' Fogarty said. 'We have an important visitor.'

'Important, me arse,' said Marty. 'We all know what's important to Fogarty.'

His wheezing laughter turned into a horrible racking cough.

'Ignore him,' Fogarty said. 'He's harmless enough but the old mind's gone. We'll go this way.'

The smell of burning toast got stronger as we walked down the corridor on the other side of the hall. In the small kitchenette, a woman stood over a frying pan, poking at some sausages with a fork. She was short and stocky with long, straight grey hair scraped back off her face in a tight ponytail, her huge hoop earrings almost touching her shoulders. As she turned to talk to Fogarty, she steadied herself with a hand on the counter. Her face was strangely discoloured and her cheeks had caved in. No teeth, I guessed. A refugee from a domestic war zone, her nose looked like it had been broken in several places and never reset.

'I was up in the Coyningham Road this morning,' she said in a tobacco-hardened voice. 'I'll be in my own flat in ten days time, they said, if I can keep my nose clean in the meantime.'

'You'll be missed, Eileen,' said Fogarty. 'Along with your cooking. We'll have to go down to the Silver Bullet Café to remind us of the smell of burnt grease.'

Her wide grin showed me that I was right about the teeth.

Fogarty ushered me through the adjoining dining area. A large corkboard on the back wall was covered with layers of flyers. Many of them were missing person notices. 'Have you seen this man?' 'Teenage girl missing from Navan.' Fuzzy, smiling faces from pictures taken at birthday parties, wedding parties or sporting events. Beside them was a selection of menus from Chinese takeaways and pizza delivery services.

'Room service,' Fogarty said.

Then he pointed to a couple of framed paintings hanging side by side in an alcove.

'Those are Stevie's. Stay here and I'll get some tea.'

He returned to the kitchen while I stood in front of the paintings. I propped the self portrait from Stevie's room against the wall on the floor beneath them. The paintings above were a pair. One showed a young man crouched in a shop doorway, a blue sleeping bag covering his legs and lower body. He slumped against the doorpost, his eyes closed, his hands open, palms upwards and empty on his lap. On the ground beside him was a crumpled white plastic bag.

Its companion painting centred on the figure of a girl lying back on a bleached-out timber bench, the kind they have on the boardwalk close to the Ha'penny Bridge. In the distance was a green coffee kiosk and figures of men and women walking or sitting. The grey stone blocks of the quay wall formed the background. The girl's head rested back against the wall as if she was taking in the rays of the morning sun. Long dark hair covered part of her face. She wore a t-shirt, a short skirt and ankle boots. Her legs were stretched out, her arms folded across her chest. Like the young man in the other painting, her eyes were closed. I stepped closer to see what was shining on the bench below her elbow. It was a syringe.

Fogarty appeared with a carton of milk under his arm and two mugs of tea and placed them on a table. He produced some sachets of sugar from a pocket and half a packet of chocolate biscuits from another. 'A miracle,' he said, indicating the biscuits.

I couldn't tear my eyes away from the painting of the girl.

'Looks like Kitty, doesn't she?' Fogarty said, sitting down. 'Don't worry. Kitty's no addict, just did a bit of modelling for Stevie sometimes. It isn't real.'

'It's not real.' I repeated, still staring at the painting as I sat too. 'It's *more* than real.'

Now I knew what Stevie's paintings had in common. Using some extraordinary combination of composition and treatment of light and shade, the artist had created an effect that seemed drug-induced, heightening reality, delineating and intensifying it. Even the painting from Stevie's room, with its classical style and treatment, had the same immediacy.

'They're beautiful. But really disturbing ... what are you're doing?'

Fogarty had been gazing at me fixedly for several minutes and now reached a hand towards me and touched the hair at my forehead. I flinched as if I'd been scorched.

'Sorry, it's just a bit distracting.' He held out his finger at eye level and we watched as a tiny golden spider descended from it on an invisible thread. Fogarty rose and gently dropped the spider on to a dusty artificial plant on the counter before returning to the table.

'You were saying?'

'Oh, right. Just that Stevie's paintings are quite disturbing. I'm not sure they'd be suitable for everywhere ...'

Fogarty put down his mug and sat back with a dangerous glint in his eyes.

'You mean, not suitable for the alcos and junkies of the Sunrise Hotel? You think those paintings are too depressing, maybe a bad influence?'

'Well, they might be a bit close to the bone,' I muttered. God, he was touchy about this place. So much for the truce.

'Connie, this is a hotel. It's a very cheap one, possibly the cheapest in town, but it's a hotel all the same. People pay their own money to stay here. They choose when to come and when to leave. Or not leave. See that guy over there?'

He nodded towards a tall, stooped old man who was shuffling into the kitchen.

'Harry checked in here one day twenty years ago. Hasn't been outside the door since that day, not once. He has a bunch of kids lined up to run messages for him, getting him his smokes and the few things he needs. It's possible that he'll stay in his room forever and never leave, and that's ok, it's his business.'

'So it's not like a hostel or a shelter.'

'Bingo. If our guests want to drink themselves to death or shoot whatever crap they can get their hands on into their veins, they're free to go ahead. Just so long as they do it quietly and privately and try not to mess up the decor while they're at it.'

The last bit had to be a joke.

'Ok, I get it. And you're free to plaster the place with all the depressing pictures you like.'

'We don't do rainbows and bunnies. And just so you know,' he smiled at last, 'I'm not a bleeding social worker.'

He reached for my mug.

'Finished? You said you hadn't much time. Come on and I'll show you something interesting before you go.'

I'd forgotten I'd pretended to be on a tight schedule.

'So, if you don't mind me asking,' I said as I stood up. 'who pays ...?'

'For the palatial surroundings and my handsome salary? The property is privately owned. We get by on the small charges the guests pay. It's cold in the winter and the roof leaks. But the hotel stays private and independent.'

Kind of like yourself, I thought as I followed him out. I wanted to ask him how he ended up in the Sunrise Hotel, what he was doing there and for how long. If he wasn't a social worker, then what was he? He sure as hell wasn't a hotelier working up his tourist industry credentials. Despite myself, I was beginning to get curious about Pius Fogarty.

18

MORTIFICATION

I followed Fogarty through the open emergency exit at the end of the corridor and out into the air. The daylight was blinding after the dimly-lit passageway. I stood on the metal fire escape about four or five steps up from ground level, shaded my eyes and looked down on the yard.

It was surrounded by high walls on all sides and paved with uneven flagstones. To my left, an aluminium pull-up garage gate took up most of the side wall. Beside it, a rusting rotary washing line pegged with socks slanted towards a lean-to shed. A row of wheelie bins lined up against the house wall. The sign on the wall above them had a red skull and cross-bones and the words: 'Caution. Baited area'. Tendrils of determined ivy twisted up a trellis on the whitewashed back wall.

Fogarty addressed the small group who sat smoking around a battered timber picnic table.

'This is Connie. She's getting the grand tour.'

The two thin blonde women at the table pulled on their cigarettes and looked me over before simultaneously croaking, 'How'er yiz.'

Beside them, a man in a wheelchair studied us gravely before returning to his conversation with the women.

'Over here,' said Fogarty, moving towards the far wall.

From where I stood, it seemed to be covered with some sort of mural. I followed him, passing a large national flag painted on the back of the house.

'Football support?' I asked.

He shook his head.

'Political. We've plenty of football fans here and you'll see the flags all around the place on match days. But that one was painted by our patriots. They insisted on hanging a flag outside the entrance too. You might have seen it when you came in?'

'Missed it. Do you have rules about, you know, flags and political stuff?'

'Rules about flags?' he laughed. 'They can hang their jocks from the chimney pots for all I care.' He lowered his voice as he continued.

'The guy in wheelchair over there, he's from Belfast. Kneecapped on a visit down here last year.'

He called back to the man at the table, who was looking over at us now. 'All right, Barry?'

'Aye, Fogarty. All's well.'

'Holy shit,' I said under my breath.

'It hasn't gone away,' Fogarty said. 'The punishment beatings and intimidation. Down here as well as up north. Just doesn't get reported.'

'Speaking of reporting, what about Mooney? You were going to have a chat with him.'

'I was going to kick seven kinds of shit out of him.'

'And?'

Fogarty stopped and took his time about answering.

'Let's just say that Mooney and I have reached an understanding. Another article will appear in tomorrow's rag and it'll have a more balanced viewpoint. You know why it'll be more balanced? Because I drafted the bloody thing. Mooney wouldn't know the meaning of balance if he was on a seesaw with an elephant.'

'Jesus. What did you do to him?'

'Between ourselves, I have some information on Mooney that he'd prefer doesn't become widely known right now. Don't worry, there was no blood spilled. Or at least, not very much.'

'No wonder they're queuing up to shoot you.'

Fogarty was amused.

'Who's been talking? Ok, everyone is, I know. I'm guessing your information source is Kitty. A girl with a wild imagination. Don't believe everything you hear from her. Or from anyone else around here. There's a lot of old talk going about and most of it is rubbish.'

'So you're the only one I can trust, is that what you're saying?'

'Pretty much.' He might have been joking. It was hard to tell.

We skirted a stack of brown plastic chairs in the corner surrounded by a scattering of cigarette butts. A couple of used syringes glittered amongst the weeds in the shore. Fogarty stopped.

'They should be in the syringe bin. Hey, Miro!'

He called to a tall young man who had pushed up the metal gate on the far wall and was sweeping around the bins with a yard brush.

'Over here. And say hi to Connie.'

The young man came over and held out his hand to me, smiling shyly.

'Hello, I am Miroslav. I am from Minsk.'

'Miro helps out around here,' Fogarty said. 'He's a handy guy. If you ever need anything moved or something fixed, Miro's your man. Electrical engineer, no less.'

'Any good with coffee machines?' I asked.

'Maybe,' Miro laughed.

'Come on,' Fogarty said, moving ahead. 'This is what I wanted to show you. It's our graffiti wall.'

The wall was around fifteen feet long and ten feet high, every inch of which was decorated with written, hand-drawn and spray-painted tags, symbols, pictures and messages. About a third of it was covered with a grid of black-framed boxes, each box containing a handwritten message or note. I read a couple. There were entire life stories there scrawled in a couple of sentences or just a few words.

'RIP, Kelly, – missin ya girl, June '11.'

There were a lot more RIPs and a lot more 'missin ya's.

A smaller section alongside was filled with political symbols and slogans. Further down the wall seemed more artistic and random.

'Was this planned?' I asked.

'It just happened. A few years ago, some of the guests started writing up messages and painting pictures and graffiti tags on the wall. They left behind their paint and spray cans, others started to use them and it caught on. Soon we'll need to get more wall.'

'It's incredible,' I said, passing the crudely-drawn genitalia enlivening the middle section and pausing at a section devoted to religious and mystical images and objects. Holy medals and rosary beads had been attached to the surface in places. Small nooks and crannies were stuffed with slips of paper, prayers presumably, and petitions. A little painted shrine depicted a bearded saint with his hands upheld, palms facing outward.

'Padre Pio,' Fogarty said. 'Miracle worker to the poor. The Padre's been falling down on the job lately, though. Miracles for the poor are in short supply around here.'

Beside Padre Pio was a simple but more accomplished image of another male saint. He was kneeling, his hands joined in front of him in prayer. He was wrapped around with rusty chains and ropes which dug deeply into the flesh around his chest, his arms and his legs.

'That's Matt Talbot,' said Fogarty. 'You know – the local candidate for canonisation. He was a reformed alcoholic from the tenements who devoted his life to prayer. He lived just up the road from here.'

'Was Stevie religious?'

'Not at all, at least as far as I know. Why?'

'Because he painted this – look at his signature.' I pointed to the minuscule 'Stevie H.' which, at least to my weak eyes, was barely visible beneath the picture.

'You're right.' Fogarty said, frowning as he peered at the name. 'I never noticed that.'

'What's the story with the chains?'

'Mortification of the flesh. An extreme type of penance. When Matt Talbot eventually collapsed and died on the street – that was about a hundred years ago – they discovered the chains and ropes he wore around his body night and day.'

'Weird. Why would someone do that?'

And also, I wondered, if Stevie wasn't religious, why would he paint this? I examined the picture more closely, my nose nearly touching the wall.

'He's got other wounds besides the marks of the chains. Look.' I pointed to Matt Talbot's neck and to the back of his hand.

I stepped back and looked at the adjoining picture again.

'That other saint has them too – they're on his hands.'

'Padre Pio always has wounds,' Fogarty said. 'What kind of education did you have? They're his stigmata, the bleeding wounds of Christ. They miraculously appeared on Padre Pio due to his sanctity.'

'But these aren't like stigmata. They're the same as the ones on Matt Talbot over there. And – this sounds really stupid – they look to me like cigarette burns.'

Right then, I realised what I'd missed from Stevie's self-portrait, the one I'd taken from his bedroom and was currently secured firmly under my arm. I held it up so that I could have another look. Now I could see the cause of the pain on the boy's face.

'Well, look at that,' I murmured, pointing to the faint mark of a cigarette burn on boy's raised wrist. 'Why did Stevie put it in his self-portrait? Why did he paint Matt Talbot? What's the connection?'

My mind was racing, making wild leaps, processing flickering memories of old movie frames, something in a cult book. The name of a horror movie, what was it? *'La Fin Absolute Du Monde'*. A line from a song about the drinks and the pills not working, '*... in the morning it hurts like cigarette burns.'* I saw torture scenes, remembered harrowing reports on child abuse ...

'Connie.' Fogarty's voice came from somewhere far away.

'Look, I want you to stop poking about and asking questions about Stevie. It's not safe. I shouldn't have shown you all this, it's only encouraging you and making you jump to all kinds of crazy conclusions. There are things

going on around here that people don't want to come out –
things they'll go to any lengths to keep hidden. I tried to
warn Stevie the night before he disappeared – but he went
crazy and walked away. If he'd listened to me and stayed
here, he might still be alive. Will *you* listen to me now?'

I couldn't believe my ears. Where had this come from?

Fogarty stood in front of me and placed his hands firmly
on my shoulders. His eyes bored directly into mine.

'Could you not just stick to the scones and the pots of tea
and leave well enough alone?'

I shook his hands off me and pushed him away with all
my strength, then pushed him harder as he staggered
backwards.

'Ow! Jesus!' he howled as he regained his balance and
placed a hand on the bandage underneath his shirt, his face
twisted with pain. 'My bloody arm!'

I'd forgotten that he was wounded but by now I didn't
care.

'*You* want me to stop asking questions about Stevie?' I
repeated, my face burning. 'Why don't you just piss off and
go back to sitting on your arse in your cage – or whatever
you do with yourself. I promised Kitty I'd try to find out
what happened to Stevie and that's exactly what I'm going
to do.'

I was shaking with fury, angrier with myself for allowing
him to draw me in and play me for a fool. I should have
known. It's not as if I hadn't been warned by practically
everyone I'd met. So he thought I was that easy to
manipulate? Jesus, I'd show that arrogant bastard.

Miro had left the gate open so that he could put out the
bins. As the smokers at the table exchanged knowing looks,
I marched out onto the side street clutching Stevie's
painting, leaving Pius Fogarty standing there speechless,
grasping his injured arm.

19

TEXTS 2 TALBOT ST

The flags at the entrance to the Sunrise Hotel hung limp as I rounded the corner. The green version of the Starry Plough was tacked to a broom pole; from a narrow timber length the tricolour drooped in tatters.

'Yeah, perfect,' I snarled as I passed.

I turned on my phone as I crossed the road to the quayside. Seconds later, the phone began to jump. Three missed messages.

I was getting overfamiliar with those metal benches on the quays. I sat on one now to check my calls. Despite the day's stifling warmth, the seat felt as cold and wet as the one Mooney and I had shared last night. Finally there was a message from Aggie: 'UNEXPECTED TURN OF EVENTS. MAY BE OUT OF TOUCH FOR A BIT XX.'

No smiley face.

Jesus Christ. My heart pounded as I tried to call her but the phone went straight to voicemail. I left a message, 'Please call! V. worried. Are you ok?'

Next message, unknown phone number.

'Urgent! We need to talk, informally. Dinner tonight, 7.30. The Parlour, Hawkins Street – Anthony Brady.'

'No!' I groaned. I didn't want to have dinner or anything else with Brady. On the other hand, I didn't need any more enemies right now. Plus I might need him to check up on Aggie. I decided to wait and get back to him later.

The next message told me I had a missed call. I checked my voicemail. The male caller's words were rushed and strangled over a fractured connection. It was Jimmy Mooney, his voice shaking but insistent.

'Can't explain now but it's bad. Told you I made a mistake ...' Then he said something I couldn't figure out. It sounded like 'thud' or 'sud'.

'... putting it right,' he continued. 'You're the only one who'll believe me. It's all ...'

There was a lot of crackling, in the middle of which I could only catch '... thirteen twenty'. After that, it cleared briefly. 'Meet me in *Way To Grow* ... Talbot Street at twelve noon. You have to be there.'

Mooney had always seemed slightly crazed, but this was different. Now he sounded scared. My first thought was his run-in with Fogarty, but that seemed unlikely to cause this kind of reaction. I recalled our midnight encounter. My initial impression of him had changed at the quayside when I saw him so crushed and so ... *contrite*. I'd lured him back from the edge last night by promising him news, and, like a starving dog, he seized on the scraps of information I threw him. It gave him strength again, drove him to act. Was it my fault he was in trouble now? If only his message had been clearer. What the hell was 'thud' or 'sud' and what was 'thirteen twenty' about? The one sure thing was that Mooney wasn't strong any more, he was terrified.

I scoured my raddled brain to try to remember what I'd said that had caught his attention last night. The missing sketchbooks. And something else ... I couldn't remember. There was no choice, I'd have to meet him. I checked the time. He'd called me at eleven and said to meet him someplace on Talbot Street at twelve. It was half eleven now. I could see the steamed-up windows of the Silver Bullet Café across the road a little further down from where I sat. I'd just enough time to drop by and check up on Josie and Kitty.

As I pushed open the café door, I spotted the foreigner again, the one who was in the café yesterday. I still couldn't figure out how I knew him. He sat in the same place as before, the corner opposite the door, drinking a can of Coke, examining a map. He looked up as I passed, then returned to his reading. Aviator sunglasses on top of his close-cropped head, he looked fit and tanned, early-fifties most likely, wearing an olive green polo shirt and grey cotton trousers. Good looking guy. Who the hell was he? And what was he doing so far from Starbucks?

Without a word to anyone, I went to the kitchen and pushed the painting I was carrying face inwards behind the microwave, then ran straight upstairs to change my top, wash my face and check my hair for spiders. Five minutes later, I was back downstairs.

On a stool at the counter, Josie was concealed behind the lurid cover of a *True Detective* magazine. Viv sat at a table chatting to Christy, an old joiner, retired for years from the Port and Docks Authority. Christy drank at least a gallon of tea a day and never removed his hat, not even in bed, or so they said. Their loud comments about everyone around them could be clearly heard above the general hum of conversation. The Russian sailors sitting in the top corner were either very tolerant or didn't understand their accents.

Some of Stevie's friends were back, five or six of them, sitting around their usual tables. Kitty perched on a third table nearby, talking animatedly, her legs crossed. She jumped down as soon as she saw me. 'You've been gone for ages – I hope you're getting somewhere,' she hissed at me.

'I'd get there faster with a quick coffee,' I hissed back, pointing at the door. She grabbed a take-out cup.

A warm, sweet smell rose from something bubbling in a large aluminium pot on the hob and a gentle rhythmic knocking came from within. Must be Josie's coddle, I thought. The pigs' feet must be trying to kick their way out.

'Got stuck up there in Fogarty's ... gaff,' I said, accepting the hot cup from Kitty.

She grinned. I was learning the lingo.

'Are you ok looking after things? I have to go out again.'

'Just so long as you're getting somewhere,' she repeated. 'We're planning Stevie's send-off. You know, his funeral?'

'Oh right. God.' I said, suddenly worried about the painting I'd inadequately hidden. I retrieved it from the kitchen and discreetly passed it to Kitty, whispering, 'Look after this. It could be important. Hide it somewhere safe and don't show it to anyone.'

Kitty took one look at the self-portrait and said 'No fucking way!' so loudly that everyone looked in our direction. So much for discretion.

One of the girls leaned in to see the painting, blonde hair falling over half of her face, the other side of her head shaved close. She looked up at Kitty and shook her head slowly, a slight smile on her pale face.

'It's ok, Kitty. Just Stevie's idea of a joke, is all.'

Her voice was gentle, faltering slightly.

'Are you sure, Hannah?' Kitty asked.

Hannah rose and moved over to Kitty, giving her a loose hug. She was tall and very thin.

'I'm sure,' she said more firmly this time and she turned towards the door.

'I have to be off. I'll see you all later.'

The rest of them said 'See ya, Hannah' and 'Later' as she went out.

'What was that about, Kitty?' I asked. 'Is it something in the painting?'

'No,' she said and met my gaze with wide eyes. 'No, sorry, I just made a mistake. It's all ok.'

'Well, if you're sure,' I said. There was definitely something going on but I had no time to stay and worm it out of her.

'We'll talk about this later,' I said.

Once outside, I realised I had less than ten minutes to get down to Talbot Street. I'd never make it in time on foot. There was only one thing to do. I walked back through the café, out to the yard and whipped the raincover off my old Dutch bike. I contemplated it silently for a moment and downed the dregs of my coffee. People in this country hate cyclists almost as much as they hate trees. I've heard it's a deep-rooted psychological thing tied up with rejecting the poverty-stricken past and wanting to kill your father. Actually I wasn't sure about the last thing but it's something dark like that. Despite the risk, it was time to tackle Dublin's notoriously cyclist-unfriendly streets. I checked that the lock was around the base of the saddle and that the key was on my key ring.

As I wheeled the bike past the customers on my way to the door, one of them said, 'there goes a brave woman.'

Kitty was busily clearing up and her friends were preparing to go. It might have been my imagination but they all seemed more subdued now. I looked back at Kitty. She was holding her phone and watching me nervously. I got the impression that she couldn't wait for me to leave.

I pushed the bike across the road and took off down the quays in the direction of town, the huge trucks lumbering past making the whole earth shake. By the time I got to Talbot Street I was a nervous wreck. I had no idea what *Way*

To Grow was, so I walked slowly up the crowded street, scrutinising the shop fronts on both sides of the street.

They were mostly bargain stores and shops selling mobile phone covers and paraphernalia. When I reached the top of the street, I was thoroughly confused. I'd seen nothing called *Way To Grow*. I decided to go back and check the side streets. I locked my bike to a bus stop pole on O'Connell Street before heading back down North Earl Street to where it merged into Talbot Street. I checked every laneway and adjoining street all the way down to the end. It was well past midday by now. I phoned Mooney but got no reply. At the bottom of Talbot Street, just before it joined Amiens Street, I spotted Mabbot Lane. Double yellow lines ran down both sides of what was more like an alley than a street. A mixture of new apartment buildings and old warehouses blocked light from the lane and made it seem even narrower and more hemmed in. A dingy shopfront halfway down the lane had a dark green sign with a yellow-painted name hanging over it. *Way To Grow*. Other signs said 'Hydroponics' and 'Grow your Own'. Great, I thought, a Grow Shop. God knows who or what was inside, but there was no sign of Mooney anywhere else. There was no option. I'd have to go in.

20

WAY TO GROW

The interior of the grow shop was a lot bigger than the small low-key frontage suggested. It stretched back to a large, well-lit space full of bags of soil and nutrients, electrical equipment, lamps and metal containers. Two enormous potted banana plants stood at the front of the shop, their huge leaves almost obscuring the counter. Racks full of multi-coloured seed packets hung on the near wall. A sign over the seed section said 'Plant plugs available. Please inquire about bulk orders.'

The shop was bright and well-organised like a neighbourhood hardware store with a gardening section, and had the same musty smell of chemicals and vegetation. Through the foliage, I could just make out a curly-haired young man who stood at the counter sorting a pile of packages. He looked up when I entered and gave me a beaming smile.

'How'a ya?' he said in a strong Louth accent. 'Are you looking for something in partic'lar or just having a look-round?'

'Looking for someone,' I said. 'Guy called Mooney. Do you know him?'

'Is it the reporter fella?'

I nodded.

'Yeah, I know him, he's been in few times recently. Not today, though. He's doing a story on new strains of cannabis or something. The boss told me not to talk to him. Not that we're doing anything illegal here or anything. It's just that he'll twist what you say, the boss says, and if he starts to annoy the customers, we'll have to stop him coming in. Are you from the papers?'

'No, I'm from a café on the quays. Mooney asked me to meet him here – I have no idea why.'

I moved closer to the racks of seed packets to see what was on offer. Just the usual kind of vegetables, tomatoes, beans, cabbages, herbs. Nothing remotely druggy, unless I'd missed the news reports of hallucinogenic carrots or psychedelic celery. You never know with that GM.

'I didn't know there were grow shops here. I heard of them when I lived in Amsterdam, but I've never been in one.'

'Amsterdam, yeah? And you're running a café in Dublin?'

'Not that kind of café. Jesus, people round here are very quick to jump to conclusions.'

'Sorry,' he said, laughing. 'You never can tell. Most women who come in here, women your ...' He hesitated.

'Do you mean women my age?' I said icily.

'Well, there's a couple of different types, yeah? Like, there's the baby-boomer slash ageing-hippy chicks.'

'Obviously.'

'Then we might get the suburban housewives who're into gardening. But they usually go to the bigger outlets on the outskirts of town or they shop online.'

'Those suburban coffee mornings must be a lot of fun these days.'

'Ah, there's never been a shortage of drugs in the suburbs. Growing their own is little hobby, a bit of a novelty. And I hear that baking with the cannabutter is very popular with the health-conscious slash anti-smoking brigade. Nice for the dinner parties, y'know? Plus they say the weed's bringing families together again. Kind of a shared interest with the hubby and the stoner kids. Keeps them all safe at home and nicely chilled. What's not to like?'

'Well, when you put it like that ...'

'Then we get the self-medicating ones. They might have work-related stress and sure the gardening's therapeutic in itself. Or they've ongoing pain management or ... um ... women's problems. Especially at certain times of life.'

He glanced at me to see if I was taking offence again.

'Go on.'

'Course there's serious businesswomen growing on a commercial basis. They're usually involved in the bulk order end of things. I thought you might be one of those.'

'Well, I suppose I should be flattered you didn't take me for one of your ageing hippy chicks *slash* suburban housewives. And thanks for the tip on the self-medication for women's problems, I'll bear that in mind.'

'Great,' he said, smiling gently, immune to my sarcasm. 'I'm Ned, by the way.'

'Connie,' I said. 'From the Silver Bullet Café. Ned, how does your boss get away with this, legally I mean?'

'Oh, this is all totally legal. So long as we're just selling equipment that could be used to grow anything. Didn't you see all our lovely vegetable seeds? Lord, Mammy'd kill me if she thought I was involved in anything illegal. As it is, she thinks I work in the plant section in IKEA. I'm a horticulture student in the Botanic Gardens. This is just part-time to help make ends meet. I deliver organic vegetables on Saturdays too.'

'Just vegetables, Ned?'

'Now look who's jumping to conclusions!' he laughed. 'No, seriously. Look around. Do you see any bongs or drug paraphernalia? Any hemp-based products? If we stocked stuff like that, people would think we're a head shop and we'd be overrun with head-bangers looking for cannabis substitutes and all that.'

'Head shops? Are there any left? Didn't they ban them?'

'Yeah, first most of the legal highs were banned – you know, snow blow, spice, bath salts, all that stuff. Then they banned the actual chemicals to stop them being rebranded and sold as something else.'

He saw me looking at him blankly. 'All that stuff?'

'Mephedrone, cocaine substitutes, synthetic cannabis. They used to call them things like pond cleaner and bath salts. Concoctions of chemicals churned out by factories in China. They were banned here back in 2010. Some of the head shops kept going for a while by selling other stuff or they turned into sex shops to try to stay in business. There used to be head shops all over the city centre, but they're gone now.'

'Really? There's no back-street operations going on?'

'Oh, there's back-street operations going on, but they're not head shops. People would report them. Thanks to the likes of your pal, Mooney, and the rest of the media whipping up scare-stories.'

'He's not really my pal. But the legal highs are still available, right?'

'More available now than ever. Just illegal, meaning four times the price. Not that I go for any of that stuff myself,' he added. 'You just hear about it all the time.'

'So where do people get it?'

'Dealers. On the street and in the clubs. Some stock left from the head shops is being sold illegally. But people mostly order it on the internet or smuggle it in the usual ways. Some users might take a chance and order it themselves but most of them go through their dealer.'

'Jesus, this online shopping thing has really taken off, hasn't it? You mean you just go online, fill up your little shopping cart with illegal drugs, enter your credit card details and select express delivery?'

He grinned. 'Exactly. 'Course the Customs are looking out and they intercept some of it. But there's ways around the address you use. The guards are seizing the stuff all the time, but there's no shortage of it anywhere. 'Scuse me, just need to get this out of the way ...' He bent down to move something.

'Ned, does *thirteen twenty* mean anything to you?'

'Thirteen twenty? Nope. Why?'

'Just something somebody said, never mind ...'

He lifted a heavy bag of compost down to the back of the shop and returned for another one. I followed him slowly, reading the labels on the bags lined up neatly against the wall. I stopped in front of one product.

'Iguana Juice?'

'God you're very suspicious. No, it's not a hallucinogen. It's a nutrient. And before you ask, no iguanas were harmed in the making of this product. As far as I know.'

'And this. Vintage Bat Guano?'

He laughed. 'Vintage is so *in* these days. Or so Mammy says. Back home in Termonfeckin, we've whole rooms full of stuff from the nineteen seventies and eighties. Mammy thinks she'll make a fortune from selling it all on eBay. Seriously, though, have a look at this.'

He pointed to the corner where a metal table was surrounded by aluminium and plastic bins.

'My mixing station,' Ned said proudly. 'Nutrients for indoor foliage plants – that's my thesis topic for college. I make up my own mixtures to sell alongside the commercial products.'

'All tried and tested?'

'I test thoroughly and people test them for me too. Let me know if you'd like to give it a go. And if you're interested in that head shop stuff – which I really don't recommend – a fella sells bath salts out of a van just around the corner from here. He has it in a barrel ...'

The shop door opened and someone came in. Ned looked up.

'Mr Costigan! I have that message for you here.'

Ned took a fat brown envelope out from under the till and handed it to Brian Costigan who pocketed it with a nod of thanks and turned to me.

'Well, Ms Ortelius. How nice to see you again. Didn't know you were interested in indoor gardening. Something else you picked up in Holland?'

'I was just leaving. Ned, about your organic vegetables. Would you deliver down to the North Wall Quay?'

'No trouble,' he said. 'I've a flyer here somewhere with my number.'

He produced a leaflet from the jacket hanging on a wall hook. It said 'Daisy Root Organic Veggies.'

As I moved towards the door, Costigan blocked my way and said quietly, 'A word, please. If you have a moment.'

'I'm in a bit of a hurry. Have to get back.'

'It's just I have some news about your aunt. But if you don't have time ...'

He had me there. I stopped.

'I'm under some time pressure myself at the moment,' he said. 'Why don't we take a little ride and I'll fill you in?'

Costigan opened the shop door just as a large BMW pulled up outside. It was the latest model, black and shiny and driven by Dean Clarke.

'After you,' Costigan said, opening the rear door of the car. I got in, my hands clasped to the seat edge to stop them shaking, my heart pounding. Costigan sat in beside me. I was thrown backwards immediately as the black car sped the wrong way up Mabbot Lane, its tyres screeching as it careered right, swung right again and rounded down Foley Street, roaring over its cobbles before braking abruptly at the corner of Amiens Street.

21

Best Dressed Chihuahua

The BMW took an illegal right turn across the traffic and picked up more speed as it headed towards the river.

'Does Dean know this is a thirty kilometre an hour area?' I asked Costigan.

Dean Clarke grinned in the mirror.

'Thirty is bleeding parked,' he said.

He flicked channels on the radio. A news item reported a regulatory initiative from the Health Services Executive promising the usual efficiencies and cost savings. Dean switched to a music station with a rapper explaining in verse exactly why he was breaking his bitch's ribcage.

'Jesus Christ,' Costigan said, leaning across me to stare out my window. 'Pull over, Deano – now!'

He stabbed his finger at the window.

'See that dog? That's Bertie, Dessie's bowler. Dessie loves that little dog. He's even wearing the Tommy Hilfiger jacket

Dessie got him for Christmas. Dessie'll fucking crucify us if anyone sees it outside that clinic.'

Tied to the methadone clinic's railings was a fluffy white Chihuahua wearing a tiny tartan jacket. He was yapping at the cadaver-like figures of the addicts filing in and out of the clinic's doorway. A baby girl in a buggy reached out to touch him. I winced, praying he wouldn't take the hand off her.

Clarke forced the near side of the car up on to the footpath, its tyres protesting loudly.

Costigan got out and quickly untied the dog, which proceeded to bark itself into a frenzy.

'Ah here, Mister. You can't just take a little dog like that. He belongs to someone, he does.'

A couple of the addicts started to remonstrate with him and the baby girl began to cry.

Costigan shouted over to me. 'Will you go inside and get herself out? She won't come out for us but you could tell her ... I don't know ... the dog needs her or something. And don't try anything funny. Remember Aggie.'

I sat staring at him. 'What?'

'Do it,' he said, 'Like, now!'

Dean Clarke turned round and grabbed my arm, pushing me towards the door.

'You heard him. Go inside and get her out of there.'

I'd already walked up the steps when I thought to ask.

'Who? Who am I getting out?'

'Fuck's sake,' Dean groaned through the open window, putting his head down on the steering wheel.

'It's Karen,' Costigan said. 'Karen Donlon.'

I pushed the door of the terraced red-brick building at the same time someone exited. I was immediately stopped by a determined young security guard.

'Sorry, we can't admit you without an ID and an appointment. Have you got an appointment?'

I wasn't expecting that. There were so many people coming and going, I thought it was as accessible as a normal doctor's surgery. But obviously this was not a normal surgery. When I thought about it, I realised the clinic would be well-stocked with drugs and of great interest to all passing dealers, suppliers, gangs and addicts. Of course, you couldn't just wander in off the street.

I stood back and began to untie my scarf while I tried to think of something to say. Someone, presumably the receptionist, called out a question from the reception area on the right of the hall. The security guard popped his head in the door to answer her, 'Oh, right. I'll ask her.'

He addressed me a little more politely this time.

'Are you the woman from the HSE about the ...'

I remembered the radio report I'd just heard about the new regulatory procedures. 'Yes, yes, I am. Constance Ortelius, Health Services Executive.'

'They're expecting you. Sorry, they never said.'

'Don't worry about it,' I said kindly as I passed him.

Karen Donlon was bent over the clinic's reception desk but I heard her before I saw her. She was obviously upset. She ordered the receptionist to go through the appointments book for what was clearly not the first time judging by her raised voice and the receptionist's resigned demeanour.

'But he said he'd be here. Are you sure there isn't a mix-up?'

'I'm sorry. He hasn't been in today. And it's not his first time to miss an appointment. Which means ...'

'I know what it fucking means.' Karen shouted, 'it means he's fucked it all up and he's out on his ear and he's fucking fucked. That's what it fucking means. Fuck.' Her voice cracked. 'He promised me, is all. We're supposed to go together. He told me the last one was cancelled. Now he's not here for this one.' She wiped her eyes and turned as she became aware that they were not alone. Her smudged blue eyes hardened as she recognised me and when she spoke, it was through clenched teeth, her voice rising with each consecutive word. 'What. Is. That One. Doing. Here.'

I stood in the reception room doorway, ready to flee.

'Em. Costigan's outside. With the car. And your dog.'

She squinted at me. 'What?'

'If you want a lift.'

'Oh, I see. Another one of Dessie's little spies.' She brushed past me as she opened the door and looked out.

'And there's that pair of useless spare pricks. A lot of good any of them are when it comes to anything that matters.'

As my sworn enemy walked down the steps towards the car, she seemed so crushed and weary that I felt a wave of pity for her. Costigan put the Chihuahua down to open the car door for Karen, taking her handbag as she got in. In a flash, the little dog raced up the steps and, as I caught him in my arms, he licked my face all over. I was still spluttering as I brought him down the steps and handed him into Karen in the car.

'Your dog,' I said.

'Fuck you.' She practically spat at me, took the dog and looked away.

Costigan closed her car door and before I could ask him about Aggie, he got in the front with a single word.

'Later.'

The car swung abruptly off the footpath and into the traffic, disappearing almost instantly and leaving me standing there, choking on its dust.

22

SPECKLED CHERRIES

An attractive black-haired woman in a fitted red dress addressed me from the top of the clinic steps.

'Are you Karen Donlon?'

She was distracted by a dishevelled young man who saluted her as he shambled past.

'Ah there y'are, Doc. Thanks a million, Doc.'

'Oh, hi Robbie. See you next week.'

She came down the steps and looked at me inquiringly.

'No,' I said. 'If you're looking for Karen Donlon, you've just missed her.'

'Are you a friend of hers?'

'I wouldn't say that, no.'

'But you know her?'

'We've met a couple of times. The second time we met was just now, in the clinic. She seemed a bit shook.'

'She has her reasons. I'm Dr Madden. Rose Madden. I work here.'

'Connie Ortelius. I run the Silver Bullet Café. On the rare occasions I'm actually there.'

'So you're not from the Health Services Executive? And you're not here to advise us on the new regulatory procedures?'

She stood with her arms folded, looking very stern. I wondered if she'd call the guards. Store Street Garda Station was just around the corner. Maybe I could establish a routine and get taken in there for questioning every day.

'I'm so sorry,' I said. 'I realise it's a very serious thing to lie to your security guard and enter your clinic under false pretences but ...'

'Yes?'

'I'm trying to find out what happened to Stevie Hennessy and I was supposed to meet someone with information ... but instead of meeting him I was picked up by Karen's husband's ... em-employees and forced to get Karen from your clinic or they might hurt my aunt ... God, I know this isn't making any sense.'

The doctor seemed to thaw a little.

'Connie, if you don't mind me saying so, you look a bit shook yourself. How about a cup of tea inside? Can't have people collapsing on the steps, you know. It'd give us a bad name.'

You have to like a doctor with a sense of humour. I allowed her to steer me back into the clinic, past the reception area and through the hall into a bright office with a desk, a computer, a couple of armchairs and a coffee table.

'Hang on and I'll get the tea. I could do with some myself.'

I sat and checked my messages as I waited, hoping for news from Aggie. Nothing. I leaned back in the chair and closed my eyes. I had no idea what to do. If I went to the guards, what could they do? I had no proof that anything had happened to Aggie. I had nothing but thinly-veiled threats from Steyne River Securities and a text heralding her disappearing act. That, and my gut instinct telling me that something was horribly wrong. When I opened my eyes again they fixed on a notice on the wall.

Warning (PSNI)
Speckled Red/Brown Cherries.
Linked to deaths of users in Romania.
Description: Red/brown or red/grey in colour, with a cherry logo stamped on them. Contains 4-methylaminorex, a synthesised drug known as 'ice' in the USA, previously unseen in the UK.

I remembered what Ned had told me back in the grow shop, about factories in China churning out synthetic drugs, about it all going underground when the government banned the constituent chemicals. I tried to think about Stevie and the bath salts he allegedly injected. But I couldn't concentrate, I was too worried about Aggie.

The doctor reappeared and deposited a tray on the table holding a couple of mugs of steaming tea and a plate of Jaffa Cakes.

'Help yourself to milk and sugar. I see you're reading the latest warning.' She nodded towards the notice. 'The police and the health services issue them regularly. Cross-border collaboration too, like that one. Sometimes we even get them in time to spot something before it's too late. But it's impossible – you can't keep up with all the new drugs.'

'So I've heard.'

'When I met you outside, Connie, you looked slightly ... disorientated, if you don't mind me saying. Clearly something's wrong. Here, have a biscuit.'

'Everything's wrong,' I said, taking one from the plate she offered and nibbling at it distractedly. 'First Stevie's dead, nobody knows exactly how or why, and, besides his friends, nobody cares. Now my poor old aunt, who went off to Las Vegas to gamble away her pension, has possibly been kidnapped. Karen Donlon has taken a set against me and might want to kill me. I don't know if I can trust anyone, not even the guards.'

I looked at the doctor suspiciously. Why was she being so nice to me?

'It's ok, Connie. Everyone's paranoid these days. It's a natural defence mechanism. However, it sounds as if you have some things worth discussing with the guards. Your concerns for your aunt's safety, for example. I suggest a practical approach. Do you know where Store Street Garda Station is?'

I nodded, laughing bitterly.

The doctor gave me another concerned look.

'As soon as you leave here, go across the road to Store Street and have a word with them. They'll contact their counterparts in Las Vegas and at least you can get someone to check on your aunt's welfare. all right?'

I nodded again, feeling like an idiot.

'About Karen Donlon. She's a relative of a patient here and I have yet to meet her, but from what I know the poor woman has enough problems of her own. I really don't think she's going to kill you anytime soon. Do you believe me?'

'Ok.' I still had my doubts but the doctor sounded like she knew what she was talking about.

'Next, Stevie – Stevie Hennessy – that's who you mean, right? That's a whole different story. What's your connection with him?'

'He was a regular in my aunt's café on the quays. I met him when I arrived home last week. She told me to look out for him while she was away. When his body was found, his best friend made me promise to help find out what happened to him. He was special. You know what I mean?'

'Actually, I do. Everyone loved Stevie.'

'So you knew him? Nobody believes the guards will follow up on his death. Maybe you can tell me something about him. Unless ...'

I remembered I'd already blotted my copybook by circumventing the clinic's admission procedures. I didn't want to push it with the doctor, especially when she was being so nice to me.

'... it's against your regulations to give out patient information.'

'You're right. I appreciate your sensitivity. We don't give out patient information to anyone, let alone people like you who just walk in off the street. In fact,' she laughed, 'nobody walks in off the street like you! But you have Stevie's interests at heart and, let's face it, none of us can help him now. So, totally off the record, I'll tell you. Stevie completed the programme here about nine months ago. I haven't seen him since then. He was particularly highly motivated, sailed right through without a single set-back. It was quite unusual.'

'So Kitty's right – he was clean. Or at least he was until the night of his death when they say he injected himself with bath salts and got that disease.'

'That's what they're saying? Where's that information coming from?'

'It was in the paper this morning. The headline was, *"Flesh-Eating Infection Ate Teen Junkie's Hand".*'

'You're not serious. That's outrageous. Bloody irresponsible reporters. They'll cause a witch-hunt.'

'That's what Fogarty said.'

'Pius Fogarty? So he's involved in this too, is he? God, that doesn't exactly inspire confidence.'

Funny how there wasn't a female in this part of town without an opinion on Pius Fogarty.

'He's not really *involved* – more concerned about the knock-on effects on his residents. Stevie was one of them up until Friday.'

'They found Stevie yesterday, wasn't it?' she asked, looking at me sadly. 'I couldn't believe it when a patient told me earlier on. But it's been so hectic here all morning, I haven't even looked at the papers yet.' She sighed, before continuing. 'The pathologist's preliminary report can be expected within twenty four hours. It'll be available some time today, I imagine.'

'If the pathologist's report isn't out yet, where did Jimmy Mooney get the medical information about Stevie?'

'Probably some lab rat leaked it. Happens all the time.'

'But if someone in the State Pathologists' lab supplied the information, that means the newspaper article was *right* about the drugs – and about the disease?'

The doctor held up her hand.

'Not altogether. The toxicology report won't be out for five to six weeks so nobody'll know for sure about the drugs until then. However, the pathologist may have formed an opinion from the examination of the body and that could be the basis of the leaked information about the drugs. Or your reporter could simply have put two and two together and made ten.'

'Why would he do that?

'Lots of reasons. Sensationalism. The political agenda. You know, clean up the streets, that kind of thing.'

'So it might be true about the drugs but it's not definite?'

'Correct. What's of far greater importance is whether the pathologist has formed a conclusion as to the actual cause of death. Was it a drug overdose that killed Stevie, was it death from drowning – or did he die from streptococcal septicaemia? If it was either of the last two, the first one can be ruled out as a cause of death and the presence or otherwise of drugs in Stevie's system becomes incidental.'

'What was the third possible cause of death you just said? I thought the disease Mooney reported was Necro ... something.'

'*Necrotising fasciitis*. NF for short. It's a bacterial infection. When I mentioned streptococcal septicaemia as a possible cause of death, I was referring to the type of bacteria underlying NF. You know the common strep throat? The NF type of *Streptococcus* is related to it. Under the right conditions – an open wound, dirty water – it can turn into a disease that destroys cells so rapidly it seems to be visibly consuming the body. That's where it gets its flesh-eating reputation.'

'Jesus. People die from it?'

'Oh yes. But it rarely gets to that stage. It responds well to antibiotics when it's caught in time.'

'What if it's not – or if the antibiotics don't work?'

She shrugged her shoulders. 'There's some research – inconclusive as far as I remember – showing traditional Asian medicine having some effect. I think it was in PLOS One – you know, the Public Library of Science. But look, what we're discussing is speculative. NF is not unusual in the community and I've personally never had a case where it didn't respond to antibiotics.'

'You've actually treated it?'

'Absolutely. Particularly here, with intravenous drug users.'

'Stevie's hand and wrist were black and swollen, but it wasn't like that ... chronic thing ... you just described.'

'Indeed. If Stevie had the infection, it must have been at an early stage. Or the discolouration was caused by something else.'

'So there can be discolouration without any disease ...?'

'Of course. Skin discolouration is common with intravenous drug users or people who are skin-popping – you know, injecting directly under the skin. But' she paused, 'in Stevie's case that would have been impossible.'

'Why? Because he was off drugs? But it looks like they found them in his system.'

'No. Because Stevie was trypanophobic. He would never inject himself nor would he ever allow anyone to inject him. When he used heroin, he smoked it. Stevie had a morbid fear of needles.'

My phone buzzed and we both jumped. As I reached for it, Dr Madden stayed my hand with hers.

'Connie, I'll see if I can find out more about the pathologist's report. I'm assuming there's a logical explanation for all this, but if there's anything suspicious about Stevie's death, it's a case for professional crime investigators. No matter how little faith you and your friends have in them, it would be best for you stand aside and leave it to them.'

Yeah, that's what Fogarty said too, I thought. Before responding to her, I glanced at my text message. It was from Detective Nuala Rossiter. I had to read it twice before I could take it in.

'Urgent – request your assistance. Mooney in Mater Hosp. fighting for life. His last call was to you. Where are you?'

I looked up at the doctor.

'You were saying, Dr Madden, about me standing aside? Believe me, I wish I could. But I'm afraid it's far too late for that now.'

23

AN ORDINARY LUNATIC

As the unmarked police car sped up Gardiner Street heading for the Mater Hospital, I sat in the passenger seat beside Detective Nuala Rossiter while she explained that Mooney had been found unconscious on a side street off North Earl Street. Not far from where I was supposed to meet him on Mabbot Lane, I added silently.

'God knows how long he was in that condition,' she continued, swinging right at Dorset Street, then left up the North Circular Road. 'There are so many people sleeping in doorways or just lying around comatose it doesn't really register with passersby anymore – or it does but they don't know what to do about it. A worker from a nearby homeless shelter checked him and raised the alarm.'

'He couldn't have been there for more than a couple of hours,' I said. 'He phoned me at around eleven – he wanted to meet at twelve.'

I didn't mention the place Mooney had proposed for our rendezvous or any of the details of his voicemail. If there was any possibility of talking to him, I wanted to do that first.

'We know what time he called you. That was the last call he made. Do you mind if I ask what your meeting was about?'

I answered truthfully that I hadn't a clue.

'Do you know what Mooney was working on?'

'No, but I'm sure it was something to do with drugs or Stevie's death or both. What happened to him?'

'The medical examination showed that he'd suffered head injuries consistent with an assault, possibly with a baseball bat or similar object. He had another minor facial injury which he may have been suffered earlier. While the head injuries probably rendered him unconscious, they weren't life threatening. It was only when he gained consciousness, if you can call it consciousness, that the real problem become known.'

'What do you mean?'

'As soon as he came to, it was clear that he was under the influence of a substance, as yet unidentified, that made him dangerously aggressive. He kept grabbing his arm, shouting that he was burning. Once he was sedated and the staff were in a position to examine his arm they saw a small cut that had become infected. They treated the wound with antibiotics. Even under heavy sedation and dosed with pain-killers, he was clearly still in agony. When he was re-examined, the doctors realised he had developed a serious bacterial infection. He had emergency surgery to stop it spreading. We still don't know if it was successful.'

'What kind of bacterial infection?'

'We don't know.'

I was stunned. Mooney knew he was in danger. That's why he sounded so scared on the phone. What in God's name happened to him? I had no idea how I'd become involved in this nightmare. Rossiter turned into the hospital entrance and pulled into a priority parking space.

'We've got nothing out of him except moans of pain and gibberish ...' she paused, 'we're hoping he might talk to you but it's a long shot. Detective Inspector Brady has secured clearance from the hospital authorities permitting you to visit the patient for a couple of minutes only. He should be coming out from under the anaesthetic now, if he's alive at all.'

She moved quickly through the hospital reception area towards the lifts and I followed, almost running. She pressed the button and sighed before she spoke.

'To be honest, Connie, there's a strong possibility that Mooney might be dead by the time we get there. You need to prepare yourself for that. Whatever happens, I want to thank you for your help.'

I nodded dumbly as the lift doors opened.

In an empty side room, I dressed quickly in the surgical scrubs, mask and gloves that someone had handed me. Rossiter was waiting. She opened the door of a nearby room and I entered. The first thing that struck me was the foetid stench of rotting flesh overriding the hospital's pervasive antiseptic air. It was the smell of putrefaction, of living death. I wanted to throw up. I looked over at the figure on the bed. Despite heavy sedation, Mooney was moaning and breathing laboriously. Liquids – antibiotics and painkillers – fed into him through multiple tubes. His eyes were closed but he was still shaking and shuddering, bathed in sweat.

Poor Jimmy Mooney, I thought, remembering last night. He didn't deserve this, he was just an ordinary lunatic. I went to the bedside and took his hand, trying not to look at his other side which was now missing its entire right arm and hand.

'Mooney – Jimmy? It's me. Connie. You were looking for me?'

After a couple of seconds, his eyelids flickered, then flew open. His pupils were completely dilated, turning his eyes into black pools. They stared at me now without a hint of recognition. His head started to shake again and his whole body convulsed in a violent shudder.

I felt an authoritative hand on my shoulder. It belonged to a grave-faced man in a white coat. He had 'senior consultant' written all over him.

'I'm sorry but I'm going to have to ask you to leave. This visit should not have been authorised. It may harm the patient.'

'But we received clearance at the highest level – the patient has information of potential importance to an investigation.' It was Brady.

'You didn't receive clearance from me and I'm the medical officer in charge. I must ask you all to leave. This patient is in a critical condition. He has undergone severe trauma, emergency surgery and may possibly require further surgery. His life is in danger. I'll be happy to answer your questions outside. Thanks, Maria.'

He nodded to the Filipino nurse approaching Mooney's bed.

Brady hesitated for an instant, growled something incomprehensible and stalked out. I exited more quietly, following the doctor through the open door, leaving the unfortunate Mooney racked with pain in a tangle of tubes.

24

A WALK IN THE PARK

The consultant led us down the corridor and into a meeting room, where we were joined by Brady, Detective Rossiter and a colleague of Mooney's, a crime reporter who introduced herself as Lucrezia O'Leary. 'Call me Lu,' she said.

'No press!' Brady commanded.

'Do you mind? I believe I'm in charge here,' the consultant said from the top of the room. 'I'm Mr Rory Kennedy, surgeon and specialist in infectious diseases. Mr Mooney is *my* patient. I'll answer your questions in relation to his condition and it will save me time if all concerned parties are present now. If the police have additional questions, I'll deal with them later. Other media queries should go through the hospital press officer, Rachel Nesbitt. Thanks for coming, Rachel.'

He nodded to the earnest woman in a dark suit who had just entered the room, then surveyed the room before speaking.

'Mr Mooney was admitted in the early afternoon via A&E. He was unconscious and had sustained significant head injuries. When he regained consciousness, Mr Mooney was distressed, disoriented and in great pain. Re-examination identified a pervasive bacterial infection arising from a small wound on his arm. He was immediately treated with antibiotics and assigned to my team. We quickly identified the infection as deadly *necrotising fasciitis* and performed an emergency operation on the patient to remove the infected tissue and prevent it spreading. Amputation was unavoidable if we were to save the patient's life. We initially removed the right hand and lower part of the right arm below the elbow. Unfortunately we ended up having to amputate Mr Mooney's entire right arm and hope that the progression of the disease will stop there. The patient's immune system is seriously compromised and I regret to say that the outlook for Mr Mooney is extremely grave. We have been unsuccessful in our attempts to contact his next of kin and would appreciate assistance with this from his colleagues or friends.'

'He has a brother in Australia. Another in California, I think.' It was Lu O'Leary.

'Thank you for that information. We'll follow up with you. Are there any questions?'

Rossiter got a nod from Brady and put up her hand.

'Thank you for the update, Mr Kennedy,' she began. 'In your opinion, how might Jimmy Mooney have become infected with this disease?'

'This type of *necrotising fasciitis* is caused by Group A Strep bacteria.' Kennedy spotted a few raised eyebrows. 'Yes, it does sound familiar. It's the same bacteria that causes strep throat.'

Exactly what Dr Rose Madden had told me earlier. 'However, Group A Strep comes in different strains, some of them very powerful. The *necrotising fasciitis* occurs only with an invasive strain of the bacteria and usually enters the body through a wound or a cut. Mr Mooney could have encountered the bacteria anywhere. I'm afraid most cases of NF are due to sheer bad luck.'

'Mr Kennedy?' It was Lu O'Leary. 'You're a specialist in infectious diseases and have been assigned this patient. Does that mean that this disease might be highly infectious, possibly an epidemic?'

'No, it's not an epidemic.' Kennedy spoke firmly. 'It's extremely important not to sensationalise this. If we include yesterday's reported occurrence, we *may* have two instances of the infection. Two occurrences within a close time period will understandably attract some public attention. But we need to keep them in perspective.'

'Is the disease resistant to antibiotics? What if more people get infected?' Lu again.

'Antibiotics have not been effective in this case, possibly because the disease had already become chronic by the time it was treated. It is unlikely that others will become infected,' the surgeon said. 'But we'll see.'

'Oh come on,' Brady said. 'The infection is clearly drugs-related. He injected something. Must've used a dirty needle.'

The consultant considered this for a moment before he responded.

'Of course, Mr Mooney's treatment is further complicated by the presence of non-medical drugs in his system, drugs, which, as Detective Inspector Brady suggested, entered the patient's body intravenously. The location of the initial infection could be the needle entry point. But the truth is, we don't know and Mr Mooney can't tell us. We identified the drugs in his system as a combination of mephedrone and methylenedioxypyrovalerone, also known as MDPV.'

'AKA "bath salts",' said Lu. 'That's ridiculous. Mooney's a crazy bastard but there's no way he's into any of those legal highs.'

'Former legal highs,' Rossiter corrected her.

'All right. Former legal highs, then.'

'What about Mooney and Class A drugs?' Brady rounded on Lu O'Leary.

'Don't be stupid. He's into Gaelic games, for God's sake. And pints. Not pills or potions.'

'We'll see what the Drug Squad makes of the substances we've found in his flat, then.' Brady said. 'A least one packet of a suspicious-looking white powder, plus multiple traces on a number of polished surfaces. Looks like Mooney wasn't quite the Angel of Truth he pretended to be. Nor a man of morals either, if the pictures we found on his computer are anything to go by.'

'Whoa there, Detective Inspector.'

Lu O'Leary held her hand up, silencing Brady.

'Since when did Mooney become a Garda suspect? And what gave you the right to search his flat?'

'We've been watching Jimmy Mooney for some time. He's been associating with people involved with drugs ... vice, you know, the kiddie kind ... organised crime ...'

'That's his job, for fuck's sake.' Lu O'Leary looked like she was about to explode.

'... and we had reason to believe that Mooney was becoming implicated. When he was found unconscious on the street, well, along with the evidence we already had on him, it was enough to get a search warrant for his home in Phibsboro. If he survives this ...' Brady jerked his head towards the room where Mooney lay. 'His flesh-eating disease will look like a walk in the park compared with what he'll be facing in court.'

He looked around at us.

'Ok, I realise that may seem a bit harsh. But a crime is a crime, as the lady said.'

'And a bollix is a bollix,' said Lu O'Leary.

Brady let it go. 'Rossiter, stay here and keep me posted. I'm sure the rest of you have things to do.'

He touched my arm as he moved to the door. 'See you tonight, Connie.'

Rossiter looked after him with undisguised distaste, an expression she retained when she turned to me.

'Really, Connie? You're dating Brady? I'm amazed. I mean, if nothing else, he's a married man with four kids out in Skerries ...'

'And don't we envy the lucky woman who has that coming home to her,' said Lu.

Even the consultant looked appalled.

'It's not what it seems,' I muttered, looking Rossiter in the eye.

'I guess you're old enough to know what you're doing,' Lu grinned.

Rossiter relaxed and smiled faintly. 'Ok, I believe you. You really couldn't be that stupid.'

'Well, thanks for the vote of confidence, girls.'

'If there are no more questions ... I need to get back into surgery.' Kennedy said, turning to go without waiting for a response. He looked exhausted.

'Connie, I'm driving across town,' Lu said. 'You want a lift back?'

I nodded. 'Thanks.'

'Just realised I need a quick last word with the doc,' she said, as the door closed behind him. 'I'll nab him before he goes into theatre. You go ahead and I'll catch up with you at reception.'

I told Rossiter I'd call her later, then headed down the corridor following the exit signs. As I passed the nurses' station, I spotted the Filipino nurse who had attended Mooney. She called me over and took my hand.

'You are Mr Mooney's friend?'

'Well, not really. But he was on his way to meet me when this terrible thing happened. I feel I'm to blame in some way. He wanted to tell me something.'

'Yes,' she said, nodding. 'He passed out as soon as he said it.'

'As soon as he said what?'

'You didn't hear? You were the last to leave the room. I think he waited for the others to go.'

'What did he say?'

'It was hard for me to understand. Something about clay.'

'"Clay?" Really? What exactly did he say?'

'He said, "It's clay".' She nodded confidently. 'Yes, I'm sure that was it. I hope it helps you. And I hope your friend makes it.'

'I hope so too.'

As I descended the stairs and entered the reception area, I thought about the words 'It's clay'. After all his effort to communicate with me, that was the best he could do? Thanks, Jimmy, I muttered to myself. I really hope you make it because I'm definitely the wrong person to figure that one out.

'Hey Connie – over here!' Lu called from the entrance. 'Come on – got work to do!'

She led the way to her ancient, rust-covered Range Rover which was parked across two reserved parking spaces. She gave me an appraising look while starting the car.

'So what's your take on this business?'

'I hoped Mooney was on to something in relation to Stevie Hennessy's death. That's why I went to meet him.

Now all I've got is a whole lot of questions and a painting of Stevie's that may contain a hidden message. And all I'm doing is trying to keep a stupid promise I made.'

'You've got more than the cops, then,' she said. 'Let me know if you need an expert to look at the painting.'

She drove down Eccles Street at top speed, crashing the Range Rover's gears. I instinctively shrank down in the seat.

'What's wrong?' Lu laughed. 'Are you worried someone will see you in this ideologically incorrect and environmentally unsound form of transport?'

'No – no one knows me here. I'm just not used to this, um, type of car – and the driving style. You don't really see it in Holland. No offence.'

'None taken,' she said, running a red light.

'Speaking of Holland, I've just remembered my bike – I left it locked up just over there.'

I pointed ahead to the bus stop on O'Connell Street with my bike still chained to it.

'You ride a bike in this town? Are you insane?' Laughing loudly, she took both hands off the wheel to form air quotes as she intoned, 'Depressed, lonely, suicidal?'

She swerved sharply and mounted the kerb.

'Go get it. Sling it in the back.'

'Actually,' I said, opening the door and sliding out of the car, 'I might as well just cycle on home from here. Easier for you too, with the one-way system and all. And the air will do me good. Thanks for the lift, Lu.'

'If you're sure.' She seemed concerned. 'Stay in touch, Connie. I've got your number – I'll call you if I hear anything new from that nice consultant up there. You know, if it's the married men you're in to, he'd be streets ahead of that dick, Brady. No offence, as you'd say yourself.'

'Jesus, Lu. I told you, I'm not –'

'Yeah, yeah. To be continued ... Meanwhile, I need to make tracks. I have to carefully craft a news story around Mooney's condition, toning down the drugs, flesh-eating diseases etc, for our online breaking news. It's the least you can do for a pal. And I need to find enough gin to help me write the poor bastard's obituary. They want it ready for tomorrow's early edition. If we have to use it, it'll go alongside Mooney's last story on Stevie Hennessy's death. How ironic is that?'

'And you know,' she called through the open window as she pulled away without indicating, 'that last story is the best thing Mooney ever wrote.'

I watched the rear of the Range Rover as it merged into the relentless traffic. A horrible thought came to me and I stood still, gripping the handlebars of my bike. Was Pius Fogarty the last person to see Mooney before his assault? And what exactly had Fogarty done to him?

25

The Sacred Heart of Monto

I must have taken a wrong turn. Wheeling my bike down the crowded footpath, my mind was back in the hospital with Mooney, the taste of disinfectant and decay still in my mouth. The gnawing rat returned to my stomach as I tried to tell myself that Mooney would survive, that it wasn't my fault, that Aggie was safe, that we'd all be fine.

I stopped at an unfamiliar intersection with signs for the motorway and the airport, noisy with traffic heading out of town. A broad street bisected the outbound route. It had a mix of new redbrick, low-level housing, even newer apartment buildings, windowless commercial blocks with heavily razor-wired perimeters and a couple of boarded-up Victorian ruins. It was strangely quiet for a city centre street.

I leaned on my bike at the traffic lights wondering which way to go and noticed that I was the only pedestrian anywhere in sight. Looking for a street sign, I saw a large brown notice beside a cluster of trees across the road. It said 'Shrine of the Venerable Matt Talbot' and it stood in the car park of a church that was set well back from the street and surrounded by railings. Curiosity and the prospect of a momentary refuge propelled me across the road. I locked my bike to the base of the sign and stood back to read it. The words beneath the caption said, *Matt Talbot, labourer for Christ and hope for all those suffering from Addiction. www.MattTalbot.ie.*

The church was not only locked, it was secured like a fortress. White-painted wrought-ironwork protected every window and encased the porch, guarding every inch of the entrance. On the gates set into the cage-like structure, the white paint was worn away in places where padlocks rubbed against it, exposing rusted wounds. Why so much security on a church, I wondered.

'Joy-riders,' a voice said behind me. 'And other gurriers. Ramming the doorway, breaking in and lighting fires. Are you here for the removal?'

The voice came from behind a forest of flamingo-pink gladioli and matching chrysanthemums and roses. The flowers creaked in their cellophane wrappers and scented the air in a cloud around their bearer, a diminutive, elderly female.

'Is that you, Viv?' I asked, parting the vegetation to reveal a pair of bright eyes under a fresh blue rinse.

'Not my choice of colours,' she said. 'I would've gone for white or cream. And lilies'd be *lot* classier. But they wanted these, to match that American limousine of his, I suppose. If it was me, I wouldn't want a reminder. Driving that thing around Ballybough is asking for it, as far as I'm concerned. No wonder he ended up the way he did. Hold onto these while I get the keys.'

She thrust the bouquets into my arms and fumbled in the large black leather handbag that hung over her arm.

'I thought I'd pay a visit to the shrine,' I said, eyeing the notice at the church doorway for clues about the removal and its deceased pink limo owner.

It said, 'Our Lady of Lourdes Church, Sean McDermott Street. Home of Matt Talbot'. Daily Mass times: 'Monday to Friday – English language 6pm, Romanian language, 8pm'.

'Which shrine?' Viv asked as she unlocked a padlock. 'There's not just the one in here, you know.'

She pulled apart the iron gates and pushed them flat against either side of the church's doorway. Then she produced another set of keys, unlocked the main door and went inside. The clang of metal bolts sliding across metal echoed around the interior. When she reappeared, she stood beside me and looked out to the street while replacing the keys in her handbag.

'No sign of them yet? Well, it's early enough. You know,' she said, 'There was an old, old church on this spot before this one. The metal church, it was called. It was made out of corrugated iron and it was for the poor in the area and the unfortunate souls out of Monto.'

Even I knew that Monto, Dublin's infamous red-light district, was in this area until it got closed down by the Legion of Mary sometime in the 1920s. There was no sign of any of that now. At least not here and not in broad daylight.

'This church was built to replace the metal church.' Viv continued. 'Then they exhumed Matt Talbot from his grave in Glasnevin and brought him back here to rest in his shrine. People come from all over to see it. You should've been around here during the Pope's visit. You know the one I mean. Not this Pope, the other one, in the batmobile.'

'Popemobile.'

'Nobody could believe it when they said the Holy Father was coming all the way from the Vatican to Sean McDermott Street. They worked for weeks cleaning up the place, painting the lamp-posts and putting up flowers and banners and everything. On the day he arrived, the street was lined with thousands of people. And all the television and the radio stations were here, even the BBC.'

She paused and looked up and down the street as if she could see the scene in front of her still.

'When the Pope appeared at the end of the North Strand in his ... what-do-ye-call it, Popemobile ... and turned onto the top of Sean McDermott Street, a mighty roar went up from the crowd. And we waited here for him to pull in to the churchyard. He came closer and I saw his face as clear as anything in the Popemobile window – but he didn't stop, just kept on going and disappeared away off up O'Connell Street. They were very sorry, they said afterwards, but his schedule had been changed.'

'That's terrible,' I said, thinking, bloody popes, they always let you down.

'Ah, we had a great party anyway. But I felt sorry afterwards for the Pope. He really missed out, you know. Come on till I show you inside.'

She removed the flowers from my grasp and carried them up the steps. I followed her slowly, but, as I entered the church, I discovered I wasn't Matt Talbot's first visitor that day. Brian Costigan and Dean Clark were inside already. They stood facing me with their guns drawn.

I froze, shocked by the guns, then more so when I saw Viv's flowers lying on the carpet in front of the altar and Viv's handbag strewn beside them, its contents spilling out on the floor.

'Viv?' I croaked, looking wildly around the bright interior. Redbrick arches in the naves were topped by clear glass windows flooding light on to the white and red mosaic floor of the centre aisle. At the top of the church, a simple altar table was overhung by a huge crucifix on an emerald-green backdrop. Over on the far side, an open side chapel was delineated by a row of columns. In it, a clear rose window illuminated an enormous sarcophagus of limestone, brass and glass. The Venerable Matt Talbot, I presumed. There was no sign of Viv anywhere.

'What have you done – where is she?' I shouted at Brian Costigan.

'Here I am,' Viv said cheerily as she appeared from somewhere to the side of the altar, this time clasping a collection of cut glass vases to her chest and sloshing water everywhere. 'Gotta get a move on, they'll be here any minute.' She stopped, looked at the two armed men and tutted.

'Put 'em away, boys. Father Constantinescu will be very cross if he sees any of that carry-on. Why don't you make yourselves useful and show Connie the shrines.'

'Sorry, Viv,' Costigan called up to her, pocketing his weapon and nodding at Clark to follow suit. 'Standard procedure for the boss, the health and safety check. We're done now.'

He smiled at me. 'Ms Ortelius?'

'No thanks,' I said. 'I'll show myself the shrines.'

'You do that,' he said. 'And take your time. Nobody leaves till this is over.'

'There's people arriving outside,' Clarke said, peering through the glass doors while glancing at his phone. 'They're standing around waiting for the hearse. There's a TV crew at the gate. But no cops that I can see – don't know what's going on there. What happened to the ring of steel we get for all the funerals?'

'Strange,' Costigan said. 'I don't like it. We're supposed to be protected by those state-funded layabouts. Just as well we're looking after it ourselves. Are Charlie and Macker round the back?'

Clarke nodded.

Costigan spoke into his phone.

'All clear, boss. No, boss, I don't know why there's no cops. I'll send you the heads up as soon as the mourners are in.'

They took up positions on opposite sides of the church entrance, watching the doors. Trapped, I scanned the space for another exit. My only hope was the possibility of a side door at Matt Talbot's shrine. I crept up the aisle on the right hand side as Viv flew about the altar and the naves, depositing enormous and somewhat haphazard arrangements of shocking pink flowers in strategic locations.

I stopped in front of a glass case set deep into the wall. It held a silver-painted statue surrounded by photographs. White lettering on the statue's deep pink plinth read: 'The Sacred Heart of Monto.' A panel of explanatory text was mounted on a vivid cerise background.

It told me that this was no ordinary statue of the Sacred Heart, but was viewed as mysterious and possibly miraculous. When builders tried to remove it from its original location atop a building on Mabbot Lane, the statue shattered into pieces and a strange, dark cloud blocked out the sun. A sudden gust of wind, remarkable on an otherwise calm day, terrified the workers. The statue was reassembled, painted silver and installed here where its powers could be safely contained. Stories abound about the scent of roses emanating from it and its multiple miraculous cures.

Mabbot Lane again. It was only this morning that I went there to meet Mooney but that seemed like a century ago. What happened to him and to Stevie was an even greater mystery now, one unaccompanied by the scent of roses or any damned miracles.

'Any chance of a favour?' I whispered to the Sacred Heart of Monto.

The statue glittered back at me coldly.

26

SUGAR RAY

From within the side chapel containing the shrine of the Venerable Matt Talbot I heard the murmur of the crowd gathering outside, but there was still no sign of anyone entering the church. Costigan and Clarke remained as silent shadows at either side of the entrance.

So much for taking refuge in a peaceful sanctuary. Instead, I was trapped in a gangland funeral service in the company of armed men with only a couple of ineffectual spiritual entities to call upon for assistance. I started to get panicky again. There was no side door at the shrine and there was no way I was going out past those guns. I had no choice but to wait for the service to start and try to make a discreet exit while people's attention was directed elsewhere.

I took a quick look around Matt Talbot's shrine. If I thought I'd spot any connection here with the images on the graffiti wall in the Sunrise Hotel, I was mistaken. I examined the exhibition presented on a couple of freestanding panels to one side of the immense sarcophagus. Monotone photographs of a blackened skeleton, complete with rusty chains, were labelled 'Exhumation at Glasnevin Cemetery'. Others showed a religious procession and a picture of de Valera labelled 'President attends Re-interment and Blessing of Shrine'. There was a section dedicated to Matt Talbot's early life and work and samples of his surprisingly elegant handwriting. No gory images of wounds. No cigarette burns. Nothing.

I examined the sarcophagus itself, noting the tupperware lunchbox at its base marked 'Petitions'. It contained photocopied slips of paper and a ballpoint pen. You could fill out a form and request assistance from the aspiring saint. There was a slot in the sarcophagus to make a donation and post the petitions. I wondered where they went to. Some people, either in devotion or desperation, had by-passed the regular process and had gone the direct route by posting folded notes and small photos through a slit in the glass to lie inside, pressed against the polished wood of the coffin. A smiling baby looked out at me from behind the glass alongside a fading picture of two men, one young and one old.

This has to be the final stage of desperation, I thought as I dropped a few coins and my own folded slip of paper into the slot, my heart filled with the guilt of the unbeliever. I jumped as the front doors opened with a bang and heard shuffling footsteps, and a low rumble punctuated by a laboured squeaking.

I looked out from my vantage point and saw the coffin being trolleyed carefully up the centre aisle by four black-coated undertakers, who seemed to be having some trouble keeping it on track. I wasn't sure, but the coffin seemed larger than usual. The trolley wheels protested loudly as they made their way up the church to a position in front of the altar.

Two of the undertakers went swiftly down the aisle and reappeared almost immediately with armfuls of floral wreaths which they placed at the base of the altar steps. One of the wreaths spelled the letters R-A-Y in bright pink blooms.

An undertaker produced a lilac-coloured J-cloth and a canister of Mr Sheen and carefully sprayed and dusted the coffin. His companion placed a pair of boxing gloves on the lid and then reached into a plastic bag on the floor and produced a large framed photograph. That also got the Mr Sheen treatment before being positioned on the coffin lid with the boxing gloves arranged in front. I strained to see the picture. I made out the shapes of two men, one large and white, the other smaller and black. I had no idea who they were.

The undertakers melted away as the crowd entered the church. Every pew quickly filled with mourners and the main body of the church soon had no vacant seats, except for the top three pews which were reserved for immediate family. People stood in the area inside the entrance doors and along the sides. Some mourners shuffled into the side chapel where I was lurking and, as I moved to make some more space, I noticed for the first time that I had not been alone there. A man sat in the corner, at the far side of the sarcophagus, his face shrouded in shadows. I wondered how long he'd been there.

An altar girl in frothy white vestments appeared with a burning taper and reached up to light the solitary candle in a tall, brass, candle-holder that stood beside the coffin. A hush descended on the crowd.

The creak of the opening doors accompanied by stifled sobbing indicated the arrival of the grieving widow, black-ringed eyes, blonde, deeply-tanned, doped up to the eyeballs, leaning on the arm of a white-faced woman, with two bewildered little children trotting alongside clutching the fabric of her coat. The tight cluster of family pressed close behind them and they all moved like a single entity to the top of the church and poured into the first three rows of pews close to the coffin.

It looked like the ceremony was finally about to begin. The priest had already shaken the hands of the widow and family and was making his way back up the steps to the altar when the doors opened again and the sound of brisk male footsteps grew louder as they proceeded up the central aisle.

The young woman standing beside me momentarily stopped chewing her gum to exclaim under her breath, 'Jaysus. Look who it is.'

'Shurrup,' her male companion growled, his black biker jacket creaking as he turned his angry, acne-pocked face to her.

The man who now stood directly in front of the widow wore a black crombie, a loose paisley scarf, sunglasses hooked into his breast pocket and an expression of barely-contained fury in his dark eyes. Level with his position, one in each side aisle, stood the watchful Costigan and Clarke. It could only be Dessie Donlon.

The priest, standing at the lectern on the altar and oblivious to the sudden appearance of Dublin's most notorious crime boss, began the ceremony in a melodious Eastern European accent.

'Dearly beloved, we are gathered here this evening to mark the first stage of the homeward journey of our brother, Raymond Brosnan, known to many of us as Sugar Ray ...'

He was interrupted by the low moan of fear and distress that came from the widow. The priest paused to look down in concern.

The crowd was deathly quiet as Donlon reverently placed an enormous wreath at the base of the coffin's trolley. It was in the shape of a boxing ring. He then turned to address the widow.

'Sandra, I'm sorry for your loss and that your kids have lost their Da. I want you to take this to look after yourselves.' He pressed a white envelope into the widow's shaking hands before continuing. 'Ray was my right hand man, he was like a brother to me ...' He bent to embrace her.

'You hypocrite!' The white-faced woman beside the widow was on her feet, jabbing her finger at Donlon, who stepped backwards and held up one hand in placation.

'He was *my* brother and he wouldn't be in that coffin if it wasn't for you. You're not wanted here, you murdering bastard. As if torturing and killing him wasn't enough, what you did ... and you have the nerve to turn up here ...'

She drew back her head and spat. The guttering candle hissed as it was doused in flying spittle, more of which plopped on to the framed photo on the coffin and started to slide slowly down the glass. Dessie Donlon was caught in the eye and, as he moved to wipe it off, he stepped back again, colliding with the coffin. The trolley teetered and then collapsed. As the congregation held its breath in horror, the coffin tumbled to the ground and with a crack like a shot, the lid split open and the corpse rolled out.

It lay on the red carpet, the mortal remains of a huge dead hulk of a man in an expensive suit. The sickening smell of embalming fluid filled the air. The carpet around the body darkened with something liquid that seeped into it, dampening the scattered lumps of flesh-coloured putty and the wads of white cotton wool close-by. I'd never met Sugar Ray Brosnan but I could safely bet that he wasn't looking his best right now.

The original stunned silence had been replaced by a whispering from the crowd and then a low murmur. That was pierced now by the clear, high voice of a child.

'What happened to Da's mouth ... an' where's his teeth?'

And his sister cried, 'An' what's that on his face?'

The widow's moans turned into howls and the congregation pushed forward like a landslide. Some stood up to see better and pass what they saw back to their neighbours.

'Oh, my good Jaysus,' said the young woman beside me, chewing vigourously. 'So it *is* true. No wonder they had to close the coffin for the viewing.'

'What is it,' I asked her, 'I can't see. What's on his face?'

'It's letters carved into his forehead,' she whispered back, ignoring the furious glare from her boyfriend. 'There was a rumour that someone broke in to the funeral parlour and did it before the viewing. And that Dessie Donlon paid them to do it.'

'Shurrup,' the boyfriend hissed, shaking her elbow.

'Gerroff,' she said. 'I was only *saying*. I mean, carving up dead bodies. It's not natural.'

'What letters?' I asked. 'Do they spell something?'

'Course they do,' she said as if I was a halfwit. '*Ra* – that's what they spell: R-A-T.'

She nodded sagely towards the altar and I followed her gaze. Donlon was taking control. He signalled the undertakers to come up and heave Sugar Ray back into the coffin. The crowd went quiet again as it watched. With a nod, Donlon motioned Costigan and Clarke to move towards the doors. Giving his face a final wipe with a white tissue, he addressed the sister of the deceased in a hoarse voice and a tone that indicated an order rather than a request.

'We'll say no more about this, May. All right?'

There was no response.

'You're upset now, I know that, May. Like I said, Ray was like a brother to me too. Maybe he made a mistake and maybe he said something and maybe he bears the signs of that now. That's just the way things are. But as God is my witness, I did not torture him before he died and I am *not* responsible for his death. Don't worry, Sandra and May – and all of yous.'

His voice rang out around the church, his face livid with anger, as he eyeballed the crowd.

'I'll find out who killed Ray Brosnan. I'll find out who's trying to destroy my business. And you'll all know about it when I do.'

He walked down the aisle and out the doors as briskly as he had come in. I took the opportunity to push my way out of the side chapel and slip down the aisle. I closed the church doors behind me just as the priest intoned 'Lord, we come in peace to remember your beloved son, Raymond ...'

27

SWEET AND SOUR

Outside the TV cameras were waiting.

'Mr Donlon, may I ask you a few questions ... Mr Donlon ...'

The reporter had ambushed Dessie Donlon at the gate and the cameraman swivelled his shoulder-mounted camera to get a full-face close up. Costigan was there in an instant, pushing himself between his boss and the media men.

'No questions, please. Mr Donlon is a busy man. He won't be giving any interviews.'

Clarke was on the street, yelling into his phone.

'Where the fuck are you? Get your arse down here *now*.'

Back at the gate, the TV reporter wasn't giving up. He looked about twenty-eight years old and was dressed in combats, khaki flak jacket, white t-shirt and dog tags. His accent was pure South County Dublin.

'Mr Donlon, can you comment on the recent series of Garda raids on premises in Coolock and Dublin West that yielded over three million euros worth of illicit drugs, contraband and stolen luxury vehicles? What about the discovery of the cache of high spec automatic weapons in the basement of the Koochy Koo Bar and Casino on Foley Street and the subsequent arrest of a number of your employees?'

Donlon gave a tight-lipped smile and turned his back on the camera. The cameraman moved around him. The reporter ducked past Costigan and pushed his mic towards Donlon again.

'Mr Donlon, is there a connection between those events and the death of Sugar Ray Brosnan, the man some people called your lieutenant ... the man whose removal service you've just left?'

A black BMW, its headlights blazing, drove up at high speed and screeched to a halt inches in front of Dean Clarke, who was still standing out on the street with his phone to his ear. Clarke wrenched open the driver's door, hauled out the driver and shoved him aside with a dig in the stomach that was too fast for the camera to catch but vicious enough to cause the man to double up in pain.

'Let's go,' Clarke called out of the open window as he jumped into the driver's seat.

Costigan opened the rear passenger door for Donlon, who sat inside. Costigan got in the front and, just as the car was about to move off, Donlon's window rolled down. He leaned forward and, while gazing directly into the camera, spoke into the microphone that was thrust inside.

'Let's get one thing straight for your viewers,' he said. 'I'm just a local businessman, doing my honest best to keep jobs in this area. I know nothing about any of the things you've mentioned. Just like those two women over there, I'm an ordinary member of the community going about my business. You might as well ask them what you've been asking me.'

As the BMW took off down the road, the TV camera slowly turned to focus on Viv and me, standing beneath the sign for the shrine. I'd just unlocked my bike, grateful that most of it was still there, apart from its rear light, back mudguard, brake cable and the top of its bell. I contemplated the remnants of the sweet and sour pork balls that were congealing in the foil container that had been dumped in the bicycle basket. A viscous red syrup oozed through the wickerwork and dripped down on to the spokes below.

'That's disgusting,' I said.

'It is,' Viv agreed, 'And as for the altar carpet inside, what am I going to do about that? It's going to take more than Febreeze to get rid of that smell.'

She looked up in surprise as a microphone appeared before us and the reporter announced,

'I'm talking to two members of the local community here outside Our Lady of Lourdes Church on Sean McDermott Street where the removal service for Raymond 'Sugar Ray' Brosnan is underway. Ladies, you were inside the church. Can you tell us anything about the service?'

Viv opened her mouth to speak but I got in there first.

'I think your viewers would like to know that the altar flowers were truly magnificent.'

Viv beamed with pride, her cheeks as pink as Sugar Ray's limo. I started to push my bike away.

'Just one more question. Did I hear you talking just now about cleaning up the community?'

Overwhelmed by the day's events, with pictures flooding back to me of dead Stevie and almost-dead Mooney and Sugar Ray's mutilated corpse, I finally lost it with the khaki-clad correspondent.

'Tell you what,' I said as I reached into my basket. 'Here.'

I took the container of sweet and sour pork balls and their coagulating scarlet syrup and pushed it firmly into the reporter's chest, giving it a good rub in.

'Clean that up,' I said and I cycled away with as much dignity as my loudly-rattling bicycle would allow.

Josie and Kitty must have patched things up while I was away. The two of them were sitting outside the café smoking when I rattled up the road, dismounted and pushed my bike up against the wall. Josie observed me with her arms folded, head back, squinting through the smoke from the cigarette between her lips. Kitty grinned, her eyes hidden behind large sunglasses.

'Well,' I said, 'Aren't the pair of you a lovely advertisement for the café? Have you managed to drive all the customers away?'

'Hey, Josie,' Kitty said, ignoring my comment, 'I think that's Clean-Up Connie, our newest local celebrity. Didn't recognise her, it's been so long. Hey, Connie, caught you on the news just now. Lookin' good, boss! You're trending too, practically viral.'

'What are you talking about?'

'You were on the telly just now. Everyone's seen it. The Cleaner Liffeyside man called just now to say they want to make you an honorary member. Hang on, it's up on YouTube already ...' She pushed the sunglasses up on top of her head and fiddled with her phone. I reminded myself to ask her later how she came to have the latest iPhone.

'Got it, I'll just turn it up. Here.' She passed me the phone.

It was a clip from *TV News Live*, one that had been broadcast about fifteen minutes previously. The studio presenter announced, 'And now we're going live to Dublin's Sean McDermott Street where the removal service is taking place of Raymond Brosnan, flamboyant manager of a well-known inner city boxing club with alleged links to Dublin's criminal underworld. Josh Treanor reports.' Cut to the scene outside the church and a close-up of Josh in his flak jacket and dog tags, earnestly speaking to the camera.

'Raymond Brosnan's mutilated body was found on a piece of waste ground in North County Dublin on Saturday. His death bears the hallmarks of a gangland-style execution. It follows yesterday's dramatic shooting of a local hotel proprietor with alleged connections to the criminal underworld – right on the doorstep of Store Street Garda Station.'

I moved the slider to fastforward through the footage of Dessie Donlon. To my horror, amongst the images flickering past, I saw my own face looming large, flushed and wild-eyed, framed by a shock of unkempt hair. It was the face of a madwoman. Reluctantly, I pressed 'Play'.

'Clean that up,' I heard the madwoman shriek and I watched as the camera pulled back to reveal a bright red stain spreading across the front of the reporter's white t-shirt. The reporter stepped back with his mouth open, clearly taken by surprise, then recovered himself and spoke quickly and fervently.

'"Clean it up" is the message from this ordinary Dublin woman who doubtless had the concerns of her family at heart when she decided to make this protest. This is a sign ...' He pointed to the stain on his chest, keeping his finger there as he solemnly intoned, '... an expression of the depth of feeling here in Dublin's north inner city where the community has clearly reached the end of its patience with the wave of crime and violence that is devastating their lives. Josh Treanor for *TV News Live* from Dublin's north inner city.'

Cut to me wobbling down the street on my bicycle.

I handed Kitty back her phone. She was grinning even more broadly now. Josie had one eyebrow raised.

'Like it?' Kitty asked. 'Will I read you the comments?'

'No. Leave me alone. Put my bike in the yard, will you? I'm going upstairs. I need some quiet.'

'At least tell me what was that horrible red stuff you shoved in the guy's chest and let me end the online speculation – oh and here's the post.' Kitty held up a white envelope.

'Sweet and sour pork,' I said as I snapped the envelope out of her hand, '... balls.'

28

GRAND PLANS

The registered letter was marked 'Urgent' and was addressed to Agnes Moran. Obviously I had to open it, but as soon as I did, I wished I hadn't. I wished I was back in Amsterdam in my tiny apartment on Orteliusstraat, alone in that quiet space, surrounded by nothing but dying plants.

The letter was on City Council headed paper. I scanned it quickly. The words 'Compulsory Purchase Negotiations' stood out, the rest a blur of bureaucratese. There was a request to enter immediate negotiations for the compulsory purchase of the building, a proposed meeting date and the routine 'do not hesitate to contact us' ending.

I sank down on my bed, my head in my hands. Just like that, our pathetic little world was endangered. For me and for Kitty, that meant the roof over our heads along with our fragile new lives.

'Hope it's good news, Connie,' Kitty called up to me. 'God knows we could do with some around here.'

'Just boring business stuff,' I called back, trying to keep my voice steady.

'I still can't get over Mooney,' she said. 'He was a gobshite but he wasn't the worst.'

I'd told Kitty that Mooney had been assaulted and was in hospital, but left out the disease part until I got more news on his condition. More than likely, the city's gossip machine was already circulating some garbled version of Mooney's fate, feeding the rumours of an epidemic and fuelling the growing panic on the streets. Once that took hold, no amount of reassurance by sensible infectious disease consultants would stem the fear.

The suitcase with my few belongings stood in a corner of my room, still unpacked. Maybe there'd be no need to do that now, I thought, as I picked up my phone. Again, Aggie's phone rang out with no response. Her mailbox was full and not accepting messages. I repeated the call, with the same result. I sent her another text asking her, yet again, to contact me urgently.

My heart raced as I sat on the bed, reviewing the number of calls and texts I'd sent her over the past twenty-four hours. I'd already worked out that her last text to me was sent at 2.45am Las Vegas time. Why did she text me in the early hours of the morning? Dr Rose Madden was right – it was time to get the police involved.

Well, I'd agreed to meet Detective Inspector Brady in a couple of hours so that he could get whatever it was that was so important to him off his chest. I'd tell him the whole story about Aggie and maybe he'd make contact with his Las Vegas counterparts tonight. Eight hours behind us, I thought, that meant plenty of time for them to make enquiries in normal working hours. I breathed more easily. I was almost looking forward to seeing Brady later on. Almost, but not really.

Now that I had a plan about Aggie, maybe I could tackle the compulsory purchase thing too. I stood up and moved to the open window as I searched for Aleka Marr in my phone contacts. A large, battleship-grey jeep, with six aluminium boxes strapped to its roof, was parked on the footpath below, its diesel engine gurgling loudly. A sudden movement caught my eye. It was Ozzie Wolf, darting up the basement steps and into the left-hand driver's seat. I'd never seen him move so fast.

I caught a quick glimpse of the Mercedes marque as he backed to do a rapid U-turn, then sped off towards the city centre. So his other car *was* German, a vintage G-Wagen that made Lu O'Leary's Range Rover look like a candidate for an Earthwatch award.

I wondered if Ozzie had received a similar letter from the Council. They hardly wanted this building by itself, more likely they were after the whole terrace. Maybe we could stand together as a community and resist the city's plans.

'Hi, Aleka Marr speaking. How may I help you?'

'It's Connie Ortelius. You know, from the Silver Bullet Café. Aleka, when we first met, you kindly offered me advice and support. I've just received a compulsory purchase notice from the council. I've no idea what to do. Can you help me?'

There was no hesitation in her response.

'Of course, Connie. I meant every word. I'll be happy to help. I'll make some informal inquiries with the council first thing tomorrow and maybe we can meet up mid-morning to review things. How about 11am in the café? And, Connie _'

'Yes?'

'Try not to worry. It'll be ok. Something can always be worked out.'

I muttered my thanks and hung up, sighing with relief. Maybe I'd have something positive to tell Aggie when I finally tracked her down. Assuming she was ok.

'Hey, you look better,' Kitty said when I came back downstairs. 'You didn't look so hot when you got home.'

'You don't say.'

'Yeah, kind of old and grumpy. Like Josie. She's gone home by the way. Look, here's something else to cheer you up.'

She hit the button on the mechanical cash register and the drawer slid out, displaying a nice collection of legal tender, mostly twenties and tens.

'Wow,' I said, making her smile. 'And is that a fifty I see before me? What exactly are you selling here, Kitty?'

She laughed. 'A bunch of French sailors came in at lunchtime. They stayed and drank coffee for half the afternoon.'

'I'll bet they did,' I said, looking at her shining eyes, the dark circles underneath them now well-faded. The resilience of youth.

'That American guy was in again too. Must be staying around here. He never says a word, just reads his map or checks his cool-looking tablet, you know, an iPad thing.'

'I saw him earlier on. I keep thinking I know him from somewhere but I just can't place him.'

'He sits at the same table for a couple of hours every day, drinking Coke. He's ok though, quiet but not creepy. Always drops a big tip into the jar for me.'

'Well deserved,' I said. 'Any more news? Do any of your friends know where Stevie was on Thursday or Friday night?'

'I've heard nothing about that,' she said carefully, as she perched herself on her favourite table. 'But I might have something about the sketchbooks. My friend Hannah was back in. You remember her from this morning? Tall, thin blonde, slightly out of it? She had an idea about Stevie's missing backpack. She said she heard something from Shane – you know, Stevie's friend – about a new place Stevie went to paint. Shane wasn't supposed to say, but he was totally off his head at the time.'

'A studio?'

'Stevie always had someplace to work. Sometimes it was just an old shed. Once he shared a space with some other artists in a converted garage over on Dominic Street. He moved out of there a while back, said he needed someplace quieter. I didn't know about the new place, he never said.'

'Tell me about Shane,' I said kicking myself that I'd forgotten about him. Fogarty had mentioned the name when Stevie's body was recovered. 'He knows about the studio. They were good friends?'

'They were more than good friends. Were. Up till a month or two ago. They had a serious bust-up and they were avoiding one another since then. Shane took it hard. He was bad before, but he's lost it altogether now.'

'Meaning?'

'Ah, you know, the drugs and all that.'

'Do you know why they fell out?'

'Not a clue. Lovers' tiff, maybe. Happens all the time, you know yourself. Stevie was my best friend but when it came to romance he was a bit on the love 'em and leave 'em side. Didn't get too attached. Unlike Shane. He has a different kind of personality.'

'As we're on the subject of Stevie's sketches, do you want to tell me what was going on this morning when you saw Stevie's self-portrait? Where is it, by the way?'

'Don't worry. I put it in your room behind your suitcase.' She continued hesitantly. 'Like Hannah said, that painting was just Stevie's idea of a joke ...'

'How do you mean? Is it that he copied an old master but put in a contemporary twist?'

'What? No. It's that he painted a picture of himself with that mark on his hand.'

'Mark? Oh, you mean the cigarette burn. Does it mean something?'

For a moment, she flattened the surface of the sugar in the sugar bowl with the back of a teaspoon using small circular motions. Then she spoke quietly, focusing on the sugar.

'There was this ... thing, a while back. A kind of a weird trend. I heard about that mark then. It was supposed to be a sign of having kind of ... specialist interests, if you know what I mean. It wasn't Stevie's thing at all.'

'So that's why you were surprised at the painting.'

'Yeah, but Hannah's right. Stevie was having a laugh. He did that in his paintings sometimes, you know? Put in little private jokes and stuff.'

'Ok, and if Hannah's also right about the possibility of Stevie's missing backpack being in his studio, how do you think it got there from the Sunrise Hotel locker? Would Stevie have taken it himself?'

'Must have. I definitely left it in the locker. By the way, you're not the only one looking for Stevie's sketches. Bloke came in here today asking about "Stevie Hennessy works", as he called them, especially works in progress. Said he'd pay highly for any drawings or sketches. I don't think he was Stevie's collector, didn't seem the type.'

'Stevie had a collector?'

'Yeah, a guy with something to do with Trinity College. He bought a lot of Stevie's paintings. I never met him. And before you ask, I don't know his name. Unless ... it might be Gordon something. Stevie mentioned that name sometimes.'

'Would Shane know the name?'

She shook her head. 'Most of the time Shane doesn't know his own name.'

'Why am I only hearing about all this stuff now?'

'You never asked.'

'But this is very good, Kitty. I think we may be getting somewhere. It shouldn't be too hard to track down that collector. Through him, we'll find Stevie's studio. And his sketchbooks. You and Hannah'd better get Shane for me –'

'No one knows where he is.'

'Find him, Kitty. And I'll find the sketchbooks.'

'And then what?' Kitty asked, her eyes on the sugar bowl.

'If Stevie asked you to take care of his sketchbooks and then, sometime on Friday he went to the trouble of taking them back and moving them, possibly to his studio, those sketchbooks must be important. When we have them, I'm sure we'll be closer to finding out what happened to Stevie.'

'Ok,' said Kitty. She didn't look convinced, but that didn't bother me. Now I had a plan. Several plans.

29

MY ENEMY'S ENEMY IS MY ENEMY

A violent scratching at the door shattered the silence of the empty café. I froze and slowly closed my laptop.

It was six-thirty and Kitty had gone out to meet her friends before starting work for Ozzie's club. She'd made me promise to meet her afterwards and fill her in on my non-date with Brady.

'Don't get too cosy with him. Prick thinks he's God's gift,' she said, shaking her head in disbelief as she exited.

The scratching became louder and increasingly frantic. I crept towards the door, not sure what I was intending to do, when I heard a familiar yapping outside.

'Well, hello Bertie!' I said and opened the door. The little dog did its jumping-into-my-arms trick again. 'What has you here?'

But it was obvious what had brought him here. A man in a black leather jacket stood by the wall, his hands in his pockets. A black BMW was parked at the kerb, its engine running. Through its darkened windows, I could just make out the shapes of two men inside. Costigan and Clarke.

The man was motionless, his tension as palpable as his expensive cologne. I didn't need to be told who he was but he told me anyway.

'Good evening, Ms Ortelius. I'm Dessie Donlon.'

He moved into the light and I saw that he was younger than I'd thought from earlier on in the church, probably in his forties and of medium height, well built. His well-cut, dark hair was greying at the temples and his face had the burnished gleam that results from a recent visit to a high-end barber.

'I'd like a few minutes with you.'

It was not a request. He walked past me into the café, leaving me to follow with his dog still in my arms. The café door swung closed behind me.

Dessie Donlon waited, his hands hanging by his side, his face dark with anger.

'I am not a patient man,' he said. 'And I am rapidly becoming very, *very* pissed off with this situation.'

He came towards me and I automatically backed away, terrified. He reached out his arms and gently removed Bertie from mine, placing him on the ground. The dog trotted off to explore the kitchen. His owner continued to advance towards me until I backed into the wall and could retreat no further.

'Now,' Dessie Donlon said, staring into my eyes, his nose almost touching mine, his breath on my face. 'I want you to tell me everything you know about this disease that's going around. Where it came from, how it's passed around, what the cure is – and who or what is behind this fucking ... annoyance.' He turned and slammed his fist on the table beside me.

I jumped. My knees were about to buckle and dizziness overwhelm me when he wheeled around and resumed his tirade from a few feet away.

'Before you start to lie to me, do I need to remind you that you are in an extremely vulnerable position?'

I shook my head.

'Good. Because I could destroy you this minute, very easily. And I can make you and your aunt and your little Chinese pal suffer beyond your worst nightmares. Am I making myself clear?'

My voice came out as a squeak. 'Yes.'

'So what are you going to do?'

'I'm going to tell you everything I know.'

'Good idea,' he said, and sat on a table unbuttoning his jacket. As it opened, I saw something bulging in the inside pocket. I didn't need an introduction to what that was, either.

'I don't have a lot of time,' he said. 'So spill.'

My mind raced. What had brought this on? He must have heard about Mooney. I needed to distract him from thinking of ways to make me and Aggie and Kitty suffer beyond our worst nightmares. I took a deep breath and started slowly.

'The disease that Stevie Hennessy had when he died has claimed a second victim, Jimmy Mooney, the journalist. He's fighting for his life, following surgery in the Mater. The doctors don't hold out much hope ...'

'Go on.'

'Mooney had drugs in his system.'

'Oh yeah?'

Good, I had his interest. He mustn't have heard any of the details about Mooney. 'He'd taken bath salts.'

'Bullshit,' Donlon snapped. 'Coke. E maybe. Not fucking bath salts. Now give me the truth or I'll ...'

I held up my hands, like that was going to help me. 'No, no really. They did the analysis in the hospital. That's what they said it was. MDPV. Possibly by injection.'

'That sounds like total crap.'

He reached into his inside pocket and extracted the handgun. He examined it briefly before clicking something and levelling it at me.

'Last chance,' he said.

I began to shake uncontrollably.

'I heard there might be a cure ... like an antidote.'

I have no idea where that came from. I was clutching at straws. And then I went ahead and made it worse.

'There may be something in Stevie's sketchbooks, the missing ones.'

A violent hiss came from the behind the service counter followed by a sharp metallic clang. Donlon's arm swung round and his weapon went off with a deafening explosion.

'What the fuck ...?' he yelled. He dropped to the ground instantly, taking cover behind a table. He crouched there, his weapon pointed towards the kitchen.

'You,' he said to me. 'Go see what's over there.'

Hands raised, I moved slowly towards the kitchen, keeping my eyes on Donlon. From behind the counter came a little whine. I looked at the floor.

'Ah, the poor little thing ...' I said, bending down to pick up Bertie's inert body while muttering reproachfully to Donlon, 'It was only the bloody coffee machine.'

I carried the fluffy bundle over to the table in front of Donlon and laid it down.

'Look what you did,' I said.

Donlon looked stricken. He stood up and replaced the weapon in his pocket.

'Is he ...?'

'Dead? I don't know. He's not moving, is he? But there's no sign of blood that I can see. Maybe he had a heart attack.'

'Ah, Jaysus,' Donlon said.

I stroked the little body a couple of times. Suddenly it gave a shudder and the tiny dog lifted his head and licked my hand.

'Hey, he's ok,' I said. 'It must have been the fright.'

Bertie rose to his feet and staggered unsteadily across the table to Donlon.

The café door swung open and Costigan appeared, a gun in his hand. He stopped and surveyed the scene, taking in me first and then Donlon sitting on a chair with Bertie in his arms.

'Sorry, Boss.' Costigan said, puzzled. 'Thought we heard a shot.'

'Nothing to see here,' Donlon said, his voice hoarse. 'Fuck off back to the car.'

We sat in silence for a few minutes after he left, listening to the clock tick. Donlon put Bertie down and we watched as he scurried about sniffing at everything. The gang leader's tone was marginally warmer when he spoke again.

'Look,' he said. 'I'm fond of the little fella, you know? Reminds me of one I had when I was a kid. Not a Chihuahua. There were no Chihuahuas in Crumlin in the nineteen eighties.'

He clicked his fingers. Bertie looked at him and wagged his tail.

'Seems fine now. Thanks for your ... help. You have a way with him.'

'You're welcome,' I managed to say, my throat dry. 'Do you mind if I get some water?'

'Go ahead'.

I filled a water jug at the tap and returned with a couple of glasses and a bowl. I poured a glass for myself and one for Donlon and placed the bowl of water on the ground for Bertie.

Donlon waited for me to finish gulping down the water before speaking again.

'Now,' he said. 'About that antidote. That *is* interesting. It could change everything. What it is? Is it available?'

I shook my head. I couldn't remember what Dr Rose Madden had said.

'Honestly, I don't know. I think I heard some mention of traditional Chinese medicine. But I'm not sure ...'

'Chinese? Does that young one you have working here know about this stuff?'

My blood ran cold. Now what had I done?

'No, no. Kitty grew up in this country. She hasn't a notion about Chinese medicine. You have to believe me ...'

Dessie pointed an index finger at me and I shut up.

'Ok, I understand,' he said. 'What about those sketchbooks you mentioned? Is there something there that'd help with this?'

'There might be. Look, I really don't know. I'm just trying to find out what happened to Stevie. His sketchbooks went missing from the Sunrise Hotel around the time he died. He used to put all kinds of little messages into his pictures. If he knew something, he might have ... But when you think about it, he couldn't have known about the disease or its antidote, could he? Otherwise, he would have used it.'

'If he had time,' Donlon said, thoughtfully. 'This disease is bad for business. All the panic about it, it's getting worse. It's putting the customers off and it's destroying our credibility as an organisation. I want it to go away. I need to find this antidote.'

'But the disease isn't really infectious, the doctors said. There's only been two cases ...'

Donlon gazed at me pityingly.

'Nobody but a fool or a child would believe that crap they're putting out, those so-called "assurances". We're not fucking stupid, are we?'

He had a point. To lose one homeless teenager to a mysterious killer disease was unfortunate, to have a second case, within twenty-four hours, involving a well-known gentleman of the press ... that was unbelievable.

'And anyway, from my point of view it doesn't matter if it's an epidemic or a bleeding flash in the pan,' Donlon continued. 'It's what people believe that matters. My customers, my competitors. And ...' he added bitterly, 'my fucking wife.'

'Karen?' I said before I could stop myself.

Donlon regarded me with renewed interest.

'You know Karen? Are you friends with her?'

'We've met. I don't think she regards me as a friend.'

'All the same,' he said. 'That would be very helpful.'

'What would?'

'If you were to talk to her ...'

I was shaking my head.

'... reassure her about the disease. Repeat that crap you said from the medics. If that doesn't work, tell her about the antidote. Tell her you're helping me to find it.'

He picked up my phone beside the laptop and keyed in a number.

'Here,' he said handing it to me. 'It's ringing. Talk to her.'

I was still shaking my head when I heard Karen answer. I cleared my throat.

'Hi Karen, this is Connie Ortelius from the Silver Bullet Café. Your husband ...'

The line went dead. I held up the phone to Donlon so he could read the screen showing 'Call ended'.

'She hung up.'

'Probably drunk. Try her again later.'

'I really don't think so. Karen doesn't like me. Actually, for some reason she kind of hates me.'

'Makes two of us,' he said, rising to go.

'Sorry?'

'She hates me too. But I want you to call her anyway. She's losing her mind about that useless young fella, just because he's been missing a couple of days. 'Course he's off partying with those fuckers he calls friends, junkie fucking sleazeball queers.'

I winced, waiting for him to start slamming his fist on the table again.

'She thinks he's in danger, that he'll get the bloody disease. As far as I'm concerned, if he gets it, he bloody deserves it.'

'Is he your son?'

'Biologically, yes. Any other way, no. Little bastard, making a show of me. He hates me too. Happy families, eh? Give me gangland warfare any day. Come on, Bertie, time to go.'

He scooped up the dog and made for the door. He turned as he opened it and said, 'Contact me day or night if you get any information. Anything at all. I put my number in your phone there too.'

I nodded dumbly.

'By the way,' he said, 'How's your aunt? Haven't seen her for a while. Hope she's keeping well!'

And then he was gone, leaving me staring at the 'Open' sign that swung like a noose on the back of the door.

30

A DATE WITH THE LAW

I don't know how long I sat there, shocked and paralysed by the gang leader's barely-contained violence, the sound of gunfire still ringing in my ears.

I ignored the first call from Brady and the second one. Then, desperately retrieving the shreds of my master plan, I texted him a lie that I was on my way. Ten minutes later, I'd showered, thrown on some makeup and my least crumpled dress and was running down the quays towards town. My only defence against Donlon was to keep my date with the law.

The tiny restaurant was buzzing, and on a Monday night too. The recession was over for some. For others, it had never existed.

I scanned the room for Brady and spotted him at the far end. He sat facing the door and the empty chair in front of him. He raised a hand to catch my attention.

'Sorry,' I said. 'You got my text? I had a visitor I couldn't get rid of.'

'No problem,' Brady said, with a forced smile. He skewered the last seared scallop and curtly indicated that I should sit. I could hardly blame him for being angry, I was at least forty minutes late.

He looked me up and down and gave a little nod. Presumably I'd passed a test of some kind. He wore a smart shirt and tie with his usual expensive watch and a new haircut. For the kind of man who wouldn't be seen dead with a woman who didn't reflect his style, he was certainly lowering his standards with me.

'Can I order you a drink?' he said. 'Some wine?'

I shook my head, still reeling from my encounter with Donlon. 'I'll stick with the water, thanks.'

I noticed that Brady was doing the same. He saw me checking his glass.

'Working tonight,' he said. 'Press conference at nine. There's a lot going on.'

'I've seen the reports. Multiple police raids, seizures of drugs and contraband. Congratulations. You're on a roll.'

'Thank you,' he said and motioned the waiter for a menu. 'For a long time we could do very little, mostly due to the cutbacks. Now we're making more progress.'

He handed me the menu. 'Sorry I had to go ahead. Would you like to order something?'

I'd eaten nothing since a nibbled biscuit with Dr Rose Madden earlier on, but stress, bad company and recent gunfire seemed to have spoiled my appetite. I shook my head. 'I'm not hungry at the moment.'

'You're a cheap date!' Brady laughed.

'This is not a date. If you remember, you said you wanted to see me about something.'

'I also said it can be a date if you want it to be a date.' He smiled into my eyes, his anger forgotten. 'But yes, I wanted to see you alone. You see, I'm concerned about you.'

'There's no need for any concern,' I replied evenly. 'I'm a grown woman. I can look after myself.'

'I'm not so sure about that,' he said. 'I believe that your judgement may not always be the best.'

'What are you talking about?' I laughed to hide my rising panic. How much did Brady know about me?

'You may be in danger of associating with people who are ... problematic. Who might even do you some harm.'

'What people?'

'People like Fogarty. Like Ozzie Wolf. Look,' he said, wiping his mouth with a napkin and taking a drink from his glass. 'I'm going to give it to you straight. First Fogarty. He's not what he seems.'

'Fogarty's just a customer.'

'Even if that's true, you should know what you're dealing with. Pius Fogarty has a violent criminal history. He was shot yesterday as part of an ongoing gangland turf war.'

'Mistaken identity, I heard.'

'Not according to my intelligence. Look, I shouldn't tell you this. The CCTV footage is unusable unfortunately, but eye witnesses have described a jeep like Ozzie Wolf's driving away from the scene.'

'Now that's ridiculous,' I said eyeing the colourless liquid in his glass and wondering if he was drunk. 'Ozzie's a social butterfly. The nocturnal variety – a social moth? Whatever he is, he's not a hit man.'

'We believe the attack came from a vehicle on the far side of the road, a foreign jeep with left-hand drive, like Ozzie Wolf's. A gunman in the passenger seat would have had a clear shot of the victim. It's a possibility. The alternative is Steyne River Securities or a rival gang. We'll know more when the ballistics report comes in.'

The Ozzie thing sounded like pure hokum, but he'd struck a chord about Fogarty. That Kevlar vest of his had been niggling at me. It was hardly normal attire for a hotel proprietor, even in my neighbourhood.

'You might think Fogarty's a rough diamond with his homely hotel and his waifs and strays. But back in the day, he ran a security firm, an independent outfit with deep connections into the criminal underworld. Four years ago, Fogarty was charged with murder. The case was dismissed on a technicality and Fogarty walked.'

'You mean he was innocent?'

'I mean he was lucky. After that he took to the drink and moved in with the other low-lifes in the Sunrise Hotel. Eventually he got a caretaker position there, a job requiring minimal work and affording him full freedom to continue his shady activities. We keep him under regular surveillance.'

I tried to look disinterested but it was a struggle. I could have done without the disturbing revelations about my neighbours.

'As for Ozzie Wolf. Sure, he's a charmer, if you're into nancy boys. In reality, he's involved in dubious financial activities using his international contacts in Germany and elsewhere. You know his parents are German diplomats? They live in a kind of a castle in Dalkey, looking out over Killiney Bay.' He snorted loudly. 'Ozzie Wolf thinks he's untouchable. But there'll be no diplomatic immunity for him when the time comes.'

I sighed and considered offering to top up his glass of vitriol.

'And what has any of this got to do with me?'

'I'm doing you a favour, Connie. There are people ready to take advantage of unsuspecting newcomers like yourself, and, if you don't mind me saying so, you seem to be walking blindly into their clutches. I'm in a good position to see what's going on. I can help you, but only if you help yourself and work with me.'

'You can help me in what way?'

'There are changes coming to this town,' he said. 'The quaint old ways, the two-bit hoodlums with their miserable semi-tribal networks ... they're about to be swept away. Global interests will not tolerate the kind of chaotic approach to law and order we have in this city. And about bloody time too. As a law-enforcement officer, I lost patience a long time ago with a system that allows the likes of Dessie Donlon and his gang to thrive.'

He sat forward, fists clenched on the table, his momentary good humour dissolved.

'Have you any idea what it's like to see the puzzlement in the eyes of international business people when they hear about the latest armed robbery, the latest murder and the whole place erupting in endless feuds? This town is like the OK-fucking-Corral on Groundhog Day. They see junkies shooting up at the entrance to the International Financial Services Centre and men and women of all ages lying about in doorways, off their heads and raving. They're accosted by droves of beggars, the likes of which you wouldn't see outside of the slums of Calcutta. Well, no more – it's over. In the future, there'll be no place for local gangs and their supporting cast – that army of the ... the undead. Beggars, addicts, dealers, robbers, seventeen-year-old gun-toting contract killers ... And there'll be no place for those throwbacks, Pius Fogarty, Ozzie Wolf, with their illicit activities operating in a semi-legal twilight. So Connie, you need to decide.'

I studied him, unsure how to respond. I couldn't care less about his grand plan but he'd sown a few seeds of doubt in my mind about my neighbours.

'Come on, Connie. Whose side are you on?'

'Right now, I'm on the side of trying to survive,' I said.

'Ok, so what has you going around asking questions about that drowning victim, Stevie Hennessy?'

'Do you want to take me downtown for questioning now?'

'No, sorry, I didn't mean to start interrogating you. It's just that I can't understand what an intelligent woman like you is doing with this ridiculous amateur investigating carry-on. I mean, where are the rest of the Five-Find-Outers-and-Dog?'

'I'm a bit old to be one of the Five-Find-Outers. But I have a bike with a basket. If I got a hat and a cape, I could be Miss Marple – do you think?'

'Ok, be like that if you want. I'm only trying to give you a bit of friendly advice. This is not the time or the place for amateurs to be poking about. I'm looking after things and that's all you need to know.'

I decided it was time to see what he was able to look after.

'Ok, Detective Inspector. You know Aggie – my aunt? She's gone missing in Las Vegas. I haven't been able to contact her for over twenty-four hours. I'm worried that something might have happened to her. I'm afraid someone from here may want to harm her.'

Brady was utterly unconcerned.

'Who in the name of God would want to harm Aggie Moran?'

'Well, I don't know. She's been in some kind of stand-off for a long time with Dessie Donlon's Steyne River Securities. Maybe they've kidnapped her.'

Once again, I decided not to reveal my recent visits from Dessie Donlon and Steyne River Securities and the threats they'd made. Brady'd probably blame me for hanging out with low-lifes.

'Donlon?' Brady repeated. 'He's got enough on his plate at the moment. And I happen to know that very soon he'll have a lot more to deal with. There's no way Dessie Donlon has abducted Aggie. That's ridiculous. You see, that's exactly what I mean. You're well-intentioned but you're completely naive and seriously clueless.'

I felt my face burning. Now I felt stupid. And seriously clueless.

'All right,' he continued, 'I can see that you're worried about Aggie. I'll make contact with the police in Las Vegas as soon as I get into work. Write down her hotel name and what she was doing. You know, places she might have been, things she was doing, people she met or mentioned.'

He reached into the pocket of his jacket on the back of his chair and brought out a pen and a small notebook.

'Here,' he said, opening the notebook at a blank page and handing it to me. 'Put it down on this. I'm sure she's fine. They'll find her off playing the slot machines. Or in a bingo marathon or something.'

He didn't know Aggie, I thought, as I scribbled down some details and passed back the notebook.

'Great,' said Brady. 'Now you can do something for me. Will you keep an eye on Fogarty and on Ozzie Wolf? Let me know anything unusual they might say or do?'

Oh, here we go again, I thought, my heart sinking. Now I was being recruited as a police informer.

I jumped as my phone buzzed.

'Do you mind?' I asked Brady as I found my phone. 'It could be Aggie.'

He nodded to go ahead and called a waiter for the bill.

The message was from Lu O'Leary: *Mooney dead. Never regained consciousness. Witnesses say he was attacked by Fogarty this am. Call me ASAP. Lu*

Brady saw my expression. 'Something wrong?'

'I just need to make a quick call. Sorry, I'll be right back.'

I went outside and called Lu. She started asking questions the minute she heard my voice.

'I can't talk here,' I said as quietly as possible. 'Brady's breathing down my neck. Remember our non-date? He's heading into work in a few minutes and I'll be able to escape.'

Lu was insistent. 'I need you to help me understand what went on between Mooney and Fogarty this morning. It's very important. Where are you – Hawkins Street? Meet me in Mulligan's of Poolbeg Street in ten minutes. It's right beside you.'

She hung up and I was left staring at her text message. Mooney dead. Stunned, I leaned against the doorframe, trying to take it in. The restaurant door opened quickly and someone came out and crashed straight into me. My phone flew out of my hand and fell straight into the gutter.

'God, I'm sorry! Here, let me get it.' Brady bent down and picked up my phone before I could reach it. He produced a tissue from somewhere and, holding the phone up high, proceeded to wipe it clean. The message from Lu was still on-screen and clearly visible.

'Give me back my phone,' I said between gritted teeth.

'There you are,' Brady said, handing it over with a grim smile. 'No harm done, I hope. You need to be careful taking your phone out on the street like that. Anyone might come along and grab it.'

He had read Lu's message. I bet he wasn't happy to find out about Mooney that way. He took out his own phone and stabbed at its screen with his index finger.

'I have to go. Shame our meeting was spoiled by delays and interruptions. And that you didn't get a chance to sample the fine cooking. Another time, perhaps?'

'Sure, another time,' I said with no enthusiasm.

Brady put away his phone and focused a cold look on me.

'You won't forget what we discussed? You'll choose your friends more wisely. And you'll contact me with any news regarding your unsavoury neighbours. We have an agreement.'

I stared back at him. I'd just remembered the last person I knew who had an agreement with Detective Inspector Brady. It was Jimmy Mooney.

'You keep your part of the deal and I'll look after you,' Brady said. 'If you don't, you may find yourself in trouble.'

He shrugged on his jacket and walked away.

Feeling sick, I watched the departing figure of the detective. When he read my message from Lu, it included the alleged attack on Mooney. Which meant I'd accidentally ratted on Pius Fogarty. Brady's new informant had already produced the goods.

But Brady wasn't finished with me. He stopped at the corner and called back.

'Forgot to mention, I had a voicemail today from a police officer in Amsterdam in relation to yourself. I'll get back to him tomorrow. You wouldn't happen to know what that's about, would you?'

He didn't wait for an answer but crossed the street and disappeared into the shadows.

31

Version Control

By the time I pushed open the door of Mulligan's, Lu O'Leary was already sitting up at the bar with a pint in front of her.

'How did you manage that?' I asked. 'You were in your office when we spoke five minutes ago.'

'It's one of my many skills,' she said. 'You look terrible – what are you having?'

So Brady had got to me and it showed. Soon, I'd need to make up my mind: play along with him or leave the country. Tomorrow would tell.

'Thanks, I'll have the same as yourself.'

It was many years since I'd last sampled the second best pint of Guinness in Dublin. Lu ordered a couple of them and slid down from her bar stool.

'Come into the backroom,' she said. 'We need to talk.'

She gave a nod to the barman who said he'd drop the pints down to us.

In the spacious room behind the lounge, hung with mirrors, dark old prints and mismatched lighting, three of the four enormous wooden tables were free.

'Sign of the times,' Lu said as she took possession of the table at the far left-hand corner, with a strategic view of the entrance to the front lounge as well as the doorway to the bar on one side and the toilets and outside smoking area on the other.

'Back in the old days this place would have been packed, even on a Monday night.'

'When the *Irish Press* was still going?'

She nodded. 'And the *Sunday Press* and the *Evening Press*. Place used to be full of journalists. And printers in from next door on their tea-breaks. The newsprint was backwards or upside down at times, but there were great stories. And great writers.'

She raised her glass to a wall-mounted picture that was just visible through the door to the front lounge. It was a gold-framed, black and white photograph of a craggy-faced man holding what looked like a glass of milk.

'*Brandy* and milk,' she noted authoritatively. 'Imbibed by a man who, whatever he may have done, he never abused an apostrophe.'

'Unapologetic apostrophes?'

'Exactly.'

She shook her head slowly. Then she took a folded page from her laptop case and placed it carefully on the table in front of her.

'We'll get to that in a minute. Have you seen Pius Fogarty recently?' she asked.

I shook my head, thinking not since I'd assaulted him this morning. In retrospect, that was not something I was proud of, even if he did ask for it. Worse, I'd accidentally handed Brady information implicating him in Mooney's attack. I prayed Fogarty wouldn't find out, not least because he was a known criminal and a possible murderer.

'Fine, let's talk about Mooney then,' Lu said. 'I want to go back over the times he spoke to you.'

'All right,' I said, 'I met Mooney for the first time yesterday in the Silver Bullet Café, a few hours after Stevie Hennessy's body was found. Mooney came in to interview me but ended up ranting about the locals and the crime-infested neighbourhood. A good old jeremiad, I believe it was.'

She smiled.

'The next time was last night, in the Eight Bells. He was arguing with Brady. They'd both had a few drinks. Then Mooney made a pass at Kitty and there was a bit of a row.'

'And you were involved?'

'I'm afraid so. You know, Lu, I used to lead a quiet life. But lately, whenever there's any trouble around, I seem to land right in the middle of it.'

She laughed. 'You should be a journalist. You'd never be stuck for a story.'

I thought back to last night in the pub, squirming internally at the memory of Fogarty's amusement when he saw me in Brady's arms.

'Mooney was upset with Brady, as if Brady'd reneged on an agreement with him. Brady was ... dismissing him and Mooney didn't like it.'

'So how did it end up?'

'Mooney quietened down and left.'

'So it looks like Mooney and Brady had an arrangement to exchange information. That's not unusual. Journalists and cops need each other at various levels. Synergies, as they say. I wonder what happened to end it ...' Lu tapped her pen on the table for a moment. 'And that was the last time you saw Mooney – but you heard from him again?'

I didn't want to go into Mooney's drunken near-suicide in the middle of the night. The man's entire life was about to be scrutinised in public and some things should stay private.

'He phoned me this morning around eleven,' I said. 'He was agitated and wanted to meet straightaway, in a place just off Talbot Street. Turned out to be a grow shop.'

She nodded. 'Yeah, that's not as odd as it might appear. He had to keep up-to-date with the drugs scene, it moves so fast. He was working on a big story. But why did he want to meet you so urgently?'

I'd been thinking about that. Apart from the two of us making a kind of connection the previous night, we had nothing in common. I'd laughed at his dire warnings when I first met him. God, I felt bad about that now.

'He knew I had an interest in finding out what happened to Stevie Hennessy. When he phoned me this morning, I thought he'd found something and was going to share it with me.'

'The guys in the newsroom sensed he was on to something,' Lu said. 'But he wouldn't tell them what it was. And Connie –' She sat back, folded her arms and squinted at me. 'Why do I get the feeling you're holding back on something too?'

I was holding back on a lot of things, but it occurred to me just then that Lu could help with one of them.

'You're right,' I said. 'I'm sorry. There's something I forgot to mention to the guards and it's got me worried. That's why I didn't tell you up front. You see, I missed that call from Mooney this morning. He left a voice message telling me he wanted to meet me. He sounded scared ... and he said some stuff I couldn't understand ...'

'Jesus, Connie. I'm usually the last one to worry about legalities, but in this case ... you have to hand that voice message over to the guards, assuming you haven't deleted it. Otherwise you'll be done for withholding evidence, obstructing the course of justice, all that shit.'

'I know, I know. I'll do it in the morning. I haven't deleted it.' I said. 'But before I report it, can you just listen to it, see if you can make sense out of what Mooney's saying?'

I quickly accessed my voicemail and handed her my phone. She pressed it to her ear and listened, her dark eyebrows slanted in a frown. Then she put down the phone and closed her eyes, sighing, 'The poor bastard.'

'Lu, "thirteen twenty". What did he mean?'

'No idea,' she said. 'Could be a price – like a sum of money, or a time – like a train time. A serial number, a code number, a year ...? Let me think about it – and the rest of the message too. Can you send it to me? There's something there that sounds familiar but I can't place it.'

Then Lu picked up the folded paper in front of her.

'Which brings me to Mooney's last story. According to the guys in the office, Pius Fogarty appeared at Mooney's desk first thing this morning. He grabbed Mooney by the front of his shirt and planted him one, right smack in the face. Mooney went down – he was the worse for wear from the night before – but Fogarty pulled him up, threw him back on his chair and wheeled him in front of a computer. He told him his article was irresponsible and would make innocent people suffer.'

Lu shrugged her shoulders and took a sip before continuing.

'Then Fogarty produced a page with an alternative version and, even though Mooney's nose was bleeding heavily, he stood over the poor schmuck and made him read it. Then he told Mooney to rewrite the story based on it, to do the right thing.'

'And the other people in the office just stood by and watched?'

'It's the newsroom, Connie,' Lu said. 'They like to see a bit of action.'

'That's how the story was revised?'

'Yeah. But even without all the fisticuffs, it seems that Fogarty was preaching to the converted. Mooney read Fogarty's version and started to work on it, with Fogarty watching him. I heard Mooney just knuckled down, typing, moving text round, trying not to bleed on the keyboard. What a pro.'

She shook her head and gazed into her pint before drinking deeply.

'And the story got submitted, or whatever you do?'

'Yeah. Then the pair of them went off quite amicably. The job done.'

'Together?'

'Together. That's the last time anyone saw Mooney, until ... you know,' she paused. 'Although, it wasn't the last time Mooney was in contact with the newsroom.'

'Sorry?'

'Just before eleven o'clock that morning, he submitted a new version of the story.'

'Just before he called me? What was different about it?'

'That's the problem,' she said. 'We don't know yet. With our submission system, you do everything online – upload articles, edit them and submit them. Before his original article was processed, a new version came in and replaced the first one. Here's a printed copy of the new version, the one that'll appear in the morning paper and online sometime tonight.'

She opened the page and glanced through the text. 'That's the trouble these days, a quick once over and everything goes in more or less as is. There's no sub-editing, in the traditional sense at least. It's not the same for every reporter, of course. But a senior guy like Mooney, he has authorisation to access the document after the editor had seen it.'

'Online? Using his phone?'

'Our system's not fully mobile yet. Mooney would have used his notebook and wifi to go online and make his changes.'

'Isn't the earlier version of the article stored somewhere in the system? Surely, somebody can access it and compare the versions.'

'Sure, there's a paper trail. But it's not accessible to everyone. Only the senior execs can get in there and they're not around until the morning. I tried to contact one of them, but got no response yet. And I want the information now.'

'So no proper version control in your online submission system,' I said disapprovingly.

We sadly contemplated our empty glasses and the impending digital dark age.

'I'll get this one,' I said and took the empties with me up to the bar.

'Same again?' the barman said.

'Thanks,' I said and then I saw him.

In the front lounge, down the long length of wooden counter, sitting by himself over a quiet pint, was Pius Fogarty.

32

THE GREAT THIRST

I took a deep breath and carried the drinks back to Lu O'Leary.

'I know how we can find out what Mooney changed.' I said as I put down the pints. 'Fogarty's here. He's sitting at the end of the bar.'

'No way,' Lu said. 'Who's he with?'

'No one at the moment, as far as I can see.'

'Quick,' she said, thrusting the printed page into my hand.

'What do you mean?'

'For God's sake,' she said. 'Go over there and show him the article. Ask him what's different about it. Do it now before we lose him.'

'Me? Why not both of us?'

The prospect of approaching Fogarty alone after our last encounter was not something I welcomed.

'Yes, you. This is a one woman job. Besides, you and Fogarty have a kind of a thing going on, don't you?'

I nearly choked on my drink.

'A what?

'Never mind,' she grinned. 'Just do it. I'll go through to the bar, I know some people over there.'

She nodded towards the door on the right, where I could hear laughter and the rumble of male voices coming from the bar. 'Old friends,' she said as she rose, taking her pint with her. 'Permanent fixtures.'

She waved encouragingly from the doorway before disappearing through it.

I sat there for a moment, shaky and nauseous. The last time I felt like this I was seriously seasick. I crept unsteadily towards the counter, and peeked through to the front lounge. Fogarty saw me immediately and, remaining expressionless, raised his glass to me.

No escape now. I picked up my drink, squared my shoulders and walked past the row of men seated along the bar.

'There you are,' Fogarty said as I approached. He didn't seem at all surprised to see me.

'So how are things?' he went on, pulling over a free bar stool. 'Any news?'

It was as if nothing had happened. I scanned his face for clues to what he was thinking. He looked me in the eye and gave nothing away.

I cleared my throat. 'How's your shoulder?'

'Despite the most recent assault on it, I'll survive. Thanks.'

'Look, I'm sorry about that. I didn't mean to hurt you ...'

He waved his hand.

'Forget it,' he said. 'Water under the bridge. Drink?'

Without waiting for a response, he caught the barman's eye and held up two fingers.

'Thanks,' I said and then, hesitatingly, 'did you hear about Jimmy Mooney?'

'I did,' he said and sighed. Finally, some humanity beneath the mask of insouciance. 'The poor fool. They got him in the end.'

'Who did, who got him?'

'The bad guys, Connie. That's who got him.' He shook his head, staring at the rows of bottles on the wall. As one of the bad guys himself, he didn't look like he was celebrating.

'Was it connected with Stevie's death?'

'To be honest,' he said, 'there's so much happening now, it's hard to know. I'll tell you this, though. Mooney knew he was in trouble. He'd got too close to the truth and he was going to be stopped. And I'll tell you something else. I don't know what he did or who he met but after I left him this morning, Mooney deliberately and knowingly went out to meet his fate. It was suicide.'

This was a new side to Fogarty. Sincere, open and honest were not the usual words that sprung to mind when his name came up. I decided to see if he'd continue in this mode if I pushed him. I unfolded the page Lu had given me and placed it on the counter.

He glanced at it briefly.

'It's the article, the one we rewrote this morning. What about it?'

'Look again,' I said, 'it's not *exactly* the same article you and Mooney worked on, the one Mooney submitted when you were there. This is a later version. Mooney resubmitted this sometime around eleven this morning. It superseded the earlier version. Any idea why he would have done that – or what changes he made to the article?'

He picked up the page and frowned while reading it carefully. He shook his head and went through it again word by word, tracking each one with his finger.

'Nothing's jumping out at me. Any change he made was minor, if not, it'd be obvious.'

'Whatever it was, it had to be significant in some way, otherwise why would he bother to resubmit?'

'The only thing I can see is that quotation or whatever it is at the end.'

Fogarty held the page up and ran his finger along the very last line. It was centred and in italics but it didn't have quotation marks.

'Let me have a look,' I said, taking the page. The last line said: *Clay is the end and Clay is the beginning.*

'What is it? Are you all right?' Fogarty noticed my hand shaking. I put down the page.

'Nothing, I'm fine,' I muttered and sank down on the bar stool. The words 'It's clay' roared in my ears, the last words Mooney may have spoken to anyone.

I took a deep breath and scrutinised the text again. The final line was completely unrelated to anything that went before.

'This quotation, it wasn't in the original?' I asked.

'I can't remember. It's the kind of thing Mooney might have tacked on to the end. He liked to sprinkle his work with classical quotations from Shakespeare and the like. He could be writing about a gangland contract killing where some poor fucker gets hit in front of his kids at a filling station and Mooney'll throw in *"What a piece of work is a man ..."* He was always at it. Probably felt it lifted the prose, ennobled it or something.'

He took a deep draught and tilted his glass, studying it for a moment.

'Do you know what?' he said. 'We are a nation cursed by literature.'

'And by bar room philosophy.'

'Agreed,' he said and examined the page again. 'Like I said, I can't be sure that line wasn't there when we submitted the piece at around ten this morning. I allowed Mooney artistic licence to change the wording and add his signature style, so long as the thrust of it was what I wanted. If he added a line at the end, it may not have registered with me. But I can check it.'

'What do you mean?'

'I printed the version we submitted. You obviously think this is important – that Mooney took the time to make the change and send it in. And you think Mooney was on to something.'

I nodded.

'As it happens, so do I.'

He stood up and drained his glass.

'The printed version's back in my place. I'll check it and I'll let you know if I find anything. Can I keep this page?'

I nodded. 'Go ahead. That quotation at the end sounds familiar ... What's it from?'

'Beats me,' he said and called over the barman.

'Hey, Tommy, what do you make of this?'

The barman came over and read the line on the page.

'Sounds a bit like Kavanagh, but it's not. The structure is similar but the words are wrong.'

'Patrick Kavanagh?' I asked.

'Yeah,' said the barman. 'Reminds me of the first line from *The Great Hunger*. Only it's not. Maybe it's biblical.'

He went off to serve a customer.

'The barmen here know everything,' Fogarty said. 'If that line was in the article all along, it was one of those typical

Mooney embellishments. He could have slung it in on the spur of the moment and garbled it. I'd put him under a bit of pressure.'

A bit of pressure from your fist, I thought, but kept it to myself. I rose to go too. I'd just realised the time. I had to meet Kitty.

'But if it wasn't in the first version,' I said, 'and it was the only change, well, it would mean something, wouldn't it?'

'It would. Are you heading off?'

'Kitty's finishing work down on Middle Abbey Street. It's her first time since Stevie's death and she's nervous. I promised I'd meet her.'

'I'll walk you to the bridge,' he said. 'It's on my way.'

It seemed the most natural thing in the world. I hadn't forgotten about Fogarty's murky past. Or that he was recovering from a recent gunshot wound from when somebody tried to kill him. I suppose I should have been more careful. But it looked like our truce was back on. The bridge was only two minutes away, literally around the corner. What could possibly happen in that short time?

33

LOVELY

I turned to the barman as Fogarty made for the door,

'Would you mind telling Lu O'Leary I had to go? She's in the bar. Tell her Connie'll call her later.'

'Certainly, love,' the barman said. 'Take care, now.'

I had no time to go round to Lu and even if I had, I wasn't inclined to inform her I was going anywhere with Fogarty. I could just imagine her eyebrows arching with amusement.

Outside, Fogarty was standing in the doorway, carefully looking first one way and then the other. Without taking his eyes off the dark street, he gestured for me to come forward.

'Looks ok,' he said. 'Come on.'

'Aren't you being just a tiny bit dramatic?' I said as we moved away from the light of the doorway and past the ugly office buildings that dwarfed the old pub and disfigured Poolbeg Street. A few posters fluttered from the office gateway opposite from when the building was occupied by housing protesters.

'You can't be too careful,' he said, as he walked closely by my side, grasping my elbow firmly. He looked over his shoulder.

'Something's wrong. I can feel it ...'

'You're making me nervous.'

'Good, you should be nervous. I keep telling you to be more careful. You keep going the way you're going and you'll need a personal bodyguard.'

'Are you applying for the position? I hear you used to work in security.'

'Ha!' he said, 'That was a long time ago. What else did you hear?'

For once, I kept quiet.

'The trial. What are they saying these days? Not that I care.'

'I just heard something about you being accused and ... um, acquitted.'

Fogarty checked behind him again and, still holding my arm, he stopped walking.

'As you're so interested ... I was charged with the murder of Eddie Riordan, my business partner. Eddie'd got involved in some dodgy transactions with some powerful people. He was in too deep, never told me a thing. Hardly a day goes by without me thinking about him. I lost my business, my home, everything. But worse than all that, I lost the best friend I ever had.'

I noticed he omitted to say he was innocent of the charge. But if I'd thought Fogarty was distant and detached earlier, there was no sign of it now. I couldn't see his face but his voice was tight with pain.

'I'm sorry,' I said. 'I –'

Fogarty had tensed. His fingers dug into my arm.

'Quick,' he said. 'Move!'

An engine roared and tyres squealed as a car appeared from nowhere and tore down the empty street at top speed. It was heading directly towards us.

Fogarty half-dragged, half-pushed me into a recessed doorway as the car mounted the footpath and drove straight at us. It missed us by inches and only then because we were flattened into the back of the doorway. If we hadn't moved the instant we did, we would have been dead. The car swept past, screeched to a halt and then reversed rapidly, stopping just beside the doorway. There was no escape, we were trapped.

Fogarty moved to shield me from what was coming. Pressed against me, I felt his heart thumping, his body taut, his breathing short and fast. And no Kevlar vest. Over his shoulder, I saw the car idling at the kerb, its engine running, its headlights turned off, its dark windows obscuring the identity of its occupants. The window on the front passenger's side slid down slowly. In the darkness, I saw the flash of something metallic, but it vanished just as quickly. The dark window rolled up again and the car took off at high speed, screaming around the corner and off down Townsend Street.

The smell of burning rubber filled the air in its wake. I began to shake from head to foot. To my horror, I felt hot tears coursing down my face. Oh for God's sake, I told myself, don't be so stupid. Despite all I'd been through, I hadn't cried in years. I didn't know I still could.

'It's ok. It's all right now.' Fogarty was holding me so tight I could hardly breath. He pulled back a little to look in my face.

'Ah God,' he said and he pushed back the hair that was sticking to my face.

'They're gone now. Don't worry, they won't be back.'

He used his fingers to stop the tears streaming down my face. And then he leaned in and began to kiss them away, his mouth moving down slowly to find mine. One of his arms wound tight around my waist, his other hand cradled my head, his body pressed hard against me. Caught by surprise, I forgot to breathe for an instant. Then my shaking stopped as I reached for him, lifting my face to his.

'Well, isn't this lovely.'

A familiar male voice announced the unwelcome appearance of Detective Inspector Brady.

Fogarty pulled away from me, slowly and gently, briefly touching my face before turning to Brady.

'Fucking cops,' he said. 'Never there when you need them. Then they show up when you definitely don't.'

He glared at Brady. 'Where were you about two minutes ago when we were deliberately run down by a car and were possibly about to become the victims of a drive-by?'

'I've no idea what you're talking about,' Brady said. 'I saw no car. But I can tell you where I was. I was informed you'd left Mulligan's and I was on my way to find you, Pius Fogarty, to take you in for questioning.'

'Are you arresting me?'

'I have the power to arrest you if you do not cooperate.'

'What the hell for?'

'We want to question you in relation to the grievous assault causing serious bodily harm on the journalist, Jimmy Mooney at his place of work at nine o'clock this morning and again, at a place unknown, at between eleven and eleven thirty this morning.'

'You're joking.'

'I am deadly serious. We have witnesses for at least one of the assaults. I want you to come with me to the station now.'

Brady spoke into his radio.

'Yeah, I've got him here. Poolbeg Street, outside the Corn Exchange apartments. Yes, where the *Irish Press* used to be. You can drive round.'

The headlights of an unmarked police car appeared at the end of the street. Detective Nuala Rossiter was driving. She pulled in to the kerb beside us and stopped the car, leaving the engine running. She got out and stood beside the car, carefully taking in the scene. Fogarty clasped my hand now, his fingers tightly coiled round mine. I didn't want to let go.

Rossiter glanced at me curiously before opening the door of the rear passenger seat.

'I have to go with them, Connie,' Fogarty said as he disentangled his fingers from mine. 'Are you ok? Will you be all right?'

I finally found myself able to speak again, just about.

'Yeah, yeah. I'll be fine.'

'They were just trying to scare us, that's all,' he said.

I managed a smile. 'They did a good job.'

I knew he meant that if whoever was in that car really wanted to kill us, they would have done so.

Fogarty put his arms around me again. It was the most comforting thing I'd felt in a very long time.

'Call you later,' he said.

'Let's go,' Brady said. 'Come on Fogarty, you're about to help the police with their inquiries. Again.'

As Fogarty got in the car, Brady continued. 'And Connie, thanks for informing me about your friend here assaulting Jimmy Mooney. That was very helpful. I'm looking forward to more useful tip-offs from you, as we agreed.'

He might have hit me I was so shocked. It had at least the same effect on Fogarty, judging by the look he gave me through the open car door. Brady closed the door and then got into the passenger seat beside Rossiter, who had already started the engine. The police car vanished around the corner leaving me standing, stunned, on Poolbeg Street.

34

TENNER

'Tenner.'

I was propped against the wall, wondering if I'd stopped shaking enough now to be able to walk, still trying to process what had just happened with Fogarty. A young man had stopped on the far side of the street.

'Excuse me?' I asked.

'Tenner,' he said again. 'For ... you know.'

It slowly dawned on me what he was proposing. He was slight, probably in his early twenties, with cropped fair hair and a sharp little pinched face like an unsuccessful rat. Despite which, he seemed quite self-assured. I tried to muster my dignity and make an appropriate response.

I cleared my throat. 'You're barking up the wrong tree, young man. And anyway,' I continued, ever-helpful, 'you're in the wrong place for, em, what you're after. You'll need to go up to Mount Street or Fitzwilliam Square, somewhere like that.'

What was I doing, acting like a tourist advisor for the little shit and me in a state of nervous collapse? The guy walked away up the street, his hands in the pockets of his light raincoat. My phone buzzed and as I fumbled for it in my pocket, I looked after him. A wave of incredulous rage came over me. What did he mean, a *tenner*? I knew times were hard and all that. But a fucking *tenner*?

He halted at the top of the road and our eyes met.

'Are you sure?' he called back, as if concerned that I was missing an important opportunity. Then he dug his hands deeper into his pockets and walked away.

The text was from Kitty.

'Where r u? Break-in at the cafe. Call me NOW.'

I called her.

'Are you all right, Connie? I was worried something'd happened to you. Hannah phoned. She said the cafe shutter's pushed halfway up and kind of crooked. And the door's wide open. Where are you – are you in the café?'

'No,' I said as calmly as I could. I'd begun walking. 'I'm on –'

I looked up to check the street sign.

'Hawkins Street, just turning the corner.'

Now I could see the lights and the traffic along the river. 'I'm coming onto the quays ... there's a bridge ...'

'Rosie Hackett Bridge,' Kitty said. 'I'll meet you on it, I'm coming up the other side. Are you ok? You sound a bit weird again.'

Not half as weird as I feel, I muttered to myself.

'Jesus!' she said when she caught sight of me. 'Your eyes! What happened to them? You haven't been crying, have you? Did somebody hurt you?'

'No, no,' I forced a laugh. 'Something in my contacts – stings like mad when it happens. Come on –' I flagged down a passing taxi, 'we'd better get home.'

'North Wall Quay, as fast as you can,' I told the driver.

He took a quick look at me in his mirror and must have decided on the basis of what he saw, to forgo the usual 'Out for the night, ladies?' type of banter.

'I'll have yiz there in a jiffy,' was his sensible response as he started the meter, raised the volume on the radio and took off like a rocket. An R&B guitar filled the car as the singer sang '*Everyone acts crazy, Yes or no means maybe ...*'

'Cheers, Rory,' I whispered, watching the lights in the river flash past as we were thrown backwards and the taxi sped down the quays.

'You're smiling now, Connie,' Kitty said. 'Are you sure you're ok? Apart from the break-in, is anything else wrong?'

'Everything's wrong, Kitty.' I was laughing now. It was probably hysteria. I gave her an edited version of events, leaving out the fact that Mooney had died.

'Fogarty was arrested for assaulting Mooney this morning. The guards think he had something to do with Mooney getting attacked later on in the day too.'

'No way! And how's Mooney now?'

'No better,' I said, truthfully.

It had just occurred to me that my voicemail from Mooney could possibly exonerate Fogarty from the later assault charge. My phone battery was about to go. I'd forward it to Rossiter later.

'How was the non-date? Did you find out anything from Brady?'

'I found out that everything they say about him being a bollocks is completely true.'

'That's nothing new.'

'I know. But afterwards I met Lu O'Leary, you know, the journalist? She thinks there's something important in an article he wrote, one he first wrote with Fogarty and changed later on. But we don't know because Fogarty's been arrested and we need to see the original article Fogarty printed out.'

'I'm not with you,' Kitty said.

I was about to explain but as the car slowed at the North Wall Quay I lost the power to speak. Silently looking out at the Silver Bullet Café, I paid the driver. The hateful shutter had been forced open and now hung at an awkward angle, slightly buckled. I almost felt sorry for it. The café door swung wide open and gaping, its lock smashed and broken.

'Good luck, girls.' the cabbie said as he drove off. He sounded like he meant it.

Kitty and I stood at the door, neither of us keen to enter.

'When did Hannah call you?' I asked.

'Just before I called you,' Kitty said. 'Maybe about a half an hour ago. She noticed it on her way past, you know, to Recovery.'

'To where?'

'Recovery. It's a new thing Ozzie's hosting next door on Monday nights. That's what I was repping for tonight. Listen –' she put her hand to her ear and leaned in the direction of the club next door.

'I can't hear anything,' I said.

'Exactly! It's quiet. Very chilled. You should go.'

'Nice try, Kitty. You're a good rep, but clubs are not for me.'

'How do you know?' she said. 'All kinds of people go there. You'd be surprised.'

'I really, *really* need to go to bed now. But what if there's somebody still inside? Would thirty minutes give whoever broke in enough time to do whatever they wanted and get away?'

I made up my mind and moved towards the door and the darkness within.

'I'm going in.'

35

GAVIN

Inside the café was quiet except for the sound of trickling water. I crept slowly towards the light switches and listened again. Nothing. When the lights came on, my heart sank at the scene before me. Every drawer in the kitchen had been emptied, every cupboard turned inside out. Even the fridge had been rifled, with food containers and drinks removed and lined up in front of it, its door left gaping. That's where the trickling came from. The only thing that was left undisturbed was the till. It was not that kind of break-in.

I closed the fridge door and checked the storeroom. Again, the smaller items had been taken out and piled up on one side, the larger boxes were up-ended. In the toilets, the tops of the cisterns had been removed. The laundry basket stood empty and the washing machine looked like it had been disembowelled, with wet towels and tea towels spilling out, some coiled on the floor. The unlatched back door and shed door swung gently. They'd gone through everything in the yard, including the bins. Whoever broke in was looking for something and knew exactly what it was. I noticed that the cellar door remained locked and was glad they'd missed it, as I had no desire to ever go down there. Then I heard a cry from the kitchen.

'Connie! Look at the coffee machine!' Kitty pointed with astonishment at the bullet hole in the side of the machine.

'Oh, that's ok,' I said. 'Somebody shot it earlier on.' Pity they didn't disembowel it too, I thought, regarding it with loathing.

Kitty started to say something but then clearly thought the better of it. She picked up a milk carton.

'Will I start putting things back?' she asked.

'Maybe just the food,' I said, holding my phone. 'I'd better call the guards.'

I by-passed the regular emergency services and went directly to Detective Rossiter. As I reported the latest incident from the North Wall Quay, I heard her sigh. She sounded tired.

'All of our cars are out at the moment, Connie. We're completely swamped. Just make sure the place is secure and leave it. I'll get someone down to you as soon as possible, but it might be the morning. Sorry.'

'Leave it? And go where, exactly?' I muttered, staring at my phone as the battery died and with it the possibility of forwarding Mooney's voicemail to help Fogarty. I plugged it in to the charger in the kitchen and waited for signs of life.

And then I heard it. A sound coming from upstairs. I shushed Kitty and pointed upwards. There it was again. A definite rustling, then a muffled thump and the sound of movement.

'Oh God!' Kitty said, terrified. 'Call Detective Rossiter again. Tell her to come and help us.'

'She can't,' I said. 'They've no one available.'

I listened again. I could still hear the rustling.

'Look, we can't stay down here cowering all night. I'm going to go up there as quietly as I can and have a look. You go to the door and if I'm not back in five minutes, run and get help.'

Kitty nodded and moved to the front of the café.

I couldn't believe what I'd just said. The words seemed to come from a different person. With the greatest reluctance and a pounding heart, I moved towards the stairs. A thought occurred and I went back to examine the selection of kitchen implements hanging from hooks on the rail above the cooker. My hand hovered over the choice of weapons, passing over the spatulas and ladles, finally selecting a black cast-iron frying pan. I added a small sharp knife from the drawer. Not ideal, I thought, but an improvement on a cake slice and a hell of a lot better than nothing.

Brandishing the frying pan in one hand and the knife in the other, I went back to the stairs and crept silently upwards, stopping every couple of steps to listen. The noise had stopped.

On the half-landing where the stairs turned, I looked through the open doorway of Kitty's room. Even in the dark, I could see clothes, shoes and books thrown about everywhere. Nothing unusual there, I thought. Good luck to anyone trying to rifle through that.

The little bathroom beside Kitty's room had been well turned-over too, but there was no sign of life anywhere. As I rounded the bend on the stairs to go up to my room and so-called office, the noise started again. I grasped the hand rail and jumped as the frying pan clanged against the bannister. The knife clattered as it landed somewhere below. The noise in my room changed abruptly to a series of thumps, then stopped again.

'Who's there?' I called. 'The guards are on their way. They'll be here in a minute. Come out and show yourself.'

I grasped the frying pan more firmly to give myself courage and called out again, this time more confidently.

'I'm warning you. I have a weapon.'

I heard a strangled sound and peered through the doorway. The window was open and the lace curtains billowed in the breeze. It was dark, but the light coming through the window from the streetlight outside was enough to show that my room had been ransacked. My suitcase was emptied, my few clothes dumped out and my books and papers scattered everywhere. Out of the corner of my eye I saw a movement. There was something on my bed.

'Stay where you are,' I said, 'And don't move!'

I snapped on the light.

The gannet gave a strangled squawk and made a couple of hops. Then he lifted his tail and deposited a milky glutinous blob on my sheets.

'You dirty bastard,' I said and went for him with the frying pan.

The gannet flew up to the top of the wardrobe and stood there, silently observing me with an injured air.

I looked around for something to throw at him and stopped. I scanned the far corner of the room. Something was missing.

Kitty appeared behind me and spotted the gannet on the wardrobe.

'Jesus, what's that? It's feckin' ginormous. Is it an eagle?'

'It's a bloody pest and I'm going to wring its neck the minute I get my hands on it.'

I went over to the corner and poked around, hoping that what I thought was missing had slipped down beneath the mess on the floor.

'Plus it reminds me of a horrible ex-boyfriend from years ago. He was a rugby player. They have the same crooked beak and disgusting habits. Should have wrung his neck too. Gavin.'

'Huh?'

'The boyfriend. He was called Gavin.'

'Oh right. What are you looking for? Is something missing?'

I did a last check and turned to her as soon as I was sure.

'Yes, something's missing. It's Stevie's painting.'

We searched her room to make sure the painting wasn't just misplaced, but it was definitely gone. So that's what the intruders had been after. And presumably they turned the place upside-down looking for more pictures or sketchbooks.

'Kitty, you know your friend who noticed the café had been broken into?'

'Hannah.'

'Did she see anything else? Anyone inside, a car outside?'

'She didn't say, but we could ask her. She's in the club.'

'You mean next door?'

I chased the seabird down off the wardrobe with a mop and he hopped out the window, but remained on the windowsill. Looking around at the chaos, I realised that the likelihood of getting any sleep here tonight was remote. Rossiter had advised me to secure the place and leave.

'Ok, Gavin,' I told the gannet as I pulled down the window sash. 'You're on sentry duty.'

He appeared to take the instruction on board.

I grabbed the sheets off my bed and threw them in the washing machine, asking Kitty to make sure any perishables were back in the fridge. Then I found a piece of string, pocketed my phone and headed for the door.

'Come on, Kitty,' I said. 'We're going clubbing.'

The last place I needed to be was somewhere full of drunken revellers, heaving bodies and pounding music, but we had nowhere else to go. I ineffectively tied the door closed with the string and went to yank down the shutter. As I did so, I saw a reflection in the window of a crazy woman, her face streaked with mascara and her hair sticking out in all directions. She wore a dress that was once reasonably presentable but now looked like something out of the recycling bin.

'Who cares,' I muttered. 'Apart from the neighbours, it's not like I'm going to see anyone I know.'

36

TONIC

The bouncers flashed their gold fillings and smiled their most diplomatic smiles as I followed Kitty up the steps to the front door of the club. If Recovery@Stalag17 had a smart dress code, they were waiving it for the neighbours.

'Come on,' Kitty said, grinning widely as she linked me. 'Let's go find Hannah.'

She led me through the marble-tiled hall with its internal fanlight, creamy plasterwork and peacock wallpaper into a huge space with a bar running most of its entire length. Soft light bathed the room, its tone altering slowly from warm rose to gold. Sofas and wing-backed armchairs were arranged in groups on the wide timber boards and around the enormous open fireplaces blazing with burning logs. The room was at least triple height in places. Exposed brickwork went all the way up to the roof through bleached joists and past floating ceiling roses hung with ornate old brass chandeliers. Metal and timber stairways ran between the floors, and an antique brass-and-mahogany lift glided up and down through the levels. Along the bar, altar candles burned in tall candelabras and hundreds more candles flickered throughout the space on every surface and at every level.

At the far end of the room, a projection of a rolling seascape covered the entire back wall with waves gently lapping the skirting boards. An extremely tall African man stood at a keyboard, motionless except for barely perceptible finger movements, making strange but melodic sounds that were almost hypnotic.

'He says he's Somalian shaman. An actual witchdoctor,' Kitty said. 'Look, there's Hannah.'

She pointed to a group, some sitting on a large green velvet sofa, some on a threadbare oriental rug in front of it. Hannah smiled when she saw us and I let Kitty go ahead to talk to her while I stood for a moment and looked around.

Kitty was right, people of all ages were here. If they'd had a card school, Aggie would be right at home. I felt that horrible knot of anxiety in my stomach again as I thought of her. I checked my phone for news from Brady. Again, nothing.

'Constance! Don't look so worried, you're in Recovery now!'

It was Ozzie, first air-kissing me and then determinedly steering me by the arm towards the bar.

'You need a special Recovery tonic,' he said. 'I insist.'

He gave a nod to one of the barmen who was busily cutting limes and muddling bunches of mint. The drink, when it appeared, was bright green and foaming. I took a tentative sip, watched by the barman and Ozzie, my solicitous carers. It was delicious and instantly invigorating.

'So good,' I smiled through a pale green moustache, feeling better already.

'Let me show you around,' Ozzie said, taking my arm again and marching me down the room.

'It's not always pretty like this. This is only for Recovery, which is something I decided to provide as a public service. You picked a good night. Most of the other club nights are a little more teutonic – steel mesh curtains and iron candelabras, very different sounds. Still cool and alternative, of course. People rely on me for that sort of thing.'

'It's not at all what I expected,' I said.

'Naturally,' Ozzie said, leading me up a short flight of timber stairs past a landing to another stairway. As I went to follow him to the next level, I heard someone call my name. I looked back and saw Lu O'Leary having drinks with some people in an alcove. The permanent fixtures from Mulligan's, I assumed.

'Hey, Connie,' she called again. 'Come back! I have something for you.'

'I'll follow you up,' I told Ozzie and went back to Lu.

'What, no Fogarty?' she said. 'I'm disappointed.'

I shook my head violently, as if to shake off the memory of recent events on Poolbeg Street.

'Did you find out the difference between Mooney's articles?'

'No, Fogarty got called away somewhere,' I said, hoping my vagueness wouldn't make her suspicious. 'He said he'll take a look as soon as he gets a chance.'

'Pity,' she said. 'Look, here's the number of an art historian friend of mine. She'll help you figure out what Stevie was up to with that painting.'

I took the number and promised I'd call the art historian in the morning, not mentioning that Stevie's painting had been stolen. I didn't want to think about that. In the past few minutes, I'd been feeling less panicky, no doubt due to the therapeutic effects of Ozzie's Recovery tonic. I didn't care, I just wanted to stay that way for as long as possible.

'Oh and Connie,' Lu called me back again. 'I think I figured out one of the things Mooney said in your ... *voicemail.*' She stage-whispered the last word.

'Go on.'

'It's not "thud", it's "fud". You know, F-U-D.'

'Ah, yes,' I said with no idea what she was talking about. 'Brilliant. Thanks, Lu.'

I went up the stairs after Ozzie. Almost at the top, a large bull of a man pushed against me as he rushed past, nearly knocking me down. The behaviour was completely out of place here, as was the man. Detective Inspector Brady's face was scarlet, his eyes wild with anger. He and I looked at one another in surprise for a moment. As he started back down the stairs without a word of apology, he muttered, 'Jesus, you certainly get around.'

'I could say the same for you,' I called after him. 'And what about Aggie? Did you ...'

'Not fucking now,' he said as he disappeared around the corner.

I stared after him. There's a guy who could do with a Recovery tonic, I thought. He probably hadn't even bothered to call Las Vegas.

I wondered where Ozzie had got to and wandered along a gallery which was bordered with a timber balustrade and had an excellent view of the whole ground level. I saw Kitty and Hannah down there amongst their friends, chatting and laughing. A couple of familiar-looking figures perched at the bar, engrossed in conversation.

'Oh God, no,' I thought, 'not Karen Donlon and Tanya.'

But even my arch-enemy seemed to be relaxed here with no fire-spitting or death threats in evidence. All the same, I thought I'd steer clear of her just to be on the safe side. Then

I recognised Dr Rose Madden's red dress amongst a group of dancers. I examined the liquid in my glass wondering if it had miraculously improved my eyesight. The doctor danced around with her arms outstretched and I smiled, happy to see her happy. She spotted me as she turned and whirled closer.

'I sent you ...' she called. But I couldn't catch the end of her sentence.

'What?' I called back. 'I can't hear you.'

She laughed and, miming a phone call, shouted, 'Tomorrow!' before spinning back to the other dancers.

I strolled further down the gallery and peered into a semi-enclosed space which was like a small private meeting room. Inside, a long refectory table held a couple of tall silver candelabras, platters of fruit and decanters of wine. Silhouettes of five or six people encircled the table, most of them with their backs to me. In the centre, clearly visible and facing me, was Aleka Marr, with her arm around Ozzie in a casual but proprietorial way.

'Wow,' I thought, backing away, not wanting to intrude. 'The rumours about Ozzie and Aleka are true.'

But it was too late for my discreet withdrawal. I'd been seen.

37

ALWAYS OPTIONS

'Connie!' Aleka called me from the table. 'Over here! Come and join us.'

She smiled and pulled up a chair.

'Here, have something to drink. Have you eaten?'

She poured me a glass of wine and loaded a plate with cheese, figs, quince jelly. I realised I was starving.

'Meet my colleagues,' she said. 'I've roped them in for Bicknor Day on Friday, whether they like it or not! This is Claude Leyton. Genius civic designer.'

Aleka indicated the man directly opposite her. It was the good-looking guy from the café, the American I thought I recognised every day for the past few days. Now I remembered where I'd first seen him. It was on the flight from Amsterdam. He was my rescuer, the passenger in the next seat who'd tackled the dental tourist pest and made him shut up.

'Hi,' I said. 'I think we've met before.'

He met my smile with a questioning look in his warm, hazel eyes. He didn't recognise me and was trying hard not to be rude.

'I'm so sorry,' he said, shaking my hand. 'I'm afraid I'm a little tired and I don't ...'

'My mistake,' I said. 'Terrible eyesight. I've confused you with someone else.'

'*Nobody's* like this guy,' Aleka said. 'I should know, we go *way* back.'

She put her arm around my shoulder and gave me a squeeze. 'I love bringing my favourite people together.'

Aleka enthusiastically introduced David Donaldson, Rick Kornell and Nathan Penrose. International cookie-cutter corporate types, they were healthy, handsome and practically robotic. Besides Leyton himself and Nathan Penrose, an African American with an accent from the Deep South and the build of a prop forward, it was hard to tell where they were from. If the other two were American, they were not of the talkative variety. Penrose feigned some interest as we shook hands. Donaldson and Kornell just looked bored and uncomfortable. I was sure we'd all been on the same flight from Amsterdam last week.

'How do you like it here?' I asked for something to say.

Zero response. I wondered if they'd heard me.

'The guys arrived only a few days ago,' Aleka said. 'Since then they've had a very heavy schedule, not a minute's rest and no time for any sightseeing. I think I have them worn out already.'

She smiled all round.

'Was that Detective Inspector Brady I saw going down the stairs?' I said to break the silence again.

'He had to leave,' Aleka said. 'Busy man. He's been a great help with my Bicknor Programme but he's totally overstretched at the moment. Claude's taking over the arrangements for Friday.'

'Ah, the Bicknor Programme,' I said, unsuccessfully pretending I remembered anything about it.

'Don't tell me you're not involved in Bicknor Day – and my Bicknor Programme has passed you by?' Aleka said in mock horror. 'I don't know how you've escaped. On Friday we have an event in St Patrick's Cathedral reinstating the medieval commemorative brass of Archbishop Alexander de Bicknor. You *must* come. I'll arrange an invitation to the unveiling and the banquet afterwards. Everyone will be there!'

'Alexander de Bicknor?' I repeated, dimly recollecting snippets of media coverage about the discovery of his missing memorial. I'd never heard of him until yesterday. Not that I was any expert on medieval Dublin clergymen but he sounded totally obscure. I decided they must be running out of people to honour.

'He was a man of unbelievable energy and vision,' Aleka said. 'Hounded by actuaries and a victim of political disfavour, his reforms and far-sighted civic ventures were forgotten for centuries. You know he founded this country's first university, the University of St Patrick's? It's high time his name was properly commemorated. What better way than the Bicknor Programme to improve life in central Dublin?'

Ozzie disentangled himself and rose to his feet.

'Sorry, Aleka. I have to look after something,' he said, raising her hand to his lips. He smiled at her slowly. 'See you in a little while, darling. Connie, I'm leaving you in good hands.'

There was no trace of the alley cat antagonism I'd witnessed between Ozzie and Aleka earlier. They made a striking, if unusual couple, the golden girl of commerce and the young prince of darkness. Even the age difference seemed to add to their allure. It still appeared an odd relationship, but who was I to talk about odd relationships?

Ozzie walked down the gallery and stood at the balustrade for a few seconds, surveying the scene below, before moving down the stairs.

'I'm glad you're here, Connie,' Aleka said. 'I was just about to contact you. Look, something's come up and I can't meet you in the morning as planned. Do you mind? I'm really sorry.'

'Not at all,' I said. 'I know you're busy.'

'I feel terrible – but now that you're here ...' She turned to her guests. 'Guys, you won't think I'm rude if I talk to Connie for few minutes, will you?'

Again, there was no response from them, but Aleka seemed to communicate with her business associates via telepathic means.

'Thanks, guys,' she said and, leaving them to their personality deficits, turned her full attention to me.

'Now, Connie, I made a few calls as I promised. That compulsory purchase notification you got is the real deal. Is Aggie back yet?'

I shook my head.

'You'll have to act on her behalf and respond to the communication. Tell them you'll enter into negotiations. It won't commit you to anything but'll buy you some time. Otherwise they'll take legal action and move to take over the property anyway. Sorry about putting it so bluntly, but there's no other way to say this.'

'And what about the negotiations? Is there an option to say no, that we don't want to be "purchased"? Leave things the way they are.'

'Well,' she said slowly. 'There are always options, but in this case they're pretty limited. You won't be able to leave things the way they are. You can play for time for Aggie's sake. But even that will take work.'

I couldn't believe it. How was I going to tell Aggie? She'd left me in charge and only days later her sixty-six-year-old business was heading for closure.

'You're saying there's nothing I can do?'

'There may be something ...' Aleka was thoughtful. 'Maybe something similar to the route Ozzie's taking – you know he's also received a letter from the Council? The ownership of this building here is legally unclear, which makes it problematic. Missing deeds. I don't know if you're in the same position.'

'No, Aggie owns the building from back in the year dot – and I'm pretty sure she has the deeds and proof of purchase.'

'No good, I'm afraid,' Aleka said. 'Won't make any difference to the council's compulsory purchase plans. If anything, clear ownership makes it easier for them.'

'What's Ozzie going to do?'

'It's a bit circuitous, but it should work out so that he can stay in business for a while at least. He's going into partnership with me. Heartbeat will nominally take over the building.'

'Don't the Council want to redevelop the property?'

'They do. That's inevitable. You and your neighbours are in a prime location at a time when there's huge demand for space and very little availability. For Ozzie, our partnership means the changes can be negotiated over time.'

I drank some wine and tried to absorb the information. I didn't want to be rude, but being able to buy a little more time didn't seem like much of an improvement to me.

'You could do this for me – and Aggie?' I asked without enthusiasm.

'I'm not sure. I probably shouldn't have said anything. I have to be careful not to be seen to bend the rules or do favours for friends.' She gave my arm an encouraging squeeze. 'But if you're interested, I'll see what I can do. What do you think?'

'I'd be interested in anything you can suggest,' I said.

'Cool,' she said. 'Meanwhile, don't forget to respond to that notification.'

I promised her I'd respond, and then something else occurred to me.

'Is the Sunrise Hotel under threat too? I mean, would Fogarty have got one of those letters?'

'He may have,' Aleka said. 'But the Sunrise Hotel has even more immediate problems, largely due to the behaviour of its manager ...'

Her phone buzzed and she pursed her lips as she checked it, then looked back at me.

'You know, I'd be very surprised if the Sunrise Hotel survives for much longer.'

38

MEMENTO MORI

Four am and there I was, alone in a nightclub, too tired to sleep and too scared to go home. How bloody pathetic.

Aleka had rushed off after her phone call, having given me a consolatory hug and assuring me that everything would be all right. I wanted to believe her. Her colleagues were gone too. Strains of music and the murmur of voices rose from the floors below, but this level, including my alcove, was completely deserted. Stalactites of wax hung from the candelabras and the almost-spent candles battled to stay burning, their feeble light flickering, like a faulty old movie projector, over the debris on the table. Something was floating on the surface of my wine, it looked like an insect's broken wing. I pushed away the wine glass and my plate of flaccid fruit and congealed cheese, feeling sick.

In the bathroom, I splashed cold water on my face and felt a little better, so I did it some more. The cool breeze coming from the open window felt even more refreshing. I stepped up on the cream-painted heating pipes that ran around the room just above skirting board level and pushed the window open fully, leaning my elbows on the sill and thrusting my head and shoulders out as far as I could, greedily drinking in the night air.

It was still dark. Dawn wouldn't be for another hour or so, but there was already a sense of lightness in the sky around the dark hulks of the neighbouring deserted buildings, defusing the shadows on the derelict site behind us that wouldn't be derelict for much longer. A newly-arrived crane crouched over next door's construction site. I raised my face to the fresh sea air and closed my eyes, then opened them again as I heard a car door close and the murmur of voices somewhere down below.

The window was set into the side of a return and overlooked the side street running alongside the building. My view was partly obscured by the high, stone boundary wall crowned with the locally-ubiquitous razor wire. Stretching out as far as I could, I saw, illuminated by a streetlight, the roof and front section of a car and the figures of a man and a woman standing beside it. I stiffened and caught my breath. The car was Detective Nuala Rossiter's, the one we'd travelled in to the Mater Hospital. The couple's identity was unmistakable. I didn't need to see their faces to know it was Nuala Rossiter and Pius Fogarty. They stood close, engaged in intense conversation. I watched, almost choking, as Fogarty put his arms around her and held her in a deep embrace, their shadows merging. Finally, she whispered something, got in her car and drove off. Fogarty stood under the streetlight for a moment. Then he moved across the street and was lost to sight.

I began to breathe again, hard and furious. I'd been beating myself up over that bastard being stuck in the police station, feeling guilty and thinking that I'd betrayed him. Well, he was obviously well able to look after himself – and he had certain sections of the police force looking after him too. This explains a lot, I thought, my face burning despite the cool air. No wonder Nuala Rossiter had reacted so strangely whenever Fogarty's name was mentioned. God knows what else the pair of them were involved in. I drew back from the window and turned to go, completely forgetting that I was standing on a pipe about a foot above floor level. Stepping out into thin air, I seemed to hover for a second and then slammed down on my knees on the hard tiled floor. Pain rocketed through my body.

'Ow, ow, ow ...!' I howled as my vision darkened and the pain intensified. Instead of passing out, somehow I struggled to my feet. I hobbled out the door, bent almost double, clawing at the walls for support, stricken with physical and emotional agony.

'Here, allow me,' a quiet male voice said, and I felt a pair of strong arms around me, holding me straight. I looked up into the calm face of Claude Leyton, who apparently was rescuing me for the second time.

He half-carried me to an open timber deck on the far side of the return. It was probably a smoking area, but there was no-one out there now. A wood-burning stove glowed in the corner beside a seating area and it was here that Leyton guided me, helping me into a rattan chair. I moaned as quietly as possible as I bent my knees to sit.

'Can I get you anything?' he asked, still standing.

'Jesus. Sorry, I mean, no thanks,' I said as I prised off my shoes and slowly eased my legs onto a stool, raising the hem of my dress to inspect the damage. The dress was torn, my knees bruised and bleeding and starting to swell alarmingly.

'Oh God,' I said as I glimpsed something sharp and gleaming in the middle of the mess of blood on my right knee. 'Glass. There must have been broken glass on the floor ...'

'Sit back,' Leyton said, pushing me gently by the shoulder so that I was well back in the seat. 'Let me have a look.'

The light from his phone revealed a large, evil-looking shard embedded in my flesh.

'Yuck,' I said. 'That's disgusting. I'm so mortified ...'

Leyton took something from the inside pocket of his light cotton jacket. I heard a metallic click and saw the glint of a pair of tweezers.

'Don't worry, it's perfectly clean,' he said. 'You might want to look away now.'

He might have been a surgeon, so sure and deft was his removal of the glass, so fast I hardly felt it.

'There,' he said, holding the bloodied shard to the light, still gripped by his tweezers, and rotating it. 'Nasty thing. You're lucky it didn't get in too deep. Doesn't look like you need stitches. Let me check ...'

He dropped the piece of glass into a waste bin nearby and placed his tweezers on a small table. He tore open the cover of an antiseptic wipe and bent to dab at my wounded knee. 'This may hurt a little.'

'You're very kind,' I muttered, trying not to yelp at the sting of the chemicals on my raw flesh.

'It's fine,' he said. 'Rest it for a while now, and try and get some ice on it for the swelling. They may have some downstairs.'

He cleaned his tweezers and his hands with another antiseptic wipe, dropping that too in the waste bin, and replaced the tweezers in a silver box.

'So,' he said as he took a seat beside me.

'So, yourself,' I said. 'Why did you pretend you didn't recognise me from the plane?'

'I'm sorry,' he said. 'I just like to keep some things to myself when Aleka's around. Don't get me wrong, she's a wonderful person and a great friend. She's just a little ...'

'Over-involved?' I said. 'I've noticed. It's ok about the plane. I just felt a bit stupid, but that's not unusual these days.'

The last bit was supposed to be a joke, but he nodded at me seriously.

'I've seen you around,' he said. 'That little café of yours ... there's some pretty unsavoury customers going in there. You're on your own there, right?'

I sighed. 'My aunt's in the States for the week, but there's been no word from her. I'm worried that she's in trouble but the police here are too busy to check.'

He hesitated before saying, 'Look, if you need help, I have some contacts through work, state departments, local sheriff's offices ... I could drop by tomorrow.'

'Yes,' I said. 'Yes, please. That would really help.'

We sat silently for a moment, listening to distant sirens.

'That was you at Matt Talbot's shrine yesterday, wasn't it?'

'Yes, it was,' he said, 'I love history, especially folk history. Shrines, relics, all of that. It's one of the perks of travel, you learn so much.'

'And what did you learn from the Venerable Matt Talbot?' I asked, hoping he hadn't seen me posting my petition to the saint. If he did he probably thought I was a religious nut as well as an accident-prone magnet for trouble.

'Well, I learned that there are people here who still believe they can receive direct favours from those who have passed on. You see that in many cultures. What's interesting is how various societies invoke it, the differences – and the similarities. The shrine of Matt Talbot wouldn't be anything without his bones. Those kind of relics, not just reminders of the person but actual parts of them, are used all over the world, sometimes to make miracles happen.'

'What did Aleka call you, a civic designer?' I asked. 'You sound like an anthropologist.'

'I'm just an engineer, an environmental engineer,' he said. 'Specialising in reconstruction of civic communities in post-emergency situations, you know, like after wars or natural disasters.'

'Is this a post-emergency community, here in Dublin?'

'Hardly at all,' he said, 'I've seen a lot worse, believe me. No, I'm on my way home, been away too long. Aleka asked me to break my return journey for a few days to help with her project. She loves hosting events, you know, public spectacles, entertainments, games. Says it's all about impact and fun. But she has a lot on her plate right now. She knows my interest in history and knew I couldn't resist a visit. But after this, yeah –' he stretched, then shook his head. 'It's home for this boy. Home and staying there.'

'Where's home?'

'Wisconsin. Got a small-holding there, pasture, some forest. My wife, Laurie, she's with her Mom till I get back, her and my two sons. Here, I'll show you a picture.'

I watched as Leyton reached for his silver box, guessing this was probably the most conversation the man had had with anyone in a long time. His voice sounded strained and kind of rusty, like it had seized up though lack of use.

Leyton handed me a photograph of a pretty, dark-haired woman, who looked like she was in her mid-thirties. She was smiling down at two gap-toothed blonde boys and a laughing golden retriever.

'They look lovely,' I said dutifully, handing back the photo. He replaced it carefully in the silver box. I saw that it had a number of compartments inside.

'Interesting box,' I said. 'It looks like a cigarette case, but obviously it's not.'

Leyton made no response but instead rotated the box in his hand. I saw an inscription on the front in the midst of some intricate decorative work.

'What does it say?'

He paused before saying, 'Memento mori.'

'Oh,' I said, surprised. 'I've heard of such things. Is it Victorian?'

'Earlier, eighteenth-century. It's a family heirloom, passed on to me by my mother, who got it from her mother. I carry it everywhere. It's my good luck talisman.' He smiled at me for the first time.

'So, apart from your family photos and your tweezers, what else have you got in there? You're not using it as a traditional memento mori box, I suppose?'

I'd read about the strange custom of retaining physical reminders of deceased loved ones. Locks of hair, sometimes woven into jewellery, rings and brooches with representations of skulls and skeletons, photographs of the dead loved one, with or without coffin. Reminders of their deaths, and equally, reminders of your own. *Memento mori* – 'Remember you must die'.

'Not exactly,' he said. 'But I have to keep what I inherited. There's a strand of hair from my great-grandmother. Some other things ... Incidentally, her hair is almost exactly the same shade as yours. Hair doesn't decay. Bones and teeth are the same, possibly nails. My guess is that's why they're used as relics for saints and invested with all kinds of powers. They are precious artefacts because they're the only genuinely permanent thing about a person. That's why there's so much wrong with artificial substitutes. In terms of what I was talking about, that's not just an insult, it's more like a sin. But I guess you think I'm pretty weird, right?'

I hadn't the heart to tell him that unlike his great-grandmother, my particular shade of chestnut was entirely thanks to L'Oreal Paris. Semi-permanent Copper Glow, to be precise. And yes, he was pretty weird, but no weirder than many around here and a good deal kinder. I was about to tell him so when Kitty burst into the deck area and practically jumped up and down on the timber boards in front of me.

'Where were you?' she shrieked, her eyes alight. 'I've been looking for you everywhere! The Sunrise Hotel's on fire. All the residents are out on the street. They're evacuating the building. Come on!'

She hauled me to my feet ignoring my howls of pain and dragged me towards the door.

'Hang on, Kitty. Just a minute,' I said, turning back. Leyton sat quietly in the corner, the glow of the stove and the brightening sky behind him illuminating his unperturbed face.

'Thank you, Claude,' I said. 'You were very kind – and most interesting. Don't forget one thing, though.'

He looked at me with one eyebrow slightly raised.

'*Memento vivere.* Remember to live.'

He raised his hand in another mock salute and flashed his rare smile as Kitty pushed me away down the corridor.

Day 3

TUESDAY

39

POST RECOVERY

'Nobody died,' said the old man wearing spotty pyjamas and a pink plastic raincoat. 'Or got hurt or anything. There wasn't even a decent explosion.'

'Or flames shooting out the windows or flying glass,' said his companion in a dressing gown. 'I remember when there were real bombs going off in this town.'

As the sky brightened, we shivered on the quayside and reflected quietly upon declining national standards in improvised explosive devices. It was generally agreed amongst the temporarily-evacuated residents, who waited on the quayside drinking hot beverages from paper cups, that the source of the fire was a bomb and not a very big one.

There was no real fire damage. I heard the biggest problem was trying to get Harry out. He was the guy who hadn't left his room in twenty years. He'd barricaded himself into his lair and refused to talk to anyone except Fogarty. Nobody wanted to break it to him that Fogarty had been arrested, and, as far as they were aware, was still being held in either Store Street Garda Station or the Bridewell. I knew better, but said nothing.

In the end, Harry won and didn't have to move an inch. He hung a triumphant flag out his window, made from bedclothes and possibly a section of the skirting boards. Everyone cheered and clapped.

The fire brigade had tackled the fire in the basement quickly and efficiently and then gave the building a thorough check. As soon as they'd issued the all clear, the hotel residents wandered back to their rooms to resume their abnormal lives. Even though the Fire Department had yet to make a public announcement, Lu O'Leary had already submitted her news story.

'Incendiary Device in Docklands Hotel. Dissident Republican Group Suspected.'

'Republicans? Seriously?' I asked her as we stood outside watching the action. 'Why would a republican group, dissident or otherwise, want to firebomb the Sunrise Hotel? Where do you get this information?'

'Sources close to the fire,' she said and smiled as she handed a cup of tea to a tall, young firefighter.

I remembered my visit to the Sunrise Hotel and the flags and political slogans I saw painted on the walls. I remembered the man in the wheelchair in the hotel's backyard, the man Fogarty said had been kneecapped. Maybe the dissident republican idea wasn't so crazy after all.

As dawn broke over the city, the Silver Bullet Café looked even more run-down and forlorn than usual. The buckled shutter and broken door didn't help. Feeling like a traitor, I turned my back on it and slunk back into Stalag 17. I'd tackle the café later. I just needed to lie down and close my eyes for an hour or two.

The ground floor of the club was empty and overhung with that dismal sense of post-party desolation. Kitty was asleep somewhere. Lu O'Leary was engaged elsewhere doing in-depth research with one of her sources. No one else was about.

Then Ozzie appeared offering a warm herbal concoction. I was almost asleep as he led me to a sofa in front of the dying embers of a fire and handed me a rug. The projection on the back wall had changed to a forest scene, with light shining through rows of trees, their leaves moving gently above a woodland floor of ferns and mosses. The Somalian shaman was still playing his keyboard or at least his fingers still made those tiny movements over the keys. But there was no sound that I could hear, just a general sense of peace.

I asked Ozzie about Aleka and he smiled and said, 'Darling, she's extraordinary in ways you couldn't possibly imagine.'

'Why was Brady so angry?' I asked. 'And what's the story with Aleka's dull friends?'

'Just Aleka stuff,' Ozzie said. 'And Brady's always worked up about something. Bit on the over-zealous side. Plus he's not happy about being dumped.'

'Being dumped by Aleka? For you?'

Ozzie laughed. 'Being dumped by Aleka for Leyton.'

As I was trying to take that in, Ozzie sat down beside me and asked how I was doing. So I told him. About Aggie going missing and Steyne River Securities and about Karen Donlon and the compulsory purchase notice and poor Jimmy Mooney. I told him about Brady and Donlon and the car attack and about Fogarty getting arrested. I hope that's all I said about Fogarty. And I hope I said nothing about Amsterdam and the things I was trying to forget.

Ozzie listened, his arm resting lightly around my shoulders as he gazed up at the ceiling fan, a huge black ship's propeller slowly rotating. Somewhere in the middle of it all, I fell asleep. I slept for what could only have been a couple of hours, but it felt as good as if it had been for several days.

Kitty woke me by plonking herself down on the sofa and shaking me violently.

'Hey, Connie. Wake up – guess what?'

I half-raised myself and tried to prise open my eyes with my fingers. There was no sign of Ozzie. I looked at Kitty in a blur. Damn, I'd fallen asleep with my lenses in. They were still in there but it felt like there was sandpaper on the inside of my eyelids rubbing my eyeballs raw. I needed eyedrops, fast.

'Fogarty's back.' Kitty went on. 'He sent Miro, the new guy, over to fix the lock on the café. And Josie and Viv are in there cleaning up. They even fixed up my room.'

'For that alone they deserve a medal – or one of those plenary indulgences they're always doing,' I said, stretching, keeping *schtum* about Fogarty and wondering why, despite being well-rested, I felt like I'd been in a road accident.

'They deserve one of the *what*?'

'Plenary indulgences. Like sentence remission in purgatory. What time is it?'

'Just after nine.'

I got up off the sofa and shrieked with the pain. I sat down again, took a quick look at my knees and groaned. I should have listened to Leyton and packed them with ice before I went to sleep. Now it was too late, they were swollen and black and it hurt to even look at them. I stood up carefully and my dead phone, which must have been lying underneath me while I slept, now fell and clattered across the floor. I realised at the same time that I had no idea where my shoes were. I sat down again and buried my head in my hands and groaned some more. 'This is all just too *hard*!'

'Why don't you stay here and rest for a while?' Ozzie said gently as he materialised from nowhere. Kitty picked up my phone and started searching for my shoes.

'I can't,' I snapped at him. 'I have important things to do. Very important things. I just have to remember what they are.'

A passing truck-driver honked and shouted an extremely rude comment as I limped the short distance from the nightclub to the café next door. I was barefoot, half-crippled and three-quarters blind. My face and hair were a state, my green dress torn and crumpled. Kitty had run on ahead, possibly out of embarrassment. Ozzie was coming after me to help, even though I'd told him not to.

Josie leaned her sweeping brush against the wall as I approached and folded her arms.

'You're going the wrong way, love,' she said. 'The Sunrise Hotel is that way.'

'Not now, Josie,' I said through gritted teeth.

'And what kind of hour do you call this to be coming home? The cut of you. I don't know what your poor aunt would say.'

The young man who was tidying his tools at the café door glanced up just as Ozzie caught up with me. I recognised him as Miro, the handyman from the Sunrise Hotel and thanked him for his work on the locks.

'Is no trouble,' he said. 'Fogarty, he said I should come.'

I was about to ask him to look at the coffee machine when he beckoned me closer and said in a loud whisper, 'I have message for you. Your aunt, she will be ok, you keep looking after things.'

'What?' I whispered back. 'What do you mean? Who's this message from?'

But Miro's attention was focused elsewhere. His gaze was locked upon Ozzie, who had just arrived. Wordlessly, Miro dropped a spanner into his toolbox and walked past me, stopping in front of Ozzie. He placed his hands on Ozzie's shoulders, and stared intently into his face. Without shifting his gaze, he opened the top buttons of his shirt and, grasping Ozzie's hand, placed it inside his shirt on his bare chest. Ozzie's eyes opened wide, but he said nothing. Then Miro's arms slipped around him as he moved his mouth down to kiss the curve of Ozzie's neck. Ozzie closed his eyes but otherwise remained absolutely motionless.

Viv appeared at the door in her flowery house coat and looked at Josie, who rolled her eyes and lit a cigarette.

'All right, boys, get a room,' she said. 'The rest of us have work to do.'

My hopes for a functioning coffee machine receded as Miro and Ozzie slowly walked away, arms wrapped around one another. I sighed and went inside.

40

Turning the Corner on Crime

'Well, that was weird,' Kitty said from the chair she stood on. She slammed the portable TV on both sides with her hands and stepped down to view the results. The screen flickered and came on. 'I'll say one thing for that Miro, he works fast. And I'm not talking about the locks.'

I shrugged and plugged in my phone, willing it to charge quickly, desperate for news from Aggie, or from Brady about Aggie.

The phone came on, but no messages appeared.

I was running out of options and I was running out of allies. I had no doubt as to the source and the meaning of Miro's whispered message. He was clearly working for Dessie Donlon. Look after things for Donlon and Aggie will be ok. And if not ...

Mooney was dead, Brady was a dead loss, Ozzie was otherwise engaged and Fogarty was hardly likely to help me now, was he? Now that he thought I was in league with Brady and had shopped him to the cops about Mooney. He thought I was a rat. And I knew that he was involved with Detective Nuala Rossiter, that he was more than a little bit dodgy and that he was a dirty, lying, cheating bastard.

Lu would have to learn about Mooney's article some other way because I had no intention of contacting Fogarty now or anytime in the future. In fact, avoiding Pius Fogarty altogether seemed like an excellent idea.

'Are you not listening to me?' Kitty said. 'Touch of the morning afters, is it? I just told you that last night's fire is on the news. Now you've missed half of it. Look.' She turned up the volume.

Josh Treanor stood with his back to the Sunrise Hotel, microphone in hand, sporting vintage Desert Storm combats and a red bandana.

'Gardaí have just confirmed earlier reports that this was an attack by a republican breakaway group based in Northern Ireland. As yet, we have no explanation as to why this particular hotel was targeted. Josh Treanor reporting from Dublin's North Wall Quay for *TV News Live*.'

'Thanks, Josh,' said the female half of the studio newscaster duo. 'But despite this incident and our top story of the tragic death of award-winning crime journalist, Jimmy Mooney, it's not all bad news today. The Garda task force on organised crime is reporting unprecedented success in its recent crack-down on gangland operations. At a press conference last night, Detective Inspector Anthony Brady announced, "We have turned the corner on Dublin crime."'

Cut to a clip from the press conference with an assured Brady spouting statistics on his recent police raids, and the resulting arrests and seizures of drugs and contraband.

The reporter immediately returned to the community disquiet around the death of Jimmy Mooney from the same disease as the homeless youth whose body was found on Sunday. Referencing mounting fears about the disease and yesterday's shooting of a hotelier on Amiens Street following the killing of Raymond 'Sugar Ray' Brosnan, she asked, 'Have we turned the corner on crime and entered an era of chaos? Regrettably, Detective Inspector Brady was not available to comment this morning.'

The report ended with a quotation from the last article of the 'late, great' Jimmy Mooney: '*The war on crime is an economic war that bloodies our streets daily, where the forgotten cannon fodder are the poor, the vulnerable, the young and the innocent. Our first duty is to protect them and in this we have failed.*'

I gaped at the TV. Mooney was right. It was a real war and the likes of Dessie Donlon would fight to the death to defend their territory. I'd not only failed in my duty to protect those around me, I'd actually endangered them. I'd somehow propelled Mooney on a course that ultimately resulted in his horrible death. I'd failed to get the guards to even start trying to locate Aggie. Due to my foolhardy remarks to Donlon about Stevie's missing sketchbooks, I'd accidentally planted the idea that some clues to his death might be found in his sketches. Donlon was so desperate, he was prepared to grasp at straws. He already had the painting from the break-in, I was sure of it. If he got his hands on the sketchbooks before I did, he'd find nothing about an antidote to the disease, because there *was* no antidote. And then he'd take it out on Aggie and on me and on Kitty too.

I remembered what I had to do. I had to find those sketchbooks before anybody else did. Everything else would have to wait. By now, whatever was in the sketchbooks was completely incidental, I needed them for bargaining power and nothing else mattered.

'Sorry, Mooney,' I whispered. 'I'm going to have to put you and Stevie on hold.'

A 'call me' message appeared on my phone. I paused for just an instant before deleting it. 'You're on hold too, Pius Fogarty. Permanently.'

I stood up, walked to the window and looked out. Kitty was out there helping Josie with the bins. I had to think fast. When I'd told Kitty that the sketchbooks could be in Stevie's secret studio, I was just trying to show her I was making a bit of progress. But when I thought about it now, that studio idea was all I'd got. I thought about the six-inch paint brush amongst Stevie's belongings. He had to have been working on a large work to need a brush like that. And he'd need a studio for a large work.

Apart from the elusive Shane, the only other person who might know the studio's location was Stevie's collector. I picked up the phone and called Lu's friend, the art historian, fully aware that Dessie Donlon wasn't the only one grasping at straws.

41

BOY BITTEN BY A LIZARD

There'd be something wrong with me if I wasn't paranoid at this stage, I thought, justifying the taxi fare to the National Gallery. I looked over my shoulder as the taxi crossed the Samuel Beckett Bridge and drove down the south quays. As far as I could tell, I wasn't being followed.

The taxi pulled up outside the Clare Street entrance to the Gallery and I walked in through the soaring, light-filled Millennium Extension. I had arranged to meet the art historian, Karalyn Hughes, in the Gallery restaurant at eleven o'clock. It was only ten-thirty and I was too restless and nervous to stand around waiting. A guide swept past me leading a small tour while sonorously intoning '... fascinating discovery of this intriguing palimpsest ...'

I decided to follow them and further my education while killing a few minutes. I caught up with the group in a darkened vestibule signposted 'A Medieval Mystery.' The guide, a self-important art history graduate student with a summer job and a Salvador Dali moustache, stood in front of a large, decorated brass panel that glowed golden under a soft spotlight. The figure represented on it was that of a bishop with his mitre and crozier. An image of another brass panel portraying a populous family was projected on the wall alongside that of the bishop.

'What we are looking at here,' announced the guide, 'is the lost monumental brass of an archbishop dating from the mid-fourteenth century. Discovered by construction workers last week, embedded in a house wall in Temple Bar, this artefact is on temporary display here in the Gallery before it is relocated to a permanent location at the end of the week. Here, we see the figure of an archbishop under a straight-sided canopy with pinnacle and shafting. His hand is raised in blessing and he holds a cross-staff with trefoil terminals in his left hand. The marginal inscription in Latin clearly identifies this work as commemorating Alexander de Biknor. The brass was probably originally located in St Patrick's Cathedral and was stolen or sold off sometime in the following century. While memorial brasses are numerous in England, they are very rare in this country. This one is extremely significant not only because of who it portrays, the brilliant and tragic Bicknor, fourteenth-century Archbishop of Dublin and Lord Chancellor of Ireland, an Englishman, favourite of Edward II, a former treasurer of the Crown. And a peculator ...'

'Percolator?' I said aloud without thinking, haunted by my aunt's evil coffee machine.

The guide stifled a sigh as he assessed the class troublemaker. '*Peculator*. An embezzler of public funds. He was found guilty of financial malfeasance. Ultimately pardoned by the King, it has been suggested that Bicknor may have been a victim of circumstances.' He turned to indicate the projected image beside the brass panel.

'As I was saying, the significance is not only due to the person portrayed, but because of this fifteenth-century image on its reverse side, of a merchant, his wife and their twenty-two children, behind which the Bicknor brass remained hidden for six or seven centuries. This palimpsest ...'

He sighed again as he saw my hand shoot up and correctly guessed my question.

'Yes, a palimpsest is usually understood to refer to a piece of vellum which has been wholly or partly scrubbed of its original text and overwritten, retaining traces of the original beneath. In archaeology however, the term denotes something created for one purpose and later reused for another, in this case, a monumental brass re-engraved on its reverse side.'

I lowered my hand and muttered thanks while staring at the palimpsest – something created for one purpose and reused for another. 'Clay is the beginning and Clay is the end' resounded in my head like a tolling bell. I rose and left the vestibule and its shining brasses. It was eleven o'clock, I had a splitting headache and another art historian to meet. The guide did not look as if he was going to miss me.

I spotted her immediately. She told me on the phone that she'd be wearing a multi-coloured jacket and sitting at the back of the restaurant. Looking like a woman from a Renoir portrait, Dr Karalyn Hughes' dark eyes danced with fun, her blonde curls cascading around a porcelain doll face. She stood to shake my hand, and greeted me in a voice that was deep and slightly husky.

'I hope you're not expecting much,' she said. 'Based on what you asked me on the phone, I feel like a terrible fraud. Nineteenth-century ecclesiastical art is my area, not contemporary art or Caravaggio and his imitators. But maybe I can point you in the right direction.'

'That's fine. I'll be honest with you too,' I said. 'There are other people interested in my artist's work, dangerous criminals who've already stolen one of them. Just say no if you'd rather not get involved.'

'Don't worry. I can look after myself. Here, have a look.'

She opened her handbag under the table and I saw a metal canister nestling inside.

'Pepper spray?' I tried not to laugh.

'Mace. For my field trips. You've no idea how many pervs are lurking round old church cemeteries. Show me the paintings.'

'I wanted to ask you something else too, about a collector ...'

'First the paintings. You said you only have photos on a phone. It's not ideal but I'll do my best.'

My priorities had shifted from the paintings – now I just wanted to find Stevie's studio. I fought back my impatience and passed her my phone. The first painting was Stevie's self portrait.

'That's the one that was stolen last night. The boy portrayed is the painting's artist, Stevie Hennessy.'

'That's nicely done,' Karalyn said. 'You guessed correctly, it *is* styled on the Caravaggio, "Boy bitten by a lizard". Couldn't be anything else. Caravaggio has influenced artists ever since his own heyday in the seventeenth century. His paintings are so immediate, he seems to reach right out to people four centuries later. Extraordinary, really. But this is very clever.'

'Can you see the mark on his hand?'

'Yes,' she said, expanding the image while talking to herself. 'The artist is clearly drawing attention to it, although it's presented very subtly. What's its significance? Is it ... a burn mark?'

She flicked backwards and forwards through the four photos, enlarging one or two of them to have a closer look. The first two were of Stevie's paintings from the dining room in the Sunrise Hotel. 'Boy and Girl With Drugs', I called them.

'There's no doubt that your Stevie was very talented. He liked to capture the drama of everyday life, didn't he? He's certainly a master of composition. And he's excellent with light and colour.'

She moved to the image from the graffiti wall in the Sunrise Hotel, the portrayal of Matt Talbot wrapped in chains and with burn marks on his hands and neck. She enlarged that too and examined it in detail.

'Clearly the same artist, but this time imitating religious iconography, replacing the stigmata with those burn marks. They're obviously important to him and carry some meaning. Any idea what it might be?'

'I was hoping you could tell me if it has any artistic relevance. Otherwise it might relate to a local subculture.'

'I don't know if the burn shape corresponds with an established art symbol, but I doubt it. I'll check with my colleagues but your subculture theory seems more likely. Tell you what, while we're here, why don't we go upstairs and look at some art? We might get inspired!'

The last thing I needed was to waste time wandering around an art gallery but my art expert had already headed for the stairs. I followed her upwards, moaning quietly with the pain from my still-sore knees.

The upper level was surprisingly busy. Elderly couples and tourists moved about systematically, dutifully reading the printed information beside the paintings. Droves of schoolchildren congregated in gangs. Summer camps, I guessed. The schools wouldn't be back for another week or two.

At the top of the stairs we went through the sliding glass doors under the sign 'Masterpieces from the Collections.'

In the first room, Karalyn enthusiastically pointed to Fra Angelico's *Saints Cosmas and Damian and their Brothers Surviving the Stake*, a scene depicting the attempted martyrdom of a cluster of saints perched on a pile of firewood. They were miraculously untouched by some odd-looking tongues of flame, to the obvious disappointment of the spectators. Beside me, a particularly self-satisfied Judith casually held up the dripping head of Holofernes which she'd just lopped off. My twitching anxiety was not helped by being surrounded by bloodthirsty artworks.

Karalyn propelled me into the next room and stood me in front of Caravaggio's *The Taking of Christ*, the painting that was dramatically discovered twenty years ago in the dining hall of a religious order just a few streets away. It was centred on the back wall and was attracting a lot of attention. A young woman sat on a bench with pencils and a small sketchbook, copying the faces of Christ and Judas. I wondered if Stevie had ever sat here doing the same thing.

The wall-mounted information mentioned Caravaggio's realism, the crowded picture space and his famous contrasting light and dark, the *chiaroscuro*. And it noted that the figure holding the lantern is believed to be Caravaggio himself, the artist casting light on the scene. I thought, that's what Stevie was trying to do too, in his own way.

I stepped back to view the whole painting, a dramatic freeze-frame of a shocking event. The traitor, Judas, has just landed the hateful kiss. The face of Christ looks resigned and unutterably sad. The armoured soldiers have already moved in to arrest him. His best friend is running away.

That's exactly what betrayal looks like, I thought. I knew both sides of that story. I cringed when I thought of last night, of Fogarty's tenderness and my response and how it all ended in cold-blooded betrayal. Or at least that's how it would have appeared to him.

I began to feel light-headed and wondered if it was the after-effects of Ozzie's drinks last night. And then I saw something. Was I imagining things or was that a mark on the right wrist of Christ, just below the sleeve of his robe? Alarmed security wire ran all around the room about four feet from the walls. It was impossible for me to get a closer look.

I glanced at the painting to the right, of *David and Goliath* by Gentileschi, clearly influenced by Caravaggio. I scanned the figure of the giant, who was squeezed uncomfortably into the frame, and then that of the boy, David. He had a round mark on the inside of his left ankle. I moved quickly from one painting to the next. In *St John the Baptist in the wilderness* by Borziani, St John is naked except for a strategically draped cloth – and I saw a mark on his left arm just above the elbow. On the opposite wall, Ribero's poor old *Saint Onuphrius*, who wouldn't have looked out of place in the Sunrise Hotel, had a mark on his lower back. In *Kitchen maid at the supper at Ammaus*, by Velazquez, the pretty servant girl had a strange mark on her left cheek just below her eye.

I felt a touch on my shoulder.

'Connie, are you ok?' It was Karalyn, regarding me with some concern.

'All of them have a mark somewhere on their bodies. Look.' I went around the room pointing at the paintings. She followed and eventually caught up with me.

'They're not the same kind of marks as the ones in Stevie's paintings,' she said firmly, steering me towards the bench.

'They're not?'

'Definitely not,' she said. 'I think you need to take a little break.'

She sat me down and smiled kindly.

'Am I losing my mind?' I asked her.

'Possibly,' she said. 'Would you'd like to get some air?'

'No, no.' I said. 'I just need to think. I'm getting desperate, making connections where there aren't any. I have to try to make sense of all this.'

'Take it easy,' Karalyn said. 'Maybe try another tack. Didn't you have some other questions you wanted to ask me. Did you say something on the phone about clay?'

'Yes!' I said. 'The word "clay". What does it mean to you? In art, I mean.'

'Well, if you're talking about painting, that's easy,' she said. 'Clay is used to make pigments – you know, the colours of paint.'

'Go on.'

'Well, clay has always been used in art, going back as far as the cave paintings. But especially with Renaissance and Baroque painters, they used different kinds of clay for different purposes. So for example, they used clay from Sienna called *terra rossa*. You've heard of burnt sienna? And the ochres – those are the clays used to make earth colours. And the red earths – based on red clays and boles, which were used for gilding. They used clay from Verona and other places for painting flesh. That was green earth or *terra verde*. And they used white earth or white clay pigments or kaolins for painting grounds ...'

'Whoa, whoa! Tell me more about the flesh one, the green earth.'

'I can recommend a book on the composition and proportions of minerals in green earth and other pigments if that's what you need.'

'Thanks but I don't need that right now. What was it used for again?'

'Medieval and Baroque Italian painters used green earth for underpainting flesh tones. They used it to neutralise the pinks and reds of the flesh colours. By painting a layer of green under the pinks, they could avoid creating a kind of a "sunburn" effect in the flesh of the figures they painted. Look at Nicholas Poussin's body of Christ over there.'

'His body looks kind of green,' I said.

'Exactly,' said Karalyn. 'The top layer of paint which would have had the pink tones has faded away leaving a greenish colour.'

'*Clay is the beginning*,' I said. '*In the beginning was the word, and the word became flesh ...*' I continued automatically, dredging up some distant lesson, '*... and he now became man, who was hitherto clay.*' I was trying not to get over-excited again, but it seemed like I was getting somewhere. 'This is interesting. Is it what Mooney was on about? Would Stevie have known about clay and pigments. Would Mooney?' I was thinking aloud.

'Most artists would,' Karalyn said. 'Some contemporary artists still grind and mix their own pigments.'

Maybe Stevie did that too. I wished I knew what it all meant. But I pulled myself up – first, I needed to find Stevie's studio.

'One last question, Karalyn. I'm looking for a particular art collector. Someone who'd buy student work like Stevie's. He may have a connection with Trinity College. Gordon something, possibly.'

'It has to be Gordon Wentworth,' Karalyn said. 'Gordon's well-known for buying works from emerging artists and making a killing on them. He's got a really good eye. He used to lecture part-time in Trinity, but he stopped that a year or two ago. I haven't seen him for ages. He left to focus on his private gallery on Denzille Lane. It's not far from here. I'll write it down. The Wentworth Gallery. You'll see the sign.'

I couldn't believe it. Finally a bit of luck.

42

DENZILLE LANE

Denzille Lane was only five minutes from the Gallery. I left my art historian at the entrance, having carefully looked up and down the street for anything suspicious or threatening. I was getting as bad as Fogarty. Karalyn clearly thought I was mad, but she agreed to get back to me with any further insights she might have on the paintings.

I crossed the road at Lincoln Place, again at the top of Westland Row and, limping over the uneven pavement, headed straight down Fenian Street to where it joined with Denzille Lane. I saw the sign immediately. The Wentworth Gallery was painted in gold letters on a black background. The mews had a flat, brick facade, a large garage-style door, a smaller door beside it, a big square window above and an intercom. I buzzed the bell and waited. No response. I tried again and heard footsteps and someone fumbling with the door on the other side. The door opened and a young woman came out in a hurry.

'Sorry,' she said as she brushed past. She was Eastern European. Blonde, slim and tired. 'I'm late.'

I watched her walk quickly down the lane the same way I'd come up, while I held the door open with my fingertips. There wasn't a sound inside. I wondered if anyone was home. I entered and heard the door close softly behind me.

It was a modern, architect-designed conversion. I was in a large reception room with sofas and recessed lighting. Natural light flooded the room from skylights, reflected in the polished boards. The walls were white and covered with paintings and drawings and textile wall hangings. As I made my way towards an arched doorway at the far end, my foot kicked something small and soft. It flew across the room and bounced off the far skirting board. I picked it up to have a look. It was a champagne cork. I walked through the archway and up a step into a small internal courtyard, noticing that its terracotta-tiled floor was strewn with more corks. Smoke rose from within a grove of potted palms in the corner accompanied by a strong smell of burning cannabis. There was still no sound. I tiptoed to the corner and, parting the foliage with my hands, peered through the palm fronds.

A large male in his sixties with a greying black beard and hair to match, lay back in a hot tub with his eyes closed, smoking a little silver pipe.

I cleared my throat.

'Gordon? Gordon Wentworth?'

The man raised himself slightly in the water revealing a pair of bright red nipples nestling amongst thick, black and silver chest hair. He removed the pipe with one hand and lifted his other hand to wave in the direction of the reception room. The voice rumbling from his barrel chest was a deep, rich baritone.

'There's a little bonus for you on the table, petal. Now run along!'

Hope she got more than a tenner, I said to myself. I pushed past the palms and stood in front of the hot tub.

'Gordon? Would you have a minute?'

He raised one of his bushy black eyebrows and opened an eye.

'But you're not – what's her name. Who the hell are you?'

'I'm Constance Ortelius. I'd like to ask about someone you know. Stevie Hennessy.'

There was a moment's silence and then the man sighed.

'Ah. I thought someone might come along eventually. All right. Give me a minute. You might like to fetch the coffee? It's in the kitchen. Mine's black.'

Wentworth stood up in the tub and stretched, giving me the full frontal, with rivulets of water running off his copious body hair. Then he turned and clambered out, offering the rear view too. I tried not to wince visibly.

I returned from the kitchen with a couple of mugs of black coffee from a silver Moroccan coffee pot that I'd found on the stove. Wentworth was now roosting on the edge of the tub with his legs apart, a tiny towel more or less around his loins. He'd exchanged his pipe for the remnants of a cigar that was in the ashtray and he puffed on it thoughtfully while giving me the once over.

'Well you're not what's-her-name, but you're not too bad. Reasonably fuckable.'

'Gee, thanks,' I said, handing him his coffee.

'Oh don't be insulted,' he said. 'I mean it as a compliment.'

'You're too kind. But Gordon, I don't have a lot of time and I need your help. I told you, it's about Stevie Hennessy.'

'Poor boy,' Wentworth said. 'His was a great talent. His paintings were already attracting international attention. I'm so glad I bought as many of them as possible when I did. I've been getting a lot of inquiries, especially now that he's ... you know. Would you like to see some of them?'

He pulled on a short bathrobe and towelling slippers and, with his coffee in one hand and his cigar in the other, moved with a rolling gait towards a steel spiral staircase, kicking the corks out of his way.

'Sorry about the mess,' he said. 'Bit of a party last night.'

'Please tell me you're not going to invite me to come up and see your etchings,' I said, although I was really more worried about my aching knees.

His laughter rumbled above me as he ascended the stairs.

'I hope I'm not that predictable,' he said.

'I hope so too,' I thought as I followed him, carefully not looking up.

The large loft-like gallery space adjoining Wentworth's living quarters was filled from floor to ceiling with paintings. Even so, Stevie's pictures stood out from the others and not just because there were so many of them grouped together. It was because of that immediacy of Stevie's work, its intensity. These works were similar to those in the Sunrise Hotel, scenes from the city's street life presented from a very personal viewpoint.

'Fabulous, aren't they?'

There was no doubt that Wentworth genuinely loved Stevie's work. Those paintings meant more to him than just some good investments and I guessed that was quite unusual with the collector.

'Of course there were others he wouldn't sell me. A series of landscapes I wanted that were quite extraordinary, unlike anything else he's done. But he had all kinds of excuses for not selling them. He said he wanted to finish the series or that he was too close to them etc., etc. I suppose they're still up there in his studio.'

He'd just said the magic word.

'Gordon, I need to go to Stevie's studio. Have you been there? Do you know where it is?'

Wentworth hesitated before replying, pondering something.

'Look, Stevie was very secretive about his studio. I think I'm one of only one or two people he allowed to set foot in it. For starters, he was there illegally, so he had to be careful. The other thing is, well he was in a bit of trouble. He seemed to have annoyed some people ...'

Wentworth noticed my interest.

'I'd rather not get into that now. The only reason I'll give you any information is because I fear for the paintings. They could so easily get lost or damaged. Losing Stevie was bad enough. Losing his work would be a double tragedy. At least if I go with you, I could photograph and catalogue them. And you can be the witness that I don't steal anything!'

'You'll take me to Stevie's studio?'

'Yes,' he said. 'I think I must. We'll go there now.'

Now we're really getting somewhere, I thought, as Wentworth finally went to put on some clothes. It was progress on two fronts.

43

THE STUDIO

'Spencer Dock,' Wentworth told the taxi driver.

'I don't believe it,' I said. 'Stevie's studio's been right under our noses all along.'

We travelled back across the river to the North Wall Quay, home of the Silver Bullet Café, the Sunrise Hotel and all of Stevie's old haunts. We drove past the café and turned left on to New Wapping Street. Wentworth instructed the driver to pull in at the corner of Mayor Street.

'We can walk from here, otherwise it gets complicated with the tramways,' he said as he heaved himself out of the cab. He'd brought his briefcase and an expensive-looking camera with a tripod in a carry-case. It looked like Stevie's studio was somewhere in the streets directly behind the North Wall Quay. The area was dominated by a huge empty site surrounded by a wooden hoarding, a site scheduled for a massive building project. It couldn't be there. After that you came to the shiny Spencer Dock developments, with their very own tram station and dinky designer park. Surely it couldn't be there either.

Wentworth knew where he was going and marched along purposefully while fending off my questions about Stevie and the people Wentworth had said he'd annoyed. Eventually he stopped to adjust the strap on the tripod case and took the opportunity to tick me off.

'Now, petal,' he said. 'I'm not going to say this again. There are some people I have to deal with as part of my business who can only be described as dangerous. I'd be taking a terrible risk if I told you anything about these things. It's best for both of us if I say no more. Look what happened to Stevie.'

'So you're saying Stevie was at risk from some of those people. Do you think they were responsible for his death?'

'God, you're an awful woman. Do you never give up? Ok, I'll tell you this, but only because I feel terrible about it. I was at a party last Thursday night – I won't say where. And I saw Stevie and his on-off boyfriend, Shane getting ejected by the security. Stevie seemed off his head and I was surprised because, to the best of my knowledge, he'd been off the drugs. The two of them were practically carried out. I was with a new client and I was avoiding one of my ex-wives so I couldn't go after them. That was the last time I saw Stevie.'

'Who was at the party?'

'Oh, everyone.'

'Whose party was it?'

Wentworth had stopped outside a new and very empty office building. It was fifteen storeys high, tall for the still relatively low-rise area. There was a huge 'Office Space To Let' sign running across it from top to bottom diagonally. It was designed to look like a ribbon on a gift-wrapped package.

'Stevie's studio is in the penthouse.'

'In there? How did he get past security? Isn't there CCTV and all that?'

'He had an arrangement with the security guard. Stevie could be very persuasive, you know. And commercial lettings were non-existent until recently, so there was no demand for the space. But ... there's something wrong here. I can tell.'

'What's wrong? Come on, let's go in and see.'

I was desperate to get in there and get off the street, where we were way too visible.

'No. No, I can't. Look at the door,' he said, pointing. 'It's wide open. I've never seen it like that. I'm sorry but I'm not going in there.'

'Oh for God's sake,' I said, marching up to the door. I was getting tired of pandering to Wentworth. 'The guard's probably out having a smoke. I'm sure he's just around the back. But if it makes you feel better ... '

But the security guard wasn't having a smoke and he wasn't round the back. The door of the security office gaped open. I knocked on the timber door surround saying, 'Excuse me?' before looking in. The security guard was slumped over his desk with half of his skull missing. Dark blood soaked into a copy of the free daily advertiser underneath his head and sprays of blood and jelly-like clumps stuck to the nearest wall. The man was stone cold dead.

I backed out the door, hand clasped over my mouth, my gorge rising. Holding the wall, I gasped for oxygen, then slowly turned, witlessly, to warn Wentworth. But Wentworth was gone. I looked up and down the street, but there was no sign of him. For a man of such large physical presence to vanish so quickly, he had to have a pretty spectacular flight reflex. Gordon Wentworth's finely-tuned instincts went way beyond his ability to spot promising artists. I wished I had them.

I returned to the empty office building and stood outside the security guard's office, considering my options. For an instant, I considered calling the guards, but where would that get me? More close encounters with Detective Inspector Brady? No thanks. It had been just over twenty-four hours since I'd last been in the interrogation room in Store Street station and I was in no hurry to go back there. Anyway, I hadn't time. This was no coincidental, random crime. There was nothing to steal in this building. It was conceivable that the security guard was the victim of a contract shooting – anything was possible in a town where everything and everybody was connected. But the likelihood was that whoever broke in here and killed the guard was after one thing – access to Stevie's studio. I had a good idea who it was and what they wanted.

I'd lost the race. I'd moved as fast as I could, I had the best of expert advice and even a bit of good luck in the end, and still I'd lost it. The bastards had got here before me and I had no idea how they did it. Now I also had the brutal killing of a blameless security guard on my guilty conscience.

Needing confirmation of my failure, I entered the lobby and pressed the lift's up button. Its doors opened immediately. I tried the other lift and its doors opened too. A small safety precaution. I got into the nearest one and pressed the button for the penthouse.

A recorded woman's voice with an English accent startled me with her sudden 'Doors closing' announcement. The doors opened on the fifteenth floor and I stood there for a moment, listening. There wasn't a sound. The door opposite the lift was wide open.

I had to shade my eyes against the dazzling light when I entered the penthouse. I was in a vast glass box positioned on the very top of the building with a wide timber wrap-around deck outside, accessible through sliding glass doors. All of the glass doors were open and the wind coming through from all sides blew papers and drawings around the room and out through the doors to the open skies. Stevie had rigged up lengths of white sailcloth over the roof glass and part of the glass walls to diffuse the light. A row of huge canvases stood propped against the walls. They were covered in paint, depicting – landscapes, was that what Wentworth called them? I'd look at them properly later, I thought. I had something else to do first.

I could see that Stevie had tried to create order in this place, to make a space where he could create freely, but what I was looking at now was chaos. The studio had been ransacked as thoroughly as the café was the night before. Boxes of art materials were emptied on the floor. Tubes of paint and soiled cloths and bottles of solvents littered every surface. Canvases had been pulled out of the places where they'd been stacked. Portfolio cases lay open on the floor with their contents spilling out. A sudden gust of wind blew more papers off the trestle table in the middle of the room. I ran and closed the sliding doors and suddenly the room became still and quiet. I began to search every inch of the place but it took no time to find what I was looking for. The green backpack that Kitty had described was under a metal trolley. There was no mistaking it. It was the backpack Kitty had stashed in the locker in the Sunrise Hotel, the one that had contained the sketchbooks, the one that had gone missing. And now it was empty.

Well, I wasn't surprised. What had I expected? I had led a dangerous criminal gang to believe that the missing sketchbooks contained the key to an antidote for a disease that was threatening to destabilise the city and disrupt their power base. Of *course* they were going to stop at nothing to find it. I felt like such a fool. Donlon must be examining the sketchbooks right now. I wondered what he'd find in them. Nothing about a disease or its antidote. He was going to be furious when he discovered the truth. And now I had nothing to keep him from following through with his threats to Aggie.

I walked around the studio. All my hopes had centred on finding this place. I'd even hoped to find some explanation to Mooney's fixation with clay. The connection that had seemed a possibility in the National Gallery, the use of clay in paint pigments, now looked like foolish, wishful thinking. I checked Stevie's paints, most of which were in tubes on the floor. I touched a mound of deep green on the paint-covered top of the metal trolley. It was oil paint, squeezed from a tube, a dry skin on its surface but still soft underneath. I saw no sign of minerals or pigments, in powder or other form, that could be ground up and mixed for paint. Another dead end.

I sank down on the floor in despair, staring hopelessly at the sky through the glass roof. What was I going to do?

Directionless, my eyes wandered across Stevie's large canvases leaning against the opposite wall. At first they appeared to be abstracts rendered in muted blues, greens and greys. But Wentworth had called them landscapes and slowly I began to see what he meant. What had initially looked like meaningless shapes were actually definite natural formations. The six huge canvases made up a series. All had the same composition and all had the same subject. I realised it was a lake. The shape and the position of the lake was similar in each painting but its appearance and colour varied. From painting to painting, the lake changed from tones of blue to green and back again. From water to grass to water. Each painting was beautiful in its own right, but together they were riveting. Now I understood what I was looking at. The subject was the turlough, the disappearing lake from Stevie's childhood that Kitty had told me about.

With tears running down my face, I gazed at the paintings and at the only place in his short life where Stevie Hennessy had known safety and love.

I blew my nose and stood up. It was time to go, but before leaving, I wanted to pick up the papers that still blew around the deck. It was the least I could do. I opened the sliding doors and went outside, collecting the drawings that had gathered in corners and pressed against the walls. When I straightened up, I was stopped by the panoramic view of the city around me. I saw church spires as far away as St Patrick's, the Wicklow and Dublin mountains cradling the town, the blue sea dotted with ships over on my left, the sun warming the red-brick buildings and the river shining through it all. And I realised, this is a beautiful place; and also, I should never have come back.

I bent to pull out a sheet that was jammed under a large plant pot, knocking over the pot as I did. The compost spilled out over the boards. I put the papers I'd retrieved on the trestle table inside and went back out to clean up. The compost was dry and warm and as I scooped it up with my hands and pushed it back into the pot, I thought about Ned Kinsella in the grow shop. I remembered his mixing station, its bins full of soils, the surrounding shelves lined with containers of liquid and powders, the whiteboard scrawled with names and measurements. All of which Mooney would have been aware of. And Mooney had arranged to meet me in the grow shop, just after he'd possibly written a cryptic message about clay. I stared at the soil in my hands and then rubbed them together quickly to brush it off. I had an idea.

Before leaving, I carefully photographed Stevie's large canvases individually and as a group. While I was doing so, I noticed there was something different about the last one. The boundary of its lake was in tones of grey and the shape, though similar to the others, was angular, less natural. I stopped and scrutinised it. It definitely represented something made of stone or concrete, like an urban equivalent of Stevie's disappearing lake. If there was someplace like that in the city, it wouldn't have been just attractive to Stevie, it would have been like a magnet.

I took the lift to the ground floor and, deep in thought, headed as quickly as my injuries would allow in the direction of the Silver Bullet Café. There were still a few straws left for me to grasp.

44

DAISY ROOT

Without the drawback of banjaxed knees, it would have been a five minute walk from the empty office building to the café. As it was, I speed-hobbled most of the way in just under double that time, keeping well in from the road and as much out of sight as possible. On the way, I called Daisy Root Organic Veggies, the only number I had for Ned Kinsella.

'Ned, it's Connie from the Silver Bullet Café. We met yesterday.'

'I remember, you're the one from Amsterdam,' he said. 'Is it vegetables you're after?'

It was not, but I thought I'd better make it worth his while.

'Yeah, go on. Vegetables would be great.'

'How about I start you off with a sample box, unless you need something in particular?'

'No, no. Nothing in particular. But I need them extremely urgently.'

'You need nothing in particular extremely urgently?'

'Well, yes. In the next few minutes or so.'

There was the briefest pause on the other end.

'Righty-oh, ten minutes then.'

I stopped before the corner and looked around it carefully. No cars were parked close to the café or on the quayside opposite. Nothing was coming down the road. Nobody was lurking in the shadows as far as I could see, but of course, that wasn't very far. I scuttled around the corner and inside the café without incident.

Viv and Christy were the only customers. They sat drinking tea at their usual table in the middle of the room. Kitty and Josie were clearing up after what looked to have been a busy lunchtime. I put my finger to my lips as I approached them.

'I need your help, Josie,' I said quietly. 'Have you got a minute?'

Kitty came over close and said in my ear, 'The guards were here this morning just after you left. Detective Rossiter was annoyed that we'd cleaned up. She wanted to talk to you.'

'I'll call her and tell her we couldn't leave the place as it was.'

'I told her that already. And they wouldn't have found anything anyway. It was a professional job.'

Josie brought a pot of tea and some cups with her and put them on the table before sitting down.

'Are you all right?' she said.

'Ah, yeah,' I said.

She knew well that I was lying.

'Kitty, did Stevie have a special place that he liked to go to? Not his studio, I mean someplace different.'

'God, maybe he did. He did these disappearing acts all the time, but I never asked him where he was. He needed time to himself. He never said anything about it, he just came and went. Why? Have you found something?'

'I found some more of his paintings. Here they are on the phone.'

I handed it over to Kitty. She examined the paintings with a frown.

'Is it a pool? I don't recognise it.'

'Josie, can you take a look? You know this area inside out.'

Josie checked the photos and shook her head.

'It's a particular *kind* of place, Josie. Maybe these photos aren't helping, you'd have to see the paintings themselves. Let's see ... do you know anywhere around here where there's water ... that goes up and down?'

'Up and down?'

'Yes. Or in and out.'

Josie looking at me as if I was an idiot child.

'Connie, love,' she said slowly. 'All the water around here goes up and down – and it goes in and out. With the tides. The river's tidal all the way up to Islandbridge.'

'That's not what I meant. I'm looking for someplace where the water is enclosed ...'

'And the water goes up and down?'

'Yes, or in and out.'

Josie considered this for a minute.

'What about a lock, like on the canal? They have to be able to raise and lower the level of the water on the locks. You know, the water goes up and down?'

I think she was laughing at me.

'The Royal Canal sea lock is down the road,' she said. 'They have it all done up now. I saw a boat going through it only the other day.'

'Ok, I'll check it out,' I said, although I was pretty sure the place I was looking for wasn't a lock.

'Could it be on the other side of the river? What about the old Poolbeg harbour, over there in Ringsend? It has a wall around part of it and the tide comes in and fills it up.'

'Ok, that's sounds good. Anything else?'

'I'm sure there's other places,' Josie said. 'I'll have a think. But there's been a lot of changes around here. I don't know the area as well as I used to.'

'I have to go out again but I won't be long. Call me if you think of anywhere else.'

The door opened and Ned Kinsella came in with a large cardboard box.

'Veggie delivery,' he said placing the box on the table in front of us. He looked around and smiled at Kitty.

'Nice place.'

'Thanks, Ned. That was quick. This is Kitty and Josie.'

'I don't often get emergency calls for random veggies,' he said.

'It's you I need, Ned. Your expertise. I'm interested in clay.'

'You remembered about my compost! Yeah, I know a bit about clays.'

'What if I told you that a man who was very sick with a ... a bacterial infection on his skin –'

'– wanted to use clay as a cure?' Ned offered.

'Sorry?'

'He could use clay to cure the disease. Isn't that what you were getting at? Some clays are anti-bacterial. They're good with those kind of diseases.'

'Seriously? Could you use them instead of antibiotics?'

'Or along with antibiotics, yeah. You have to be careful though, some clays could have the opposite effect. There's a special kind of green clay that's been tested and it works, though they're still trying to find out how it does it.'

'Green clay, green earth, *terra verde*,' I said to myself.

'*Terre verte*,' Ned corrected me. '*French* green clay. *Terra verde* is Italian. They're related. Both have a lot of iron in them.'

'Can you get some of this special clay, I mean quickly?'

'First you want emergency vegetables and now it's green clay! I've none in stock, but I'll check with my supplier. Shouldn't be too hard to get. How much do you need?'

'I've no idea.'

'I'll see what's available,' he said, turning to go. 'I'll text you.'

'Hold on till I pay you for the vegetables.'

'The first box is on the house,' he said as he left.

'Lovely,' said Josie as she peered into the box, delighted. 'And finally you're bringing some nice young men into the place too. Makes a change from the usual crowd of latchikoes you seem to attract.' She gave Kitty a knowing look.

I grabbed a glass of water in the kitchen and as I gulped it down, I noticed a small padded envelope on the counter. It was addressed to me, care of the Silver Bullet Café.

'What's this?'

'Sorry, I forgot,' Kitty said. 'It arrived this morning.'

I shook open the envelope and a small cardboard box fell out. I checked for a note but there was none. The writing on the box seemed incomprehensible but maybe I just couldn't focus with Kitty fidgeting about, opening cupboard doors and dumping things in the sink in front of me. I pocketed the box, thinking I'd open it later. I went to get my bike.

'Where are you off to now?' Josie asked. 'You're a bit like that watery place you were talking about – in and out all the time.'

'I know, sorry,' I said. 'But I won't be long. I want to have a look for the watery place.'

Kitty's tension was palpable as I wheeled my bike past her towards the door.

'Are you ok?' I asked her.

'Ah yeah,' she said. 'I just have this funny feeling – it's probably after the break-in. I feel jumpy. Like as if someone's watching us. I keep looking out but there's no one there.'

'Don't worry. Everyone feels like that after a robbery. Invasion of your personal space and all that.'

I didn't tell her that I felt exactly the same way, and it wasn't only because of the break-in. Outside the café, I considered calling Rossiter but I had no time for a lecture on the wrongs of interfering with last night's crime scene. And the memory of her with Fogarty last night was definitely off-putting. Instead I texted her with the message, *'Apologies for the café clean-up. It was out of my hands. Urgently need your help to locate Aggie, missing in Las Vegas for 48 hours. Brady has the details. Thank you.'*

I'd already pressed 'send' when I remembered my promise to Lu to inform the guards about Jimmy Mooney's voicemail. I'd do it later. I checked the street carefully again before painfully heading off on my bike towards the Spencer Dock Sea Lock.

I found it a short distance away, where the Royal Canal joins the river, right beside the tilted glass barrel of the Convention Centre. The lifting bridges looked like they were still in working order. I walked my bike down the landscaped walkway beside the lock and stopped to examine the huge lock gates. Impressive as it was, I knew the lock was not the place for Stevie. It was far too open and exposed, too noisy to be a refuge.

I thought about the south side of the river and Josie's idea about the old Poolbeg Harbour. It sounded as if at least part of it was open to the sea. Again, that seemed too open for what Stevie had portrayed in his pictures. All the same, I was about to head to the East Link Bridge to cross the river and check it out when my phone rang. It was Kitty.

'We asked Christy. He's thought of someplace else. Here's Josie.'

'Hower'ya love,' she said, 'didn't we forget all about the dry dock. Up in Alexandra Basin. The water goes in and out. And it goes up and down. Isn't that what you wanted?'

Yes, that's what I wanted. I got directions from Josie and cycled back up the quays to the roundabout at the end. Instead of turning right to cross the East Link Bridge, I took a left and the next right onto Alexandra Road. I was heading for Dublin Port. About two hundred yards up the road, I stopped and looked at the sign on a pair of steel gates. It said, Dublin Graving Dock. As I stood there, a message came through on my phone: *'Need to talk to you urgently. Please come down to Store Street asap. Nuala Rossiter.'*

Not now, Nuala, I thought and put my phone on silent.

45

GRAVING

I looked through the blue steel gates and knew I was in the right place. Something about the light and the colours here made me sure that this was what I'd seen in Stevie's painting, the last one in his turlough series. From where I stood, I could see part of the vast basin of the dry dock itself. It was drained of water and an enormous green ship sat perfectly balanced within it with no visible means of support. Its red keel and underbelly looked naked and raw, ready for surgery. The dry dock was bigger than a football field, like a giant, grey concrete swimming pool with a royal blue metal railing running around its perimeter. It wasn't very lake-like, but I had no doubt that this was Stevie's urban turlough.

I locked my bike a little way down the road and returned to the gateway. This time I entered, passing the 'Authorised personnel only' sign. A large white machine shed on the right stood with doors agape. Above the doorway, a sign said 'Dublin Graving Docks.' Outside it, a group of men unloaded a large piece of unwieldy equipment off a small truck with its engine running. Down on the floor of the dry dock some men in hard hats and high-viz vests were conducting an inspection beneath the belly of the ship.

I walked into a single storey timber-clad building beside the gate and knocked on the office door. A voice told me to come in.

'Hi,' I said. 'I'm Karalyn Hughes from Trinity. You got my email asking if I could come here this afternoon to take some pictures of the dry dock?'

'Sorry?' The poor man hadn't a clue what I was talking about and neither had I.

'I'm researching, um, Dublin's twentieth century industrial architecture. I was talking to somebody on the phone last week. Was it you?'

'No, it wasn't me.'

I smiled brightly as he looked me over.

'Here's my card,' I said, handing him the business card Karalyn had given me in the National Gallery. God forgive me, I thought, and I hoped Karalyn would too.

'Ok,' he said. 'The only thing is, most of us here are knocking off at four. If I can get someone to show you around, I don't see why not. No harm for more people to know about this place. Here,' he handed me a high-viz vest. 'Put this on and I'll see if one of the lads outside is available.'

He was gone for only a couple of minutes when he returned with an older man. I was staring at a garbled text message I'd just received from an unknown phone number. It said: '*Snt hainosankyuto.*'

Pure gobbledygook, I thought, shaking my head as I looked up at the men.

'Paddy, meet Karalyn from Trinity. She's doing some research on the dock and she wants to take a few pictures.

You can show her around. I have to head off, so I may not be here when you're done. I'm Richard – call me tomorrow if you need anything else.'

I thanked him, then followed Paddy outside.

He started by showing me the pile of flotsam banked up at the end of the dry dock, a mountain of rubbish that came in with the ships and got left behind when the dock was drained.

'God knows what you'd find down there,' he said.

I looked over the railing at a ton or so of cans and plastic, bags, bottles and containers of all shapes and sizes. Lying on top of the pile, looking surreal, was a safety man – one of those yellow 'wet floor' signs – its flattened shape like the chalk outline of a victim's body.

Paddy pointed out capstans and stag's horns and fair leads. He said the dry dock was nearly sixty years old, opened in 1958 by the President of the day, Sean T. O'Kelly as a major piece of national infrastructure and a source of great pride. There'd been an older dry dock alongside it, a Victorian structure built from cut stone, ascending in tiers like an amphitheatre. That was filled in five or six years ago and now a tarmac car park occupied the site. So much for the national pride. Paddy said this dry dock was destined for the same fate, the plan was to close it down in the near future to make more room for visiting cruise ships. So that's what Richard meant when he said that more people should know about it.

'But doesn't everything come into this country by ship? Cars, fuel, food, everything. Where will the ships get fixed if this place is gone? It's the only functioning dry dock in the country, right?'

'Right,' Paddy said. 'They'll have to go to Poland. Globalisation, I think they call it.'

'Madness is what I call it,' I said.

Paddy laughed. 'It's the way things are around here. They want to clear the docks area and make way for new developments and apartments. And cruise ships.'

'I thought the government was trying to create jobs.'

'Maybe, but they don't seem to want fitters and welders and guys who can make things. Even though it brings money into the city, it doesn't fit with the plans so it has to go. Here, you should see this.'

He pointed at a grey building with a sign that said, 'Number 2 Pump House.'

'The control centre. Come in and have a look.'

We passed through a blue door into a room floored by a metal grid, with a stairs going down it to another, similar level below. On the floor stood a series of large blue cylinder-shaped structures, each one sitting on its own black metal stand.

'Those are the pumps,' Paddy said, proudly. 'Still working perfectly after sixty years. There's engineering for you!'

Over on the far side of the room, was the control panel with a row of round dials and a panel of switches and buttons.

'The original controls – also working perfectly.'

He explained how the ship was floated into the flooded dock, secured carefully and how the floating gates were put in place and sealed shut.

'The caisson gates – I'll show them to you in a minute.'

I listened to Paddy about the workings of the dry dock, but I was looking out for something else. Looking for some sign of Stevie.

We left the Pump House and walked to the far end of the dry dock, to the outer sill, as Paddy called it. A yellow iron ramp led to a timber bridge that spanned the width of the dock. We crossed it, stopped halfway and looked down. The depth was indicated by white numbers written on the dock wall, going down in a line. Thirty three feet.

I peered down a round hole in the bridge that was protected by rails and saw water at the bottom, the depth of the dry dock's floor.

'That's the well,' Paddy said. 'It collects water. You're standing on the floating caisson gates. When they're in position, after the ship has entered the dock and been secured, the caisson gates create a seal and the water in the dock is pumped out.'

'How long does it take to drain the dock?'

'About five hours.'

I took pictures of the caisson gates and the well and the stairways along each wall that ran down to the bottom of the dock, each with its rusted handrail. Paddy showed me the small powerhouse as we walked beneath the dry dock crane, still standing on its original massive iron girders. The crane looked like it meant business with its huge hook hanging over us.

We'd walked the whole way around the dry dock and were almost back where we started. Paddy nodded over towards a high fence and the carpark beyond it.

'That's where the old graving dock is. It was built a hundred years before this one. Now they're talking about uncovering it again and turning it into a tourist site. And closing down this one that's bringing in money and jobs.' He shook his head. 'I'll never understand what goes on in their heads. I'm sorry but I have to go now. Is that ok for you?'

'More than ok, Paddy, thanks a million,' I said. 'I don't want to hold you up, but would you mind if I take another picture or two back there?'

I pointed back to the area around the crane.

'Ah, you seem the sensible type,' he said. 'You'll hardly go climbing up into places you shouldn't. Go on, just don't be long. I'll head on – I'll tell the guy on the gate on my way out so he knows you're still here. Everyone else has gone.'

I had one last question for him.

'Have you ever seen anyone drawing or painting here?'

'You know, there's been one or two artists about. I don't know their names ...'

'Did you ever see a young one, a teenager, with blond hair?'

'Ah, yeah, that kind of rings a bell. But you should ask the security guy – he knows everyone, whether they're supposed to be here or not.'

I thanked him and went back to the crane. I didn't need to talk to the security man just yet. I picked up the piece of charcoal I'd spotted on the ground and tapped on the window of the small shed beside the power house. I heard a rustle inside.

'Hi Shane,' I said. 'It's Connie from the Silver Bullet Café. Are you ok?'

46

THE GAME

'Do you want to tell me what happened, Shane, the night Stevie died?'

There was no response.

'It was Saturday night, wasn't it Shane? You must want to talk to someone ...' I paused. 'Don't worry, I won't tell anyone if you don't want me to.'

'Don't tell me Da,' Shane said, terrified.

'I won't tell your Dad, I promise. But you have to tell someone, Shane, for Stevie's sake. Do you know that his body was found? Back up the river, not far from the Silver Bullet Café. Nobody knows what happened to him. They're saying all kinds of bad things about him in the papers. You don't want that, do you Shane? You're the only one who can tell us what really happened. Come on out and talk to me.'

I sat down on the top of a capstan, one of the blue revolving metal cylinders that Paddy had shown me earlier. And waited.

After a few minutes, Shane shuffled out and sank down in front of the shed. He sat there in silence with his back propped up against the wall. He looked as if he hadn't slept or eaten in days.

'Got a smoke?' he asked eventually.

'Sorry, I quit a while back.'

He stared at me uncomprehendingly. When he began to talk, his voice was thick and slow.

'I've been going over it and over it,' he said. 'It's been doing my head in. We went to this party that Stevie was invited to – on Thursday. It was full of old farts – so fucking boring. I just wanted to get out of there. I was pissed off with Stevie, but he wanted to see someone about his pictures, maybe that Gordon weirdo, I don't know. I went off up the stairs by myself and swallowed a tab someone gave me. I don't know what it was, but it was bad, really, bad. I couldn't breathe, thought I was having a heart attack, thought I was going to die. Stevie came and found me and he was helping me, when these people came into the room and closed the door.'

'What people? How many?'

'Haven't a clue. Three or four of them, maybe. One of them was arguing and they didn't see us on the floor. They took stuff out of a bag and put it on the table. I thought they were dealers and they were talking business. Stevie tried to get me to shut up so they wouldn't see us. But I must have made a noise and they came and they found us. It was all my fault. It would never have happened if it wasn't for me ...'

'What happened, Shane?'

'I think one of them said something like. "now's your chance – here's a couple of junkies that have just fallen into our laps." They tried to sit me up on a chair, but the poxy yoke I'd taken made me all limp like a rag doll and I kept falling over. Another one said they should get rid of us, that we'd heard too much. But the first one said no one would believe a pair of dirty junkies. And do you know what they did?'

I shook my head. Shane clasped and unclasped his hands, struggling to speak.

'They held Stevie down, stretched him out and, like, whacked him with something. One of them said to get his hand, that he was a perfect little guinea pig.'

Shane clutched his hair in his shaking hands and held them there while he screwed his eyes closed.

'What happened then?' I asked after a few minutes.

'Stevie went off his head. He was roaring so much that they knocked him out with, like a stun gun or something. Whatever it was, he went unconscious. Then they called some other guys and they carried us out and dumped us down some laneway. It was morning by the time I came to and Stevie was gone. I found him in the Sunrise later on, he was arguing with Fogarty. He packed his stuff, said he was leaving and that everyone should leave. He said he was going to see Kitty and he was getting his money from Ozzie and then he was off.'

Shane paused for a minute before continuing. Now his voice was strained and high-pitched.

'I don't know where he spent Friday night, maybe in the studio, though he never wanted to sleep there. Somebody said they saw him back in the Sunrise on Saturday morning but they couldn't be sure. I searched everywhere. In the end I found him here at the dry dock. This was his favourite place. He started coming here a few months ago to draw or just sit and look at the water. The security guy knew him and turned a blind eye. When I got here, he was sitting over there, close to the edge. He'd pulled off his t-shirt and he was staring at his hand, he just kept staring at his hand. It was turning black and he was burning up. I tried to get him to go to a doctor but Stevie said it was too late, that he was dead already, dead without his hand. It must have been close to midnight.'

'On Saturday night?'

Shane nodded. He was on his feet now, staring into the vast empty concrete cavity.

'The dock gates were open and the tide was coming in, flooding the place. Stevie loved the dock when it was full. The ship that was here was ready to go out. There was hardly anyone around, couple of guys over the far side finishing up, the ones on the ship busy getting her going. There was no moon and it was really dark – just the safety lights around the dock and the light in the ship's engine room. Stevie stood up and said he wasn't going to be used by them, he said he wouldn't be part of the game. I didn't know what he was talking about. He walked right to the edge and – he disappeared. I don't know how it happened, if he jumped or if he slid down that stairwell there and slipped into the water. I just know there wasn't a sound, not a splash. I thought I saw him in the middle of the black water out there, floating, not swimming. Maybe he was in too much pain from his hand or maybe he'd hit his head or something. But the ship's propeller began to turn. I thought I saw his body swirling around behind the ship, being sucked out after it. There was nothing I could do. I fell apart ... couldn't call out, couldn't get help ... I wish I'd gone in after him now. I wish I was dead too.'

Shane sobbed soundlessly while I sat in silence, trying to take in what he'd just said.

I had to ask, 'Shane, what was the game Stevie was talking about?'

Shane shook his head.

'I honestly haven't a clue,' he said. 'I'd tell you if I knew. But I'm stupid like that, no cop-on. Useless, my Dad says.'

'You're not the only one who's useless, son,' Dessie Donlon said as he appeared in front of us. 'You've found your match with herself.'

47

MAKING A MONKEY

Dessie Donlon was not a happy man. But then, none of us at the dry dock was happy that afternoon. Shane immediately went into shutdown mode, probably his default behaviour in the presence of his father. He folded his arms, clammed up, avoided eye contact and became completely expressionless.

I tried to look unsurprised, as if I knew all along that Shane was Donlon's missing son and that Donlon was likely to show up at any minute. Somewhere in my confused brain there must have been an inkling that Donlon's missing son was the same person as Stevie's missing boyfriend, I just hadn't quite joined up the dots yet. Why did I have to do all the work, I complained to myself. Would it have been too much to expect that Kitty or Fogarty or *anybody* could have told me?

I thought Donlon was going to hit me straightaway when he walked right up and stood about six inches in front of my face. I instinctively put out my hands to try to protect myself. He pointed his index finger at me and, still glaring into my eyes, deposited the black holdall he was carrying at the open door of the shed beside us. He reached inside the holdall and, without taking his eyes off me, took out two battered spiral bound A4 sketchbooks.

'Stay, Bertie,' he said to the little dog peeping out of the holdall.

'Now,' he said through clenched teeth as he thrust the sketchbooks into my arms, his face white with rage. 'What the *fuck* made you think you could make a monkey out of me? I'm Dessie Donlon. I run this town. *Nobody* takes me for a fool. Look at those sketchbooks and tell me right now, where is the *fucking* antidote?'

I opened the nearest sketchbook and breathed in sharply. I flicked through the pages. They were covered in grotesque drawings of people, it was like Hieronymous Bosch met Goya's black paintings. There was something familiar about many of them, but I hadn't time to examine them properly.

'Mr Donlon, I'm very sorry. But if you remember, I did say to you that if Stevie knew what the antidote was, he would have used it to save himself. I didn't think it was in the sketchbooks, that was your idea. No, please, don't get mad –'

Donlon lashed out and belted me across the face so hard that I was thrown off the capstan and hit the shed wall hard. The sketchbooks went flying across the ground. Shane didn't move a muscle.

'*Don't* talk to me about whose idea was what,' Donlon said, advancing on me again.

'No, no,' I said, desperately trying to pull myself up and out of his way. I tried hard to stem the dizziness and not black out. Especially since I'd just realised something. That last text message I'd received wasn't garbled, and now I knew who it came from. I held up my hand.

'I have the antidote here.'

He stopped.

'I have it here in my pocket. Can I get it out to show you?'

'Ok, but don't try anything stupid.'

I was done being stupid. I was going to give him anything he wanted. I reached into my jeans pocket and took out the small box that had arrived earlier today in the envelope addressed to me. Donlon snatched it from my hand and read the label.

'What's this shite? Some kind of homeopathic bullshit?'

'*Hainosankyuto*. It's been tested and shown to be effective against *necrotising fasciitis* – the flesh-eating disease that Stevie Hennessy and Jimmy Mooney had. It'll cure strains of the bacteria that are resistant to antibiotics. It's well documented. You can read about it in PLOS One. That's the Public Library of Science,' I gabbled, remembering as much as I could from what Dr Rose Madden had told me in her clinic. 'Very reputable journal – open access too.'

I felt my jaw carefully, wondering if it was dislocated. The side of my face was swelling up. I was afraid to say any more for fear of unleashing more violence. I certainly wasn't going to mention anything to do with clay and its antibiotic properties. He'd think I was trying to make a monkey out of him and break my neck on the spot. Then he'd probably go after Ned and kill him too, just for the heck of it.

'Go on,' Donlon said.

'It's a traditional Japanese treatment for infectious diseases, based on ancient Chinese medicine. Scientists have tested it with the kind of bacteria that cause our flesh-eating disease. They found that it's effective both in curing the disease and in preventing it. So if you're worried about Shane, you should get him to take three to six of these every day before meals.'

I thought it sounded convincing considering at least half of it was made up.

Donlon laughed derisively.

'You don't think I give two shits about this useless waste of space here, do you? I leave that to his mother. Once he started shooting that crap into himself and hanging out with those ponces, that was it for me. Dean Clarke out there is more of a son to me than he is.'

He gestured towards the road outside. Costigan and Clarke must be waiting in the car, I thought. Again, there was no response from Shane Donlon. Obviously his father's less than loving opinion of him wasn't breaking news either.

Instead, somebody else spoke.

'So why don't you tell her why you really want that antidote, Donlon? I'm sure Connie'd love to know.'

It was the voice of Detective Inspector Brady and it came from above us. Donlon reached under his arm but before he could get there, a shot exploded, ripping into the ground beside him.

'Drop your weapon,' Brady roared. 'And get down on the ground.'

Brady was up on the crane ladder, just below the platform. He was partially concealed behind one of the crane's supporting girders. Donlon wasn't having any of it. He ran underneath the crane and started firing through the structure at Brady. He hit a cable and the crane's giant hook plummeted down until it stopped and swung about dangerously at about my height off the ground. I grabbed Shane, who was still standing as if he was paralysed, and ran, doubled-up, dragging him with me to take cover behind the capstan.

Donlon and Brady were playing cat and mouse around the crane. Brady kept taunting the gang leader.

'Why the panic about the disease, Donlon? It's because you know it's over for you and your lot, isn't it? You're desperate, you're trying to keep control but you know you're finished. We have a whole new approach now, and with it we can out-gun you, out-manoeuvre you and put you out of business. Permanently. You and all the other fucking parasites.' He spat out the last word.

Donlon laughed from behind one of the crane's thick steel legs.

'You're just another crooked cop, Brady. You and I both know that you've lost control of your "new approach". You thought you were a partner, but you're nothing but a puppet. Look what happened to Mooney. Did your partners consult with you about that? Did they tell you about their meeting with him in that office on Marlborough Street? The guy was riddled with cancer already, did you know that? He hadn't a chance. And as for that Hennessy kid ... You know, I've done some fucking horrendous things in my day, and I expect to burn in hell for them. But I'm not a fucking hypocrite.'

'Sure, Donlon.' Brady's voice dripped with sarcasm. 'You're proud of destroying generations of families through drugs, using the homeless as mules; the vice, the trafficking, the killing.'

'And you're going to make things better?' Donlon shouted back. 'All those ambitions you had, your studying, your hard work. What did it get you, you loser? A pay freeze, a ban on promotions, no recruitment for years, no resources.' Donlon laughed. 'I'd like to thank the government for its assistance on behalf of Steyne River Securities!'

Brady's shadow moved about up there as he silently positioned himself. Donlon ran to the far corner of the crane's base, squinting up, his weapon aimed skywards.

'You want to watch out, Brady,' Donlon continued. 'You thought your *business* connections with their resources and their expertise were the answer, but you know better now, don't you? You've been played for a fool. And using me as your trophy is not going to work now, Brady, because it's too late and you're in way over your head. I'm disappointed in you, Detective Inspector. Did you not do any research? Check out that stupid nickname and see what you find. Jesus Christ, I've been called a psycho once or twice and it takes one to fucking know one.'

'What nickname? Who's he talking about?' I muttered into the rusted metal column my face was jammed against.

'That's enough,' Brady finally retorted. 'You're playing for time, Donlon, but you might as well give up now. Don't think those clowns in your beemer are going to come and rescue you. You won't be seeing either of them again.'

Donlon stopped for an instant and glanced over in the direction of the gate and his car. It was long enough for Brady to take aim and fire. The noise of the three-round burst was deafening. Shane and I covered our ears, cowering down behind the metal capstan as the air filled with the smell of burnt sulphur. It sounded like Donlon was hit, I couldn't tell how badly. He dropped his weapon and swayed, trying to keep upright.

Brady clambered down the ladder and jumped the last few steps. He moved towards Donlon and lowered his pistol to take aim again. Instantly a wild yapping started as Donlon's dog shot out of the black holdall and began nipping Brady's ankles. Brady tried to kick the animal out of his way. Donlon reached, grabbed the huge hook and swung it. It came straight for Brady but he ducked out of its path and straightened up again, shooting three times in rapid succession. He got Donlon in the chest. Donlon staggered backwards, regained his balance, then fell to his knees, blood spreading across his shirt front. The yapping had stopped. Little Bertie lay flat on the ground, motionless. I must have made a noise because Brady swivelled round and raised his gun again, this time in my direction.

'I'm sorry to do this, Connie, but I have no choice. Come on out, don't make me come and get you.'

I didn't move.

'Come on, Connie.'

Shane and I watched, frozen, as the great hook swung back towards Brady from behind, slamming him on the head and jamming its sharp end into the back of his neck. It lifted Brady up, squirming and screaming and swung him out over the dry dock and back again. Donlon was on all fours, coughing blood, but somehow he wasn't finished yet. Holding his chest with one hand as if he could staunch the blood that now covered his entire shirt front, he reached for his gun on the ground beside him. It slipped from his blood-soaked fingers but he held on to it the second time and loosed a single shot at Brady up above. It hit the side of the crane. He turned to where we were crouching.

'You fuckers,' he muttered. 'You see who's in charge round here? You see!'

Then the automatic gunfire started. It came from above, from somewhere up beyond the car park and it sprayed Donlon in the back with such force that he toppled over, propelled sideways with the impact. He rolled once and fell face first over the side of the dry dock. After a second, I heard the crunch of his body hitting the bottom.

The automatic gunfire resumed, this time directed at Brady who was still swinging by his neck from the hook. The bullets hit him repeatedly, making his arms and legs jump in a macabre dance like an electrocuted marionette.

A covered stairway was directly behind our hiding place at the capstan, the one Shane thought Stevie slipped down. It was like a tunnel and led to the floor of the dry dock. While the gunfire was focused on Brady, I pushed Shane down the steep, slippery concrete stairs and followed him, the two of us sliding and falling until we grabbed the rusted handrail and clung there, terrified, as we listened to the noise outside.

And then it stopped. I waited about five minutes before creeping up the steps to see if it was safe to come out. All was quiet except for the creaking of a chain above me. I didn't want to look up at Brady. His shadow swung gently backwards and forwards over the dry dock, its floor painted with an arc of his blood. Donlon's crumpled body was down there too, spread-eagled atop the flotsam at the far end, like more debris from the sea. Little Bertie's body lay still on the ground.

'Poor Bertie,' I said to him. 'Brave dog trying to save your rotten master. He didn't deserve you.'

As I bent to stroke his side, he stirred and I realised he'd fainted again. I picked him up and he licked my nose. Then I heard a noise behind me and froze, ready to run for cover again.

'Hell-OOOO,' a voice called out. 'Is anybody there?'

48

ASHES TO ASHES

There was no mistaking the wearer of those white skinny jeans, strappy sandals, spray tan and diamonds. It was Karen Donlon. She stopped the minute she saw me standing there in the midst of the carnage.

'Why am I not surprised?' she said.

'It's not how it looks, Karen,' I said, possibly even more terrified of her than I was of the guns. 'It wasn't me.'

She glanced up at Brady, still swinging gently on his hook, and said, 'Jesus.'

Then she looked into the dry dock and saw Dessie down there, lying amongst the flotsam. She studied him for a few minutes and clicked her tongue.

'Well now,' she said. 'Isn't that the end of a bleeding era.'

I bet she was already planning her outfit for the funeral. Plus her future career as widow of the great man, Dessie Donlon, another local candidate for canonisation.

She lit a cigarette and said, 'Where's my son?'

I called him. 'Shane, it's safe to come out. Your Mum's here.'

Shane appeared at the top of the steps, his dark hair in his eyes, his face pale, wearing a smile for the first time since I met him. He walked over to his mother and she put the cigarette between her lips and held out her arms to hug him.

'There you are, son.'

'How did you find me?' Shane asked.

'I was following that one,' she said, indicating me with her cigarette. 'Thought she was having an affair with your father. Well, she has a reputation for that kind of thing.'

'Excuse me!' I said, outraged.

'I parked in an entrance up the road and waited there while she went in here. Then Dessie's car pulled up outside the gates. Dessie left Costigan and Clarke in the car and had a word with the security guard. He must've frightened him off because the security guard went off down the road and didn't come back. Then Dessie walked in here. I was sure I'd caught the pair of them in the act.'

'Oh for God's sake,' I muttered. Karen ignored me.

'I was about to come in and confront them when I saw that bollix Brady arrive. He went straight up to Costigan and Clarke like he was going to have a chat with them. He got them to roll down the window and then he took out a gun and shot the pair of them up close and without any warning.'

'In broad daylight – on a busy road?' I still couldn't get over Brady. He must have lost his mind.

'It happened real fast and I didn't hear a sound. Used a silencer, I suppose. Then he went in through the gates here.'

That explained it, I thought. Brady had slipped past us and climbed the crane while Dessie was threatening me.

'After a while I heard the shooting,' Karen continued. 'I waited till it all went quiet and then I came in.'

'How did you know I was here?' Shane asked.

'Well, I didn't. I'd been putting pressure on Dessie to find you. I was terrified you were going to get that disease Stevie had. There was a rumour that there was a way of fighting it – an antidote. I told Dessie about it and he got real interested. That's when he started dropping into herself here and following her about. I suppose I should've copped it was something to do with the antidote but I was a bit paranoid at the time, especially about herself. Her number was in Dessie's phone. She even phoned me one night and mentioned him. She just kept showing up everywhere. Sorry.'

'That's all right,' I said.

'Dessie wasn't getting anywhere and, speaking of paranoid, he was going up the walls about the disease *and* about some new crowd coming in on his patch. Sugar Ray was tortured, his teeth pulled out before he was killed, and next thing the cops were raiding every one of Dessie's operations. And still no sign of you, Shane. Then I found an address for a place on Spencer Dock written on a piece of paper in your room.'

'The studio,' I said. 'That's how Dessie found it before I did!'

I thought about the dead security guard and how he mustn't have agreed to play ball with Dessie. Or maybe he wasn't given the option.

'Yeah, I told Dessie to check it out. He found Stevie's sketchbooks there and after that he wasn't bothered about looking for you, the bastard. The only reason I knew you were here, Shane, was because the minute I got here I spotted your jacket through the door of that shed there.'

Karen pointed and we saw the sleeve of a red cotton jacket in the shed doorway.

She walked to the edge of the dock and considered her dead husband. Then she took a last drag from her cigarette, flicked it away and watched it spiral down to land on top of him. 'Ashes to ashes,' she said and turned to go. 'How about we get out of here.'

'Hang on,' I said.

I went over to her and handed her Bertie.

'Your dog,' I said.

She took him in her arms and studied me for a moment.

'Thanks,' she said. 'Come on and I'll give you a lift. You're hardly going to cycle back after all this.'

Shane collected his jacket and some other stuff from the shed. I ran around and picked up as many of the sketchbooks' pages as I could. Some of them had blown as far away as the caisson gates at the other end of the dock, some were floating out on the water beyond it.

Karen's silver sports car was across the road and we had to pass the black BMW to get to it. Through the open window on the driver's side, I saw the two slumped bodies.

'Jesus,' I muttered.

The pavement shook as a convoy of articulated trucks rumbled past us towards Dublin Port. Passenger cars sped in the opposite direction towards the city. Why had none of them stopped? Surely someone had heard the gunfire. What was wrong with people in this town?

I got in the car beside Karen, with Shane and Bertie in the back, and looked back to the dry dock. Then I found my phone and, making sure my number was withheld, was about to make an anonymous call to the emergency services when I felt a sharp slap on my arm.

'Don't be stupid,' Karen said. 'Use a new phone, for God's sake. Here ...' She reached into the glove compartment, pulled out a phone in a plastic wrapper and tossed it back to Shane. 'Set that up for her, son.' she said.

He passed me the device and I made the call while eyeing my co-travellers carefully.

It was only a few minutes drive to the café. Karen pulled in opposite it and Shane gently removed the new phone from my hand, and broke it in pieces. He got out and slung it over the quay wall into the river. I remained seated, there was something else I needed to ask Karen.

'Who was firing the automatic weapon? You know, from up above the car park.'

'Don't look at me,' she said and she laughed. 'I haven't a fucking clue.'

I hesitated a moment, before deciding I had nothing to lose. 'You wouldn't know anything about my aunt, would you? Like, if Steyne River Securities had kept her somewhere or had ... had hurt her?'

'I know nothing about my husband's business,' she said firmly, her eyes fixed on the rearview mirror.

I got out and was about to cross the road when she called me back. She'd rolled down her window.

'Wait,' she said. 'There *is* something I can tell you. You know when I was following you, thinking you were carrying on with Dessie?'

I nodded.

'I wasn't the only one watching you. Just thought you should know.'

49

QUASIMODO

I pushed open the door and limped into the café. The throbbing of the helicopter overhead and the clamour of squad cars racing up the quays filled the room. It was quiet when the door closed behind me again. The customers gawped, their coffee cups paused in midair.

'Your face!' Kitty said, horrified. 'Jesus. What happened?'

'Fell off my bike,' I muttered. 'I'll just go and clean up a bit.'

When I looked in the mirror, Quasimodo looked back at me. One side of my face was completely swollen, a huge bruise spreading across it, the other side was scraped and covered in dried blood. One of my eyes was half-closed. My face must have hit the ground when Dessie Donlon sent me flying. My shoulder and back hurt so much, I couldn't walk straight. I was a wreck, but it could have been worse. I could have been dead like a lot of the people I'd met recently.

'Four in the past couple of hours,' I said to Quasimodo. 'Five if you count the security guard earlier on. A bloody bloodbath. And it could have been me and Shane too.'

I shuddered, remembering Brady swinging from that hook like a piece of meat. Brady, who'd gone completely over to the dark side. He'd killed Costigan and Clarke in cold blood. And I knew he wouldn't have thought twice about pulling the trigger on me back there. You'd expect that kind of thing from a gangster like Donlon. In fact, with only a mangled face and a few bruises, I reckoned I'd got off lightly with him. With Brady, I wondered what drove such a dedicated police officer to do what he had done. Donlon taunted him about his frustrated ambitions. And maybe he had financial pressures? I remembered his belief that he could clean up the city faster and better, for once and for all. He wanted to impress his friends in the financial and business sector. I wondered about those connections. I thought about his anger as he rushed past me in the club last night. Ozzie said it was because Aleka had dumped him for Claude Leyton. That made no sense whatsoever.

And I wondered who was responsible for the automatic gunfire that finished off Brady and ultimately saved me and Shane. It could only have come from the tall office building I'd seen across the car park next to the Dublin Graving Dock property. I'd given the building a quick scan on our way back to the café. The sign on its front said 'Dublin Port Co.' and there were plenty of lights on and cars parked around it. Donlon's men couldn't have been responsible. Donlon had followed me to the dry dock, leaving Costigan and Clarke in his car and taking his beloved little dog with him. He hadn't been expecting to meet any trouble, just planned to dish it out – to me.

No, someone else was in that building, someone who knew who we were, who was well-prepared and well-armed. Whoever it was had to have been watching some or all of us. I knew I needed to make some calls and ask questions. I also knew I should phone Detective Rossiter. But not yet. First, I wanted to talk to Kitty.

By the time I went downstairs, the café was empty. I heard Kitty rummaging around in her room. The TV was on, tuned to a reality show that Kitty was addicted to. I found the disintegrating remote and, wielding a skewer, stabbed the space where the off button should be. Instead the channel switched to the news. Josh Treanor, wearing a khaki-coloured, multi-pocketed body warmer over a t-shirt and cargo pants, stood with his back to a pale blue crane and spoke with urgency into the camera.

'Another day of violence in Dublin's north inner city where distinguished senior police officer, Detective Inspector Anthony Brady, died in the course of his duty fighting the scourge of the city's criminal gangs. The body of the Dublin crime boss, Dessie Donlon, was also found at the scene here at the dry dock in Alexandra Basin. Detective Inspector Brady was responsible for the recent spectacular success of the gardaí, leading a series of well-publicised raids that cut right into the heart of the crime boss's empire. Those raids continue tonight and it looks like Dublin city's gangster era may finally be coming to an end. This is Josh Treanor for *TV News Live* from Dublin's Docklands.'

Some bloody hero. I felt sick, remembering Brady's last words to me: 'I'm sorry to do this, Connie, but I have no choice.'

I stabbed the remote again and it flicked to a panel discussion direct from daytime TV's graveyard slot. A group of experts was discussing Archbishop Alexander de Bicknor.

'You can't apply a twenty-first century world view to medieval times,' proclaimed a dapper professor with a shaved head and a trendy leather jacket, its collar artfully turned up.

'So you're saying there's no substance behind what the media are calling The Bishop's Curse,' the host said. 'It was an outlook not peculiar to Alexander de Bicknor but something to do with the medieval view of social order?'

'Yes, and don't forget, there was another angle. In focusing on vagrants and the idle poor, Bicknor could control the mendicant friars who also depended on charity and begging. He needed them as a workforce for his newly-established University of St Patrick's.'

'Casualisation of academia from the outset,' retorted a tired-looking woman historian with a bitter laugh.

'Jesus, Kitty, would you ever turn this thing off?' I slid the loathed remote across the counter as she came in. She picked it up, pointed it and the TV screen went black. She put it down and sighed.

If I looked strange, Kitty didn't exactly look herself either. I hobbled over to her and made her sit down and talk to me. She was agitated, her eyes darting in the direction of every sound.

'Connie, remember earlier on I said I thought we were being watched? Well, a couple of times today when the place was empty, I thought the bell on the door rang – as if someone had come in. But there was no one there. Another time, I saw a shadow at the window, but it was gone when I looked again. I must be going crazy.'

Her dark eyes were full of fear. No more smart arse attitude. She jumped when I touched her arm.

'I was glad when your American friends came in and stayed for a long time,' she said. 'They've only just left. He was asking for you, you know, the George Clooney lookalike.'

'You mean, the Clark Gable lookalike. Oh, never mind,' I said to Kitty's raised eyebrow.

'He left something for you. In the bag in the kitchen. I think he likes you.'

'You think every man who walks in here likes me,' I said as I went to retrieve the bag. 'That's not how grown-up life works. Everyone has an agenda.'

I smiled as I looked into the bag and saw my shoes. I'd forgotten all about them. I opened a card with an invitation to a gala dinner for Bicknor Day on Friday. On the back was a note in clear, open handwriting: 'I really enjoyed our conversation last night. I hope you did too. Please do me the great honour of being my guest on Friday. Claude.'

Beneath the message was an underlined mobile number.

'Why the hell not,' I thought. He was pleasant, easy on the eyes, had perfect manners and he'd offered to make enquiries about Aggie. Plus he was no friend of Brady's and that was all the better. After all the horror and the mayhem, doing something normal and civilised sounded good. I reached for my phone to respond but it was dead again. I went to look for the charger while saying to Kitty, 'You need a rest. Why don't you take it easy tonight?'

She shook her head. 'I promised Ozzie I'd rep tonight. I'm still trying to find anyone who might have seen Stevie the night he died. But now I'm scared. Will you come and meet me there, Connie? Please?'

I'd been going to tell Kitty about what I'd learned from Shane, that she was right all along about Stevie, that he had, effectively, been murdered. I was going to tell her about the sketchbooks. But now I hesitated. Partly because she was so nervous and tired. But I was also wondering why she hadn't been fully open with me about Shane. I decided it would keep until the morning and I'd had a chance to think about it all.

'No problem,' I said, even though I felt like going straight to bed.

'My pitch is Williams Lane, do you know it? It's an alleyway between Middle Abbey Street and Princes Street. If I'm not there, I'll be around the corner on Litton Lane, between North Lotts and the river. It's close to where the competition is, the other clubs. I'll text you – maybe around midnight?'

'Ok,' I said. 'Are you sure you're all right? Is there something you're not telling me?'

She shook her head but I knew her well enough by now to know when she was lying.

50

FUD

There were no customers, everyone had left early. Outside on the quays was strangely quiet, with practically no traffic. But through the bathroom window at the back came a sporadic din of sharp bursts and crackles. I phoned Lu O'Leary but could hardly hear her against the surrounding racket of sirens and shouting.

'Can't talk, Connie, it's madness here,' she yelled into her phone from a few streets away. 'There's a running battle here on Ballybough Road. Same in Cabra, Coolock, Crumlin, West Dublin. It's the post-Donlon turf war. Community leaders claim armed militia activity but the Garda Commissioner denies all knowledge. And that disease ... people are panicking ... I have to go.'

I locked up the café and pulled out my laptop to do some research, still thinking about everything that Shane told me about what happened to Stevie, about the party they'd attended on Thursday night and what happened to Stevie.

His account explained how the drug got into Stevie's system. But I wondered how reliable Shane's memory was.

I thought of the allegations that Donlon had thrown at Brady at the dry dock and what he said about Mooney. If Mooney had cancer, I guessed that was the information Fogarty had on him that Mooney didn't want known. So that was what the consultant meant when he said Mooney's immune system was compromised. No wonder the bacterial infection killed him so quickly, he hadn't a chance. Mooney told me he'd made a mistake and he was going to fix it. He must have known that, as a cancer patient, if he became infected with *necrotising fasciitis*, it would run through his system at lightning speed and would be unstoppable. He must also have known that two deaths from the disease within twenty-four hours would ring alarm bells and attract attention, especially if one of the victims was a high profile journalist. Maybe he hoped it would attract the wrong kind of attention for the people whose plans he had decided to destroy. Fogarty said Mooney's death was suicide. I was sure now that Mooney had deliberately endangered himself by going to that meeting in Marlborough Street. Suicide by criminal.

I looked up 'FUD', one of the things Mooney'd said in his voice message, as confirmed by Lu. My search results returned Fear, Uncertainty and Doubt, a strategy to influence public opinion by spreading negative or false information. Alternatively it's a Scottish vulgarism for female genitalia, but I discounted that. The deliberate use of disinformation to control people through fear sounded about right.

I remembered Mooney's newspaper headline, 'Flesh-Eating Infection Ate Teen Addict's Hand.' That was FUD. Mooney's rant about the drug-fuelled crime explosion and its impact on trade and tourism. That was more FUD.

Mooney had been deliberately spreading fear through his articles, fear, uncertainty and doubt about crime in the city and about its most vulnerable people, the addicts, alcoholics, the mentally unstable on the streets, the homeless. Then he changed, he realised he'd made a mistake. That night when he was going to throw himself in the river he said he'd been stupid, that he'd been taken for a ride. That meant somebody had persuaded him to propagate the fear. Who was it, I wondered, and why?

I tried to figure out what had happened to Mooney to make him realise his mistake. That conversation with Brady in the Eight Bells had made him angry. Brady had cut him loose that night, said he was on his own. I guessed Mooney had been collaborating with Brady to spread the fear and that Brady had been feeding him information to support it as part of his plan for wresting back control of the city. Later on, Mooney was so filled with self-loathing, he was prepared to kill himself. That's why he didn't resist Fogarty's rewrite the following morning. Now I remembered what I'd said to him when I got him away from the river's edge the other night. After I told him about the sketchbooks, I'd mentioned Stevie's warning that everyone is in danger. Mooney had made me repeat it. That was the point that Mooney decided to sacrifice himself, I was sure of it.

'Don't you worry,' he'd said to me. 'I know what I have to do.'

Now I knew what he'd had to do too. Fight FUD with FUD. Counter-FUD. By getting himself infected, he deliberately heightened the level of public anxiety. No amount of dead homeless teenagers would have had the effect of a dead member of the media with a household name.

On a whim, I searched for 'thirteen twenty' and 'Dublin'. I was surprised to find a podcast about medieval Dublin vividly describing what the city was like in the fourteenth century. It hadn't occurred to me that Mooney might have been referring to the year 1320. It was a real long shot, but worth checking out if only to eliminate it from the possibilities. According to the podcast, 1320 was a year when Dublin was recovering from war and devastation of apocalyptic proportions. Coincidentally, it also seemed to be the heyday of Alexander de Bicknor, the Archbishop of Dublin. I listened to the podcast and checked out a couple of articles about Bicknor, finally understanding what was meant by The Bishop's Curse.

I cleared my work table and spread out the remnants of the sketchbooks I'd retrieved from the dry dock. All of the eight loose pages were crumpled and dirty. Half of them were destroyed by dirt and water and were completely illegible. At least one of the remaining four pages was blood-stained. Brady's blood, I assumed, trying not to think about his bullet-riddled body swinging from the crane, its blood draining out onto the concrete far below.

That wasn't the only way Brady featured in the sketches. I recognised his face amongst several others in the smudged but detailed pencil drawings. Brady must have been desperate to get the sketchbooks too, there was no way he was going to let those drawings fall into the wrong hands. And there were other faces I recognised on the pages, people I'd only seen pictures of on the news or in the papers. Stevie's talent was his ability to capture a likeness and to make reality appear more real. There was one face that appeared in the sketches more frequently than any of the others, someone who was very real. And the cigarette burns were there too.

Soon I was on the phone and I wasn't making social calls.

When I was done I had a list of names to match some of the sketches and I had a lot of detail on one of them. I checked parish records online, phoned Lu O'Leary and a contact in Amsterdam, leading to another in New York.

I spread out my notes on 1320 in Dublin and on Archbishop de Bicknor and my jottings on FUD. Then I looked up Matt Talbot and his shrine to check again for any connection with the burns. I found none, but to my surprise, I saw that his website had an online version of the petition. Anyone could submit their request by filling out a form, just as I had done on paper the day before. I smiled as I thought I'd send him a reminder. I started writing:

> *Dear Venerable Matt Talbot, I hope you don't mind me asking but I was wondering when you think you might get around to considering my request (submitted yesterday in hardcopy).*

It's funny that sometimes when you start typing you keep going almost without thinking, as if your fingers have an independent need to communicate. I looked at the page I'd written with interest, especially the sentence, *'Clay is the beginning and Clay is the end.'* I shook my head and went to delete it by pressing the 'Close without saving' button. A window appeared saying, 'Thank you for your petition. May God bless you.' The damn thing had been sent. I was staring at the screen in astonishment when the banging of an open window at the back of the café made me look around. I realised it was pitch dark and I'd been sitting there for hours. And I'd just missed a text from Kitty: *'R u on ur way?'*

I ran out the door while texting a response.

I made it to Middle Abbey Street by ten past midnight. No running battles, no police presence here. Just the distant chorus of sirens from all directions. The sound of music and laughter carried out onto the street through the open doors of a club on my left. The bouncers and a couple of girls were smoking quietly around the entrance, but inside the night was in full swing. It had that feel about it, the energy and optimism of a night out just before it all turns sour and depressing.

I passed the side entrance to Penney's department store and stopped outside a grand old building with a square, white-faced copper clock extending out above its entrance. The clock had the name 'Independent House' written on it and it could be read from either side by people coming up or down the street.

To the right of the building's entrance were three old postboxes set into the wall with labels etched in their brass surrounds saying 'Letters and Box No. Replies' over one of them and 'Competitions' over two of differing widths. All of the postboxes had the word 'Push' printed on their flaps and a little metal hood to keep off the rain. The brass surround had been corroded by the weather over the years, its surface patterned with blotches and bubbles and as if it had been attacked by acid. The name over the postboxes was 'Independent Newspapers Limited' with smaller lettering for 'Irish Independent', 'Evening Herald', 'Sunday Independent'.

The building was empty and abandoned. Its copper clock hanging proudly over Middle Abbey Street was stopped. Steps led up to its entrance, a carved stone doorway. A blue sleeping bag lay crumpled along the top of the steps but its occupant was nowhere to be seen. There was an opening, a partly-covered alleyway, running between Independent House and the next building. A single overhead light at its entrance illuminated the street name, Williams Lane. I checked my phone to make sure this was where Kitty asked me to meet her.

I looked down the lane. Dirty brick walls lined its sides all the way down to the dim rectangle of light at the far end. The rest of the interior was in darkness. Kitty wasn't at either end of the alley. She was nowhere in sight.

I texted her to let her know where I was. I wondered why she'd asked me to meet her there at all. Surely she had friends who'd be much better suited to the job. Neither the time nor the place was suitable for anyone over the age of forty, with the possible exception of street cleaners or cops, none of whom were around at the moment. My phone buzzed again and I checked it, thinking it was Kitty. But the text came from Karen Donlon.

'Look you did me a favour finding Shane and all. So I'm returning it as a one-off. No one in Steyne River Securities knows anything about your aunt. That's all I'm saying. Do not contact me. I mean ever.'

I read the words but couldn't take them in. If Steyne River Securities didn't know about Aggie, what the hell had happened to her?

'Spare some change, Missus. Anything at all, Missus.'

The homeless guy appeared out of nowhere and took me completely by surprise. So much for my observation skills. Anyone could have jumped me. I'd really have to pay more attention.

He was young, late teens, early twenties. With his tousled brown hair, bright eyes and a shy smile, there was something sweet and gentle about him. Thinking of Stevie, I reached into my jeans pocket, feeling for the change I'd raided from the tips jar earlier on. As I dropped whatever I found there into his outstretched hand, he said 'Thanks, Missus, thanks very much.'

I muttered 'Good luck' to him and he shambled off towards O'Connell Street. I walked in the opposite direction past an amorous couple welded together in a doorway and a group of teenage boys heading to the nearby club, laughing loudly.

I turned left on to Liffey Street, then left again, hoping that walking would bring some clarity to my tumult of confusion over Aggie. Now I really wished I hadn't agreed to meet Kitty. She said if she wasn't on Williams Lane, she'd be on Litton Lane, between North Lotts and the river.

I walked down the narrow, cobbled street feeling increasingly fearful. This really wasn't a good place to be alone. It was too dark, too quiet, too full of creepy old warehouses and the back entrances to buildings on Middle Abbey Street on one side and those fronting the quays on the other. I walked along the middle of the street, staying clear of the dustbins and the parked cars and the dark gateways.

I was about to turn right onto Litton Lane, the narrow street that ran down to the river and the boardwalk, when I heard a movement behind me and froze. I heard it again and ducked down behind a parked van. After a few seconds, I peered around the back of the van. A hunched figure stood in the middle of the intersection of the streets, looking up and down. Looking for me. Someone was following me.

51

WILLIAMS LANE

'Missus, where are you? I have something for you.'

It was the young homeless guy I'd given my change to a few minutes ago. There was no way I was coming out. I'd been subjected to one violent attack within the past eight hours, I wasn't about to present myself for another one. I stayed behind the van, hoping he couldn't hear my heart pounding.

'Come on, Missus. It's something belonging to you. You gave it to me by mistake.'

He moved under a street lamp and stretched out his arm, holding his palm open to the light. There was something in his hand but I couldn't see what it was. He stood there, motionless in the streetlight. I examined him and assessed my chances. He was very thin and shorter than me. Judging by his pallor, he might not have eaten in a while and was probably sick. I reckoned he wasn't that threatening after all.

'What is it?' I called from behind the van.

'Come and see,' he said and turned his open hand towards me.

I emerged from my hiding place and walked slowly across the lane to where he stood. His eyes shone as he smiled and tipped something into my open hand.

'You see,' he said. 'You gave it to me. With the money.'

I looked at the small white object in my hand.

'What is it?'

'You know,' he said, 'must be your kid's. From you being the tooth fairy, like.' He said it shyly, he was really only a kid himself.

'You'll want to hold on to that,' he said as he turned and walked back the way he'd come.

I looked after him, amazed he'd taken the trouble to find me and return such a thing. He thought it was important but I'd never seen it before. It meant nothing to me. I stared without understanding at the tiny tooth in my palm. The sudden beep of my phone startled me into almost dropping it.

'*On Wlms Lane. Whr u?*' It was Kitty.

As I rounded the corner back to Middle Abbey Street, I saw Kitty across the road at the entrance to the laneway. I waved and her pale face looked back at me, her expression nervous and unhappy. Not much of a welcome. She stamped the hands of a couple of scantily-clad, drunken girls who teetered on impossible heels. As they staggered off, she went to come and meet me, finally smiling. Then she stopped, as if she'd forgotten something, turned and darted down the alleyway.

'Kitty!' I called after her. 'What's going on?'

I ran across the street to the entrance to Williams Lane. Kitty was down at the far end of the alley, her slight figure silhouetted in the rectangle of light. I called her again and was about to walk down to her when there was a sudden noise. Two dark shapes appeared from the left of the far entrance and grabbed Kitty, bundling her away. Her stifled screams stopped and were replaced by silence. I tore up the alley, shouting her name, ignoring something metallic that clattered away from under my feet. I dropped my phone as I ran, hearing it hit the ground in the darkness. When I got to the end, I looked in every direction for any sign of Kitty or her abductors. Directly opposite me, taking up most of a high wall, a metal garage gate was firmly closed. To the left was the closed exit to a multi-storey car park owned by Arnott's department store. To the right, the direction in which her abductors had taken Kitty, I looked up the empty street to O'Connell Street. Clery's shutdown, dead facade was just visible through the kerbside trees across the road. There was no sign anywhere of Kitty or the men who'd taken her.

For an instant, I was paralysed. Then I forced myself back into Williams Lane to try to find my phone and get help. Feeling about the ground in pitch darkness halfway up the alley, I picked up a small metal cylinder, about the size of a lipstick. I pocketed it and kept searching for my phone, moving my feet carefully in case I stood on it. Miraculously, one foot touched it gently and even more miraculously, when I retrieved it and pressed the button, the light came on. The screen wasn't even scratched. At least I could call for help, just as soon as I got out of that claustrophobic tunnel.

At the entrance to the lane, under the dull yellow glow from its dirty, wire-covered roof light, I examined the metal tube I'd found on the ground. It was a club stamp – like the one I'd seen Kitty using. She must have dropped it.

I pressed it on the back of my hand, the way I'd seen Kitty do, but there was no mark. I put it away and fumbled for my phone with shaking hands.

'Hello, Emergency Services,' a rushed female voice answered. 'Please provide your location and the emergency service required.'

'Middle Abbey Street, Williams Lane. I need the guards. Someone's been abducted.' She switched the call before I'd finished the sentence. As soon as I heard the words 'Bridewell Garda Station', I launched into a description of what had happened.

The Garda officer sounded tense.

'Look, I'm sorry ... I've taken down the details you've supplied along with your contact information but to be honest, all of our units are already attending to multiple emergencies across the city. Priority incidents. I'll see what I can do but right now I can't give you any information on when we can get someone down to you.'

I stared at the phone in disbelief, thinking that surely a reported kidnapping should be seen as a priority. But not in the Bridewell, or at least not tonight. I thought about Brady and how he'd gone over to the dark side. How did I know all the guards weren't like that? Detective Nuala Rossiter seemed ok when I first met her, but even then I felt there was something about her, that she was hiding something. On balance, if she was foolish enough to hook up with Fogarty while in full knowledge of his criminal record, I guess it was her own look-out. I called her number feeling almost sorry for her. It went straight to voicemail. Damn. I left a terse message telling her it was urgent and asking her to get back to me.

I stared into the laneway, willing Kitty to appear, almost seeing her standing there laughing as she explained it was all a joke. But there was no sign of her. It was over ten minutes since she was carried off. Those men could be hurting her ... I didn't want to think about what they might be doing. I got my phone out again and scrolled down through the list of contacts, stopping at one.

Ozzie Wolf answered with a 'Bad timing, Connie. I'll have to get back to you.'

'Help, Ozzie! Don't hang up – Kitty's in trouble!'

I figured Ozzie would know what to do. Kitty had been repping for him after all, he was responsible for her out there. Or so I thought. He listened to my account of where I was and what had happened and remained silent for a few seconds. When he spoke, he sounded quite unconcerned.

'Are you sure she was abducted? Why would anyone do that? Naw ... it was just some of her mates having a bit of fun. Don't worry, Kitty'll show up, she can look after herself. She's probably downstairs in Stalag 17 as we speak. Come on down yourself, Connie. Have a drink. You really need to lighten up, you know.'

'Well, that's a great help, Ozzie. Thanks so much. Maybe I should call your girlfriend, Aleka and see if she'll pull some strings with the guards for me? Or should I try *her* friend, Claude Leyton, and see if *he'll* take me seriously?'

There's nothing like poking a guy in a sore spot to get a reaction. Ozzie was being way too nonchalant for my liking. Plus all of a sudden I felt like doing a quick probe on the Ozzie and Aleka thing. His tone was rather less offhand when he replied.

'Don't bother Aleka, she's totally tied up tonight. The Bicknor Day is looming and all that ... If you're not happy with my take on all this, why don't you call Fogarty? He's probably hanging around doing nothing. Call him. Tell him to come and get you – or get a taxi. Do it now.'

'Fogarty's the last person I'd call at a time like this. Or ever,' I said, haughtily. 'Come on Ozzie, help me!'

'Don't stand around there, Connie. I'm serious. That's the best advice I can give you right now. I have to go.'

He hung up. Useless, I thought, filled with dismay. He really couldn't care less about Kitty or me. But what had I expected? I shook my head and reluctantly searched for Fogarty's number. I hesitated, took a deep breath and texted. That way I wouldn't have to hear his voice. Almost immediately his message pinged back.

'*Stay there. Conceal yourself. I'm close by. With you in 5.*'

I pressed myself into a shadowy tattoo shop doorway directly opposite the entrance to Williams Lane. Hiding my dimmed and silenced phone under my top, I peeked down every few seconds to check the time. Two minutes ... three ... four ... five ... six ... Fogarty was taking too long. Where the hell was he?

Something odd was going on in Independent House, the grand old building across the street. The empty newspaper print works at one end was blocked up with barred and boarded windows and a rusting shuttered door. The front of the building seemed quiet too. The bolted front door and blacked out windows made it look empty and as quiet as the grave. But there was a feel of something about it, like a sound that was a pitch beyond the human ear.

A man entered Williams Lane from the far end and disappeared into its dark interior. He didn't come out. If he was having a piss, it was taking an awful long time. Another figure appeared, also at the far end, walked into the darkness and vanished just like the first one. One minute I saw his silhouette against the light, just like Kitty's earlier on. Next thing, as his shape merged into the gloom about halfway up the lane, there was a brief flicker of light and he was gone.

Still no sign of Fogarty. But I'd been thinking while I was waiting. It had taken me only seconds to get to the bottom of the alley after they grabbed Kitty, yet there wasn't the slightest trace of anyone when I got there. I heard no car or any form of transport leaving Princes Street. That meant Kitty couldn't be very far away. I decided to go back into Williams Lane to see what was going on. I stood in the middle of the empty alley, close to where I'd found my phone, and looked up and down, utterly bewildered. Just as I thought, those two men had vanished one after the other. And then I felt a whisper of movement in the wall behind me. A dark figure melted out of the building and my hand was grasped with an iron grip. A torch snapped on and I pulled my head back, wincing in the expectation of the beam that was about to expose my face. Instead, my wrist was wrenched around and the light raked across the back of my hand. I looked down. A luminous mark glowed on my skin. It was the shape of a cigarette burn. Of course – a UV club stamp, I thought as I was pulled inside.

52

HEALTH AND SAFETY

Inside the huge old building, I found myself in deeper darkness. A blue emergency lamp glowed from above a closed door but gave out little light. There was silence except for the sound of breathing. I wasn't the only one in the room. I held my breath, wondering what I'd got myself into now and how I was going to find Kitty. I was sure she was somewhere inside this place. I tried my phone for some light but the damn thing was dead again. Great. Even if Fogarty showed up, he'd never find me here and I had no way to contact him.

The door opened and the light from a torch moved across the speckled terrazzo-tiled floor and up the walls, illuminating corners of the high-ceilinged room. An old centre-light-fitting cast skeletal shadows across the walls. The torch beam shone up and down the shapes of two other people in the room besides me. I guessed they were the men who had entered via the alleyway before me. I should have been scared then. Hell, I should have been terrified. But I'd picked up on something from the others in the room, something that counters fear. It was anticipation.

'No talking. Put these on,' said the tall figure holding the torch. He bent down and threw a bundle at my feet, then did the same to the two men.

'Regulations,' he said. 'Health and Safety.'

We obediently donned the vests and pull-up safety trousers from the bundle.

'All of it,' he said, throwing us some footwear. 'Including these. We'll look after yours.'

I'd already found a pair of heavy gloves on the ground in front of me along with something else I couldn't identify. I held it up to the emergency lamp to get a look.

'Goes over the head,' the figure said. 'Safety hood.'

'This seems totally over the top,' one of the men said as he bent down to put on the boots. The accent was affluent, Southside, professional. He had a point. It was around one o'clock in the morning and it looked like we were in for a guided tour. Surely it wasn't Culture Night already.

'I said no talking. As soon as you're ready, follow me.'

He exited, leaving the door open, and waited while we shuffled out after him, creaking in our safety gear.

'Close your eyes,' we were commanded at the other side of the doorway. The sudden hiss of an aerosol spray took me by surprise. I felt its sting on the skin around my eyes that was left exposed by the hood. A chemical smell filled the air.

'Just an additional precaution,' our strange guide said. 'You never know with the hair products these days. The men are the worst. Follow me.'

We lumbered after him through a vast, dim hallway and up an ornate staircase with angular, brass balustrading. Art Deco, I guessed. As we ascended, the deep silence of the lower level was replaced by a continuous, dull sound coming from deep within the interior, accompanied by a smell I had difficulty identifying, one that was familiar but out of place. It was warm for the time of night.

Our guide paused on the landing before a large, solid oak closed door.

'You first,' he said, pushing me in front. 'Next you and you.'

He stood behind us, his massive bulk blocking any possible retreat.

'Now,' he said. 'When I open this door and say "Go", you must push past the curtain one by one and wait on the other side for me to join you. Do not stop. Do not attempt to go back. Now –'

His huge arm reached past me and pressed something on the door, causing it to open slightly. 'GO!'

I pushed past the door into a passageway and immediately encountered a heavy, grey leather curtain hanging from floor to ceiling. I drew aside the curtain and jumped backwards the instant I glimpsed what was on the other side.

'MOVE!' roared the guide from behind.

I moved, pushing past the curtain and shielding my eyes from the glare and the fumes behind it. Roaring and scorching, the short corridor was ablaze on all sides, including the ceiling and the floor.

'Come on,' said the guide. 'You're well-protected.'

He ran down the corridor, the flames licking his legs, and stopped at the far end.

We all hesitated. This did not look safe, protective gear or not.

'You need to move or you'll be incinerated,' he roared again. 'The safety gear will not protect you for long here. And there's no way back. Come on – quickly.'

There was no option but to go forward. I stepped onto the burning floor and felt the intense heat through the safety boots. I ran as fast as I could, eyes closed, gloved hands over my face. I looked through my fingers for an instant and thought I saw tongues of fire on my cuffs. I ran faster and reached the end first, the two men a few seconds behind me. The guide pushed us through another fire curtain and the air filled with steam and the stench of burnt water as we were sprayed by shower jets.

'Take off the gear and leave it here,' the guide said.

I put up my hand.

'Yes?' he said, his arms folded, leaning against the wall.

'Impressive show,' I said. 'Though I don't know how you handle the insurance. How do we get out when we want to go home, will we need to go through all this again?'

'You'll leave when you are allowed to leave. Like everyone else.'

He pulled off his hood and I saw he was smiling. I also saw his face. It was a mass of badly-healed scar tissue, no nose or eyebrows, lidless eyes. I looked away quickly.

Without fire retardant safety gear there was no way out, at least not the way we came in. I was trapped, with no idea what this place was or what I was doing here.

My companions did not seem to share my anxiety. They'd stripped off their safety hoods and protective clothing and were eager to move on.

'Where's it all happening?' said the guy who'd spoken earlier, a smooth, cosmopolitan type, aged anything between forty-five and sixty, with a Portuguese golf course perma-tan and glossy mahogany-tinted hair.

'Yeah, let's see the action,' the other guy said. 'It's taken long enough to get here. And it bloody cost enough.'

He was older, maybe in his sixties, with a neat grey goatee and a luxuriant thatch of steel grey hair, carefully blow-dried into a bouffant. He gently pushed it back into shape when he removed the safety hood. Just as well hair products were factored into the safety precautions. The guide turned and we followed him through another fire curtain to a gangway that bridged a huge open space. More flames, this time in an arched open tunnel running the entire length of the metal gangway. Now I identified the familiar smell I got earlier. Burning gas. It was running through the metal frame that arched around the gangway, with holes drilled for the gas to feed the flames licking all around it. But that's not what struck me most about this place, that's not what brought me to a dead stop.

Even before I got there, even before I heard it, I *felt* it. Funny how it needed no introduction: absolute savagery, devoid of humanity, beyond evil. The dominant noise was a primitive, rhythmic beat underlying the zoo-like sounds of humans behaving like predatory animals. A huge cage suspended from the roof, dripped with something viscous, the faces beneath howling and demonic. Inside, the shapes of creatures which might once have been human, circled and slashed one another, lumbering lumps of meat. In the dark of the yawning roof space hung a huge neon word: BURN.

The vast space had many levels and led to tunnel-like spaces filled with dark figures, moving in a slick blackness. I saw half-naked girls and boys, with eyes like bottomless pools, being mauled by fat-fingered old men, their lascivious eyes glistening. Shouting and pushing came from a balcony where intense gambling was underway with violence pending. God knows what the stakes were.

Our guide stopped and pointed to stairways running off the gangway.

'Off you go,' he said. 'You'll be alerted when it's over. Special procedures around departures are applied. For discretion and security.'

My companions were panting with excitement. They didn't need any encouragement to take off down the nearest stairway. I moved to go down there too even though it was the last place in the world I wanted to explore. But I was here to find Kitty and I hoped I wasn't too late. I was stopped by a strong grip on my arm.

'Not you,' the guide said. 'You have to come with me.'

53

THE LONGFORD LEADER

Melted Face marched me along the flaming metal gangway to a doorway at its far end. I hoped his plan was to check my club membership and throw me out. On second thoughts, it was hardly the kind of place that would have a bunch of rejects standing around outside, smoking and hurling casual abuse at the bouncers. If you were ejected from this club, being able to stand at all might be a problem. And Melted Face looked like he had a different plan in mind for me anyway.

I tried to see beyond the flames and the fumes, hoping to find a chance to escape. Somehow I had to lose my sinister tour guide and get the hell out of there.

A slow, rhythmic drum beat acted as a backdrop to the clamour of voices, the shouting and cheering around the fight cage and the shrieks and groans coming from God knows where. A man staggered past me in manacles, driven on by the lash of his masked slave-master.

On the other side of the door was a landing with an large industrial lift. Melted Face pushed the lift button with one of the three fingers remaining on his gauntlet-clad right hand. As the lift, clanking ominously, started its descent from an upper story, a group of people joined us on the landing, all hooded or masked. One of them was complaining loudly.

'I have to get out of here,' he said. 'I'm claustrophobic. I can't be stuffed into a dark dungeon like that. I swear, I'm having a panic attack. You have to help me.'

He reached out his hand, grabbed my arm and said, 'Get me out of here.'

There was no mistaking the dazzling gleam of the ultra-white teeth. It could only be my fellow passenger on the flight from Amsterdam, the dental tourist.

'There's a body down there,' he hissed at me. 'Don't know if it's alive or dead but they're just stepping over it like it was the most natural thing in the world. God knows what's going on in this place. When I got the invite, I thought it'd be the usual oul' BDSM craic, you know, like you'd hear about down in the golf club. But this crowd've lost the plot altogether.'

He made a sudden bolt for the door but was immediately apprehended.

'Take him upstairs,' Melted Face said, and he turned to the distressed Longford man, who gaped at him with his mouth open. 'Don't worry, sir. They'll look after you up there.'

As the terrified man was hustled away gabbling his protests, his dental work flashed like a beacon in the fog. I stared after him – and finally I understood what had happened on that flight from Amsterdam. Why hadn't I seen what was in front of me all along? The passenger in the seat next to me had forced the old man to shut up about his teeth – but not because it was bothering *me*, as I'd thought at the time. It was because it was bothering *him*. Him, as it turned out was Claude Leyton, my new friend and confidante. Porcelain implants offended Claude Leyton, he'd told me as much himself when he said that artificial substitutes weren't just an insult, they were a *sin*. The whole idea conflicted with his sense of the natural order of life and death, of decay and of permanence. I hadn't realised at the time just how strongly he felt about it.

I remembered his silver *memento mori* box and the strand of hair he'd mentioned. He said hair doesn't decay after death, at least not for a very long time. And he said teeth are the same. Then something else occurred to me. Wouldn't that make teeth suitable as a kind of *memento mori* too? A pretty gruesome one, but no less so than hoarding dead people's hair. Relics like that have a special meaning for the people who keep them. Sometimes they believe they have special powers, like the bones of saints. Like the little milk tooth I had in my pocket. I felt it now in my fingers, its smooth surface, its sharp edge. I remembered how it looked in the homeless guy's palm as he held it out to me, pearl-like, opalescent and shining under the streetlight. Despite the intense heat around me, suddenly I felt icy cold. The little tooth had been amongst the coins I took from the tips jar, that's how it came to be in the change in my pocket. Now I understood who the tooth had come from and why it was in the tips jar. Even if Kitty had found it first, she would have shown it to me. It was meant for me, a message and a warning. *Memento mori*, remember we all have to die. Ashes to ashes, as Karen Donlon had said. Earth to earth.

And that reminded me of something else. Back at the dry dock, Donlon said something about a nickname. I had a pretty good idea now who he meant and what that name was.

The lift juddered to a stop and the doors were hauled back from the inside. Two men and a woman shoved past me, laughing and pushing a boy in front of them. The boy's pale face turned to me, his huge drugged eyes unseeing as he reached out blindly, his bare white arms and thin chest patterned with spots. They rushed him through the door and along the gangway before I realised that the marks on his body were cigarette burns. Yep, it was all coming together now.

'Let's go,' Melted Face growled. He clutched my elbow and, before I could pull away, I was in the lift and we were going down. The lift shuddered and clanked its way past steel-sheeted walls, studded with rivets that I could only just make out in the darkness. Then it bumped to an abrupt halt and my self-appointed lift attendant pulled across the metal gate.

'Your stop,' he said.

He pushed me out and, as I stood there trying to figure out where I was, the lift went back up. I reckoned we hadn't descended all that far, two floors maybe. That would mean I was on the ground floor or a lower ground floor.

As my eyes adjusted to the gloom, I scanned round a colossal empty concrete space. The smell was of damp, of diesel and of the river even though it had to be two blocks away. I heard the slap-slap of water washing against a wall nearby and the faint drone of an engine.

Two large metal chutes curved downwards from the roof to the floor. Metal pull-down gates lined the back of the space, light seeping under them from an outside source. Now I knew where I was. It was the ground floor of the rear of the building. This was the old newspaper loading area, backing on to Princes Street. This could be worse, I thought, I could find a way out of here. It was only when I heard a sound in the shadows that I remembered I was brought to this place for a reason.

'Who's there?' I called.

There was no response. With my back to the lift I moved closer to the shadowed area and almost fell straight into a pile of black rubbish sacks. When I reached out to steady myself, my hand touched the plastic and instantly recoiled. Whatever the sack contained was solid and heavy and deathly cold. I backed away from the pile and saw, a little way past it, an up-ended wooden crate. On top of the crate, watching me, sat Kitty,

It was only when her voice came from deep within the shadows, that I realised Aleka was there too.

54

ONE-MISSISSIPPI ...

'Hey, Connie. Great to see you! Even if you're looking a little the worse for wear. We hoped you'd find your way here, didn't we, Kitty?'

Kitty's head was bowed, avoiding eye contact.

I gaped at the two of them, dumbfounded.

Aleka looked as incongruous there as a prom queen sailing down a city sewer in a yacht. She wore smart beige trousers, a light white cami top and a thin silver chain looped around her neck. Her cream, leather-strapped sandals showed toenails encrusted with sparkling stones. On the floor beside the toes was an expensive-looking laptop/hand-luggage combo. She had everything required for a business trip besides the airport.

Kitty was clearly less than thrilled to see me. Without saying a word, she stared at a black polycarbon carry-case that lay open beside her on top of the crate. The interior of the case was filled with grey protective foam, embedded in which were two rows of moulded spaces. Each space contained a yellow plastic tube about the size of a fat magic marker.

As I struggled to regain my power of speech, Aleka's manicured fingers reached into the open case and plucked out one of the yellow tubes. She tossed it lightly in her hand and smiled.

'Kitty's been very helpful. She takes instructions well, very quick on the uptake. Which is more than I can say for you, Connie.'

'What's going on, Kitty?' I finally managed to ask. 'I came to find you, I thought you were in danger. I didn't expect ...'

'Oh, you feel bad,' Aleka interrupted. 'You're confused. But Kitty will explain, won't you, Kitty?'

Kitty's face was still turned away, shrouded in shadows. She used the back of her hand to wipe her cheek.

'All right, I'll do it,' Aleka said and she gazed at me for a moment, still smiling. 'Connie, I'm sorry to put it so bluntly, but Kitty kind of used you. She had her own agenda, all about punishing that wonderful father of hers.'

'He's not my fucking father,' Kitty said. 'I was adopted, remember? Except they dumped me – like I told you, Connie.'

Her eyes blazed at me as if I was responsible.

'I was just gone twelve when Mum found out about the abuse, she freaked out – and blamed *me*. She threw me in the car, drove me into town and dumped me out on O'Connell Bridge. I don't know how I survived that night. Next morning, I met Stevie and he saved me. I heard afterwards my Mum drank herself into St Pat's and never came out. I always swore I'd kill him, my adoptive father.' She spat out the last two words.

'*Adoptive* father. Whatever,' Aleka said and continued in a sing-song tone as if she was telling a bedtime story to a child. 'When she got wind that Daddy was on the scene, little Kitty got her friends to go to some of the interesting parties he frequented, to spy on him. Her best friend died from being in the wrong place at the wrong time, but all Kitty wanted was his sketchbooks, for blackmail or revenge – or both. She'd seen her father's face in a drawing and she was desperate for more details to help her track him down. That boy's death was all your fault, Kitty, you know that? You got him involved. You sent him to that party.'

'It's not true ...' Kitty was sobbing.

'Now it *is* true, Kitty, you know it is. And you were very clever about roping in poor old Connie, having her running about looking for the sketchbooks for you, asking questions, creating all kinds of diversions.'

Aleka took a step away from Kitty and spoke to me with false confidentiality. 'Of course, she knew you'd never get anywhere, Connie. She's a street smart kid and you're ... not. Now, that old auntie of yours is a different story, but thankfully she's out of the way.'

'Did you have something to do with Aggie ...? Do you know where she is? She's been missing for days.'

'Has she?' Aleka murmured dryly. 'Well, I hope it's not temporary. Perhaps Donlon and his idiot gang managed to get something right in the end.'

'I hate you,' Kitty shouted at her. 'You're the worst person I ever met.'

'You see?' Aleka said to me. 'I told you she was smart. I *am* the worst person you've ever met. Kitty had put two and two together about the clubs, like tonight's rather excellent example.' She paused and smiled. 'Location is so important. This event is just a little hobby of mine, but I like to get things right. So, I guess Kitty picked up on some street talk and the irksome graffiti that kept appearing from time to time ...'

'... the cigarette burns,' I muttered.

'There were plenty of signs, despite our strict policies on confidentiality and admission. Plus one or two casualties found in the river a while back, thankfully unidentified.'

'I didn't know *she* was running the clubs, Connie,' Kitty interrupted. 'I'd heard rumours that they were happening. Like she said, you pick up on things ...'

'And you didn't feel like mentioning anything to me?' I said.

I remembered her reaction when I showed her Stevie's painting and her vague response to my questions afterwards.

'I was going to. But then Aleka came to me in the café yesterday and she asked me if I was trying to find someone. I don't know how she knew about my father. She said she'd help me, but I wasn't to tell anyone. She said first I'd have to rep for a special one-off club tonight.'

'Rep for this place? She just said it has strict admission policies.'

'I wasn't repping to get in guests,' Kitty looked miserable. 'I had to ...'

Aleka cut in. 'Kitty stamped the regular punters on the street for Ozzie's club. And at the same time, using her BURN stamp, she selected certain types who might be suitable as ... participants.'

'Participants ... types?' I asked, my brain in turmoil.

'Types who wouldn't be missed. Flotsam and jetsam. People prepared to do anything for drugs, money or human contact – especially the kind that involves pain. We have our own sources but we always need more. There's such a demand, especially amongst our professional classes. They're all just hankering to re-experience, you know, the daily floggings by the Christian Brothers or something. This ...' she opened her arms as if to embrace the entire building, 'takes it to a whole different level. It makes your average

BDSM dungeon look like introduction to embroidery with the Irish Countrywomen's Association.'

She laughed. 'For our clients, the experience is life-changing.' She flicked a glance at the dark sacks beside us. 'For some of the participants also.'

Kitty flinched when she saw my look of disgust.

'I didn't know what it was like in here, Connie. Ok, I had an idea, but not really ... and the only one I stamped to get in here was my friend, Hannah, because she wanted to come with me. And that homeless bloke, who said he was going in anyway.'

'Don't mind her, Connie. Little Miss Innocence here was going to do whatever it took to get to her father. He's a powerful businessman and a very stupid person and he's in here somewhere. Kitty came to me and offered to rep for me. In return for my help, she agreed to help me get you here too.'

'Shut up, Aleka,' Kitty shouted, banging her hands against her ears. 'You're twisting everything.'

'Easy, Kitty ...' I said.

Kitty took a breath. 'Aleka told me tonight that she found out what happened to Stevie. She said if I got you here, she'd tell us both together. But I wasn't to let on to you, just get you here. So I did, but when I saw you outside, I got worried and ran away. That's when they grabbed me and brought me here ...'

'... and they made it easy for me to get in here too. It was a trap,' I said. 'Why did you bring us here, Aleka? What do you want?'

'Like Kitty said, to tell you what happened to the boy,' Aleka said patiently. 'I like to do things personally, you know that, Connie. And I like to leave things clean. I have to go away soon and this is convenient for me, that's all.'

I looked around again just to confirm that we were still in a dark, dank empty space with no obvious street access. Convenient for what, I wondered.

'Kitty, why don't you come over here to me?' I tried, but Kitty hesitated, looking from Aleka to me and back again. Hopeless, I let it go.

'What's in the case, Aleka?'

'I was about to show Kitty,' Aleka said, examining the tube in her hand. 'The case was part of a haul of goods seized by the guards following a raid on a premises owned by Steyne River Securities.' She held up the yellow tube. 'This, Kitty, is how it is possible for your friend to have been injected.'

'So I was right,' Kitty said. 'Someone injected him with drugs! You mean Donlon's gang – but why would they do that to Stevie?'

'It's an auto-injector,' I said as everything finally became clear. 'Like an epi-pen. But tell the truth, Aleka. That carry-case you've got there – it wasn't found in a Garda raid and it didn't belong to Donlon's gang. And the auto-injectors don't contain just drugs, do they, Aleka? They're part of your plan ...'

'Very good, Connie. You're finally getting it. This is a special auto-injector, different from the usual epi-pen. It's the latest model, based on the US Military's ATNAA, the Antidote Treatment Nerve Agent Auto-injector. It delivers two drugs, or in this case, one drug and one ...'

'... bacterial disease,' I said. '*Necrotising fasciitis* and MDPV – bath salts.'

'You can inject the disease along with the drug?' Kitty stammered.

'Yes, with some variants in terms of dosage,' Aleka said. 'So simple a child could use it.' She raised the tube higher, demo-style. 'You just remove the safety cap on top here.'

She flicked off something blue. 'Form a fist to hold it correctly. And ...'

'You're quite the expert there, Aleka,' I cut in. 'And you took the opportunity to test it on a guinea pig when you and your friends caught Stevie and Shane at that party. Then your people did the same to Jimmy Mooney – but Mooney was clever, he set you up, deliberately sacrificed himself. I know what you did and I know how you did it. I even – God help us – think I know why.'

Aleka paused, holding the auto-injector at eye level. 'I seriously doubt that,' she drawled.

'You killed him!' With a wild shriek, Kitty flew at Aleka from the side, tearing at her face.

Aleka wheeled round and lunged at Kitty with the auto-injector, but the girl was too fast. Kitty grabbed Aleka's arms at the wrists and tried to push her away. I threw myself between them, forcing them apart with all my strength, but Aleka slammed me away with her shoulder, then turned and stabbed Kitty in the thigh with the auto-injector. She managed to keep Kitty's hands away with one arm while holding the auto-injector in place and counting 'One-Mississippi ... two-Mississippi ...'

I was back in there grappling with her arm before she got to '... five-Mississippi.' I pulled her arm back, yanking out the auto-injector from Kitty's leg. Aleka grabbed me by the throat with her free hand and tried to turn the auto-injector on me. I had no idea if it would work a second time but I wasn't taking any chances. I put all my energy into keeping that device away from me. As we struggled, the auto-injector flew up into the air, spinning away before finally dropping out of sight amongst the pile of black sacks. Aleka pushed me hard. I was thrown backwards down onto the floor, twisting my leg and scraping my hands as I reached behind to break the fall. As I raised myself up, all my earlier injuries woke up and screamed. Kitty was on her feet, backing away unsteadily, her arms stretched out to ward off Aleka. Aleka stepped back, closed the polycarbon case with a snap, picked it up and swung it at Kitty with all her strength. Its hard corner struck Kitty full-force on the side of her head and knocked her to the floor.

'No, Aleka!' I shouted.

But Kitty lay on the ground in front of us, completely motionless.

55

The Sandbox

Aleka replaced the case on the crate and smoothed an invisible wrinkle from her jacket sleeve. Kitty's nails had left a long, livid stripe on her cheek, beaded with tiny droplets of darkened blood. It must have hurt like hell but she didn't seem to notice. She pushed a few stray hairs off her forehead and regarded me calmly with her aquamarine eyes.

'It'll be nice for Kitty to have some company where's she's going,' she said. 'The rest might not be quite so chatty.'

Her gaze passed over the mound of plastic sacks. Sliding down the old newspaper chute, a heavy black sack was followed by a smaller one, joining the pile behind us. Dark liquid seeped out of them and collected in a small pool on the floor. So she was planning to ship us off with the rest of her human remains. I had to get us out of there.

Aleka placed herself between me and Kitty's prone form on the ground. In her hand was another auto-injector.

'I know you think you've worked out everything, Connie. Kitty thought you were getting nowhere, but that's the youth for you, isn't it? They want everything instantly. In the end, you did quite well with the sketchbooks. It's just as well most of them were destroyed. All those important people with all those perversions. So easy to manage. The people, I mean. Their perversions are out of control.'

'Is that it, Aleka?' I asked. 'All of this BURN thing ... your "entertainments" ... it's just so you can manipulate people? And what about your precious Bicknor Day? I suppose that's a sign of how far you've been able to get with the bigwigs and the city planners. It's not a tribute to Alexander de Bicknor, it's really a tribute to you, isn't it?'

She smiled.

'I could never figure out why you've made so much fuss about an obscure fourteenth century bishop. Especially Alexander de Bicknor. You know he wasn't exactly Mr Squeaky Clean – especially when it came to the public finances. Haven't we enough present-day public traitors – peculators! – without having to dredge up one from the past and literally put him on a pedestal?'

'Oh, don't be so petty,' Aleka snapped, her smile gone. 'Yes, Alexander de Bicknor was accused of fraud and embezzlement. But he was a man of vision and that's a quality that's always been in short supply in this country. He had the imagination and the balls to change things during tough times, get them back on the right footing. He's an inspiration for our times.'

'He was another bloody bastard who abused his position. He banned beggars from the city at a time when the countryside had been laid waste. You know that, don't you? What about his famous sermon in Christchurch when your ballsy Bicknor put a curse on the "idle poor" of Dublin. A curse, incidentally, that looks like it's just as powerful seven hundred years later.'

'Nonsense. Those people were already cursed. Don't you know anything about living conditions in medieval times? And barriers to progress, whether in the middle ages or now –'

'– should be eliminated? That's what's behind that disease and your nasty little auto-injectors. You're planning to wipe out the homeless ...'

'Oh, please. Don't be so dramatic – and give me a bit of credit. Wipe out an entire section of the population? That's the stuff of comic book megalomaniacs. And anyway, it would be far too expensive. Unnecessary, too. All that's required is to make the city centre less comfortable for certain kinds of people, encourage them to leave town and stay away. That would result in a better place, wouldn't it? Better for business, for tourists, for ordinary people who don't want to be hassled by aggressive beggars every time they put their noses outside the door.' She raised a hand before I could interrupt. 'I know what you're going to say – violence, gang warfare, innocent victims. Some collateral damage is inevitable. But something has to be done – and think of the positive side.'

'So it was all about FUD,' I said as she crossed her arms patiently, and leaned against the wall. 'Fear, Uncertainty, Doubt. The disease was a way to escalate it. You planned to infect enough people to scare away the undesirables. And it had the added advantage of making Donlon and Co. paranoid and vulnerable. Combining the disease with a drug like bath salts was a master stroke, guaranteed to get you the support of the terrified public and their representatives. Very clever.'

'Thank you,' she murmured modestly.

'And you used journalists like Mooney to spread the panic. Jesus, Aleka, but a flesh-eating disease? It's beyond belief.'

'I know, but it captures the imagination, doesn't it? Broken Windows Theory is never going to work in this town – people round here wouldn't notice if the neighbourhood windows were in smithereens or covered all over in rainbows and fairy-dust. Everyone's too busy pretending to fall into potholes and file fake compensation claims.' She saw my sceptical look. 'Or the white collar equivalent.'

'So what's in it for you, Aleka?' I asked. 'You don't need the money. You've nothing to prove. And don't tell me you think you're making the world a better place. Is it a power thing or are you just bored?'

Aleka laughed. 'Don't underestimate financial incentives despite what I told you before. Think of all the property freed up when the hostels are vacated, just when the prices are going up again. And we absolutely won't tolerate state-owned properties being occupied by ballad singers and do-gooders on behalf of the homeless. But that's of secondary interest. Connie, you should understand that there are people who are attracted to disorder and chaos. We can't help it, it's in our DNA. Some of us are drawn to war zones or to scenes of natural disaster ...'

'Like vultures,' I said.

'Vultures are misunderstood creatures. They are persecuted, endangered due to myths that they are evil. In reality they perform essential clean-up operations for Nature. Without them, the world would sink under the weight of its own rotting detritus. They are not responsible for the mess they sanitise. Any more than I'm to blame for the corruption here. It was here before I arrived, aided by a culture of sycophancy and looking the other way. For me, there's an excitement that comes with chaos and the possibilities it throws up. And before you go all judgemental on me, being attracted to disorder and confusion is not unusual. Isn't that why people watch the news? Maybe you're like that yourself, Connie, drawn back here despite yourself.'

'Oh, so this is where you tell me that you and I are really quite alike.'

'Don't be ridiculous,' she laughed. 'We couldn't be more different.'

'Well at least we can agree on that,' I said. 'Because no matter what way you spin it, it's all just a great big power thing with you. Plus a chance to indulge in your nasty little games. You'd never have scope like this in Chicago. It would be too risky and you wouldn't jeopardise your political ambitions. But here you can do anything you like. Engineer situations to exploit people's appetites and then ruin them, rewrite history with the help of a few toadying cultural gurus, develop your own brand of ethnic cleansing meets urban renewal. And while you're at it, exact revenge for the wrongs you believe were done to you in the past.

'You flatter me,' Aleka beamed. 'I'm sure I'd never get round to doing half the things you say. But I see you've been delving into my murky past. I'm *dying* to hear what you found out.'

I must have been staring at her.

'Oh come on Connie, I haven't got all day. I have to be somewhere. Let me start you off ... You probably want to begin at the beginning: Ballinard, County Roscommon.'

I took a deep breath, consolidating the strands of information I'd been gathering all evening from parish records, newsroom stories, court reports, financial data, people ... when I called in old favours from a scattered network I'd almost forgotten I had.

'Angela Maher. You were born in Ballinard, County Roscommon. Your parents were simple farming people. They must have wondered where they got you from. You were born to dominate, to hurt and to control. Your teachers left you alone, schoolmates treated you with fear.'

Aleka nodded encouragingly. 'Good, this is better than I'd hoped. Go on.'

'A relationship with a married local politician and businessman left you, at the age of eighteen, with a deep derision of those in power, a baby left in care and a one-way ticket to Chicago. Political and business contacts were set up to look after you – and keep you out of the way. You went and you left your former lover dead by his own hands, his family ruined, his business destroyed. You studied law and excelled in your career. Having made a fortune in US housing repossessions, you returned to Dublin. Your involvement in Heartbeat Housing Services was a puzzle for me at first. But it's getting clearer now.'

'Indeed. And you're going to share your insights with me, no doubt.'

'Post-boom Dublin was swollen with thousands of vulnerable people – dispossessed, defenceless, desperate people. Undocumented migrants were still arriving here by the container load. They were ripe for the picking. This city was a – a sandbox for sadists, a dream destination for a sociopath like you. How could you resist?'

'Not bad, Connie.' She seemed genuinely pleased. 'Maybe I should keep you on as my biographer. You're right. This country rejected me when I was weak and helpless. It's nice to come back and be in control this time round. And the more weakness and apathy, the greater the control. I couldn't have done it alone. Politicians, financiers, the media, they all helped. Look at Mooney, the award-winning campaigning journalist, hitting the front page with his daily exclusives. Too, too easy.'

Her lovely eyes danced with amusement. 'And Brady. High-calibre, but so bitter and so troubled, personally and professionally. He thought he'd advance his career by cleaning up the city and defeating the gangs. But he hadn't the stomach for it. Tried to back out when he saw the pros in operation. He didn't realise that there *is* no going back.' She sighed. 'Too bad I put so much work into Brady, only for him to end up being such a let-down. People around here are so unreliable.'

The picture of Brady swinging from that hook at the dry dock came back to me. I thought of my non-dinner date with him and how confident and brash he seemed then, the moment just before everything went out of control. Brady was in too deep, but it wasn't Brady who killed Stevie or Mooney. Everything Mooney had said to me made sense now – or almost everything.

'But there's one person you can rely on, isn't that right, Aleka? Another vulture, like you. The one who killed Mooney. Who helped you kill Stevie. The one who killed and tortured Sugar Ray Brosnan. Who supplied the weapons, the equipment, the auto-injectors and the disease ... You have another name for him.'

'Remind me,' she said, ignoring my question. 'Who's Stevie?'

I wanted to hit her but she had the auto-injector. Instead I gritted my teeth.

'He was the teenager you killed to test your disgusting disease. You know, I discovered that Stevie was born in Ballinard in February 2000. Wasn't that the year you left, Aleka – *Angela*? Ballinard is a very small place – isn't there a chance Stevie could have been your son?'

Aleka sighed and looked utterly bored. If she made a response, I never heard it. We both jumped as the lift clanged to a stop and the gate slammed open. Ozzie Wolf didn't give me as much as a glance as he strolled across the empty space towards Aleka. I stared at him in shock.

'That's all sorted now,' he said. He looked down at Kitty's body lying still on the ground. 'And I see you've been doing some sorting out yourself.'

'Aw no, Ozzie. I don't believe it.' I stared at him, feeling sick.

'Sorry, Connie,' he said, with a shrug. 'But, you know the story, business being business.'

He turned back to Aleka. 'The others are upstairs in the boardroom. Looks like the briefing is coming to an end. There'll be a bit of clearing up to do after the demo.'

Aleka smiled at him approvingly.

'Good,' she said, checking her phone. 'The next container is loading in an hour. Make sure this pair are in it, along with the rest of the mess.' She spoke into her phone, 'Yes, send Trevor down. Glad the training went well. Roll out the next phase. I'll be in touch.'

Aleka put down her phone and spoke to Ozzie.

'You took care of that nuisance, Fogarty?'

Ozzie nodded. 'He was on the street outside here, looking for herself.' He inclined his head, indicating me.

So Fogarty had come to help me after all. He was just too late, and now they'd got him too. He was the only one who hadn't betrayed me, I thought, looking at Ozzie in despair.

Aleka's tongue flicked across her lips. 'I'd have liked to look after that one myself. But there just aren't enough hours in the day.'

'To do what, exactly?' The familiar voice of Pius Fogarty came from the darkness at the rear of the lift. As Fogarty stepped forwards into the light, I noticed Ozzie had moved back, positioning himself between Aleka and the door to the emergency stairs.

The last thing I heard Aleka say was, 'Ozzie, you little shit.'

There was a noise from the top of the chute and another black sack slid slowly down to join the others. At exactly the point when it reached the ground, the walls shook with a deep rumble and parts of the ceiling began to fall. The lights went out and sparks flew out of the lift. There was complete darkness for about two minutes until the dim emergency lighting came on. It took only that instant for Aleka to be gone. A metallic clang was followed by the sound of running footsteps. And the drone of a boat engine receded into the distance.

As the dust settled, I ran over to Kitty to push the rubble off her face.

'She's breathing,' I said, clearing her nose, mouth and eyes. I tried to prop her up. Ozzie and Fogarty pulled at the iron gate in the floor, but it wasn't budging.

'The steps here go down to a channel. I see water lapping against the bottom step.' Ozzie said. 'But this gate's bolted from the other side. She's gone – and we can't go after her. She must have had a powerboat waiting!'

'Unbelievable.' Fogarty growled.

'Yes,' I said. 'Like a prom queen sailing down a city sewer.'

56

LESS OF THE MYSTERY

Kitty moaned loudly as her body twitched all over. I put my arm around her shoulders and held her tight. Fogarty walked over and looked down at us, his expression clearly indicating that we were not a pretty sight. One unconscious teenager partly propped up against a concrete pillar. One older woman kneeling alongside her, who'd just survived a hand-to-hand fight with a maniac wielding a dual-purpose auto-injector, and looked it. He began to shake his head, still studying me while holding his phone aloft, trying to find a signal.

'No,' I said, rising to my feet to face him. 'Oh no, you don't, Pius Fogarty. You can keep your disapproving looks to yourself. If you'd got here faster, this wouldn't have happened.'

'If you'd listened to me and hadn't got involved in the first place, this wouldn't have happened. God, what happened to your face?'

'Never you mind about my face. Who else was going to do anything? You were too busy with your own shady activities, getting yourself shot by Steyne River Securities, sneaking around with Detective Nuala Rossiter, no doubt perfecting your own personal style of sex, lies and police corruption ... assaulting Jimmy Mooney, getting yourself arrested and then disappearing off the face of the earth. Very helpful altogether.'

Fogarty looked at me pityingly. 'You're way off, Connie. I wasn't shot by Steyne River Securities, it was staged to look like that – to fake escalating gang violence while getting rid of me at the same time. They missed me by a miracle, not because they were driving a left-hand drive jeep as was reported. It was because they made an uncharacteristic error, drove on the wrong side of the road and had to swerve away. Foreign. I'm guessing the ballistics report will show the ammo is US military issue.'

'You're saying you were shot by the US military?'

He really was quite mad, I decided.

'No, I'm saying I was shot by a group of contractors hired by Aleka. And as for your theories about Nuala Rossiter ... She was convinced that Brady had gone rogue and asked me to watch him from the outside, while she kept an eye on him internally. She met me in the pub on the corner of Store Street and Amiens Street just before Brady called her in to help him question Kitty. She insisted that I wear the vest. And it turned out that she was right on both counts. Brady was up to his neck in it with Aleka and it worked well for him for a while. But Aleka brought in her own people to speed things up. They were the ones who tortured and killed Sugar Ray Brosnan – not before extracting information from Ray along with most of his teeth. They made it look like it was done by a criminal gang, feeding Donlon's paranoia. The Garda raids that followed were based on the information from Sugar Ray and made Brady look good while making Dessie Donlon very upset indeed. Of course, if you hadn't told Brady while you were on your date with him that I attacked Mooney I wouldn't have been arrested and a lot of things would have turned out differently.'

'I did *not* have a date with Brady – and I did *not* tell him anything. He grabbed my phone and saw a text from Lu O'Leary.'

Fogarty raised an eyebrow. 'If you say so. Anyway, Brady went after me. But he had a change of heart later that night in the Garda Station when he was questioning me. He realised that I wasn't responsible for Mooney's death – and I'm guessing he had a good idea of who was. That was when he also realised the whole thing was going off the rails. He went to the nightclub to try to persuade Aleka to back off, but instead she dumped him. Brady needed to show he was boss and his best way to do that was to eliminate Donlon himself. That's why he followed Donlon to the dry dock. Brady killed Donlon and Donlon's men killed Brady. You should know this. Apparently, with your talent for trouble, you happened to be there too.'

'Wrong on two counts,' I said. 'I didn't just happen to be there. I figured out that the dry dock was Stevie's refuge and I found Shane Donlon there. He told me what happened to Stevie. And Donlon's men didn't kill Brady. The automatic gunfire that killed Brady was fired indiscriminately from a distance. Donlon was already seriously injured but it finished him off too. There's no way Steyne River Securities would have been responsible for that, it must been those contractors you mentioned.'

'Now, children,' Ozzie intervened. 'No more squabbling. Fogarty, you'll get a phone signal over there, where Aleka was standing. And by the way, Connie's right. Steyne River Securities didn't kill Brady. And it wasn't the contractors either.'

Fogarty and I had been glaring at one another. Now we turned our angry eyes on Ozzie, asking almost in unison, 'What do you mean?'

'There's a third element involved,' Ozzie said. 'That element was responsible for the automatic gunfire at the dry dock resulting in the deaths of Brady and Donlon.'

'What do you mean, *element*?' I asked.

'How do you know this?' Fogarty asked while punching a text message into his phone and moving to the spot beside the crate to send it. I guessed he was contacting Rossiter.

'Aggie,' Ozzie said, looking at me uncomfortably. 'She sent me a kind of a message, from Palm Beach.'

'*My* Aggie? She's in Palm Beach. She's safe?' I started to shake with anger. 'I was worried sick about her. Jesus Christ, Ozzie, why didn't you tell me?'

'She didn't want you involved. She said the less you knew, the safer you'd be. She'd received information from her Russian friend in Vegas ... who happens to be the head of a big international ... let's just say, organisation ... that something serious was on the cards for Dublin. I received a message in the form of a person ... with a sign.'

'Less of the mystery,' Fogarty snapped, looking furious. 'What person, what sign?'

'The person was Miroslav Ziniak. He was the messenger from Aggie's Russian friend. The sign that I could trust him was a matching tattoo, his and mine.'

'Not Miro?' Fogarty said. 'Ozzie, you should have told me ...'

'Miro from the Sunrise Hotel? He has a fake Russian prison tattoo like you?' I said stupidly.

'He has a real Russian prison tattoo like me.' Ozzie said and touched a small section of the larger tattoo on his neck. 'Mine's concealed within the fake one. Miro's is on his chest. The mark of an initiate. It was done to me forcibly when I was a teenager and jailed in Ukraine for ... never mind. I'll tell you another time. It was before I was rescued by my grandfather and sent to live here with my foster parents. The tattoo is a bond. It makes us brothers.'

'A bit more than brothers,' I noted remembering their meeting outside the café. Ozzie grinned.

'A brotherhood of fools and madmen,' Fogarty said, seriously angry. 'Did Aggie and her Russian friend tell you that Miro arrived here from a psychiatric unit in Lithuania – in a facility for the criminally insane? I was monitoring him in the Sunrise Hotel, giving him odd jobs and keeping him close-by. Are you telling me he's at large and ... *armed*?'

'A bond is a bond,' Ozzie said simply. 'And yes, Miro was instructed to get involved by Aggie's friend. Miro followed Connie, stationed himself on the office building roof overlooking the dry dock and when the time came ...'

'... he shot up the whole place, first finishing off Donlon and then killing Brady,' I said.

I wondered exactly how many people had been following me and watching my movements. It's a wonder they didn't all get together and hire a coach.

Kitty moaned again, more loudly this time.

'As if it wasn't bad enough letting Kitty out on the streets repping last night ...' Fogarty fumed at Ozzie.

'And cosying up to Aleka ...' I added. I still hadn't recovered from the shock of seeing Ozzie walk out of the lift, apparently in league with Aleka.

'... have you any idea how serious this is?' Fogarty finished.

'Actually, I do,' said Ozzie as another large lump of masonry fell from part of the ceiling nearby. 'Miro's been in this building for the past two hours, planting multiple explosive devices. You can see it's started already. He doesn't know we're here and he probably doesn't care. This whole place is going to blow.'

The air hung thick with dust and rancour as we stood and glared at one another in suspicion and rage. Then each of us looked around quickly.

'We have to get out of here.' Fogarty said, stating the obvious as he ran to the metal doors at the back wall, feeling their edges for a way to open them. 'Ozzie,' he shouted. 'Get something to open these gates.'

Ozzie didn't move but stood patting his pockets and looking sarcastic.

'Oh I'm sorry. I seem to have forgotten my angle-grinder,' he said, muttering 'plonker,' under his breath. He hadn't forgiven Fogarty for calling him a fool.

Fogarty ignored him, instead he started clearing the fallen debris that blocked the door to the emergency stairs. Ozzie relented after a few seconds and went to help.

'Kitty's starting to come round,' I said, as the girl stirred, her eyes half-open. 'God knows what state she'll be in when she does. She got injected with half a dose of Aleka's concoction, the bath-salts-slash-flesh-eating-disease thing. We have to get her to a hospital.'

The two men turned slowly round to face me.

'What did you just say –?' Fogarty said. 'Kitty was injected with bath salts? And *what* else?'

'*Necrotising fasciitis* – the infection that Stevie had, the disease that killed Mooney. It was injected with dual-purpose auto-injectors. Look, there's no time to explain. It's part of a plan to create panic and clear out the city. The thing is, Kitty may be infected now – we need to get her to a hospital. Plus she'll be affected by the drug when she wakes and God knows what form that's going to take.'

Fogarty groaned. Ozzie looked stricken as he spoke.

'That's what was being demo'd in the boardroom upstairs. I saw the auto-injectors on the table. I didn't know what they were at the time. They've got at least two people up there. One of them is Kitty's friend, Hannah.'

'We've got to get them out of there, ' I said.

'Are you crazy?' Fogarty said. 'We'll be lucky to get ourselves out of here. Plus Kitty needs a doctor like you said, and urgently.'

'We have to try to rescue Hannah and anyone else they've got up there. We could split up.'

'I'm with Connie on this,' Ozzie said. 'We have to stop them.'

Ozzie might be as slippery as a bucket of eels, I thought, but there was no doubting his determination to do the right thing here, even if it meant endangering himself.

'You two go,' I said. 'I'll look after Kitty, I'll try to get her out.'

Without waiting for a response, I helped Kitty to her feet and supported her while she gained her balance. She muttered something. She was definitely coming to. We almost fell over as another rumble shook the floor. More black rubble fell from the ceiling. The lights flickered again. One of the chutes buckled and looked dangerously close to breaking up. It was wet underfoot. Water from the underground channel had risen to the level of the iron gate and was spreading slowly across the floor.

'We'll have to go up to the next level,' Fogarty said. 'We'll get you out the front door if we can.'

'Ozzie, you lead, you know the building best. I'll take Kitty, you take this.' Fogarty threw me Kitty's backpack. I caught the backpack but it was so heavy I nearly dropped it. I looped its strap around my shoulder, wondering if it contained all of Kitty's earthly belongings. Fogarty went to help Kitty, but she brushed him away and moved unsteadily towards the lift, muttering to herself. She stood for a minute gazing at the electrical sparks fizzing in the lift's interior before turning around again. Between Fogarty and me, we shepherded her gently towards the door to the emergency stairs on the far side of the room.

'I'll go first and see if it's safe,' Ozzie said, opening the door.

But before he'd gone another step, Kitty took off. She pushed Ozzie out of the way, threw the emergency door wide open so that it hit the wall and raced up the stairs, shouting 'Hannah!' as she disappeared upwards into the darkness.

57

VIEL SPAß

Ozzie raced up the narrow steps after Kitty, grasping the iron handrail as it twisted upwards.

'Come on,' his voice came down through the gloom. 'It's safe so far.'

We reached the next level and saw Ozzie with his shoulder to the door. It opened a couple of inches and then wouldn't budge. Fogarty passed me on the stairs to push alongside him. The two of them put their whole strength into it but it was no use, the door was stuck.

'Something's blocking it.' Fogarty said. 'We're trapped.'

'What's out there,' I asked. 'What can you see?'

'It's the entrance hall,' Fogarty said, squinting through the narrow gap. 'The main stairs has collapsed. The landing up above is on fire – I see flames up there and a lot of smoke. We can't get out here.'

There was no choice but to continue climbing the stairs and hope we'd find a way out further up. Ozzie loped up to the next level and shouted back down to us.

'No go,' he said, coughing through the smoke seeping around the fire door. 'This whole floor's on fire. I can feel the heat. Come on – we need to get past here quickly. Are you ok, Connie?'

'Just give me a second,' I said as I reached him, leaning against the wall to catch my breath. My eyes and throat were burning. I would have killed for a drop of water. 'What is it, what are you staring at?'

Ozzie pointed at the door-frame beside me. Floating from a knot in the timber was a wisp of violet hair. 'She ran through there.'

I put my hand on the door.

'It's too dangerous, Connie,' Fogarty said. 'You can't go after her.'

'Watch me,' I said, already through the doorway, throwing Kitty's bag behind me. 'Ozzie, take this. Fogarty, you go on up to the boardroom and get Hannah. And Fogarty? See if you can find a way out.'

'Jesus Christ – why won't you listen to me?' Fogarty shouted after me, his voice hoarse with frustration. 'Ozzie, get her back, with or without Kitty. They can't get far in this heat. And give me the bloody bag.'

'Here,' Ozzie said, throwing Fogarty the bag as he followed me. 'See you upstairs – hopefully.'

I found myself on the first floor landing looking down at the collapsed staircase into the entrance hall. It was exactly as Fogarty had described, smoke-filled, with flames licking the bannisters where the stairs used to be. The only way Kitty could have gone was through the panelled oak door on my right.

Eyes streaming, trying not to breathe, I ran to the door, opened it and walked straight into the huge grey leather fire curtain. Last time I was here, I wore full fire retardant safety gear. This time I had nothing. But the corridor was in darkness, no longer alight except for some spluttering blue flames along the ceiling pipework. I raced through it blindly, guided by my outstretched hands, and crashed straight through the heavy fire curtain at the far end.

If I thought it was hot outside on the landing, pushing past that fire curtain was like opening a furnace door. I stopped instantly, holding the leather sheet. A few more steps and I'd be back on the flaming gangway, this time without any protection. The noise was deafening: the spitting and crackling of multiple fires, the crashing of metal falling from a height, the shrieks and roars of people below in terror and pain. Black smoke filled the space. I could scarcely breathe now and my eyes were scorched from the fumes. They stung like hell when I rubbed them but at least my vision cleared enough to see ahead.

'Kitty!' I called to the slight figure moving across the gangway, encircled in the tunnel of flames. Where the metal tubing that arched over the gangway had shifted and concertinaed in on itself, fountains of flame gushed upwards into the darkness. Kitty halted when she heard me and turned, her eyes too-bright and wild. Whatever effect the drugs had on her, she didn't feel the blaze or the flames licking at her body. If she didn't move, she'd be burned alive.

'Come back, Kitty,' I screamed over the infernal noise. 'You're going the wrong way for Hannah!'

She took a step towards me and then stopped, her attention drawn to something in the space beneath. The smoke cleared for an instant, long enough for me to see a ragged line of former-revellers moving towards the far side of the area. Old Melted Face was down there, the fire officer from hell, effecting emergency evacuation procedures.

But it wasn't the sight of Melted Face that had frozen Kitty in her tracks and caused her to lean out over the side of the gangway.

'Daddy!' she cried. A man looked up from the throng below. He was a white-haired, late sixties executive type, currently dishevelled and very frightened. His mouth gaped at the sight of his daughter above him, surrounded by flames.

'Kitty,' he mouthed as he stopped.

I was on the gangway before I was aware I'd decided to act. Daddy or no Daddy, if I didn't get Kitty off that gangway, she'd start to cook – and because of the drugs, she wouldn't even know it. I ran as fast as I could to keep from being burned, vaguely aware of Ozzie's voice behind me, calling me back.

'Come with me, Kitty,' I said when I'd almost reached her, dancing on the spot to protect my feet, ignoring the smell of scorched fabric and hair that rose from me. Kitty wrenched her eyes away from the man below just as a falling girder struck the gangway with a sharp jolt. Immediately, there was a terrible groan of straining metal.

'Connie, Kitty! Get off that gangway, it's going to collapse.'

I looked behind me and saw Ozzie had come out past the fire curtain and stood at the start of the gangway. His eyes followed Kitty's down to the scene below, the line of evacuees filing past Kitty's father. Ozzie must have recognised some of them as he leaned over and shouted, '*Viel Spaß, Meine Herren!* Another great investment, *ja?*'

Two men looked up furtively as the line slowed to a standstill.

'Quickly, Kitty, we have to go!' I knew I couldn't stay there any longer. If she didn't come with me now, I'd have to leave her.

Just then, a length of metal tubing broke away from above our heads and swung about wildly, gushing burning gas like an out-of-control flamethrower. It swung around, then turned and pointed directly at me. I knew there was no escape, I was about to be burned alive. Uselessly, I covered my head in my arms and crouched, awaiting annihilation.

But it didn't happen. I took my hands from my eyes and saw that, suddenly, miraculously, the jet of flames had changed direction and Kitty was recovering her balance on the gangway. She must have jumped and whacked the tubing away from me. It swung out again wildly, detached itself further from the structure, then twisted downwards towards the people beneath, engulfing them in flames. I turned my face away but still heard the terrible scream from below, 'Kitty ... BAAAABY ...'

The gangway started to break up. I reached out and grabbed Kitty's arm and dragged her off it and through the fire curtain just as the whole structure came apart. Ozzie stood back and helped us through, then paused. He turned and stood at the fire curtain, watching as the unfortunates below were showered in a hail of molten metal and flaming gas.

'What are you doing – come on!' I yelled at him.

'Bearing witness,' Ozzie said, still staring down. Then he turned to me slowly, his face ghastly grey but with a thin, peculiar smile. 'It's just, they said we'd never burn the bond-holders.'

'Jesus, Ozzie,' I said, pushing Kitty back down the dark corridor. 'Get down here. And close over that fire curtain and the door too if you can. Keep back the smoke.'

I had a fit of coughing on the landing as I headed for the emergency door. 'We can't stay here. Fogarty's gone up to the next level, we have to go too.'

I covered my mouth and closed my eyes against the acrid fumes billowing around us, feeling my way upwards with the hand rail while pulling Kitty behind me. Ozzie brought up the rear, keeping an eye on Kitty in case she decided to do another runner. She was quiet now, dull-eyed. At least she'd lost the crazy energy from the drug – maybe it was wearing off. I didn't know if she was aware of what had just happened with her father. Adoptive father. All I knew was that she had saved my life.

The sound of Fogarty coughing came from somewhere above us. Ozzie's hoarse whisper was right beside me.

'We're coming up to the second floor – where the boardroom is. I'm going up past you to take a look.'

But Fogarty's voice shouted back down. 'Stay together. I'm just ahead of you. Come up slowly.'

We arrived in a huddle a few steps below the door on a turn of the stairs. Fogarty was hunched down, peering through a chink in the door. His face was half-covered in a makeshift smoke mask he'd made from his shirt. As he inched the door open with his shoulder, he held up one hand to tell us to stay back. He held a gun in the other. The leather shoulder holster criss-crossed over his black t-shirt held a magazine pouch. As it turned out, it was just as well.

58

CLAY IS THE BEGINNING

The emergency door swung open, exposing Fogarty and the three of us skulking behind him just as a group of men emerged through a fine, wood-panelled doorway on the corridor. Claude Leyton's men, Nathan Penrose, David Donaldson and Rick Kornell didn't look bored any more. They were in a hurry. One of them carried a heavy black polycarbon case, the other two pulled larger cases on wheels.

'Guns, or drugs or those fucking disease pens,' Fogarty muttered. He shouted to us to get back as the men in the corridor turned. Fogarty flattened himself against the stairwell wall, practically standing on top of me.

Kornell pulled out a handgun, squeezed behind a column on the far side of the doorway and took aim at Fogarty while ordering the others to take cover. With a deafening noise, his gun went off and splintered the side of the emergency door. He adjusted his aim and fired again but not before Fogarty had shot at him.

At the same time, another explosion rocked the building. The corridor floor split across in several places. As the floor rose up beneath Kornell, Fogarty's shot ripped into the underlying plaster and timber which was now exposed. Kornell roared for his comrades but it was too late. The section of corridor on which they stood, along with the entire rear of the second level, collapsed into the space beneath it.

The men screamed as they fell, clutching the air with open hands, their baggage spiralling around them. A huge void, vast and black, had opened in the space beneath. The red neon sign dangled crookedly above, the word 'BURN' a dull glow.

Ozzie's dark eyes stared in horror as he held on tight to Kitty. My hands were over my mouth, I might have screamed but no sound came out. Fogarty was the first to move.

'Come on,' he snapped. 'God knows what's going on up above. We have to go *now!*'

We crossed the remaining section of the corridor. Fogarty pushed open the panelled boardroom door.

'In here,' he said. 'At least we're no higher than the second level. There's bound to be a window, maybe some way to get out.'

Inside the boardroom, it looked like a routine business seminar had just ended. A long polished timber table was positioned in the centre of the room. On it, a still-humming projector focused on a wall-mounted screen with a Powerpoint slideshow running on auto. Successive slides showed maps of the city centre, statistics and locations of homeless shelters and methadone clinics. A step-by-step chart headed 'Administer two drugs simultaneously' outlined the technique of dual auto-injectors. A timeline for the Bicknor Project, highlighted Friday's unveiling of the memorial to Alexander de Bicknor in St Patrick's Cathedral. Each slide carried the logo of the Bicknor Project.

On the table's surface was an untidy collection of paper coffee cups, scattered printed pages and an iPad in a black plastic cover. Most of the surrounding chairs were pushed back and empty, but two of them were still occupied. Fallen forward, with her thin body almost doubled up and her head on the table, was a girl with blonde hair. It was Hannah. I couldn't tell if she was dead or alive. One of her arms was bent under her head, the other stretched out in front of her. Beside her open hand was an auto-injector.

I checked the figure seated beside her. His body was slumped back in the chair, arms hanging down, his face turned away. There was something about him that seemed familiar.

'Oh no,' I said as I went to his other side, lifted his chin gently and pushed back his brown hair to get a better look at his face. It was the young homeless guy I'd met earlier, the one who had asked for change, who'd followed me to return the milk tooth he thought was mine. He felt deathly cold. He wasn't breathing. An auto-injector lay at his feet on the floor.

I touched Hannah lightly on the side of her neck and felt a faint pulse. Her chest rose and fell slowly, she was still warm. Unconscious but alive.

'What the fuck is going on here?' Fogarty said, stooping to examine the auto-injector on the floor. He dropped Kitty's backpack on a chair where it opened and something slid out, landing on the floor with a thump. I picked up the heavy, wet lump and peeled back its thin cling-wrap, releasing a smell of iron and minerals like petrichor, the perfume that comes from the earth after it rains. I pressed into the lump and examined the resulting indentation of my finger. Clay, green clay.

'Kitty must have got it from Ned Kinsella,' I said but Fogarty wasn't listening. He stood staring at the bodies, the auto-injector in one hand, his handgun in the other.

'They were dual-injected with the drug and the disease,' I explained. 'He's dead, probably got a higher dose and had no resistance. They were used as live demonstrators in a sick training seminar. Those bastards.'

A noise came from the open window and a male voice spoke softly.

'It's just a job, Connie. We're professionals and this is what we do.'

It was no surprise to hear his voice. I knew he was close, I'd felt it. A figure emerged slowly from the shadows around the deep-set window-frame.

'Get down, all of you,' Fogarty roared, as he took cover behind a filing cabinet. He pointed his gun at the figure, saying, 'You at the window, stop or I'll shoot.'

'Oh, I don't think you will,' Claude Leyton said. 'You might as well show yourself, Fogarty. Or those kids will get it. One of them is still breathing, for the moment at least.'

Ozzie and I had hit the floor under the table, painfully aware that its timber surface would be no protection against bullets.

'Connie and Ozzie,' the man said. 'Get up and stop being ridiculous. Fogarty, come out where I can see you.'

Fogarty slowly appeared from behind the cabinet. He kept his gun levelled at the man at the window. I met Fogarty's eyes and he shook his head slightly. I stayed put. Ozzie didn't move.

'Is that little Kitty down there?' Leyton continued. 'She doesn't look herself. I'm sorry to see that. Did she and Aleka have a falling out?'

Kitty rose to her feet at the sound of her name. I tried to pull her back down but she shook me off and stood beside

Hannah, stroking her hair. I had no choice and stood up too. I heard Fogarty's sigh behind me.

'You bastard, Claude Leyton,' I said. 'Or should I call you Clay?'

'Who the fuck is Clay?' Fogarty said.

'Claude Leyton,' I said. 'Clay is his *nom de guerre*, his nickname.'

Fogarty looked at me blankly.

'Mooney tried to tell us in that line he added to his article,' I continued. '"Clay is the end and Clay is the beginning." The first part means that clay can end the disease, cure it. Mooney knew that and that's why he sent me to Ned in the grow shop.'

'What?' Ozzie and Fogarty said simultaneously while Leyton raised an eyebrow.

'The second Clay in Mooney's article has an uppercase "C". Obviously it's a proper noun, a person's name. A man named Clay "is the beginning", the source of the disease and of the "solution" to the city's human problems. He is Claude Leyton, Aleka's right-hand man.'

'You know all this because of a capital letter?' Fogarty said.

'Of course. I was an editor for fifteen years,' I said. 'I pay attention to letters. And Mooney was a pro, he would have typed it like that deliberately. Then, when Donlon said Leyton had a nickname ...'

'I heard his men call him Clay once,' Ozzie said. 'He's a cold-blooded killer, works under contract. But Fogarty, you and Rossiter knew that, didn't you?'

'We knew Leyton and his men were contractors,' Fogarty said. 'Brought in by Aleka when she thought Brady wasn't moving fast enough. But we thought it was all about taking out the gangs. We had no idea of the connection with the disease. That's diabolical.'

'Mooney tried to tell us,' I said to Fogarty. 'After he left you yesterday morning, he arranged a meeting with Leyton and his men. But first he phoned me to try to meet me afterwards. Then he went online and made that addition to his story ... before walking to his death.' I turned to Leyton. 'That was stupid of you, injecting a journalist.'

'He knew everything,' Leyton shrugged. 'He insisted on meeting us and practically forced Rick Kornell to do it. And yes, you're right about the nickname. My friends call me Clay. As you said, it's a kind of *nom de guerre*.'

Leyton still had his gun levelled at Kitty's forehead. Fogarty stood motionless with his weapon aimed at Leyton. The American had something in his other hand, something in a white tissue.

'Pass me that box on the table, Connie, will you? I need to keep something safe.'

He glanced at Hannah's face for an instant and I saw something there I hadn't noticed before. A dark trickle of blood ran from her mouth.

'Just a little souvenir,' he said, and he raised the tooth to his lips and ran it lightly along his own bottom teeth. 'I like to bring back a little reminder or two. This is so pretty. The calcium-deficient ones are beautifully fragile. A tooth is a part of ourselves, isn't it? Like a ... bit of our personality. But permanent, a relic. You know what I mean, don't you, Connie. I explained last night. You understand.'

'No,' I said, 'I don't understand.' I thought I'd was going to be sick.

Just then another explosion went off and part of the ceiling above us collapsed, showering us with plaster. As soon as the debris stopped falling, I raised my head and squinted through the rising dust. A light breeze came from the open window. Claude Leyton or Clay or just plain Sicko was gone.

Not again, I thought, not another one who thought he could do whatever he liked and get away scot free. Well not this time.

I called to Ozzie. 'Quick, get some of this green clay on Hannah. I'll do Kitty.'

It was time to undo the damage, time to stop the bastards.

59

CLAY IS THE END

With his weapon raised, Fogarty ran to the spot at the window where Leyton had been. He lowered the gun and moved to look out the window but a shot rang out immediately and hit the mirror on the opposite side of the room, shattering it to pieces. I pulled Kitty back down on the ground. Ozzie dragged Hannah on her chair into the corner and lowered her inert body to the floor.

Fogarty looked out the window, muttering, 'He was standing on the clock a minute ago.'

He darted another quick look outside. 'Can't see him. He's climbed up above us. I think he's heading for the roof. Have these guys got a chopper?'

'They've got everything,' Ozzie said. 'But the roof's at least four floors up.'

'This building has balconies and decorative pediments all over it,' I said. 'It'll be easy for him to climb from one to the other.'

Fogarty looked into the face of the dead young man and shook his head. 'Right,' he said, heading for the door. 'I'm going after him. I'll try to cut him off from above.'

'That makes no sense,' I said, 'You'll never make it. It's full of smoke out there – you'll just suffocate. Leyton's better armed, he's probably better trained and he's even crazier than you are. There has to be a better way – just give me a minute to think.'

Fogarty paused, then bent and snatched up something that had fallen off the table. He turned it over briefly before pressing it into my hands.

'Your minute's up,' he said and then he was gone.

'Jesus Christ,' I yelled after him. 'Why does no one listen to anyone around here?'

The door swung closed behind him. I looked at the silver box he'd given me and then at Ozzie, the still-dazed Kitty and the unconscious Hannah. Fogarty could take his chances up there but for the rest of us, we needed to find an alternative to being roasted or smothered on the stairs or buried alive in the boardroom. Another shot blasted outside and then another. I ran to the window.

'Stay back from there,' Ozzie shouted.

I ignored him and cautiously peeked out. As far as I could see, no one was on the ground or to either side of the window. There was a slight drop down to the metal gantry that went out four or five feet to the clock. That's where Leyton had gone. He'd climbed on top of the clock and, I guessed, used it to reach the ornate stone pediment projecting about a foot out from the wall above the window. The pediment blocked my view of everything above it. I quietly put my leg over the windowsill and placed my foot on the metal gantry below. Clasping the window frame, I leaned right out. And then I saw him. Leyton was standing on the pediment, looking upwards. I leaned out further to see what he was watching. It was Fogarty. He was on the highest ledge, grasping with one hand the metal railing that ran along the top of the building. I ducked as something hurtled past me and hit the ground with a clatter. Fogarty had lost his weapon and it looked like he was about to lose his footing too. Leyton had plenty of room where he was, enough to step back and take careful aim. His heels were almost over the side of the ledge. I slid my whole body out of the window and crouched on the gantry. I needed something. I felt my pocket and found Leyton's silver box, the one Fogarty had handed me.

I tapped the glass gently to get Ozzie's attention and pointed at the table. He understood and lobbed me a lump of green clay, left over from applying it to Kitty's arm. I slapped the clay around the silver box and formed it into a heavy ball. Then I stood up straight and threw the missile at Leyton with all my strength.

Leyton must have been pretty confident up there with his target completely defenceless and in clear sight. The last thing he expected was a projectile from below slamming into the back of his head. It couldn't have hit him very hard and it couldn't have hurt him even a little. With my lousy eyesight, it was a miracle it struck him at all.

I shrank back when I heard his surprised grunt. And then his gun went off. The recoil was all it took to make him lose his balance. He teetered for an instant on the edge of the pediment, his arms windmilling as he desperately tried not to fall. He failed. He dropped heavily off the ledge with a shout and almost immediately met one of the taut metal cables that secured the clock to the wall. I threw myself back into the room as Leyton's blood rained down from above. I crawled back to the window and looked up in horror, my hand over my mouth. Leyton was almost decapitated, his head partially severed from his neck like a lump of cheese neatly sliced by a cheese wire. He hung there making a horrible gurgling sound as the cable dug deeper into his neck.

'Ozzie,' I screamed. 'Jesus Christ, what did I do?'

Ozzie ran to the window and thrust his head out, immediately withdrawing it as more blood spurted down. He turned and faced me, gripping my arms and regarding me with undisguised admiration. 'You got the bastard.'

Just then, Leyton's body slipped off the cable and dropped to the metal gantry below. Unbelievably, he was still alive, just about. As his bloodied hand moved to grip the metal rail, his open eyes stared at me. The gantry buckled and tilted, pitching his body to the side. It slid off and hurtled down, hitting the street below with a dull crunch.

The clock and its gantry began to break away from the wall, slanting downwards with a strained groan. The metal cables bolting it to the wall snapped and the entire structure came loose. It swayed for a moment before disintegrating and falling, crashing down on the body of Claude 'Clay' Leyton. As more masonry followed it to the ground, I remembered Fogarty, who I'd last seen dangling precariously from the roof railing. Now that there was nothing to stand on outside, all I could do was lean out the window as far as I could and squint upwards. He was no longer up there. The railing around the roof was bent and broken. Judging by the flames shooting from the top windows, the fire had spread to the upper stories. I checked the ground but there was no sign of Fogarty.

Then the window surround on which I sat shifted and the window frame cracked and split apart. I had just enough time to fling myself back into the room before what was left of the window's glass shattered and tinkled down on the floorboards. Bricks from around the window began to drop out.

Ozzie put Hannah's limp arm around his neck and pulled her to her feet. 'We've got to get out of here. Can you take Kitty?'

Sure I could take Kitty, I thought as I grasped the stupefied girl's hand and pulled her clear of the plaster falling from the ceiling. But where the hell could we go?

Leading Kitty, I followed Ozzie to the boardroom door and came to a dead stop beside him on the threshold. The floor outside was gone. The corridor had completely disintegrated and only a thick steel joist remained in its place, the only thing connecting us to the emergency stairs. The stairway was tantalisingly visible, only six feet away but across an abyss. The dark void yawned beneath us, full of smoke and flames, the neon BURN sign now partially burnt out and sparking like an almost-spent firework.

'We can't get across there, not with the girls,' Ozzie said.

'We have to try. We can't leave them.'

I listened to my own words as if they came from a stranger. The thought of crossing that steel girder made me want to throw up. With my vertigo and non-existent balance, even getting *myself* across would be unlikely. Ozzie was right: helping the two drugged teenagers over there was an impossibility. I realised that Ozzie would probably have no problem walking along the girder. It would be easy for him to abandon us and no one would be any the wiser. A huge burning beam crashed from the roof into the darkness below. I yelped in fright and felt a hand holding me tightly by the scruff of my neck. Ozzie gave me a shake and I closed my eyes, expecting to be shoved out into empty space to fall, with Kitty and Hannah behind me. Why wouldn't Ozzie just go ahead and save himself?

'Connie,' he said and I opened my eyes. Ozzie's black eyes bored into mine, his free hand grasping my shoulder. 'Let's work together for once. Shall we?'

I swallowed and nodded. But I still couldn't face the crossing. And then I had an idea. 'Is that girder hot?'

Ozzie reached down and touched the metal joist. 'Hot, but not burning hot,' he said.

'Kitty, mind Hannah,' I told the girl, pointing at Hannah's slumped form where Ozzie had deposited her at the boardroom entrance. She stared at me blankly but sat down beside her friend and held her hand. 'Good girl,' I said. 'Ozzie, help me. We need to build a bridge.'

Both of us glanced anxiously at the hole in the bellying ceiling as he followed me back to the boardroom table. We tipped the table on its side, knocking the projector to the floor along with the recently fallen rubble and everything else on its surface. We dragged the table across the room on its side and angled it towards the doorway.

'We need to slide it along the girder,' I said. 'See that bit jutting out on the far side? If we can line up the table and get it to sit on that, we have a bridge.'

Ozzie looked doubtful. 'It's worth a try but we better get the balance right or it'll fall and it might take us with it. Plus it'll burn.'

'Not if we're fast enough.'

We both knew it was a long shot. To use the table as a bridge, we'd have to push it straight out until it was halfway across the girder, then swivel it around ninety degrees and slide it to the left, getting it to lie lengthways along the girder. At the swivelling stage, the only way to control it would be via the nearest table leg.

We inched the table backwards and forwards to get it through the doorway, then lowered it, surface down, legs up and pushed it across the girder. I gripped the two closest legs, asking 'Now, how are we going to turn it?'

'Like this,' Ozzie shouted above the din of the inferno below. He stooped and untied a grey cable from one of the table legs. When he pulled it, the table leg on the far left moved slightly. 'Thought this might help us steer if I tied it to the legs. It's from the old light fitting that fell down with the ceiling.'

'Go for it,' I said, eyeing the fraying length as he tugged, waiting for the snap.

'If the table's weight gets unbalanced on either side, it'll tip over and fall. Push your end out as I pull this end in. I'll say when.'

A plume of smoke accompanied by a strong smell of burning timber rose from the underside of the table. Ozzie nodded at me.

'Ok,' he said. 'Go – gently ... gently ... gently ... Stop!'

The table was one third of the way across when it became unbalanced and pitched dangerously. I angled it back on course.

'Again,' he said. 'Gently ... gently ...'

We had the table about two thirds of the way across when it became impossible to control. It was too heavy and too long. Ozzie and I struggled to hold it, both of us dripping in sweat. Then I heard a noise behind me.

'Oh God, no,' I said. 'Stay there, Kitty. Don't move.'

She was confused and didn't seem to have heard me. She walked out beside me and looked around.

'Where am I? What have you done to me?'

'Jesus, Kitty,' I yelled, trying to keep my focus on our only chance of getting out of there. 'Get back and stay there.'

'Take it easy, Connie. Concentrate on the table or we're going to lose it.' Ozzie said.

Kitty swayed uncertainly, staring into the chasm without understanding. Her gaze travelled back to Hannah's slumped form, still out for the count.

'What the fuck,' she said and teetered on the brink.

'No! No, Kitty,' I said and let go of the table leg, turning to push her back.

Our makeshift bridge slipped to the side and see-sawed wildly while Ozzie tried to catch it by the leg. As it slid further, a leg caught Ozzie under his t-shirt and pulled him with it.

'Oh God, no!' I howled, powerless to do anything to save him.

'Hey, I got it,' said a deep Eastern European voice as Ozzie pulled himself free. The table righted itself and the end furthest away from us lifted and slammed down on the solid ledge on the other side.

'There's your bridge,' Miro said, 'now get the fuck over it.'

We practically fell down the stairs to the next level. The door to the entrance hall was unblocked now and stood ajar. I burst through it and stared at the street lights outside the open front doors as I gulped in a lungful of cool night air. As we staggered out and tumbled down the steps, I was yanked upright and pushed across the road and into a doorway.

'Get down, all of you,' Miro said. 'The building's going to blow.'

There was a mighty rumble and the ground shook. The tram tracks buckled and split and a hail of rubble and broken glass rained down upon the street. The building known as Independent House had imploded and collapsed in upon itself.

'Fogarty,' I remembered. 'Where is he?'

A strong arm helped me to my feet. It was Miro, our criminally-insane rescuer from Minsk.

'Over there,' he said, pointing across the road. 'Look.'

I strained to see the figure emerging from the dust cloud that billowed from the building. I took some steps in his direction but stopped. I'd just noticed something.

'Hang on!' I said and pointed at the pile of twisted metal on the ground. Underneath it, Leyton's broken body lay still, with his head twisted at an unnatural angle. One of the corners of the square, copper-framed clock was embedded right into his chest. Its white face, with its immobile hands, sat atop him like a bizarre garnish on a butcher's tray.

'What are you staring at?' Fogarty asked, as he limped across to join me.

'The clock,' I said. 'It's the time ... look at the hands.'

'That clock's been stopped for about ten years,' he said. 'It's always the same time. Twenty past one. It doesn't mean anything.'

'Oh but it does,' I yelled above the din of two fire engines belatedly arriving, sirens blaring. 'It means everything. Mooney tried to tell me. He told me the time and the place.'

'What are you on about?' Fogarty yelled back. 'What did Mooney try to tell you?'

'That it's thirteen twenty,' I said.

Day 6

FRIDAY

60

LIES, LIES AND MORE LIES

I'd seen no one but nurses for the past two days. Everyone who'd had even the slightest exposure to the disease or an infected auto-injector had been kept in isolation and under observation by the medics. Hannah had developed a mild version of the infection, but the antibiotics worked and maybe the green clay had helped too. Kitty would be back to normal once the bath salts wore off completely, although with her personality, I wondered how you could tell.

I was completely unscathed. Except for the shock and revulsion, night terrors and day terrors merging into one, reducing me to a quivering mess bathed in a permanent cold sweat. And I thought I was a basket case when I arrived home a week ago.

A short phone call from Rossiter did nothing to improve my condition. She told me about the cover-up of BURN and all that went with it. The local guards had been removed from the investigation of the destruction of Independent House and the death of Claude Leyton. The first matter was put down to a series of gas explosions, the second to misadventure. It came as no surprise that there's a whole infrastructure in place to protect the guilty so long as they're wealthy and influential. What's new? Even before we escaped from Independent House, the hellish club had emptied through multiple concealed orifices, draining out into the city like a filthy dregs. No bodies or evidence were found when the rubble was searched by the specially-designated police unit. There were no prosecutions and no media coverage. Aleka had disappeared into thin air, and there was nothing to incriminate her if she showed up anywhere; her political ambitions would be undamaged.

At least Rossiter had been able to quietly pass the information I'd given her about Leyton to her counterparts in Wisconsin. He was known to them as a sadist for hire, implicated in civilian atrocities in Iraq, Afghanistan, the Congo, God knows where else.

'He was one sick bastard,' Rossiter said. 'On his first contract in Iraq, he marched an entire village into a marsh and watched while every man, woman and child sank into it and smothered in the mud. Took one or two souvenirs from that too. And his nickname, Clay.'

A smallholding near Pine Bluff was being searched for the bodies of a missing family, a mother, two young boys and their dog.

Back here, Bicknor Day was postponed and quietly forgotten about. A hero's funeral was planned for Detective Inspector Anthony Brady, who died a martyr, protecting the city from gangland criminals. And there was still no sign of my Aunt Aggie.

But on the up side, the news told me that property prices were continuing to rise, the construction sites and their cranes multiplied around the docklands, the government promised, yet again, to tackle the housing crisis and everyone agreed that we'd come through the worst of things and were well on the road to recovery. It was back to business as usual.

Ozzie picked us up at the hospital in his grotesque sharkmobile. Kitty sat in with Josie and Viv who were already ensconced in the back, dressed once again in their Sunday best. The tutting started as soon as they set eyes on me. It was like being trapped in a demented clock shop. I glared back at them in the sun visor mirror. 'Would you two ever give it a rest? What's wrong now?'

The tutting was replaced by a resentful silence from twin pairs of pursed, fuchsia-coloured lips.

'They're just worried about you,' Ozzie said. 'You don't look yourself.'

'Oh, and I wonder why that is? I've been lied to, led up the garden path and made a total fool of. And I'm not just talking about Kitty. You have a bit of explaining to do yourself, Ozzie Wolf. About Miro and your tattoo and that whole thing about Aggie's role as – what did you call it? The "third element". And God knows what that pair behind me were up to.'

'We were going to tell you, Connie,' Viv's voice came from the back. 'But when we saw the state of you just now ...'

'... we didn't think you could take it,' Josie finished for her.

'Going to tell me what?' I snarled.

'They were in contact with Aggie,' Ozzie said. 'I didn't know that until later. I thought I was the only one who'd heard from her – and that was though Miro. I told you Aggie was the third element.'

I couldn't speak, couldn't process what I'd just heard. Aggie was safe all the time I'd thought she was in danger and practically everyone knew that except me.

'Don't be mad with us, Connie,' Viv said. 'Aggie had been warned about a threat, something so bad it would have been beyond the power of the guards to deal with. Her poker friend was the one who told her, the Russian who likes the whiskey. What's his name, Josie?'

'Sergei,' Josie said. 'He was in Dublin a few weeks back. He told Aggie to join him in Las Vegas and together they'd find a way to protect people back here. But someone was following her in Vegas, so Sergei took her to Palm Beach and she had to stop using her phone or contacting anyone in the normal way in case she'd be tracked down.'

'What do you mean, she had to stop contacting people in the normal way?'

'Remember Miro,' Ozzie said. 'He was employed by Aggie's Russian friend to act as a spy, a messenger and in the end, as a killer. He was working alone until he discovered that his tattoo matched mine, meaning we could trust one another with our lives. I already knew Aleka was up to something and I managed to get pretty close to her. But she and Leyton were thick as thieves and they let nothing slip. I pretended to partner with her on the compulsory purchase order, knowing, of course, that she was behind the whole thing. I also knew that she ordered the original fire bomb that was planted in the Sunrise Hotel. Miro found it and replaced it with a relatively harmless device, availing of in-house expertise to mimic paramilitary features and confuse Leyton, while freaking out Brady. The replacement device caused enough smoke to set off the alarm but that was all. All along, we thought Aleka had contracted Leyton and his men to oust Donlon and annex his territory plus the buildings on our row. It was only when you sent that message that it all became clear.'

'What message?'

'The petition,' Viv said. 'To Matt Talbot. You filled out the online petition and wrote about the sketchbooks and Stevie and about the parties and the burn marks and you said the thing about Clay.'

'Oh, I see,' I said. 'And the Venerable Matt Talbot told you all this?'

'No,' Viv said patiently. 'He didn't have to. I look after his petitions as well as the church flowers. He has his own email account. Aggie can access that account too from wherever she is.'

'You're kidding.'

'No. Aggie passed your information to the Russian and he sent orders to Miro. But we only heard about that part yesterday, from Ozzie.'

'So Connie, you connected the deaths of Stevie and Jimmy Mooney with Aleka and Leyton.' Ozzie said. 'It was only then that the scale of their plan became clear.'

'You could have told me,' I snapped.

'I know. But it was too dangerous. Look what was going on – Brady dead, Donlon dead and killings taking place all over the city as the criminal gangs reacted. I'd heard rumours about the BURN event scheduled for Tuesday night. Those events were a closely-guarded secret and were never held in the same location. I'd seen the graffiti and I thought I knew everything that was going on in town, but I had no idea that Aleka had harnessed a select piece of that particular scene for her own purposes. When you called me from outside Independent House, I knew that was where BURN was happening. Based on the information you put in your petition, I guessed that Aleka was going to use it as an opportunity to launch her master plan.' Ozzie darted a glance at me to see how I was taking it.

'Go on,' I said, staring at the road in front of me.

'Miro's plan was to get inside Independent House and take out Leyton and Co. using any means possible. So obviously I couldn't tell you.'

'Because?' I glared at him.

'Because Miro was the only way to do it. And Miro is dangerously insane.'

'That's why you were so strange on the phone when I called you to say Kitty was taken.'

'Yep,' Ozzie said. 'Thanks to you, I knew where BURN was, but I didn't want you anywhere near there. We took Miro's van to Middle Abbey Street. There was no sign of you but I spotted Fogarty snooping around. Miro stayed in the van ...'

'Left to his own devices, I suppose?'

'Ha! Yes, precisely. I hooked up with Fogarty, told him you were in danger inside the building and the only way to get in there was to use his help to trick Aleka. I phoned her and told her that I'd intercepted Fogarty on the street outside. She told me to "deal with him" and to come in, that she had a job for me. We got into the building with her clearance and with Fogarty posing as my prisoner. We searched for you and Kitty – that's when I saw what was happening in the boardroom. Then Aleka texted me to come down to the old printing floor. And in the meantime, Miro found a way in and went to work. His plan was to flush out Leyton and his men and finish them off, regardless of who else was in the building. But in the end it was you who got Leyton.'

'Where's Aggie now?' I asked through gritted teeth.

'Flying home,' Josie said. 'She should be landing about now.'

I stared out the window at the passing countryside, glorious in the early autumn sunshine. The golden stubble fields with their great discs of harvested hay did nothing for me as I fought back bitter tears. Under any other circumstances, I'd have headed straight to the airport to get away from this pack of liars. But I was going to Roscommon for Stevie's sake. It was the least I could do for him. Afterwards, I'd decide what I'd do.

We gathered at the centre of the turlough, the disappeared lake, overlooked by the windowless ruined cottage at its edge. You could see an outline in the green of the meadow where the water line would be when the waters rose. We promised ourselves that we'd return in the winter to see the turlough when it became a lake again.

It was a strange group of us there. Stevie's friends were like exotic transplants, the art college students and the gay boys and girls, some from the club, some homeless. Their usual exuberant banter was temporarily subdued as they contemplated their surroundings in silence. Many of them were in the countryside for the first time in their lives and looked it, with their pale faces unaccustomed to daylight, bright-coloured hair moving gently in the soft breeze, the glitter of piercings and, when they raised their shades, the blinking of black-lined eyes in the sunshine.

Karen Donlon and Shane arrived in her sports car and Bertie ran around the meadow yapping. Lu O'Leary appeared in a floppy leopard-print hat and biker boots. Going west of the Shannon must have been like going on safari to her. Gordon Wentworth appeared with an exotic-looking female on his arm. Dr Rose Madden stood quietly to one side with the nurse from the drug treatment clinic and a few familiar faces from the Sunrise Hotel. Somebody told me that Harry was there, the guy who never left his room, but I didn't believe it. One face from the Sunrise Hotel was missing and despite myself, I found I kept looking for it.

Kitty and Shane placed most of Stevie's ashes in a hollow amongst the stones that marked the turlough's swallow hole. They built some flat stones on top to keep the ashes from blowing away. Then, followed by a string of curious ponies, they walked slowly around the flat grassy space, scattering what remained.

Just as we were about to go, Ozzie's old G-Wagen appeared on the rocky green road that bordered the turlough. It was driven by Pius Fogarty and he wasn't alone. I watched as he went around to open the door and bent forward to help his passenger out. He grinned triumphantly as he led Aggie across to us.

'Look who I found,' he said.

My anger with Aggie melted the moment I saw her worried face under her magenta beret. I ran to hug the tiny figure in her purple coat and black patent boots.

'You're a terrible, terrible woman,' I said, holding her tight and inhaling her French perfume. 'How could you do it to me?'

'I'm sorry, love,' she said. 'But I had no choice.'

Most of the mourners returned to the city straightaway. But a few of us were in no hurry to leave and wandered to a nearby hotel in an old country house for food and a much-needed drink or two. For some reason, I felt a little better now. Maybe it was the pure, fresh air or the memorial for Stevie or having Aggie back again.

The hotel bar was quiet and filled with a soft light from its enormous oriel window. A glass case containing a very large stuffed pike took pride of place behind the bar. Fishing rods criss-crossed above the fireplace like ceremonial arms. Framed sets of fishing flies and photographs of men with fish punctuated the red flock wallpaper.

I ordered a couple of Green Spots and handed one to Aggie seated in an armchair at the fireplace. I sat down beside her.

'Will you have something, Nuala?' I said to Rossiter as she appeared beside me.

'No, thanks,' she said, distracted, checking her phone. She put it away, looking worried. 'I'm really sorry about this, Connie. But I've just got a message saying that someone has travelled a distance to talk to you urgently. I'm going to meet him at reception. Promise me you'll be here when I get back.'

I nodded dumbly, my heart sinking as she walked briskly out the door.

61

THE BUNCH OF GREEN RUSHES

A cop is a cop, you'd know one anywhere. Even one with shoulder-length blonde hair, long shorts, deck shoes and a baseball cap on backwards. The few locals leaning against the far end of the hotel bar stiffened automatically. The visitors from the city froze in mid-conversation, as if the centre-light-fitting with its little red lampshades had just released a bucket of rotting fish heads on the carpet.

His tanned face lit up in a smile as soon as he saw me. He reached out a strong right hand to give mine a hearty shake and moved in for the customary continental, cheek-kissing ritual. I swerved away.

'Connie!' he boomed, 'I've been having such a tough time tracking you down. It's really great to see you.'

'What do you want, Erik?' I muttered, wishing everyone would stop staring.

'You know Inspector Kuyper?' Rossiter asked, surprised. 'He's just arrived from Amsterdam. He was in contact with Detective Inspector Brady, but lost touch with us then, due to the unfortunate circumstances. Inspector Kuyper has something important to discuss with you, Connie. In private, if you like.'

'This should be good,' I heard Josie say behind me. 'He'll be after her for her immoral earnings.'

'I have *no* earnings, not even immoral ones,' I shot back at her. 'Largely thanks to this lousy cop who arrested me in my fucking office ...'

'Your workplace security called us in, Connie,' Kuyper said gently, balancing himself on the arm of a chair. 'You know that.'

'And I thought you were such a dry shite,' Kitty was looking at me almost admiringly. 'What did you do?'

I looked around. There was absolute silence. I sighed.

'I'm on the run,' I said and there was a murmur around the room. 'I jumped bail in Amsterdam, came home to escape being jailed. Not for the reason some of you think ...'

I glanced at Josie who had her arms folded with an 'I told you so' look on her face. I rose slowly and took my glass to the bar, indicating to the barman to pour the same again, before continuing.

'For years I thought I was happy. I had a good job, a loving husband, a nice apartment, holidays ... I was promoted, spent a lot more time in the office than I should have. I have no idea how long the affair was going on between Henk and Belinda. She was my friend in work.'

'Ah, no,' said Josie and Viv in unison.

'They met at one of those sham family-friendly workplace barbecues. I didn't notice. Not when my credit card was maxed out or when my savings were cleaned out. Not when Belinda hacked into my purchasing account in work.'

'Dear God,' somebody muttered.

'It was only when I was called before a staff disciplinary committee that I realised something was wrong. Of course,

I'd no proof of anything and no one believed me. I was effectively suspended, a pariah. I spent my days in my office waiting for the legal summons, slamming my little stress ball off the wall. It was yellow with a smiley face painted on it. People whispered "Burn out" as they slunk past my office door.'

'Damned shame,' said Gordon Wentworth to a general hum of agreement.

'They needed me for one thing, though. The company's global president had a particular interest in one of my journals and I had to attend a corporate event to field his questions. We were in a large auditorium, me and one hundred of the company's senior executives. The global president arrived, ancient and reptilian like King Croc, him and his young Asian wife flashing big smiles and waving at the gathered faithful while triumphalist music poured from the speakers.'

The barman regarded me carefully from across the counter. Even the pike in his glass case seemed to be listening.

'And then it came. The email from HR flashed up on my phone telling me that I was fired and had to leave as soon as the event was over, that I'd be hearing from them in relation to legal proceedings. I was staring at it when a text came in from Henk: *Hey Connie! Sorry but Belinda & I r in luv & I hav 2 divorce u. P.S. Need 2 take furniture & stuff. Know u'll be cool as always.*

'My little stress ball had rolled off the table. It bounced a couple of times before being scooped up by Belinda, who was sitting at the next table. She tossed it back to me with a sly smile. I wanted nothing more than to wipe that look off her stupid face. I smashed the ball back at her with all my strength. It missed her and hit the column behind, then shot directly and inexorably towards the podium like a tiny little bullshit-seeking missile. The global president was gloating over a giant projection of our annual profits. It hit him smack in the mouth and knocked him off balance. He toppled into the freestanding flower arrangement, hitting his head off a giant urn and fell off the dias, unconscious.'

Around the bar, a weak ripple of applause was shushed to silence. I drank again, and went on.

'They said I did it on purpose. Security was called, then the police, and I was arrested. Enter Inspector Erik Kuyper. He always dresses like a beach bum, by the way.'

'Yes, Connie, you were in a lot of trouble,' Kuyper said in his Oxbridge-accented English. 'But we sorted it out – most of it.'

'*You* made everything worse. You contacted my husband when I told you not to. You believed him, you stupid prick, when he said I was dangerously aggressive and needed to be kept sedated. He took every last cent in every bank account, every stick of furniture ... he even took my books. You believed Belinda and sent your people to raid my office and search my PC and my laptop. When King Croc recovered and the company dropped the charges to avoid publicity, you decided to charge me anyway under some public order offence crap. A kind acquaintance paid my bail and I went home. Home to an empty apartment with nothing but dying houseplants.'

'I know why you're here now, Erik. It's about the car, isn't it?'

But he had no chance to respond. I was on a roll.

'Oh, Henk loved that car. Dark blue, convertible, Audi TT. I knew he'd come back for it. And yes, Erik, I also knew that my neighbours had borrowed a tyre, with my permission, and replaced it with one of those temporary safety tyres – the type that'll get you to the garage so long as it's not too far and you don't go over sixty.'

Kuyper stood up, saying, 'Before you go any further, Connie ...'

'I admit it,' I said. 'I knew Henk would take the car. I knew he'd head straight for the motorway and bomb down it like a rocket. And I knew Belinda would be with him. Which is why, when I heard the car roar off down the street, I reached for my phone to tell him about the tyre. But something distracted me. I think it was the little spider plant in its hanging pot at the window. It looked so sick and yellow and it had a sick little yellow baby too. I found an empty wine bottle and I watered the plant and then I noticed the other sad plants and I watered them too. There were a lot of plants. Then I thought I'd trim my hair and put a bit of colour in it. It was only when the phone rang an hour or two later that I remembered about the tyre. But by then it was too late. I put my stuff in a bag, told my neighbours to take the plants and went to the airport. Jumped bail. Ran from justice. Well, here I am, Erik. I'm all yours.'

I put my wrists together and held them out. 'Take me away.'

'Connie –' Kuyper tried to stop me again.

'Come on, Erik. Attempted murder on two counts – isn't that what you want me for? Or perhaps, with any luck, Henk and Belinda have died and it's actually double murder?'

'Listen, Connie,' Kuyper said. 'Henk is still in a coma and Belinda is in a full body cast. But not because of attempted murder. It wasn't your fault – that's why I'm here.'

'Course it was. It was the only thing I did wrong in my otherwise blameless life and I'm not sorry for it. I knew the car would have a blowout and there'd be a horrendous accident on the motorway and I did nothing about it. Arrest me.'

'If you hadn't run away, Connie, you'd know the truth. The medical report showed Henk was totally coked-up when he got into the car. It went out of control and ran under the eighteen wheels of Pavel's Scania R560 before there was any blowout. Your husband ...'

'Who's Pavel? What's a Scania whatever it is? And it's *ex*-husband.'

'The truck driver, Pavel Adamik. The Scania R560 truck. Your *ex*-husband, Henk, who sustained severe head injuries as well as ... other injuries of a more intimate nature.'

He paused to meet the puzzled eyes of the seated group before continuing. 'It seems that just before it happened, Belinda was attempting a ... um ... blowout of her own ...'

'You mean?' I smiled.

'Yes, I'm afraid that poor Henk was practically unmanned.'

There was a sharp intake of breath from the males who were present. My smile became a grin.

'What about the bail-jumping? That's an offence.'

'I'm just here to get you to sign a statement.' Kuyper sighed. 'Then you're free.'

I stared at him in astonishment. After all this time, after all the fear and the worry I'd been through, I was free.

'Give me a pen,' I said.

Gravel crunched under the wheels of Rossiter's car as she and Inspector Kuyper drove away down the hotel driveway.

Kuyper waved goodbye through the open window and I called, 'Safe journey, Erik,' muttering under my breath, 'and let's never set eyes on one another again.'

I turned to go back up the front steps but stopped at the sight of Pius Fogarty, standing to one side of the door. We hadn't spoken since that morning, post-BURN, when we stood together on Middle Abbey Street, exhausted, dirty and singed, contemplating the body of Claude Leyton.

If there was so much unsaid between us then, it was even more so now. I had no idea how much Fogarty had heard of my confession in the hotel bar but I guessed from the look on his face that it was all of it.

'Don't say anything,' I said. 'I don't want to hear it. I don't want to talk to anyone ...'

'Want a lift home?' he said. 'I was thinking of hitting the road. Can't leave the Sunrise for long. The lunatics will take over the asylum and I might not get back in.'

'If I wanted a lift, I'd have gone with Nuala Rossiter and Erik Kuyper,' I lied. I'd have walked sooner than travel back to Dublin in the same car as Erik.

'Those two seemed to be getting on well,' Fogarty said thoughtfully, looking down the driveway after them. 'You know Kuyper pretty well, from what I've heard. Would he be good for Nuala? She could do with a bit of romance, I'd say.'

'Romance?' I said before I could stop myself. 'And why is that? Is she not getting enough from you or are you tired of her too? And what's so bloody funny?'

He'd started laughing, but reduced it to a broad grin when he saw that I was serious.

'Sorry, but that's so far off the mark ... and you were doing so well with your amateur sleuthing and all. So you thought Nuala and me – that we're together?'

My face was burning with embarrassment. I couldn't tell him that I'd seen them together, it would look as if I'd been spying on them. Which I had.

'Well, apparently no woman is safe around you,' I said. 'And the pair of you seem very close.'

'We *are* close – as friends. Nuala is Eddie's wife – widow now, I suppose. My partner, Eddie, I mean. I was best man at their wedding. I'm godfather to their little boy. After Eddie shot himself, after he died ... I've tried to give Nuala a hand whenever I can. And I told you, she came to me when she suspected Brady'd gone rogue, so we've been working together recently. That's as far as it goes.'

He moved past me down the steps and walked across the gravel to where Ozzie's giant jeep was parked. Taking a set of keys from his pocket, he paused with his hand on the door handle and called back over his shoulder. 'Last chance.'

I looked at him carefully and quickly weighed up the prospect of going with him against that of rejoining the group in the hotel bar, where a battalion of elderly females was undoubtedly midway though dissecting my entire life. Fogarty was the lesser of two evils.

I made him stop at the turlough again. He waited in the car listening to *The Bunch of Green Rushes* while I ran through the line of hawthorns and sessile oaks that marked the rim of the disappeared lake. I hooshed away the herd of ponies gathered around the central swallow hole and stood there for a moment, thinking about Stevie. Bending down, I looked into the small, clear pool with its sandy bottom, surrounded by rocks and rushes and flag irises. It shimmered in the sunlight and teemed with life. Pond-skaters skipped across its surface and whirligig beetles scooted about underneath, black and shiny with bubbles in their bottoms.

When the time came and the waters rose up and subsided again, some of Stevie's ashes would go down with them. They would be sucked into the labyrinthine underground water system, where the streams and rivers joined together beneath our leaky raft of an island. I wondered if some part of him would find its way back to the other river, in the city where he lived and died; the river that sustained him and reclaimed him, our poor boy from the west of Ireland.

I stooped down again and selected a stone, encrusted with white minerals and shaggy with long grey strands of bleached turlough moss. I pocketed it and walked back slowly through the meadow grasses towards the car. Fogarty stood waiting at the line of trees and held out a hand to help me up the incline. He didn't let go when I reached him, but pulled me close to him and took me in his arms.

'Now, where were we?' he murmured with his mouth on my mine, laughing as I kissed him back while pushing him towards the open rear of the jeep.

Look, there can be no expectations, I know that, and no hope either. The darkness burgeons, sure as the night, and the vultures circle, ever ready for their work. Some solace, then, however fleeting ... well, that's enough for anyone in the end, isn't it?

EPILOGUE

She smiled at the businessman in the adjoining first class passenger area, extended her seat and stretched out her long legs. The sea was blue and green beneath them, scattered with gold-edged islands. New beginnings always made her happy.

Her hand touched the armrest and she felt a surprisingly deep pain. It came from the smallest scratch on the back of her hand, nothing more. A sudden chill shook her, accompanied by a wave of fever and nausea. She sat up and half-laughed, 'Oh, surely not?'

Almost as quickly, she dismissed the idea. An hour to landing and she'd get herself checked out. As she snuggled into her thin airplane blanket, the words of her pathetic old mother came back to her. 'The devil looks after his own,' the silly woman used to say.

He certainly does, she murmured and sighed happily.

ACKNOWLEDGEMENTS AND NOTES

Huge thanks are due to the following friends, family, writers, readers and experts. To my publisher, Alan Hayes of Arlen House, the unsung hero of Irish publishing; to Daryl Slein for the cover painting and to Alice Bentley for the inside map and that cocky seagull. To Deirdre Brennan, for her advice, encouragement and never-ending support. To Dr Clodagh Brennan for her enthusiasm and invaluable medical expertise. I am very grateful to the other experts who so generously shared their knowledge with me: Dr Suzie Fitzgerald, Consultant Microbiologist, St Vincent's University Hospital, Dublin; Jerome Reilly, News Editor, *Sunday Independent*; Gerry O'Meara on homelessness, hostels and much more; Pat McManus, for the stories, the information, the guided tours – and the brief but eventful job, many years ago, in Tolka Shipping & Trading. To Dublin Graving Docks. To Paddy Wigglesworth, a good developer and a great friend. Thanks to Liadan O'Meara for her inside view of the club rep scene and the best clubs; to Síofra O'Meara for her uncompromising standards and to Doireann O'Meara for her kindness and encouragement. To Cian Brennan, Oscar Brennan and Sadhbh Brennan for *Uncharted* consultation particularly regarding flaming gantries. To Conal Brennan for the G-Wagon, Scania R560 and optimal accidents.

Special thanks to Patricia Gibney, groundbreaking bestselling crime writer, expert reader and wonderful friend; to the Irish Crime Fiction Group, especially Laurence O'Bryan, Sean Farrell – and to Jackie Walsh. To Arlene Hunt for her Crime Writing Boot Camp (with Alex Barclay, Louise Phillips, Declan Burke, Declan Hughes and Eoin McNamee – a veritable pantheon of contemporary Irish crime-writing pioneers!). Again, to Louise Phillips for the best Crime Fiction course and her continuing guidance and friendship, to Ciara Doorley on manuscript editing and to all at the wonderful

Irish Writers Centre. Also, like so many others, I am greatly indebted to Vanessa O'Loughlin of Writing.ie (aka author Sam Blake) for her ongoing help and support.

Thank you to my beta readers for their time and critical faculties, especially to John Greene of the *Sunday Independent*, again to Deirdre Brennan, Patricia Gibney, Dr Clodagh Brennan and Jackie Walsh and to Gerry O'Meara, Yvonne Desmond and Caroline McGee. Thanks to Clíona Ní Shuilleabháin for adventures in search of Roscommon turloughs; to Yvonne Desmond for tolerance and wine; to Danielle O'Donovan for the cutest hideaway in West Cork and to Rose and Mike O'Donovan for the second cutest one. To Dr Caroline McGee who bravely allowed a version of her identity to be stolen by Dr Caralyn Hughes. To the barmen and denizens of Mulligans, Poolbeg Street, those who are still with us and those who have gone before. To the printers, journalists, editors of the *Irish Press* and associated newspapers. And a very special thanks to Hannah McGee, the best friend in the world.

NOTES

The Sunrise Hotel, Stalag 17 and The Silver Bullet Café possibly exist somewhere along the North Wall Quay, Dublin 1. All of the other places are real but some have been altered slightly and one or two, like the Eight Bells pub, had to be resurrected from oblivion. Independent House lies disused and empty, as it has done for at least the past ten years. Its clock remains stopped, forever pointing to 13:20. The dry dock on Alexandra Road is now closed too, as the area awaits further redevelopment.

Archbishop Alexander De Bicknor was a brilliant administrator in fourteenth-century Ireland who established the country's short-lived first university and who embezzled an enormous sum of money from the state coffers. He also cursed the vagrant poor of Dublin. Finbar Dwyer's podcast provides a vivid flavour of those dark times in 'The Sounds of Medieval Life, a walk through Dublin in 1320', http://irishhistorypodcast.ie/podcast-the-sounds-of-medieval-life-a-walk-through-dublin-in-1320/. It is thought that De Bicknor's memorial brass was removed or stolen from St Patrick's Cathedral; it has never been recovered.

The academic paper recommended to Connie by Dr Rose Madden was this one: 'Protective effect of *hainosankyuto*, a traditional Japanese medicine, on *Streptococcus pyogenes* infection in murine model', M Minami, M Ichikawa, N Hata, T Hasegawa – PloS One, 2011, https://doi.org/10.1371/journal.pone.0022188. High quality, peer reviewed open access journals like PLoS One (and open access research repositories) are vital not only to doctors, sleuths and crime-writers, but to everyone who seeks the truth.

Homelessness has long passed crisis point in Ireland. After the bank bail-outs and the billions in taxes paid to unsecured bond-holders, thousands of Irish kids are growing up in hotel rooms eating takeaway snack boxes for their dinner and doing their homework on the floor. You'd wonder who's looking out for them and their parents now, as property prices return to boom-time levels, politicians congratulate themselves on the economic recovery – and the devil looks after his own.

ABOUT THE AUTHOR

Niamh McBrannan is a Dublin-based writer. *The Devil Looks After His Own* is her first novel and is Book One in the Silver Bullet series.

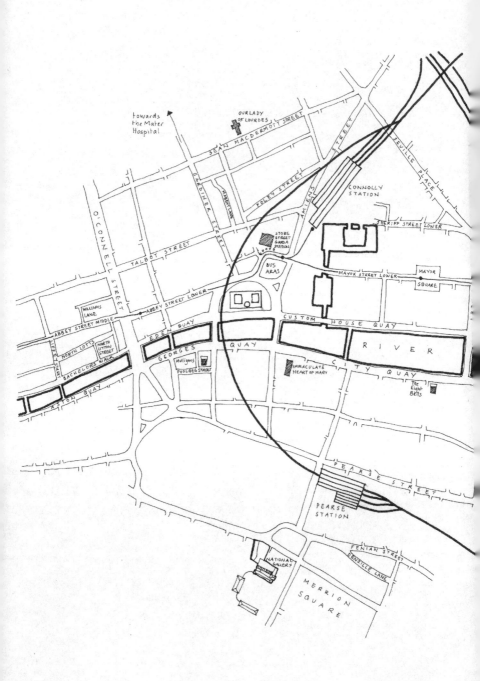